SOAR Youth Ministries

PO Box 51611 * Knoxville TN * 37950-1611
Serving Others and Reconciling

SOAR Youth Ministries

THE FREE FALL

THE FREE FALL

JANE RATCLIFFE

HENRY HOLT AND COMPANY

NEW YORK

I would like to thank the following people: My dad, who first told me I should write, even though he wanted me to be an engineer; my mom, who sent me regular checks for "this and that," even though I was old enough to be supporting myself; Blake, who will always be dear to me no matter where our orbits take us; Sherri, who listened to me read my first chapter with such glee that I thought perhaps I was onto something; Gelek Rinpoche for simply everything; Neeti Madan, who is without a doubt the best agent in the whole wide universe, and those yet undiscovered; Marc Aronson, who is exactly the editor I dreamed of: brilliant, challenging, patient, precise, and a wee bit wacky; Laura Godwin for my treasured "the"; Kim Kanner, who was the first professional to read my work and who has taught me not only the art of editing but the benefits of patience; Sue Cohn, without whose undying mental, emotional, spiritual, and financial support and friendship I would, no doubt, be in the bin or the poor farm at this moment; Lou Willett Stanek, who helped me to shape a glob of words into chapters with a plot; Kory Clarke, with whom I grew up in so many ways and who was my original brilliantine cowboy; Stephen Farrar, who would undoubtedly be on the *New York Times* bestseller list had his life played out differently; Lisa Sunshine, who shone some light when things looked bleak; Denine Polen, whose outrageously delicious meals saw me through; Elliot, Cassidy, Eva, Adam, Annabel, and Henry, whose sweet, sweet love put the rest of life in perspective; all my friends, in all shapes, sizes, nationalities, musical tastes, and head spins who rode the roller coaster with me; and to Mattie, LuLu, Tenille, Portia, Chutney, and all the others, who have brought me great comfort in times where there seemed to be none and who have caused me to laugh at the pure silliness of life.

Henry Holt and Company, LLC, *Publishers since 1866*
115 West 18th Street, New York, New York 10011

Henry Holt is a registered trademark of Henry Holt and Company, LLC
Text copyright © 2001 by Jane Ratcliffe
All rights reserved.
Published in Canada by Fitzhenry & Whiteside Ltd.,
195 Allstate Parkway, Markham, Ontario L3R 4T8.

Library of Congress Cataloging-in-Publication Data
Ratcliffe, Jane. The free fall / Jane Ratcliffe.
p.   cm.
Summary: When her family begins to fall apart, sixteen-year-old Let
is torn between two interesting and unconventional boys, as she slides
into the dark side of alcohol, illegal drugs, and sexual activity.
[1. Alcohol—Fiction. 2. Drug abuse—Fiction. 3. Sexual ethics—Fiction.
4. Family problems—Fiction.] I. Title.
PZ7.R1845 Fr 2001 [Fic]—dc21   00-59662

ISBN 0-8050-6667-5 / First Edition—2001 / Designed by Donna Mark
Printed in the United States of America on acid-free paper. ∞
1 3 5 7 9 10 8 6 4 2

For sweet Alex

I went to the woods because I wished to live deliberately,
to front only the essential facts of life,
and see if I could not learn what it had to teach,
and not, when I came to die,
discover that I had not lived.

—HENRY DAVID THOREAU

THE FREE FALL

1

My name is Violet Gwendolyn Hitchcock, but my friends call me Let. Logan says it's on account of my being too small to carry a full name, even one as corny as a flower. I came about my official name because when my parents first came to America, my dad used to bring my mom armfuls of violets from a meadow that flourished near their trailer home. My mom says my name reminds her of my dad's sweet kisses in a time of trouble. It's hard for me to imagine now that there was ever any sense of romance between them, despite the fact that my mom tries to tell me about it nearly every time the mood strikes her.

I've been thinking about the two of them a lot since I've been here—first off, because there's not much else to do. They made sure I got a single room and all, knowing how I hate strangers, but I can't hold a book, and TV is pretty much a drag. Logan brought me this old tape recorder of his. He says documenting it all might help me make sense of what's happened—which is way weird, considering I thought he'd just want to forget the whole thing.

My dad tried to sneak Whiz Bang in, but even though he got her past the main desk, some doctor stopped him in the hall, saying, "Sorry, sir, no pets allowed." My dad gave him that stone-cold stare of his—the Wall, as Logan calls it—but it didn't do much good. He had to take Whiz Bang back out anyway. I guess that stare only works on Logan and me, and of course my mom.

I figure I've been in here about a week waiting for my arms to heal back up, and I ruptured some internal organs, too. In a few more days they're letting me out, but I'm not so sure I want to go. Things have gotten pretty wound up lately. More wound than usual, that's for sure. And being in here gives me some time to think things through. I guess, looking back, it seems inevitable something had to snap, shattering my life into these beautiful fragments that keep dancing around in my head.

I remember thinking first off that God had let me down. You see, all along I had this theory I was connected directly to Him, that in fact He'd put me in charge of some things down here; most important, making sure all the roadkills I encountered got into heaven okay. And I had this whole detailed system worked out around just that, so I had figured as long as I kept up my end of the bargain, He would keep up His, too. But now that I've had time to reflect a bit, I realize He'd been watching out for me after all; I was just looking at it all wrong. And that's when my thinking started to change.

I suppose the whole thing began with me looking for the "shine." That's what I used to call that trippy kind of grace some people just seem to be born with. Radical grace, really. Electric fury. You couldn't actually see it, not the way you could see their hair color or the color of their eyes. It was more of a feeling, a vibe, just something about the way they moved, or the kind of laugh they had, or maybe the way they called out my name.

Henry Edwards was the first person I thought had it. I mean all-the-way had it, not just a little bit like some of the losers I'd dated from school. And I guess the whole thing really does begin with him. He became involved in every aspect of what happened either directly or in a roundabout way.

Our dads were partners in an automotive-consulting firm, which may sound like a bore, but they made a ton of money from it. Enough, in fact, to allow my parents to leave behind their trailer-home days and move upward and onward to the sprawling 'burbs of Peavey Lane, Billington, Michigan. Mr. Edwards and my dad didn't socialize much beyond the office though, so when Henry showed up at our house last summer, I hadn't seen him since we were kids.

To tell you the truth, I don't have too many nice things to say about Henry anymore, but back then, back on that muggy summer night—the kind only a slow, worn-down August can deliver—I thought I'd never laid eyes on a sweeter angel-man in my life. I remember thinking that even before he opened his mouth, offering me my first taste of that sweet chip on his front tooth, tender summer tongue lurking behind, which bestowed on him this slightly dangerous aura, which he kind of already had anyway, considering the way he dressed and all.

He swaggered around our living room in these black leathers, with chains that dangled from the belt loops and were connected to his wallet and his keys, and he carried some kind of swanky jackknife, the outline of which bulged in his front pocket. His boots were hitting hard against the floor, causing me to glance up from the Tat's mythology book, which was supposed to be giving me all this great insight into life, but so far was only confusing the hell out of me as I tried to sort the Roman gods from the Greeks and a couple of British kings who'd been thrown in for good measure.

The Tat, by the by, was my brother's girlfriend. I figure I'd better mention her right off, since her impact on my life was pronounced. Her real name is Anna, but I called her the Tat on account of the tattoo she'd gotten in Vegas with Logan when they ran away there a few years back. Logan says it's a red heart bordered by yellow daisies, with his name in script through the middle of it. She convinced the guy to drill it despite the girlfriend-boyfriend names doom factor. He nailed it in so secretive a place, I haven't spotted it yet. Even when she's in her string bikini.

"Evening, sir," Henry said, real polite like, his fingers steady even in motion, long and dark, offering up to my dad the envelope his dad had sent him over with; the other hand sliding up and down his chest, finally coming to rest inside the tops of his leathers. Just watching him was making me twitchy.

Out in the driveway, I could see his Mustang cooling in the heat. It was a convertible, candy-apple red. The old style, too, from the sixties, looking pretty all right to me, all glossy and thick, like an old-time rocket ship. So I started looking hard at Henry, then thinking, *Hmmm, is this what I want? Is this the shine I'm after?* Because you've got to remember all this stuff I know now, I didn't know then.

The smell of pot clung to him as he sauntered over to my dad, checking me out with a flick of his eyes. I liked the way his hair was piled on the top of his head like a Dairy Queen dip gone wrong, and as he passed me by he reeked of sweat and something more, too, working its way out through the leathers.

"You smell like marijuana, son," my dad said. "Are you sure you should be driving?"

Henry said, "Yes, sir. It's these clove cigarettes," his *s*'s snapping out like a just-lit match. He fingered a crumpled pack of Djarums that he had jimmied out of his back pocket. My dad didn't even glance at it. We were all familiar with the scent of pot on account of Logan's habitual puffing, so I knew the cigarettes didn't convince my dad, but he invited Henry to dinner anyway.

"Thank you, sir, but I've been having trouble with the headlights, and I shouldn't have her out at night." His shoulders were already facing out beyond our screen door, his gaze wandering past my parents' rose gardens, which were full of Betty Priors, Polyanthas, and Dainty Besses with petals like so many butterfly wings; their sweet summer bouquet filling our rooms as they had this time every year as far back as I could remember.

"I understand, son." My dad walked with him down the hall. "Be careful driving. I wouldn't want to see you smash up such a fine car." He laid his hand on Henry's shoulder. And in that moment, my dad seemed small and worn next to Henry, who in all his black gear looked even taller than he probably was. Which was pretty tall anyway; over six feet, I figured.

Henry nodded at my mom, and I swear gave me the up-and-down one more time, probably on account of the hot pants I was wearing, which my dad disapproved of, but it was a real roaster of a night and so far he seemed to be letting it slide. Or maybe he just hadn't noticed, which was happening more and more lately. Henry caught the door with his heel on the way out. It slammed behind him. The room vibrated a moment longer with his magnetic energy, then settled.

"My, oh, my, what a luscious-looking young man." My mom drew up beside me, adjusting her hair with smooth upward motions. I could smell her moist tan flesh pushing up close against mine, a tangle of Joy 1000, sun sweat, and the dinner she was busy cooking up. "Can't imagine how those lovely hips came from such unattractive parents." She lit up a Winston, waved her hand over my head to clear the smoke.

"Couldn't get out of here fast enough," my dad said, tearing open the envelope, "as if we were some damn leper enclave." As usual they were carrying on two separate conversations, although this time they were at least on the same topic. "And what was all that garbage about special cigarettes? I know marijuana when I smell it, and that was marijuana."

"Pot, Dad. Nobody says marijuana."

"Well, crown me the first. Now go do something useful and help your mother with supper."

So I followed my mom into the kitchen, figuring I'd set the table while she finished the salad, but I guess she figured the salad could wait.

"Don't men like that just get your blood racing?" She poked me in the side, like she always did when she talked about happening guys, which was a little too often for my taste, if you want to know the truth, being as most of them were closer to my age than hers. But the thing was you couldn't rein her in. None of us could. Our family didn't function like that. We were like those stackable Russian dolls: Open one up and there's another inside. If I were to say, "Mom, it's kind of gross when you talk about guys my age like that," who knew where that would lead, what doll lay nestled within, what we'd suddenly be discussing next, how heavy it would go, what gunky tidbits you really didn't need to know would be revealed, all because you made a passing, though seemingly appropriate, comment about a simple surface ickiness.

"Your father used to be like that," she went on. "He'd come pick me up on his motorcycle every day after school, and he'd look so magnificent in his tight leather jacket. Used to make me throb all over just to lay my eyes on him." She wiggled her hips from side to side like she was doing a little dance, then walked over to the cupboard where she stashed her cigarettes. "Of course you would never know it to look at him now. Now he looks like he never heard the word *sex* before."

She pulled out a fresh pack, sat at the table, slid the ashtray toward herself. I laid a knife and fork near her elbow.

"Now Henry has definitely heard the word *sex*, wouldn't you say, love?" She was laughing, getting this distant look in her eye. "Things are different now, though, I suppose—with all the drugs you kids have."

But she didn't say it like that was necessarily bad, more like the only thing separating her from drugs and Henry and the rest of the action was my dad and his puritanical way of life. I could tell she was about to break into her anti-my-dad rap, the one where she blames her whole doomed existence on him. It always followed hot on the heels of the romance spiel. She used to run it past me all the time, although, since I've been here, I haven't heard it once, which is another thing making me want to stay.

Why she didn't up and leave him was beyond me. *Grab your nail polish and cigarettes and Joy 1000, your pile of self-help books and the little picture of Steve McQueen you hide in your goddamn underwear drawer, and split,* I used to think when she rattled on about how oppressive my dad was. That was a big word with her, *oppression. So bust out,* I'd think. *Free yourself. Stop your complaining and go.* Of course I never said that. I never said anything really. Just nodded my head and tried to change the subject as fast as I could.

Thing was, though, when she talked like that it kind of scared me. It would drive me up to my bathroom mirror in order to search my face, hoping to find I was nothing like her. But the similarity only became more pronounced. Same wide-alert eyes. Same nose curving tentatively into the unknown. "She's a bloodsucker," Logan had warned me, sneaking up on one of my morning-mother-mirror vigils, "keep your distance."

Sometimes when she was on a roll, she'd tell Logan something secret about herself and make him swear never to tell me. Then she'd do the same to me. Like the time she bought some sexy lingerie to surprise my dad and he didn't even notice. Stuff that made you claustrophobic. Logan calls it the itch, on account of when she talks to you all oozy and secretive like that, it makes your insides get real itchy.

"Henry Edwards would be one exciting man to get to know," she said all dreamylike, blowing smoke out her lipsticked lips, staring at the ceiling. I laid out the last knife, then headed back toward the living room. Suffering from the itch, big.

My dad was still skimming the papers Henry had left.

"Hey," I said, and he just about jumped out of his skin. Clouds in his head were making him like that—jumpy, forgetful, a little out of step if you want to know the truth. He hadn't always been this way. In fact, up until a few years ago he'd been a full-on control freak, an English Mussolini of sorts, keeping the trains, or in this case his children, running on time. We had a wake-up time; a breakfast time; a say-your-multiplication-tables, recite-your-favorite-bit-of-Keats, list-the-capitals-of-the-world time; a round-or-two-of-cribbage time; a clean-your-bathroom-and-don't-leave-any-hairs-in-the-drain time; a huge sports time; a minor TV time; and, on the odd occasion, a scolding time. This was fairly rare, though, as all the rules and regulations, and carefully allotted times, reduced the amount of fuckups to a minimum, and being the engineer he was, my dad saw that as pure efficiency. We were a well-designed machine.

And while I can't say I was having the time of my life, what with every step choreographed for me, I would agree it worked well in that I understood what my father was about; I understood what he stood for: the right thing. He was a glistening pillar of right in a crumbling landscape of wrong, which was comprised of the rest of us. Then Logan took off for Vegas, and my dad seemed to crumble, too. It was as if he'd spent his whole life building his master creation, only to find it had a serious flaw and he just couldn't cope. Of course, when things became too big, he had no choice but to get involved, but until then he kept pretty much to himself. I used to think he walked away from us, floated up to the pretty clouds, because he was disgusted with his creation, but now I'm more inclined to think it was because he was disgusted with the creator.

Both my parents were somewhere in their forties, but they looked much younger. "Exercise will keep you young and keep your brain ticking," my dad would say when he woke me at 5:00 A.M. to join him for a round of calisthenics. He was into all the "up" exercises: chin-ups, sit-ups, push-ups and—in memory of his boxing days—jumping rope. "When I was your age, I was outdoors getting some air in my lungs and earning my keep. As far as I'm concerned, you kids today have it too damn easy." I knew his whole spiel by heart, too.

"Important papers?" I asked.

"They're so damn scrambled, I can't make heads or tails of them." He slapped the stack against his hand.

"Can I help?"

"Sure. Drag that marijuana wise guy back here and have *him* straighten these damn things out!"

"I guess you pretty much didn't like him." I noticed how my voice lilted at the end of sentences, making even statements sound like questions.

"Until I can straighten this mess out, I'm not too fond of anybody." He glanced up, gave me and my hot pants the old one-two, not looking very pleased.

"Logan!" My mom walked in and yelled over the banister without even a how-do-you-do to either of us. "Supper's ready."

"I'll get him." I took the stairs two at a time, Whiz Bang hot on my heels.

"Put some decent clothes on while you're at it," my dad called, his voice bouncing up the stairs behind me.

• • • •

My brother kept endless journals, stacks of them piled around his room like a fortress. He'd built wooden shutters from some old wine crates, taking down the blue-and-white curtains my mother had made years ago, and most of the time he kept them closed while he read incessantly, spread loosely across his plain white sheets like a tiger in the sun. He read, wrote, and lived beneath a single bare bulb that hung from a hook above his head. It was as though he thought if he wrote it all down on paper, the frustration of his life would just go away. Or at least he could press it down far enough that it couldn't hurt him anymore.

Logan didn't bother to hide any of his journals, either; he chose rather to let them openly gather dust as if he knew none of us had the gumption to cross him, or maybe daring us to. A couple of them did have locks, though. I knew on account of holding one in my hands, feeling the words burning a hole right through my skin as I'd stroked the worn leather; at the last minute, losing the nerve to jimmy it open and dropping it back onto the stack.

"Dinner's ready." I stood in his doorway, curving my fingers in toward my palms.

"Didn't you ever hear of knocking, Bean Brain?" Logan glanced up from the joint he was rolling, and the unsheathed light caught his fierce tattoo. *I Shall Not Want* emblazoned across his forearm, surrounded by fire and snakes and trippy flowers; not up high where shirtsleeves could hide it, but low, obvious, always there.

"I just thought you might be hungry."

I studied the outline of a hole Logan had punched in the wall during an argument with our dad, which over time had become visible again beneath the new wallpaper. I tried to remember whether dad or wall had been the target.

Logan nodded, let the rolling papers drop into the crotch of his beat-up leopard jeans so that he could focus on me more. He dressed like he worked in Vegas or something, a stark contrast to his spartan room, not to mention the odd carved knickknack or wooden oar or wicker chair of the J. Crewesque way Logan *used* to be.

I was starting to leave when Logan got all curious over Henry.

"What was the dude like?" Thick, greasy chunks of manufactured blond fell across his face. He pushed them behind his ears, started cleaning the pot again.

"He was toasted, but tried to pass it off as those cigarettes that the Tat smokes."

"Did the old man buy that?"

"Not really. He was superpolite and all, but I don't think Dad liked him much. I thought he was kind of cool, though." And I couldn't help smiling as I formed the last words.

Logan only nodded, distracted as he was by the precise tightening of his joint, sealing it with a flick of his tongue. Henry and he were the same age, but had gone to different schools on account of Butter Lane being the dividing line between districts, and even though our houses were only ten minutes apart, they fell on opposite sides.

"Remember, safety first," he said, looking up, smirking.

Logan was confusing to me then and still is, though this recent turn of events has brought us closer together in an almost primordial way. It's the way people who survive an armed robbery, say, or a devastating earthquake are said to feel about one another afterward. It's the type of connection that can't be explained or understood by outsiders; it can only be felt by the parties involved. Sometimes I can't help thinking that's why this whole thing happened—to draw Logan and me into the same orbit, rather than each of us blindly navigating within our own.

I remember watching him as he sprawled out wider on his bed, his muscles still popping even though he'd given up sports a few years back. He closed his eyes and lit up, and I was vaguely aware of his magnetic allure despite the fact he was my brother. I wanted him to come down to dinner with me, but he just didn't do things like that.

He'd show up after we were all seated, disagree with almost everything my dad said, and pretty much ignore my mom, saving what little dinnertime banter he possessed for me, but only when the mood was right. And the right mood was rare indeed.

. . . .

So I went down without him, because I knew my parents would be waiting for me, and showing up was a definite right. That's how I figured life was divided then—definite rights and definite wrongs. I was pretty clear on the wrongs on account of their being spelled out to me as far back as I could remember: B-pluses were wrong; unmade beds were wrong; sloping shoulders were wrong; idle time was wrong. The rights were what had been causing my head to spin, although since I've been here, I find I don't care so much. I believe now that it was this clear division of judgment, the not allowing for in-betweens, that got me into trouble in the first place.

Downstairs in the kitchen, I slid into my seat, back to the window, facing Logan's empty chair. My dad had brought his work papers to the table with him, and he hardly glanced up at the sight of me. My mom busied herself stirring and wiping, stirring and wiping. We were surrounded by bare white counters. No toasters. No Cuisinart. No pot holders with inspirational sayings. Everything like that had to be hauled out of cupboards where they rested, tucked inside Formica coffins, meticulous pencil outlines indicating what went where—until you needed to open a can, say, or make a pot of coffee. But the minute, the *second,* you were done, back they went, behind closed cabinet doors. "They last longer that way," my dad would explain, straining a bit as he shoved the shook-out toaster into its place. "It makes cleaning up much easier," my mom would say, wiping off the barren counter with one swift whoosh.

I stared at my plate a bit, then picked at my nails, thinking about Henry and his hot darkness. My mom plunked down a bowl of steaming pasta, the string beans in it so green, they almost looked plastic. Looking past her, I could make out the saying for the day on the fridge: "Learn to accept gifts graciously."

"Where's the meat?" asked my dad, poking around in the bowl with his fork.

"There isn't any tonight." My mom smiled a kind of fuck-you smile, so I knew right off she was seeing her shrink, Dr. Applegate, again.

"Who can eat supper without meat? It's not natural," my dad said, like he always did when it came to my being a veggie-head and all.

"Dad, it's better for you. Won't clog you up."

"I don't see any clogs on me yet." He patted his taut stomach with both hands, then scooped up a huge serving of pasta. I served myself, while my mom sat down, leaning a bit toward me, like we were in cahoots or something, like because I'm a vegetarian and she'd made a vegetarian dinner, that somehow put us on the same team.

"Pretty good, huh?" I said to my dad.

"A bit overcooked, but otherwise it's fine."

He raised his eyebrows while he spoke and leaned back in his chair, chewing his food methodically, the way you were taught that you were supposed to for good digestion.

My mom ate hers with great relish, pushing the plump carrots and sunflower seeds into her rosy-reddened mouth. I kept hoping Logan would come down. In reality, things got a little worse when he was around, but at least I wouldn't be alone with my parents.

Of course this is being told to you in retrospect, meaning I'm able to fill in a lot of particular emotions I was just guessing my way through at the time. And as I sit here now, stretched out in my narrow bed-on-wheels, I can picture that scene in my head clear as a bell. I know exactly what I was feeling, even though I was feeling it way, way down in those places we store things that we're just not ready to deal with yet, which can take a deadly and cancerous turn if you don't free them up at some point, I might add.

And exactly what I was feeling on that stagnant summer night—still clad in my hot pants, sitting between my parents, and waiting for my big brother who I knew would never arrive—was the overwhelming desire not to end up like my mom and dad, descending imperceptively into the void.

You see, I was still in search of some life-altering concoction—part pleasure, part peace, part radical grace; always full-on love. I was wanting my life to be loose, to be beautiful, open to the power that lets you breathe. I wanted to be free. I wanted to be a part of the whole.

I wanted to shine.

2

The next major thing that happened was my getting the Flame. My parents gave her to me for my sixteenth birthday, November 22, 1994. A pretty black Honda Accord equipped, I prayed to my roadkill God, with shine-finding radar.

"The mileage is top-notch." My dad handed me the keys a few days after my actual birthday because of some sort of factory delay, which had really ticked him off. "It comes with dual air bags, ABS brakes, and a built-in car alarm."

He showed me how to activate the alarm from a device on my key chain. Then he opened up the hood and began systematic explanations of the carburetor, the spark plugs, the battery, the radiator, and the alternator, which were winking at me all shiny and new, but not a word was sinking in, on account of my wanting nothing more than to take her for a spin.

"Black's so sexy, don't you think?" My mom had sneaked up behind me, while my dad was still rattling away. "I've always wanted a black car myself, but your father strictly forbade it. But now that we have this, there's no telling what kind of interstate trouble we can get ourselves into."

She nudged me with her elbow, then caught sight of herself in the fender, pushed her hair up from her face, and pouted her lips. The thing about my mom was, annoying as she could be, she was really just a bunch of talk. The only interstate trouble she'd get herself into was the wrath of frustrated drivers as she poked along in the left lane. She'd never actually *do* the things she oozed about, but her female bravado was way weird nevertheless. Black, orange, magenta, I thought, trying to ignore my mom's primping to my left, it made no difference to me what color my car was. Wheels were wheels, and as long as they were spinning forward, I was well content.

Phaëthon had probably felt the same way when he first saw Helios's chariot of the sun, I thought, mentally reviewing his section in the Tat's mythology book. Something so busting, so wild, so futuristic that he had to grab hold of the reins right then, no listening to reason, not a care for moderation—only the desire for some high-flying fun. I remembered how Helios, Phaëthon's dad, had called his chariot the flaming car of day, and I liked that. And even though my car was square and solid and safe, not a hint of the hot rod about her, I knew instinctively she was my Flame, and christened her so in my head.

· · · ·

"Pretty safe wheels, Bean Brain. No drag racing here."

Logan circled me as I sat happier than a clam in the new interior of the Flame. He scratched at his chin as if he had a beard that itched, which was a strange habit on account of his shaving every morning as though the state of the nation depended on it.

"I think it's great," said the Tat, her tits bobbing beneath her sweater. She didn't believe in bras on account of their being the ultimate symbol of America's patriarchy. She'd been through a heavy-duty feminist phase a few years back, and a couple of the less high-pressure traits still lingered. Logan and she were home from the University of Michigan and spending the long Thanksgiving weekend at my parents' house. A holiday that had lost a lot of its appeal for me since I gave up eating those wild-eyed birds. "Logan's just jealous, because his car is such a clunker." She poked him in the side, and he folded inward toward her touch.

Logan had sold his sixteenth-birthday Firebird three years back; used the money to buy a rusted-out '71 Barracuda convertible and the balance to finance his weeklong trip to Vegas. My dad had had the Firebird loaded up special, so when he found out Logan had traded it to some sleazy car dealer up on Dakota Avenue, he was furious. His cheeks were blazing red in the whiteness of the kitchen, while Logan, all cocky and beyond his reach, had smirked and strutted from the room.

To tell you the truth, I never understood why Logan went to Vegas in the first place, leaving like he did, with the Tat, as if he were headed for school. My mom had thought he was at football practice until she found the note propped up on his pillow: "Gone to try my luck elsewhere." We only knew they were in Vegas on account of the Tat's having scribbled *The Golden Nugget* across the bottom in her large, rounded swirls. A crazy exploding flower in place of the *o*.

The whole time he was gone my mom had cried and my dad had cloistered himself in the den, reading the evening paper as if Logan were just away at camp for the summer, say, sending cheerful postcards home on a daily basis, which wasn't what was happening at all, although I'm not sure exactly what was. When Logan finally came home, he was way different. Drinking a lot, flashing his new tattoo, not saying too much to anybody except to the Tat. That was when the two of them became really thick. Needless to say, the whole episode had totally freaked out my parents, and as if by divine retribution the Barracuda had conked out a week after Logan's coming home, never quite returning to a drivable state.

"Let's go for a spin," suggested the Tat, taking the words right out of my mouth, "and give my little sugar cube here time to work on his speed racer."

• • • •

En route to nowhere in particular with my almost-sister-in-law, which was A-OK with me. At the time I thought she was about as cool as they come, and I guess I'm feeling that way again, but in between these occasions of sisterly bliss, she sure did a number on my family. I fiddled around with the controls a bit, acquainting myself with all the important gizmos like lights, wipers, flip-down mirror, while watching the Tat out of the corner of my eye as she started in on this weird breathing thing. First she puffed her chest up like a nesting bird, and she remained just so, while her head drew up straighter from her spine, stray wisps of auburn hair grazing my ceiling. Then she let all the air out, like a dying balloon.

"What are you doing?" I asked after a bit.

"Yoga," she said. "It's very centering." I noticed she was wearing her hair in two long braids that hung down her chest like enchanted snakes, and she'd cut choppy bangs across her forehead. The style did lend more of a spiritual vibe to her otherwise Midwestern manner than had the former unkempt mats of grunge.

"It sure makes you sound funny."

"*Ujjayi* breathing," she explained. "It's a technique that allows you to control your breath."

"Why would you want to do that?" I glanced over at her hands, and her pointer fingers and thumbs had formed two perfect circles which were resting upon her bent knees. The Tat was always into something new, which is usually emblematic of both an active mind and a restless soul.

"Breathing is the key to our existence. All life begins in the diaphragm—the center. It determines whether you are alive or dead. It's the third chakra."

"What is that supposed to mean?"

"The third chakra is the seat of our will. Our sense of individuality. Think about when someone is rushed to the hospital and hooked up to a respirator. That respirator simulates the diaphragm—meaning that person has lost her will to live. Yoga is all about reclaiming the master controls."

I took a deep breath in, but didn't make any contact with my inner self. Did I even have one? Perhaps I was a part of that unfortunate race that had been crafted and spun out seemingly intact, when in reality we were only part human; all surface mechanisms, nods, sneezes, and regular bowel movements, when inside we were lacking the good stuff—spirit and soul and self. My mind wandered, as it so often did when presented with something that baffled it, and it usually skirted on to a topic over which it felt some control. Like right then—no doubt on account of our being in a car and all—it went to roadkills.

Roadkills had been a part of my life as far back as I could remember. I felt certain that God and I had this unspoken but precise agreement where I watched out for them and He watched out for me. But even without this bargain, I would have tried to do my best for the little critters, crushed and curled inward the way they always were along the edges of the road, their carcasses so prevalent those days that I could hardly handle the sight of another, but I always did, reeling off the please-let-him-into-heaven prayer one more time.

I had a guaranteed-to-work system figured out for the roadkills that crossed my path, or more accurately, whose paths I crossed, being as they were here first, and we were just the takers of their land. It worked like this: (a) see animal flat on side of road or in road, tail stretched out behind, head rounded in toward stomach; (b) cross myself tightly against chest in small, quiet motions; (c) say prayer: "God, allow this animal into heaven and take care of him. Let him be happy. We took away the land where he roamed, and now we have killed him. Forgive us." Sometimes here, I'd also ask God to let the critter play with

Buttercup and Rover, who were, respectively, my first kitty and the family dog who'd died a couple years back.

Sometimes I'd pass these roadkills several times a week, before they got smashed so much into the road that they were indecipherable, or another animal scarfed them down as a late-night snack, and each time I'd say the prayer. The tricky part was—because in death as in life there is always a catch—to actually get into heaven, the final cross count had to be on an odd number. One, three, or five on up, they got in; two, four, six, they didn't.

So it was a lot of work to remember who was on what number, and to give the critter on an odd number a double cross to keep them odd, but to make sure a fresh roadkill only got a single. Because every time I passed one, I had to cross myself. It was part of the rules. No crosses at all was a definite no-heavener, though I wasn't clear on exactly where my mistakes ended up.

The Tat began on some new breathing exercises that forced her stomach to and fro in hard, pronounced movements while she exhaled harshly yet rhythmically, as if she were blowing her nose to the tickings of a metronome. Under my breath, I rattled off a prayer asking that the Flame and I never hit an animal and made the obligatory pint-size cross against my chest to seal it.

My family wasn't Catholic or anything, but one of the side effects of my roadkill prescription was it forced me into considering my own death. Logan said he didn't fear his so much as the death of others, and most especially he feared somehow being involved. "Well, that could never be," I would tell him. I couldn't see him turning into a serial killer or anything. "Sometimes I get the rage, Beans," he would say, "and I get it so big and so full on, I swear it's gonna take me over." Then his eyes would turn this trippy shade of shooter-marble green, hanging heavy in his skull.

Beans was the nickname Logan called me. It was short for Bean Brain and came about on account of my not eating meat, therefore having beans for brains. The rage was what Logan called the post-Vegas, pre-pot stretch of his life, though he said it had actually always been with him and had simply had the opportunity to surface then. ("Why do you think I'm so good at sports, Beans?" he'd say, and I'd remember shirt-ripping, knee-crunching mud fights after Logan had whacked some guy in the back while tackling him, which he didn't have to do, since he was the quarterback and all.) When the rage surfaced outside of the guidelines of sports, it involved lots of screaming and punching and emotional breakdowns, and it was pretty scary, something I know Logan worked hard not to repeat.

When it got right down to it, I guess I didn't fear my own death, either, mostly because I figured if there truly was a God, and I pretty much believed there was, and He loved us the way we'd been taught, He wouldn't make it painful for us to meet Him. And if there wasn't a God, then we weren't going anywhere anyway, so what was the big deal?

• • • •

John's—ahead on the right, basking in the bluey-blue of the November sky. A crazy mix of authentic Italian overcheesed cannolis and heavy death-cream sauces magically juxtaposed with vegetarian superwonders like tofu-and-sprout sandwiches, homemade baked-in-the-sun bread, organic soups, and fresh carrot juice. Consequently it drew an odd mixture of the old curmudgeony regulars and the new hippie-head types.

"I could really go for a banana smoothie," said the Tat, having resumed normal breathing again, much to my relief. With an easy turn of the wheel, we arrived at what would prove to be an irreversible spin to my life. Irreversible because inside John's, nestled between Ma and Pa Edwards, sat my sweet Henry: waiting, pulsating. I could smell him from the tarmac parking lot—his thick, rancid odor drawing me in; smell him stronger still as the tips of my fingers turned the wooden handle of the restaurant door. Old Mrs. Edwards beckoned us over, but I needed no guide.

"Why hello, Violet, dear," she said.

And rather than answer her like a normal, well-functioning sixteen-year-old would do, I worked on squashing down the pimple near my mouth in hopes it would vanish beneath my touch.

"As always a pleasure to see you, dear."

She spoke as if this were a regular occurrence, although we seldom met, and I had been surprised she'd recognized me so easily. She probably spews out pleasantries while sitting on the bog, my dad would say after a rare night out with the Edwardses, and I was beginning to see his point.

"Now you're acquainted with Mr. Edwards and our son, Henry, aren't you, dear?"

Henry. My sweet, heart-stopping Henry paused from pushing his fries around long enough to glance up at me and smile. A dandelion ray of Henry-shine, serpentine and hot, shot through my head, down my spine, then rested between my legs. I continued on in no-talk, so the Tat introduced herself around, shaking everybody's hand and smiling that white-toothed smile of hers, which had brought on jealous fits in the most beautiful of beauties who had attended high school with her, and was no doubt stirring up similar pangs at college, too. Henry was looking even better than he had in the summer—all angles and meandering curves. Cheekbones like a mad dog.

"We're having an intimate gathering tonight for Henry at the house, and I do hope you two girls will be able to attend." I could tell the Tat was cringing at the word *girls* without even glancing her way. "I'm sure Henry would be delighted if you stopped by." Mrs. Edwards didn't even look in his direction, but reached out and patted his hand as if she were aware of his whereabouts at all points in time. I wish I'd been aware of his whereabouts for the past three months. I'd hoped and prayed and crossed every finger and toe trying to draw Henry back to my house. It never worked. But now, the ultimate birthday gift: He was inviting me over to *his* house. Or his mother was. Close enough. "Your parents have our address, dear. It's the first white house on Butter Lane past Hillstream. And, of course, be sure to bring your charming brother, Morgan."

To tell you the truth, I was damn impressed by her manners, even though she had messed up Logan's name, impressed by how easily she ignored my no-response response to just about everything she had said, impressed by her holding on to my sweaty palm a moment or two rather than pulling back in disgust.

Henry flashed me a hint of his sweet chipped tooth, and I walked away, regretting my silence, fighting the urge to turn and see if he was looking. The Tat's hips were swaying beneath her long skirt, her feet arching catlike out of her clogs. So I pushed my hips forward, too, arching my back, feeling okay, like maybe it was all about the walk. I slunk into my chair, cheeks burning, heart pounding, too excited to even order. So the Tat did it for me.

I sipped at my smoothie, swirled the bee pollen, spirulina, and ginger with my straw; listened vaguely to the Tat as she read to me from her bulky copy of *Vision of Light— the Beginner's Guide to Enlightenment.* Knowing instinctively, on some untapped level, these words held so many of my answers. Knowing this vast collection of syllables and punctuation and inflections could help me shine, but rejecting them, pushing them aside in favor of a leather-clad, meat-eating, pot-smoking, all-around busting guy. The Tat kept glancing up, too, smoothing out her hair, twisting her love beads, seeing if Henry was looking our way and smiling at me when he did.

After a bit, we split, passing by the Edwardses who were still downing their lunch, giving them a polite nod as they discussed dessert. We accidentally left the Tat's book sitting on our table at John's, the one that had been all carved up with people's initials. It made me sad to think of all those beautiful words lying there, even if I hadn't been listening to them that well, but the Tat said not to worry, she'd drop by another time and pick it up. And I found out not too long ago that that's just what she did.

3

"It might be burning, sugar," said the Tat, straightening the dress I was borrowing from her, while checking out her new bangs in the mirror. She was trying to get Logan to go to Henry's party, but Logan out-and-out refused. He sat at my desk, rolling a joint, and looked at me all squinty-eyed, like he'd bent over for a sneeze or something, and in the split second of loss of contact, I'd suddenly grown up.

"When did you start with the makeup?" He slid his hand along his cheek like he was putting on blush.

I shrugged.

The Tat took a step back trying to figure if the dress suited me or not. It was one of those hippie numbers, long and kind of shapeless, but it made me feel peaceful and centered, like my karma was in good standing. I added some more red to my already well-coated lips.

Logan said, "They're gonna stick together permanently, Bean Brain, if you put any more of that shit on."

"Are you sure you don't want to go, sugar?" the Tat asked for the hundredth time. She called Logan sugar like she was from the South or something, which she wasn't. She'd grown up right down the street from us. Logan rolled his eyes and blew air out through his lips.

"Christ, Anna, if you want to go, go with Let and her little friend. Steam on over there and have yourself a ball. Whatever. Just stop bugging me already."

He lit up the joint, clenching it between his teeth, causing him to squint up at us with smoky eyes. My room took on the familiar aroma of a sun-baked herb garden, which I was not at all averse to, although I didn't partake often myself. The Tat wavered a bit, which was weird on account of her hardly ever wanting to go anywhere without my brother. It was like they were sewn together or something, but after a minute or so of some head-scratching contemplation, she plopped down next to Logan and grabbed the joint from his hand.

• • • •

Downstairs my dad awaited me, ready to put himself through the good-father paces and sock in a lecture or two before sending his only daughter out into the heartless November evening for her first night jaunt in her good-mileage, dual–air bags, ABS-brakes, but nevertheless potentially dangerous car. Clad in his jogging gear—a big reflective stripe down both the front and back of his matching nylon ensemble made him visible at night from Peavey Lane to Timbuktu—he reviewed the safety features of the Flame. What to do if I got a flat tire, what to do if my radiator overheated, if my stick shift stuck, if I saw a pothole. What doohickey to turn, what gizmo to shut off.

"I'll get you a car phone next week," he said, "but in the meantime you're on your own. Be careful, and remember, slowly roll up to lights so that you never have to stop, keep the car constantly in motion. And if you pass anybody who needs help, don't stop. It's a sad state of affairs, but you just don't know who you can trust these days. If you get pulled over, make sure the officer shows you his badge before you roll down the window, and if you don't feel comfortable, tell him you'll follow him to the station. Don't let him bully you." I could tell it was taking all he had not to hop in the car and drive me there himself.

"And here's some Mace. I want you to carry this with you at all times. Put it in your pocket." He handed me the plastic tube, and I dropped it in my boot on account of there not being any pockets in the Tat's dress.

"A wise precaution," I said. "Never can tell what lurks out on Butter Lane these days."

"Very funny." He took his pulse before beginning his nightly run.

The thing was, the Edwardses lived about ten safety-first minutes from us, reachable by swanky, well-lit roads—no potholes, no scary intersections, all lined with rich people, alarm systems, and guards who sat in these bizarre little cottage-booths all night, on the lookout for God knows what because only a truly crazy criminal would try to break into one of these places.

"Ooooh, I see we're all ready to go." My mom walked in and waved her nails around so the polish would dry. "I just know we'll have a luscious time, won't we?" And she winked at me like she always did, shaking her hips from left to right. I motioned good-bye and split.

In the Flame I drove slowly—not like day driving—scanning the shoulder for raccoons and possums and other little scuttering night critters. I started thinking about Phaëthon again, about how he thought he could handle his father's chariot just fine. But with the first kick of the horse, Phaëthon lost control, leaving the road of the sun just like Helios had warned him not to—rising too high, burning the heavens; sinking too low, setting the earth on fire. In the end he couldn't control anything anymore, and Zeus had had to strike him down with a thunderbolt cast from his own hand. I had second thoughts concerning giving the Flame a name of such doom, but I peered through the windshield at the clear, auspicious sky and figured I was safe for a while, figured I was safe at least through Henry's party.

• • • •

Halfway to Henry's, just before Courier, my high school, I pulled off Butter Lane and onto Horseshoe Road, which after a quick curve around an overgrown oak led to Briar Path, where I picked up CJ, who, as usual, was waiting on the porch for me, even though the weather had begun to turn. There was always some trauma going on with her family, no doubt due to having eight kids and all of them pretty much burns, except of course for CJ. She kind of straddled all the cliques, like I did.

CJ's house stood amongst the other look-alike, two-story brick dwellings. Decorative-only front porches, well-trimmed bushes, and loads and loads of myrtle, a built-in fireplace inside, along with matching kitchen appliances. There were hundreds of homes like these skirting the heart of my neighborhood, and the owners were certainly well-off even by Republican standards, but somehow the monotony of it all made me sad, made me want to dart out of there the second I arrived.

CJ hopped in the car, her miniskirt flipping up with the motion. She was about as tan as a white person could be on account of her sitting by the pool all day, even in the winter if the sun was out.

"Groovy car," she said as she slammed the door shut. "How fast does it go?" The thing was, I didn't know how fast the Flame could go, so as soon as we got the hell out of CJ's sub, I slammed the pedal to the metal, and for a minute it felt like we were going backward. Then we just started wailing down Horseshoe Road, headed for the curve, hitting a hundred-plus in no time. My heart was racing big on account of my worrying about the animals I might smash (not to mention smashing ourselves if I didn't clear the oak), so as soon as I hit the high mark and we didn't seem to be able to go beyond it, I slammed on the brakes, jilting CJ's head forward like that ball and paddle game.

"Far out." CJ lit up a cigarette while rearranging her blown-out blond bangs with her fingers. She had this way of speaking like she was stuck in the '60s or something. I could understand it more if her parents were ex-hippies, but they were far from it. Her dad was one of those career-military guys, whose main preoccupation seemed to be to clean up the youth of today while his fridge was bursting with Budweiser and frozen dead-animal patties and cartons of Newport 100s; and he passed every Saturday afternoon cleaning his gun collection, which he did downstairs in the living room, right smack in front of the goddamn bay window, like it was the greatest thing in the world.

Since I'd known CJ, which was going on ten years, he'd gone from four, maybe five, little handguns to a major arsenal. "You have to be prepared for all possible danger," he'd say. Condensation from our lemonade glasses would drip down our arms as we tried to get back to the pool. "It's a jungle out there, and it's only a matter of time, before *they* tire of killing each other and start moving in on us. The way I see things, walled compounds are a must before it's too late." I was never clear on who *they* were.

CJ's mother was one of those classic brain-dead military wives, bringing her husband cold beers while he watched the tube or mowed the lawn—using one of those seated-type tractors so that he could drink and mow simultaneously. She also whipped up martinis on Sundays when the neighbors dropped by for some barbecued beef, starched her husband's handkerchiefs, ironed his underwear, oblivious to anything but what he said was so.

Thing was, as people CJ's parents were pretty much okay. In the summer she and I would hang by the pool all day, and her dad would tell us those stupid jokes fathers tell, sincerely trying to make us laugh, and I could appreciate that; and then CJ's mom would bring out pitchers of freshly made iced tea and all these watermelon balls and pineapple wedges on toothpicks. That was one thing that always confused me in life—how to separate individuals from their beliefs. And even with all the time I have to think here I haven't mastered that yet.

I kept the Flame down to a reasonable speed, and CJ had her cigarette hanging out the window on account of knowing how the smoke got to me while simultaneously flipping the radio stations around looking for her new favorite song, which knowing her was probably not getting much radio play anyway. She was concentrating pretty hard and not saying much, which was cool by me because it gave me time to check out the scenery, which was all looking different that night even though I'd been down those roads a million times before, in a million different moods. Then I started to realize it was on account of me being behind the wheel for a change, and the feeling made me chuckle. CJ looked up for a second, like maybe she was missing out on something wild, then flipped around some more.

And to tell you the truth, it was a wild feeling. The evergreens were higher, their branches stretching way wide open, astonishing the sky and the clouds and any onlooker with their magnificent twirling shades of green. Green the likes of which I'd never seen before, except maybe for Logan's eyes when the rage set in, and I was blown away by the pure beauty of all I saw.

"You look groovy," CJ said, having given up finding her song and settling on some AM station that was cranking the oldies. She rubbed the gauze of the Tat's dress between her fingers. I checked myself in the rearview mirror.

"Do I look like a loser?"

"No, darling, you look totally far out." She smiled at me, her baby-pink lips looking hot in contrast to the sky-blue eye shadow she'd rubbed on. It went clear up to her keenly arched brows. "So what does this cat do?"

"Photography."

"Wow, groovy. What kind?"

I shrugged. "Advertising, I think. You know, cars and all."

That was the thing with Detroit, everybody was working for the auto industry in one way or another, although half the time you might not know it. CJ nodded, taking a last drag of her cigarette, then tossed it onto the retreating shoulder of the road.

. . . .

The Edwards house turned out to be one of those white clapboard numbers with these carefully pruned hedges, like out of picture books of royal English gardens. I guess I'd been there a bunch of times as a kid, but it was so long ago, who could remember? Henry lived above the garage in some converted storage space that contained his apartment and darkroom. It was attached to the house by this winding, covered path, a row of miniature evergreens marking the way, but of course I didn't know that then. I didn't know much about Henry that you could actually put into conversation. All I knew was he shone so hard, it made my insides hurt.

"Nice pad," said CJ. Which it was, but CJ thought just about anything outside of her cookie-cutter abode was a nice pad, without stopping to take into account what actually went on inside of these money temples. This part of America where I lived was so rich, you couldn't begin to fathom it. You really couldn't. I used to think, if everybody on just Peavey Lane, say, gave one percent of their income to some charitable cause, we could pretty much solve half the world's problems. Then if our neighbors the next road over pitched in, we could reach the other half, too. But instead, all the money just rotted away in the banks, getting periodically shifted here or there, growing in size, but not doing anybody any good. Nobody could spend that much money on just one life. Nobody.

I eyed the mess of parked cars as we passed, figuring each one brought some happening girl, all after Henry, of course—the same as I was—but rather than back off, I charged forward, CJ at my side. "Never be a quitter," my dad would say (of course with rather different points of reference in mind). "It's a sure way to miss out on life." So even though this was not the intimate gathering I'd been anticipating—the one where Henry sat and shot the shit with me all night, before clutching my hand to his chest, proclaiming his heartfelt love, begging me to be his long-term girlfriend, with the possibility of wifedom and three beautiful children thrown in for good measure—I took my dad's advice and pressed on.

Inside, the party pulsated with all these drunk, loser college types clodhopping to some indie college music like it was really cool or something. The family room was huge and sunk lower than the landing that CJ and I found ourselves perched on—looking, no doubt, like a couple of misfits. Old Mrs. Edwards and her husband were nowhere in sight. Neither was Henry.

CJ flipped back her hair, like she always did when she was ready for action, and took me by the hand.

"Let's scarf a drink." CJ liked to drink all right, not tons, not to where she couldn't see straight or carry on a fluid conversation, although that wasn't totally out of the question, but just until she was feeling "good." I wasn't much of a drinker myself because booze loosened me up a bit too much, if you know what I mean, but right at that moment, I was feeling perhaps a tad too tense.

CJ found the bar like she was wired with radar. There was this old geezer behind it serving up drinkie-winks, and right off it made me feel kind of sad. Old people in menial jobs really bummed me out. I was always picturing my dad doing something of that sort (What if his business had failed rather than earned him all those awards lining the bookshelves in the TV room, not to mention what it had bought—the house, the cars, the tennis lessons . . . ?), or I thought about the old guy's kids and did they love him and were they proud of him, even though he had such a lousy job. I figured only kids should be allowed to do jobs like serving champagne to a bunch of overprivileged, underage losers. By the time you got to be this guy's age, you should be guaranteed a respectable position. Head of a company or something. I flashed the old guy my best smile, taking the Canadian Club and soda from his liver-spotted hand.

"So Let, where is this photo cat?" I shook my head, and we started working our way through the masses, holding our drinks above our heads, until we got lucky and stumbled upon an empty couch in one of the back rooms. "Grab a seat, darling. I'm going to prowl out the bathroom and grab some fresh ones." She finished off her gin and tonic in one gulp, then took off down this long hall while I got comfortable on the couch.

I knocked back my drink in no time, too, on account of there not being much else to do, not to mention an explosive case of nerves I had because I was going to *finally* see Henry. I swear almost twenty minutes slipped by as I alternately picked my nails and looked for CJ. Finally I decided she must have lost her way or something and got up to find her. Plus, I figured maybe I'd come across Henry en route, which was the whole reason I was at the goddamn party in the first place.

I started walking through the endless succession of rooms, squashing up skinny to fit through all the people who just kept pouring in. It was like in those flicks right before some clown yells fire and everybody just about kills one another trying to get out. After clearing the library, the living room, the study, the game room that held a pool table *and* a billiard table, and finally Henry's mom's office where she did God knows what except maybe tease up her hair and swig bourbon, I made it back to the sunken family room, only now it was way packed, and the floor was vibrating because everybody was still dancing to more lousy music. Looking way off in the opposite corner, I could make out the back of CJ's head, which wasn't too hard to do—because it was so blond, it looked like the sun had crashed through the ceiling and landed on her skull. I could tell she was having this heavy-duty rap with some guy, laughing hard with him, but I couldn't tell who.

And when I got to CJ, it was naturally Henry she was hanging with. My sweet Henry, dark and shiny as the day is long. I say *naturally* on account of CJ being a real knockout and guys always going berserk for her and this not being the first instance some guy I was into going for CJ instead. But circumstances were a little different this time around in that Henry was my big-time shiner, and I wasn't about to just hand him over to CJ on a silver platter. As I walked up, CJ kind of backed away from Henry a little bit, and they both stopped laughing, as if some applause sign had darkened.

"Darling," she said, "I was bringing you a drink, then I met this groovy cat here. But I guess you already know him anyway." She smoothed my hair down my back, then squeezed my hand like she always did when she was feeling guilty about something. "Pretty groovy, huh?"

Henry said, "Hey," and smiled.

"Hey," I said, real straight-faced. "So where's my drink?" I looked at CJ's empty hands. She just smiled and flipped her palms over, so Henry handed me his.

"Finish it," he said, "I'll grab another."

I placed my lips over the imprint his had left and downed it in a flash. Henry split to get us a fresh round, and CJ leaned in toward me.

"He's foxy," she said.

"What were you guys talking about?"

"I dunno. Nothing much."

"Did he say anything about me?"

"No." She lit up one of her dad's Newports, cupping it between her thumb and forefinger so her hand curved inward like a tunnel.

"Well, didn't you try to bring me up? Find out what he thought?"

"It's not always that easy." She blew smoke almost right into my face on account of her looking more over my shoulder than in my eyes.

Henry came back with our drinks. He and CJ clinked glasses.

"Cheers, big ears," CJ said, and laughed. Henry started laughing, too, like it was the funniest thing he'd ever heard. Then they both clinked my glass. I polished off my drink in about two minutes flat and took off for a refill without either CJ or Henry seeming to notice. CJ Jenkins was my best friend, but I've got to tell you, sometimes I wanted to kill her. I glanced over my shoulder at her busting chest heaving and ho-ing beneath her tight angora sweater, feeling my sweet Henry slipping from reach.

It turned out there were bar stations set up all over that party. Homages to the Boozeman. That's what Logan started calling bars when he finally quit drinking. I didn't figure any of the kids there were legal drinking age, not even Henry, but the Edwardses were like that. They believed kids only became addicted to the things they were deprived of or the things that were made to sound mysterious or evil. "Well, Joe must have been raised without a bloody husk of corn in sight," my dad would say, rolling his cloudy eyes.

I always thought it was weird when adults drank a lot. I figured they had these great big houses, with fancy gardens and loads of cars, a bunch of kids who were more or less good-looking and reasonably intelligent, and they were all more or less good-looking and reasonably intelligent themselves, so what were they boozing it up for? Some of them, a couple maybe, drank modestly, but for the most part, all the adults I knew really kicked them back. I mean, they got looped big-time and not just at night, either. They got looped at any old time of day. Except of course for my parents. They had a glass of wine with dinner and maybe a cocktail or two with friends, but I'd never seen them tipping over from booze, although it usually seemed like my mom wanted to, but she was afraid she'd forget where the toaster went or something.

So I ordered another drink from the same old geezer who'd served me before, thanking him about ten times over for making it and holding back the desire to inquire as to whether his kids were nice to him and appreciated that he was doing the best he could and whatnot. I considered the fact I was consuming more alcohol in one night than I normally did in a month, but given the circumstances, it felt appropriate. Even necessary. Then I began meditating on Henry. I wondered if he'd noticed I wasn't there yet, and if so, if he was wondering just where I scrambled off to. I guess at that point I'd been gone about twenty-five minutes, and neither he nor CJ was hot on my trail. I was well into my fifth mixer when CJ surfaced.

"Where'd you skedaddle off to?" she whispered in my ear, after sneaking up from behind.

"Why stay where you're not wanted?"

"What's that supposed to mean?"

I just shrugged. CJ belted down the remainder of my drink, then got us two more.

"Where's Henry?" She rolled her eyes, like who cares. "What happened to him?"

"His mother. She came and dragged him off to meet some chickie that was just his perfect match. By the by, he was wondering where you ran off to."

"He was?" She nodded while chewing on a multicolored capsule she'd just popped in her mouth. She believed you got the stuff into your system faster that way, with better absorption to boot. Like I mentioned earlier, CJ wasn't much of a boozer, not in the true sense. What CJ truly was was a popper of pills. Any kind, really—red ones, blue ones, mixed pastel tones. Made no difference. If it took her somewhere new, she was game to go.

"What are you taking tonight, girl?"

"Something to warm up my body juices, get them flowing freely, in alignment with my mind."

"Translation, please."

"Speed, darling. The juice-flower."

So what I did then was to leave CJ at the bar in the library, already rapping with some other guy, and go looking for Henry. I knew it was pretty pointless, considering old Mrs. Edwards had absconded with him, but the thing was, I was starting not to think too straight. Big fuzzy waves kept vibrating through my head, making the most illogical things seem A-OK. Which is precisely the right kind of mood to be in, if, in the short run, you need to kill some time, and, in the bigger picture, you're looking for the answer to life. I started to search the whole house, even, and most especially, the bits where the party wasn't officially going on. I was opening and closing doors like a game-show contestant when finally I hit the jackpot.

Henry. Sweet angel-man Henry. Sitting on the bed in one of the upstairs bedrooms, looking out the window, leaning forward on his knees, a rainbow of color circling his head. I waited, paralyzed behind his curved back, while searching for telltale signs of another. But he just kept staring out the window, watching the moonlight skirt across the snow, so I worked up one of those polite little coughs that girls do in the movies and jolted Henry right out of his reverie.

"Hey, Let." He looked me up and down hard. "I didn't know you were there."

"Sorry. What are you doing up here?"

"What am I doing up here? What are *you* doing up here?"

I smiled at him, trying to look some certain special kind of way I wasn't too familiar with at that point in my life, but I guess it worked because he hit the bed beside him with his hand and cocked his head to the side, motioning me over. So of course right then I got nervous as hell, and I made my way over like I had glue on my shoes.

The bed was covered in one of those slippery-type spreads with a floral pattern swirling across it. There were these two matching wicker bedside tables with iron lamps and a framed reproduction of a Hopper centered directly over the headboard. Not a speck of dust anywhere, as if the maid had just left for the day. I figured it was a guest room on account of that weird echoey vibe that rooms take on when they aren't used often. Henry's weight forced his section of the bed into a deep recess, so as I sat down, I slid up tight against him.

"So, little Let, you looking for me?" He slipped my drink out of my hand and took a sip. It was the second time that night our lips had met outside of our bodies. I felt the twitch coming on.

"Maybe." I bit my bottom lip.

"Well, how do I find out for sure?"

"I dunno."

I could smell the odor of sweaty leather rising off him, which I found out later was what he always smelled like, on account of his never taking those leathers off, except maybe for the rare weekly shower. It was like how Ryder always smelled of Southern Comfort and Ivory soap. But I'm jumping ahead, because at this point I hadn't even met Ryder.

Henry started playing with my pinkie, rolling it back and forth in his hand. I stared at my feet, my heart pounding like the soundtrack from one of those horror flicks CJ was always watching.

"So tell me, little Let, how will I know if you like me or not?"

I was wishing he'd stop calling me little Let. I thought about the Flame parked outside, assured myself I wasn't so little at all.

I shrugged again, looking at him from the corner of my eye. He kept hold of my hands, but suddenly, tilting his chin down and to the side, leaned forward and kissed me. His mouth was burning hot, not like the boys who'd been there before with mouths tasting of cold beer and chewing gum. His breathing was easy and even. He slid his hand up toward my face, then cupping it, slipped his tobaccoed thumb into my mouth.

I started to feel the pressure of his body leaning in more and more toward mine, so I concentrated on the wall behind him, the roughness of his thumb hard against my tongue. A wetness grew between my legs. My heart was putting on a hard-core drum solo, beyond horror-movie stuff and into arena rock concerts. I tried to pull my head away, but Henry had his other hand on the back of it, pushing me harder into him.

So I got into it for a little bit, his tongue feeling its way around between my lips, jamming down my throat; and the rhythm of his thumb, working in and out, in and out. His body kept getting hotter, and he slid his other hand down my back drawing me tight against him, then working it around front and up the Tat's dress. To tell you the truth, he was moving a little fast for me. I don't know if I've mentioned it yet, but at that point I was still untouched. A virgin, as it's better known. Not that I hadn't had my opportunities, but at the last minute I'd always sensed (and rightly so) the guy involved was a shine-faker, and I would split.

I tried to pull back and explain some of this to Henry, but he pushed into me more forcefully, his cock jamming into my leg, so what I finally had to do was squirm downward out of his grasp, sliding off the bed, and shoot up again a couple of feet away. I could tell from the way Henry looked at me that he was amused to say the least.

"What's the matter, little Let, you don't like me as much as you thought? Huh, baby girl?"

The thing was, I did want to be with him, just not quite like that. Not quite so all at once. I guess I was wanting at least a first date. At least a ride in his car and some rousing conversation over a bowl of pasta. But you have to understand, all the while I'm thinking this, I'm watching the pinkness nestled behind that chip of his, flicking with his laughter, hypnotizing me so to speak, as I imagined what it would feel like to have that sweet tongue wandering about my neck, say, or behind the knees like the Tat says she likes; so when he grabbed me by the wrist, I let him pull me forward and lay me across the bed. He kicked off his boots and I heard them thud against the floor while he pulled his T-shirt over his head. He arched over me, his dark nipples popping in the chill of the night, moonlight falling across his face.

I remember that night like it was yesterday, too (and in reality it wasn't all that long ago). Henry's sweet face over mine looking drawn, ravenous, like he'd been fasting for days and I was the first slice of cherry pie to cross his path. But the thing was, you see, I guess I'd actually had more to drink than I thought, because the whole time this was happening and during most of what had been happening before, the room had been spinning and the bed doing flip-flops, and then Henry himself was kind of moving in and out of focus. I tried to practice that breathing the Tat had taught me, but it just seemed to make everything worse. So what happened next was, in the midst of all of Henry's throbbing and rubbing with the cool night air on my neck, I passed out cold. And it was right at the good part, too. Right when Henry was sliding his thumb back in again and I was starting to feel the shine.

4

Bolts of bluey-blue morning light shot across my face through half-closed shutters. I stirred, finding myself alone on an unfamiliar bed, with a familiar scent, without even the slightest indentation to hint that my sweet polestar Henry had been there with me at some point in the not-so-distant past. The previous night's unfortunate turn of events came back to me with slow, methodical recall, and my head began to pound. I forced myself off the bed and began searching the adjoining bathroom for some aspirin, but came up empty-handed. So I pressed on, working my way toward home.

Downstairs the sunken family room looked like one of those after-the-bomb flicks: torn streamers, crumpled napkins, half-empty glasses of punch, but where were the people? I wanted to be long gone, too. Long gone before Henry even batted one of his angel-lids and came inside looking for a bagel and instead found me. So I grabbed my coat, which was lying neatly across the back of the couch like it was waiting for me, and bailed—knowing I should stay until the Edwardses got up, knowing that would have been a definite right, but not doing it anyway. Figuring it was a *small* definite right, an expendable one.

Right hand on the brass knob, I reached back with my left, snagging a clump of pizza and taking a bite. Nausea set in at an alarming rate. I hustled to the Flame, happy to see her again, figuring the Edwardses must have phoned my parents or I would be home by now. There was the beginning of a winter chill in the air. I glanced up at the garage, thinking about Henry, thinking about how I'd like to be up there with him right then, snuggled hard into the curve of his chest.

The ride home was long and gloomy, to say the least. I dragged it out as best I could, but I was nevertheless getting closer to my house, and to my parents. I pictured them all showered and dressed waiting for me at the kitchen table with a pot of tea, maybe even breakfast, doing their best to give the appearance of order in a situation that no doubt to them felt very much out of order.

I could picture my dad reading the paper, tennis gear on, waiting for my safe return before getting in a late-morning match with Mr. Marchers at the club. My mom would be fussing over her crosswords, a special crossword-doer's dictionary open before her, an ashtray close at her elbow. Clean of course on account of her washing it after almost every cigarette, which meant it spent a lot of time under water. And I could conjure up, plain as the breaking day on the horizon, the concern that would be radiating from their faces at the sight of me, their poor, wayward offspring, lost already at such a young age (they could be very melodramatic). Radiating and radiating, as though they could heal me with their vibrations alone.

I'd seen it all before, you see. I'd seen it with Logan when he returned from Vegas with that brand-new booze habit of his. I'd watched them radiate all over him. That, of course, was a while back. Now they just all-out ignored him. Even before he left for college, it had been like he didn't live there. Partly on account of his hardly ever leaving his room except with the Tat, and partly because I don't think my parents knew what to say to him. I think they were kind of afraid of him. And to tell you the truth, I kind of was, too. He could be real intimidating, though in a nice-enough way.

Intensely private. Cloistered. Cut off. Those are the words that came to mind then when I thought of Logan, but now I think more along the lines of *scared, lonely,* and *hurt.* He was sweet too, then and now. Like his giving me the necklace he'd made in high school, a symbol of himself he'd said, not ever taking it off until he passed it on to me right before he left for college. Not saying much when he gave it to me. Not like in the movies. No big sibling-love speech, but giving it to me all the same. Now it hung permanently around my neck.

Thinking about my parents and their fanatic radiation was depressing the hell out of me, but eventually, as I was moving in a forward direction, my house loomed before me, and what could I do but go inside? The front door creaked beneath the push of my hand, and Whiz Bang pranced out to greet me, doing her little kitty dance, the old one-two, arched spine rubbing back and forth against my calf.

Whiz Bang was pretty much my best friend, and that was taking CJ Jenkins and all into account. I'd found her when I was eleven, hidden under a truck, not coming out for anybody but me. She'd just sat there staring and blinking, blinking and staring, the way that cats do, until I had moseyed up. Then she'd scooted right into my arms. I'd emptied practically my whole savings account to have the vet fix the lump in her tummy. In return, she slept with me each and every night, nose tip to nose tip, pulled up tight against Logan's symbol on the chain.

Our house was still as a headstone, which gave me the creeps, on account of my parents being early risers; being up before them was a first. There was no morning radio buzz, no clank of dishes, not even the faint hiss of breath. I felt a little disappointed. Once home and everything, with doom and gloom heavy on my head, I wanted them to be up already: lecturing, exhorting, grounding, whatever. Just doing their parent thing, freeing me up to move on.

My head was doing a real one-two then, but the only aspirins in the house were located in my parents' bathroom. As a rule, I didn't believe in medication of any sort. You know, my body is my temple and all, but then again, my temple had been seriously violated. I remembered the Tat and Logan, in days gone by, using caffeine as a hangover remedy, so I boiled a pot of water, poured some of it over a tea bag in a cup, and let it steep for a bit, having never been able to acquire a liking for coffee.

After a while, though, I just wanted to bail. Get myself out of the house for long enough so that by the time I came back, maybe the whole thing would have blown over. The one downer was that Logan and the Tat were home, and I wouldn't get to see much of them if I split, but I figured if

I left right that minute I could get back in the early afternoon, giving my parents plenty-o'-time to forget and still leaving ample amounts to hang.

Plus you couldn't get anything past my mother anyway. She was always sensing things. Like when Logan first took off for college, there was this one night when she just couldn't sleep. She kept telling my dad something had happened to Logan, but my dad wouldn't let her call. "It's all that coffee you drink, Maude. It won't let your mind relax properly. Drink some warm milk and come to bed." Well, it turned out she hadn't been so off. Logan had gotten toasted and mouthed off to some big bruiser-type guy, who in return had belted him one, practically breaking his nose. Logan turned out to be okay, but it was weird how my mom had known something was up.

So I wrote my parents the following note: "Came home, but nobody was up. Therefore went to Hillstream for a walk. See you soon." I even drew this frilly heart and signed my name with an X and an O. Trying to sound real normal. Like I always went for walks at Hillstream at six o'clock on Sunday mornings. No biggie.

Hillstream, I should explain, is this exclusive private school near our house. Very upper-crust. It's mostly a boarding school, filled with the kids of distant and not-so-distant royalty, big founding members of corporations, and sometimes famous authors, if they came from the right family. You know, old money, not too many swanky Hollywood types there. There are a few day-doers, too, kids who live nearby and just go for classes. The grounds are massive and absolutely shocking. Low rolling hills full of nooks and crannies, places to get lost either by accident or on purpose. A beautiful rambling river where girls gave up their virginity like bubbles into the air and a great science museum where all the public schools would go on field trips once a year.

There was also a lot of cool stuff like tennis courts; and a huge lake with all different kinds of boats; and an old-fashioned boathouse with a huge veranda; and this gigantic house where the dean lived, with winding, twisting gardens of all sorts. There was one my dad particularly liked, which was done in Japanese style. Part of the grounds was open to the public, so I'd spent a bit of time there with my parents or Logan, but mostly with the Tat, who knew them well on account of one of her longer-lasting transformations involved being a major nature-head and Hillstream being the perfect place to commune with the environment.

The Edwards house actually bordered these lands, so I was heading right back into the dragon's lair, so to speak. I hadn't been able to brush my teeth (and the tea hadn't helped any), so I grabbed a pack of my mom's gum out of the pencil drawer, which was well stocked on account of her always trying to give up smoking, gave Whiz Bang a few apologetic squeezes, and split. Not a backward glance.

· · · ·

True to her name, the Flame was still warm. Six-fifteen flashed from my dashboard, so I figured I must have got about four hours of sleep. I checked myself in the rearview mirror. Yesterday's pimple was fading, but sure enough a new one was working its way up, so I squeezed it hard between my nails, watching it splat on the reflecting glass, then wiped it clean with my thumb.

The Flame, it turned out, was a pretty silent ride, which I was most appreciative of on account of the ridiculous pounding still going on in my head. Driving along, I was overwhelmed with the sudden desire to ask for forgiveness, but the thing was, I wasn't sure who to ask it from or precisely for what.

I whizzed down Dakota Avenue to the outskirts of Nottingham before realizing I was starving, so I stopped briefly at the International House of Pancakes for a stack. I remembered Logan had always eaten pancakes after his all-nighters and got real excited thinking about how I was starting to figure these adult-type things out and it really wasn't too difficult.

First off, I had the Flame, and she would take me anywhere I desired. If wanted to go to IHOP at 6:30 in the morning to cure a wicked hangover that I'd acquired trying to pick up a busting older guy (and almost had, too, except for the passing-out part, which I didn't want to think about), then that's where I was going. If I wanted to drive clear out to Wyoming, why, I could go there, too. It was easy. Just a matter of knowing where you're headed.

After wiping up the remainder of the syrup from my plate, I took off for Hillstream as planned. It just wasn't time to go home yet. I figured my parents must be up by now. My lecture stewing in their brains a few hours more, then, if all went according to plan, dissipating, thinning out, finally watering down to a "So how was the party?"

But how much time was the right amount? And how much was too much, so that it would all build up again bigger than ever?

These are the things that are hard to figure out with any accuracy, so I opted for the middle. Lunchtime. My turn would come when everyone was in a good mood, eating turkey sandwiches and cold Yorkshire pudding, feeling happy the way you always do from holiday leftovers, therefore hardly even remembering my not coming home on time, or if remembering, thinking it was okay. "Lunchtime," I said out loud, and hit the road.

· · · ·

Hillstream was deserted. Even the for-show-only guard's booth was empty. I parked in front of the Greek theater— a white stone replica of a real thing, made to look half in ruins, nestled in the thick of the woods; a low, round stage, with curved, layered benches encircling it. Through an open arched wall lay a shallow pool, almost always devoid of water, a random collection of stones filling the bottom, and a concrete statue of Artemis on one side. Off to the back, myriad paths led to various boarding-school treasures sprinkled about the grounds.

I walked around the benches a bit, climbing up, bouncing down, then up and down a few more times. After a while I sat on the edge of the pool, grabbed a handful of stones, tossed them back in, listening to the skid as they hit. I watched clouds roll by, waited for time to pass. Then I got kind of cold just sitting there, so what I decided to do was try one of the paths. I'd been on them a million times before, but always with the Tat, and to be honest, I didn't pay much attention to things like directions. I usually just followed somebody else or stayed at home.

I picked the path in the dead center, mostly for the aesthetic balance of it, but also because its twists and turns seemed vaguely familiar. It wasn't too long, though, before I had lost my way, heading toward a wrongly recognized dry streambed in the distance. I shuffled down a long hill, veered right at the bottom, then left, then right again, getting more and more tangled in the brambles, yet still not seeing any way out. The route I'd come had closed behind me, and it was getting pretty cold.

I wanted out of those woods in a big way, so what I did was to ask God to help me, give me some kind of guidance. It dawned on me that perhaps it was *His* forgiveness I'd been seeking in the car (although the reason was still unclear), so I apologized for the night before in general, promising I'd go straight home the minute I found the Flame, if he'd just show me the path. Of course I didn't do any of this on bended knee or anything. I didn't figure God went in for that. I figured that to be more of a device invented by the Church to give parishioners something to do so they didn't get bored. But I prayed just the same.

Then what happened was that the second I finished my prayer, I took a quick turn to the right, and the woods suddenly opened onto this vast clearing of dead grass. A grouping of what appeared to be dormitories were looking warm and cozy so I made my way toward them. I tried the first door, but of course it was locked, as would be the second and the third, I imagined, only I never got that far. En route I noticed a window, open just a crack, leading into what looked like a library, which was alluring because books make me feel calm and centered, feelings I kind of needed at that point.

I could almost hear the alarm going off in my head as I slid the glass pane open, but was greeted instead with more of the same eerie silence that had been shadowing me all morning. I tumbled into a room painted deep crimson, full of opulent chairs—some velvet, some leather—all facing the center, and this glamorous overstuffed embroidered couch, flanked by carved oak tables and marble-based reading lamps. I circled around a couple of times, sliding my fingers across smooth surfaces, and finally flopped straight out on the couch. I was filled with a vague sense of definite wrongness, but, at the same time, was too damn tired to stress about it.

I needed to get back to the Flame, but for the life of me I couldn't figure how to find her again. I mean, Hillstream was huge, and I was in a part I'd never even seen before. The not-for-the-general-public part. I stretched out, resting my head on what happened to be a comfortable pillow, and began counting the walls of pretty books that surrounded me.

There was quite a variety. Tall ones, thick ones, leatherbound mostly. Some looked well read, some untouched. My parents read an awful lot. So did Logan. So did I. The Tat didn't, though. Said you missed out on a lot of life that way, burying your nose in someone else's imagination. This room would have bummed her out. I continued to count. Then for a while I didn't remember a thing.

• • • •

What happened next was the beginning of the second part of the journey that led me to this goddamned hospital bed. Both parts becoming irreversibly intertwined, but it took me a while to realize this on account of being drunk a lot of the time, or hung over, or just not thinking the way I should have been. Because looking back now, I see the writing clearly on the wall. I see how I confused the shine with a lot of things it wasn't. "Life is just a beautiful journey, man," Ryder would say, "and you've got to sit back and enjoy the ride." And that really is what the shine is all about, enjoying the ride and helping others enjoy it, too, but it took me until now to realize as much.

It was that afternoon that I met Ryder. My kaleidoscopic cowboy who first came to me while I snoozed the snooze of the wayward on his school's well-worn couch. When I awoke he was there, his blondness momentarily ringed with light, and he was peering at me and scratching his nose.

"Hey, man, everything cool?"

A blink of my contacts brought his pompadour into focus. "Yeah."

At that point I didn't know who he was, and for a minute I couldn't remember where I was (amongst other things). All I knew for certain was that my head was hurting something awful and my mouth felt fierce. Gum, I thought right off, everything else falling secondary to this American need for clean breath.

He flopped back into one of the velvet chairs across the room, eyeing me with a steady gaze. Kind of nice, if you thought about it—easy, familiar, like we'd grown up together or something and he'd just stopped by my house to wake me up before going to the beach, say.

"Do you live here?" I asked after about an hour of silence.

He nodded. "Thinking of moving in, man?"

I shook my head.

"My name's Ryder. Ryder Hadley. How 'bout you? You got yourself a name?" There was a slight twang to his words, not really southern but something.

"Violet Hitchcock, but my friends call me Let. My parents flip at that, because they think it sounds like I'm fading away, like I'm going to disappear or something. My parents are a bit nuts and all, though. You know?"

I have a tendency to babble when nervous. The kind of nervous where it's sort of fun. The other kind of nervous, where you feel like you're going to die, that kind I hated. Then I get quiet and my palms sweat. Like that afternoon I ran into Henry at John's Café. Ryder just nodded, so I kept going.

"Logan, that's my brother, calls me Bean Brain on account of my not eating meat and all. Says I must have beans for brains because there's not much else going into me, but he doesn't eat that much, either, really. My dad calls me Violet, straight out, because he says it gives me the goal of being as sweet as my name."

"And your mother?" he asked, kind of tongue in cheek.

"Oh, she calls me Violet sometimes, but mostly stuff like love, or dolly girl, or missy, depending on what mood she's in."

He nodded like he knew what I meant.

"Right on," he said, "it's killer to meet you."

I smiled at him from the warmth of my couch.

"So what brings you into this neck of the woods?"

"Well, I went for a walk, and I kind of got lost, then cold, and I guess pretty much tired, too."

"Rough night?"

I nodded. He pulled a well-worn flask from his back pocket, passing it over to me with a "hair of the dog" and a smile. A cowboy riding a bucking bronco was etched on the front of the flask, and *Never Let Loose the Reins* was in script across the bottom.

"A gift from my parents." He looked at his feet. I took a swig and just about choked.

"Southern Comfort." Ryder watched me gag, and nodded like he understood just fine. "It's awesome once you get used to it. Keeps you cranking warm on a day like this. Liquid sunshine."

"Is anybody else up yet?" I handed back the flask. "I mean, don't you guys have to go to church or something? Isn't that like a dorm rule, everybody has to wear blue blazers and school ties and march off to service at the crack of dawn?" I obviously had some corny flick running in my head. Ryder, I noticed, was in Wranglers and a white T-shirt. "This is a dorm, isn't it?"

"Truth, it's a dorm. And no we don't have uniforms. That's Catholic school. Anybody up? Don't think so. Or if they are, they're still in their rooms. Bunch of late risers here. Late risers, man. Me, I'm used to riding early, so I'm up with the first rays, or before, because the before is really decent. Really beautiful, man. The true beauty. The silence we're all seeking."

He had a wild way of talking, I thought, liking it all right.

"Riding? As in horses?"

Ryder nodded.

"Where?"

"Montana, man. In Montana. My parents have a killer place there, stretching out in the glory of the Master like a kitty in the morning sun. Betty and I used to ride on Sunday mornings, bright and early, rise and shine. So it's in my blood now. On the seventh day, the day of rest, I'm up no matter what."

The sun was beating hard through the window, and I figured I looked pretty much like hell. Nevertheless, I couldn't help contemplating kissing Ryder the way I'd been kissing Henry the night before. All wet and twisty and hard. I got the vibe Ryder would have liked it, too. Something about the way he kept grinning at me let me know he would have liked it just fine.

"They had to sell the horses, though, because of all the traveling, man. Couldn't care for them right. At least not the way they needed it." He took a swig of whiskey, looking at the flask a while, thinking about something.

"Do you guys live on a ranch?"

"No, Betty and Michael have a house in town and one out on Flathead Lake, but they used to board Vengeance and Mercy at a corral outside Kalispell. It took about an hour to get there and get the horses saddled up, so Betty used to wake me around four-thirty just before the sun broke. She'd say, 'Rise and shine, Ryder honey. Creation is renewing itself.' Truth is, it was. Birds would be whizzing around, waiting to catch the sunshine on their wings, flowers starting in on their morning rush, the coffeepot gurgling away in the main house, and from my bunk, man, I'd watch that sun rise flat out over the water. Looked like you could walk right out across it and never fall in. Just keep on going till you got to the other side."

"Sounds cool."

"Yeah, it's decent, man. Betty and Michael bought this compound kind of place, all separate buildings for each room. The coolest, of course, is Michael's darkroom."

I remember how I liked Ryder right off. How he had an easy way of talking, like there was a continuous conversation going on in his head and he was just sort of musing out loud, reminiscing, letting me in on this little bit of it, but when I was gone, it wouldn't matter; the conversation would just keep flowing.

"Why does your dad have a darkroom?" I asked. Of course I was thinking about Henry. Even someone as captivating as Ryder couldn't drive him from my thoughts.

"He's a photographer." Shortest sentence to date.

"What kind?"

"Fashion, man. He does a lot of the big campaigns and shoots a bunch of editorials. He's good. You'd probably know his work." There was this weird moment of silence, then he added, "They're looking to buy a ranch now. Get the horses back," and he grinned a wide-open, teeth-sporting, eye-twitching grin.

"How'd you end up here?"

"Michael's career started really kicking and Betty manages him—you know, books all the jobs, makes sure the money's good. Anyway, they felt they didn't have enough 'quality' time for me anymore, and I have some distant crazy uncle residing out this way someplace, so they packed me off to Hillstream, man. Packed me off, probably thinking this old goat would keep an eye on me, but I have yet to meet him."

"Do you miss them?"

"In a way, man. In a way. I miss Betty a lot. She could whip up lasagna that would make our neighbor Mrs. Cordelli weep for her homeland. Made it for us just about every Sunday night, especially in the winter when we lived in town. Michael was never around much to begin with. He came and went with the wind. Like a wild stallion, Betty used to say. But, man, that implies a creature who won't be tamed. Something strong and free and cranking. Not Michael's way at all. They were actually supposed to have come here for Thanksgiving, but my kid brother got sick. Them's the breaks." He grinned again. I grinned back. Things were going all right.

After a while we heard floorboards creaking above our heads, and Ryder said that I'd better blow because girls weren't allowed in the dorms. So I sneaked back out the window, and he followed, walking me to my car, which, it turned out, was only a couple minutes away, making me wonder about my sense of direction or lack thereof. By the time we reached the Flame, I felt like I'd known Ryder pretty much forever.

"Truth, man," Ryder said, when I told him as much, "I feel the same." And he tumbled in, pulling a dog-eared copy of *Walden* out of his back pocket and tossing it on the dashboard so that he could flop more comfortably across my front seat. Sprawling out, really, like he'd been there a million times before.

"Where to?" I asked, acting on the unspoken agreement we'd made that we were headed somewhere.

"The center of solitude."

"Translation, please."

"The museum, man. To the museum."

"Isn't it closed because today is Sunday and all?"

"Yeah, but trust in me, man. I know the true way in," he said with a wink.

So I drove us up to the museum through a maze of winding, tree-sheltered roads, more like glorified paths than anything seriously meant to support transportation. The clock was flashing 11:30, which meant I was cutting it close, but an hour with Ryder and I'd still get home for a late lunch. I don't eat turkey anyway, I figured, so what was the big deal? I parked the Flame beneath the bare branches of a maple tree. A couple of squirrels foraged last-minute food while Ryder darted toward the far side of the building and jimmied the lock on this rusty door, which was pretty much obscured by an overgrown bush. A stale breeze oozed out of the doorway, flecks of dust glowing in the bright light of day.

Ryder said, "In," with a flick of his head. I shot into the darkness, and he pulled the door closed behind us. It took me a minute to gain my bearings, but when I did, Ryder took my hand and led me down this long corridor reeking of cleaning fluids and plastic, then pushed open a big old orange door, and we were in the main hall—light creeping in through these long, narrow overhead windows. We were completely alone in a space designed for multitudes.

"Holy Kamoly," I said. My feet were tingling.

"Killer, man. It's beautiful. Truly beautiful. I come here to clear my head."

The hall we had landed in held all the Native American exhibits, these life-size mannequins of Indians all dolled up in their native clothing, like loincloths and whatnot made from deerskin. The men were shown doing the hunting; and the women, the gathering and cooking, some with babies strapped across their backs. I knew they were plastic, but the thing was, in the semidarkness and eerie silence, they seemed real.

I felt this instinctive connection to the Indian way of life. Even though they did eat meat, there was a ritual about it, an understanding of where the meat came from, a thankfulness, a giving back. And the entire animal was used. Every single ounce. No waste. So unlike our times where modern grocery stores were filled with plastic-wrapped slabs of rotting carcasses, no connection made between some sucker's hamburger and that suffering cow all cooped up in a tight, narrow slot somewhere, living the most God-awful life; waiting, probably praying, for death, just so some loser could get his fill of cheeseburgers and animal-fat fries.

I started figuring Ryder must have come here a lot on account of his knowing his way around pretty well. We passed several cases bursting with stuffed bears, deer, raccoons, mountain lions, and one huge enclosure of birds frozen in flight, looking like they'd just stopped, right that second, at the sight of us. As if the moment we were gone, they'd be in full motion again. Ryder was silent. My head filled with the thumping of my heart.

In the distance a huge globe rose up, and I knew we were headed for the room with the glowing rocks. I hadn't been there since I was a kid, but I remembered that room best of all because my dad and I had gone in there so often. Every time we went, he'd take me in there right off and back again at the end, wrapping his hand around mine, leading me through the various displays, pointing out rocks he particularly liked, sitting on the center bench a minute, resting, thinking, reflecting, then up again, looking for Logan. We'd find him always on the other side of the building in the room filled with all the interactive science stuff, where you could learn how electricity works, how gravity works, how sound travels, but none of that had interested me. I'd liked the quiet of the rock room, leaning against my dad's leg, his hand tight around mine.

And it was quiet then, too, at that moment with Ryder, although none of the rocks glowed on account of the electricity having been turned off. I knew deep down we shouldn't be there. I knew this was really and truly a definite wrong, even though it didn't involve my parents directly. Or indirectly, either, unless of course we got caught.

"Do you think it's okay that we're here?" My voice, a jackhammer on a Sunday morning.

"Yeah. It's our surrender, man." He spread his arms wide as if to inhale it all in one breath.

I didn't know what he meant, but it sounded nice, and I was a sucker for words. I started thinking about Ryder spending a lot of time in here by himself, and it made me kind of sad. He was searching, too, I thought at the time. Trying to shine. But I was wrong. He wasn't trying anything. He already knew how, but it was as if the things he needed to let go of to do it all the way, complete the shine, he just couldn't part with yet. He leaned toward me for a minute, handing me the flask, and I could smell the squeaky-clean scent of Ivory soap roll off him. Not off his clothes, really—those looked like they hadn't seen water since the day his mother packed them carefully into his duffel bag—but off him: his neck, his cheeks, his skin underneath the clothes. I suddenly had the urge to kiss him again, wanting his purity on me hard. Then it was gone; fleeting as a thunderbolt.

We passed the flask back and forth, back and forth, me lying flat out on the bench, getting kind of sleepy. Ryder stretched out on the floor, started to talk about Montana again: the beauty of it, the true beauty of the Master. That was his word for God, and I liked the way he said it, too. Not as if it was someone to expect things from, rather someone to give thanks to for what we'd already been given. As if He was huge and everywhere and beautiful, which is, I guess, what they kind of teach you in Sunday school, but this was different. It was bigger. Limitless.

"It's like the shine," I said.

"Truth, man, the shine," he answered, just like he knew what I meant and all. And I guess he kind of did. The Southern Comfort was lying thicker on my brain, so I closed my eyes, just for a minute, just to clear my head, because I really did know I had to get home in time for lunch. But the thing was, I guess I'd drunk a little more than I realized. Plus I'd already been pretty tired to begin with, despite my earlier nap, and before I could stop myself, before I could hop up and get myself moving, I fell asleep again.

. . . .

So the next thing I knew, I was landing hard against the floor, smashing my elbow and knee and the side of my head. Ryder was snoozing on the floor beside me, curled up like a little kid. I looked at my watch—4:00. We'd been sleeping for hours. I poked at Ryder, feeling kind of mad at him because instead of waking me, he'd just gone and fallen asleep, too. I was dead, I figured. Right-out dead. I belted Ryder one in the arm, because he wouldn't budge, and that woke him just fine. He sat up, rubbing his eyes a bit.

"I gotta go." I made sure the urgency of my situation came through in my voice.

"Truth," Ryder said, still sitting there, his shirt rumpled and his Wranglers kind of pushed up around his boots. I starting thinking about how stupid it was he said *truth* to everything. He was just this kid, dumped at Hillstream because his parents didn't want him around, who liked to drink on Sunday afternoons, and break into the school museum. I couldn't figure out what I'd liked about him in the first place, except maybe his hair—a crazy snarl of cowboy-blondness.

"Do you think maybe you could show me how to get out of this place?" I jumped up, catching the toe of my boot on the Tat's dress. There was a slight tear of fabric. "I forgot to purchase a map at the door."

"No problem." He hopped up, too, and walked away. So I followed a few steps behind him until we reached the orange door. There was only waning sun then to illuminate our path, and beyond the door, in the corridor, it was pitch-black, so Ryder took my hand again, leading me back outdoors and to my ever-patient Flame. I took a deep breath and dropped Ryder's hand.

We climbed into the car, and I started thinking about how weird the last few days had been and feeling pretty lousy about them, too. Thinking about how pretty much everything I had done had been wrong, definite wrongs, and I hadn't done one thing to stop them from happening or to fix them when I knew they were happening or even to make amends after they had happened. I thought about the Edwardses' party and my getting so drunk and all the stupid things I'd said to Henry, my sweet-lipped angel, and messing around with him and passing out during it, forgetting all about CJ, then bailing from the Edwardses without even leaving a note, and going home and not waking anybody up, or even waiting for them to get up naturally, just taking off, eating some lousy food at the IHOP, then getting lost, and passing out again, then meeting some wackoid guy, with hair the size of a melon, who talked about the Master all the time, and breaking into a museum and getting drunk with him, then passing out yet again. My head was killing me. I wanted to be in bed, in my red gingham sheets, with Whiz Bang snuggled up against me: warm, comforting, loving me no matter what; the whole thing never having happened, because it really wasn't like me. It wasn't like me at all.

So I drove Ryder back to his dorm, following his thumb as he gestured directions, pulling up in front of the Greek theater again, and letting him out. I remember it all clearly now: him leaning in through my open window, thanking me for the lift, asking me for my phone number, and me giving it to him, writing it on a corner of one of my car papers ripped off the window on which they were still pasted, not wanting to, but not knowing how to say no, having just passed what was a pretty enjoyable afternoon with him. Somehow thinking it wasn't so enjoyable after all. Just wanting to get home and get away. Although not wanting to really go home, either, on account of home not being away, but rather being in the thick of it. Wanting Whiz Bang, and, I guess, wanting to pay up and all, because that's pretty much what you did. Avoid the wrongs at all costs, but if you stumbled and hit a few, then pay up.

And Ryder giving me his number, written on a torn corner from the book he was reading, leaving the book on my dashboard by mistake, handing me the number, telling me it was for the whole hall on account of private phones not being allowed in the rooms and all. And me taking it, looking at him hard, him looking at me, and me thinking, *What a mess. What a mess these two days have been.* Then leaning forward and kissing him lightly on the lips. Knowing he wanted the same things I did. Knowing he wanted to bust out, too, though in retrospect, perhaps his was a different breed of busting-out than mine.

And while I'd been let down to find Ryder was just like all the boys who had come before, suddenly none of it mattered: the museum, the whiskey, the passing out. I couldn't stay angry at someone who was so like me; someone who was so without the shine. We were like candles or something, useless until someone shared the fire. So I tossed his book into the glove compartment, shoved his number deep into my pocket, and headed home.

The ride back was slow and mournful, worse even than the morning version, because the situation was worse, the wrongs having doubled, perhaps tripled, even if my parents didn't know the details. It was around five o'clock when I pulled up, the house well lit both outside and in. I flipped down the visor, checking myself in the mirror, seeing if I looked anything like how I felt. And the thing was, I didn't. I looked A-OK. Healthy even, well rested, which was wild, considering what I'd just been through.

Inside, I could hear my mom busy in the kitchen, listening to old dance tunes on the radio, swirling herself in circles in between straightening shelves and wiping off counters. My dad was sitting on the couch reading the paper. He folded it in two when I walked in.

"Well, how was Hillstream?" he asked. My dad was big on sarcasm.

"Fine," I said, standing there, my stomach heavy with Southern Comfort. Not having a clue what to do or say; actually wanting to cry on account of feeling so tired and hungry and sick and overwhelmed by guilt all at the same time.

"We've been very concerned about you, young lady," he went on. "Not knowing your whereabouts has been trying, to say the least, but your mother has convinced me that since this is the first time anything like this has happened, we will let it be. Something about the natural progression of teenage rebellion. I'm not certain I agree with her, but I am willing to go along with it this one time." He stared at me, sinking each word one by one, until I felt certain his eyes had bored two new holes in my head. I waited for the inevitable punishment: a grounding, loss of the car, dishes for a week, but nothing came. Then my mom walked out of the kitchen, fixing her hair as usual, puffing on a Winston, waving the smoke in the opposite direction.

"So tell me about the party," she said, just about flooring me, bringing to life my so-how-was-the-party fantasy. "It was okay," I mumbled, feeling lousy. This was way worse than being lectured. At least if you got lectured, you got rid of the guilt. Like with Catholics and their confessions.

"We ordered some pizza. Are you hungry?" She winked at me when my dad wasn't looking as if we'd just pulled off the heist of a lifetime. I nodded even though something just didn't seem right about my parents ordering pizza while I was passed out cold with a stranger inside an illegally entered private building.

I skulked up to my room, slipped on my pj's, and finally brushed my teeth. Logan and the Tat had already left to go back to college. The Tat had laid a note across my pillow that read "Sorry we missed you. Let me know how the party went. Love and peace." I looked out the window. The Barracuda was gone. My phone machine was flashing messages, but I was too depressed to listen to them.

Downstairs again, dinner was a bust. I picked the cheese off my pizza, piled it in globs on the side of my plate; my mom chatted about this flick or that book, practically humming herself into flight, she was trying so hard to be happy. My dad was silent, probably thinking, *Here we go again;* probably thinking about Logan and when he was such a nightmare, getting all toasty drunk and smashing up things around the house when you tried to talk to him; probably thinking, *Not my daughter, too, not this again.* Finally he spoke, right over my mom. Right over whatever she was saying about the latest this or the fanciest that.

"As far as I can see, it's just damn stupid behavior, Violet, and I can't condone it. I don't know what you've been up to today, but I can smell it from here."

"Now, William, let her be," my mom interjected calmly, like she was some sort of psychiatric nurse or something and my dad was one of her patients. "She understands the situation and has already said she will take more care next time."

My dad didn't even look at her. Just sort of stared straight ahead, keeping his arms crossed over his chest. He'd learned, the same as Logan and I had, the less confronted, the less revealed, and the happier we all remained. Or so I thought at the time. Now I realize he probably thought he'd failed once; he'd let Logan slip into a place well beyond anyone's reach; therefore he doubted his ability to seal the crack before I fell through, too. I watched his pizza cool upon his plate and started feeling more depressed than ever. I felt lousy all over. Not just my thoughts, not just all the lousy memories of days gone by, but my body, too. Lousy and worn out and sick. So what I did then was I started to cry.

At first my parents didn't do anything, just looked at their plates, while I sat there, my head hanging, tears dripping onto greasy mushrooms and onions. Then my mom reached out for my hand, but I pulled away, ran upstairs, and fell facedown on my bed. Whiz Bang licked my salty cheeks for a bit before curling up on my back, cleaning her paws, and falling asleep. Once she got comfy anywhere, I'd rather die than move her, so I lay there waiting for her to stir, feeling nothing but blackness fill my head. I thought about how I had told God if he got me out of the woods, I'd go straight home. Which I hadn't. But instead of trying to figure how to make it up to God, I let the darkness charm me, sweep over me, tame my head, my eyes, my chest. Let me rest. Let me forget. Let me be.

5

Dawn. My hand cupped hard between my legs, bringing back last night's series of dirty dreams about Peter Hutchinson, captain of the football team and hard-core loser. I lay in bed a minute—or more precisely, on the bed, having never made it beneath the covers—thinking about nothing for a change; just lying there and doing some non-thinking and liking it. I watched Whiz Bang stretch out beside me—her paws pointing skyward as if in prayer, her eyes still shut against the light. Smells of culinary delights worked their way beneath my door.

"Violet, love, breakfast's ready," my mom called up the stairs.

I didn't answer right off.

"Violet, love. Are you awake?" I could hear her bare feet smoosh against each step.

"Yeah, I'm up."

"Breakfast, love. Your favorite, Oatmeal and All."

Oatmeal and All was this concoction I'd come up with to cover up the nasty taste of just plain oatmeal, which I used to think was a lot like something a mama bird would feed to her young. I'd get some oatmeal, and while it was cooking I'd add maple syrup, raisins, dried cherries, dried figs, and cinnamon, all organic of course. Then after it was cooked, I'd stick it in the freezer to cool it down a bit, before mixing in some natural applesauce and chunks of pears or mangoes or bananas, whatever was in season. Truth was, by the time you stirred in all that, you could barely find the oatmeal, let alone taste it. But it was damn good. Almost like having dessert for breakfast.

So of course my mom had taken up making it, acting like it was her invention, too, calling it Oatmeal and All, just the way I had. The thing was, she never made it quite right. Made it to her taste, not mine. But I never knew what to say: *Fuck you. You stole my Oatmeal-and-All recipe, and you act like it's yours, and you make it for me when I don't even want you to, and you don't even make it right.* On top of sounding absolutely ridiculous, it would kill her.

Downstairs, I gave her my fake good-morning smile, the one that showed all my teeth, but she seemed to take it for the real thing and smiled back, stirring the oatmeal while I sucked on my grapefruit and eyed the note she'd left on my place mat. I noticed she'd changed the Post-it on the fridge. This one read "Think before you act" and "Beauty is in the eye of the beholder." A double-header. I still wasn't feeling that great, although better than the day before. Absolutely better than that.

"So did you see *our* Henry?" Cutting right to the chase, hips in movement, my mom scooped my steaming oatmeal into a bowl. I nodded.

"And how was he looking?"

"Good."

"How about those dreadful parents of his? Were they around?" She sat down next to me, our elbows practically touching, then lit up a cigarette, holding it way stretched out to the side so as not to let it blow in my direction. But it did anyway.

"Not much."

"Well, don't be such a holdout, love. Tell me everything that happened. Did Henry ask about me?" she said with a wink, using the spoon from her coffee cup to scoop up little nibbles of my breakfast.

"I hung with Henry for a little bit. He was cool and all. I guess I had a bit too much to drink, and didn't handle it very well, so he probably figures I'm a total loser."

"Don't you love that chipped tooth of his?" She tapped on her front tooth, the end of her cigarette wedged between two glistening red fingernails. She was staring off into the distance as if there was some flick running on the kitchen wall or something, so I tried opening the note a little bit just to see what it said. She was always leaving Logan and me these notes saying she knew just what we were going through, before taking off on some bizarre tangent about her own life. Logan called it the goo. "She's oozing on you," he'd say when I got one.

"I remember when he knocked that out playing too hard on his bike as a little boy. He always was trouble." She drew out the word *trouble* like every added syllable was worth a million bucks. "Well, of course those parents of his wanted him to get it fixed, but he was absolutely stubborn about it, a real little man. No, he said, he liked the chip and he wasn't letting anybody fix it. And I was so proud of him. There was something about it, even then, that was just magnificent." She pulled her shoulders up toward her ears in a fake shiver. To tell you the truth, I was kind of surprised she liked the chip, as it seemed the equivalent of leaving the can opener on the counter, say, or forgetting to wash a pan before going to bed, which was naturally the exact reason it drew me in, in the first place.

But I was feeling sick then. And kind of mad too on account of her not even listening to what I had to say, and just going off about *her* Henry and his chipped tooth.

"I met this other guy," I said, in an effort to reestablish *mine* after my original *mine* had been snatched. It was how my mom knew so much about me.

"Really? Who?"

"His name's Ryder. His dad's some famous fashion photographer. They live in Montana and all."

"Where did you meet him?"

"At Hillstream. We sort of broke into the museum there." Her eyes got so big, I thought they'd bust right out of her head. She leaned in real close to me, lit up another Winston, pushed aside the crossword she'd been working on all morning, coming in for the kill. And I wished I'd never begun.

"What was it like? What was it like alone in there, in all the quiet and darkness? It must have been magnificent."

"Weren't you guys worried about me?" I asked.

"No. Mrs. Edwards rang us early on. Then your father drove out to Hillstream in the afternoon and found your car, so we knew you hadn't been in an accident or anything serious. Dr. Applegate says it's all just a part of a teenager's natural rebellion. Your father was too hard on Logan, and look at him now. He barely speaks to me. So I'm not going to let that happen with us, love. Dr. Applegate says you need to rebel a bit, and I'd say Henry is as fine a rebellion as they come! I say if my daughter is going to rebel, thank God it's with such a hunk!" And she clicked her tongue, making this little punch into the air with her fist.

She was twisted. But the thing was, she twisted me right up with her. Dr. Applegate was her screwy analyst whom she'd been going to on and off for the past couple of years. She thought analysis ranked high on the magnificent-o-meter. You could always tell when she was going, too, on account of her getting real feisty with Dad, maybe kicking him out of their room for a while and into the guest room next to mine. Strangely, the notes to Logan and me used to slow down when she was in treatment. I guess Dr. Applegate's office gave her an outlet for all that pent-up frustration.

I finished my oatmeal and plodded back upstairs, Whiz Bang trailing behind, feeling the ooze, too. What I did when I got into my room was to pull out my mom's note and read it right off. I believed wholeheartedly then as now in getting these types of things over with. "My dearest Violet," it began, "you are at the wondrous age of discovery, with the whole world awaiting you. You are a gentle blossom seeking the sun to help you bloom. I have sought the sun myself, and I know how difficult it is to find. My life has been full of darkness and dead vines, a careful construction of tarps and awnings blocking my light and not a drop of water reaching my roots. But you, my dear daughter, are special. You are without limits. You are my revolution. XXXOOO Mom."

My stomach went queasy. I took about as hot a shower as my body could handle. Whiz Bang flip-flopped around the back of the tub and batted at the streams of water, catching droplets on her tongue. I dried off in a hurry on account of my running a bit behind, then checked out the streaks the Tat had laid in my hair the night before Henry's party. Two fat ultrablond hunks down the front a la Mrs. Robinson. My parents had rented this old flick called *The Graduate*, which, to tell you the truth, kind of shocked the hell out of me because it's a little racy, and my parents most definitely do not have sex, at least I don't think they do, considering I've never once seen them kiss or even touch, or, when it gets right down to it, look each other in the eye.

Anyway the Tat had pulled out the bottle of bleach and the paintbrush she uses on Logan's hair, wrapping the chunks up in aluminum foil, all the while doing more of her wild breathing stuff. My dad didn't seem to notice the streaks, although they were pretty wide, but my mom thought they looked magnificent. I was modeling myself after a fifty-year-old seductress and I looked magnificent? I knew it was just a matter of time before she got the streaks, too.

So just as I was dashing out the door, thinking about how nice a morning ride was going to be in the Flame, I noticed my machine's message light was still flashing from the night before. In fact I hadn't checked it since Saturday before Henry's party. I pushed Play. First was a message from CJ wondering when I was picking her up, but I'd already left. Then there was this one from Henry, his sweet voice descending on me straight from heaven.

"Hey, baby girl. Heard you bailed on us bright and early. We turned the house inside out trying to find a trace of your existence. We're headed to John's at two, so I'll see you there. Tell Logan and his girlfriend they're invited, too."

That was the entirety of the message, delivered with the complete assurance I would show. And the thing is, I would have, too, if it hadn't been for Ryder falling asleep instead of getting us out of the stupid museum on time. I dug Ryder's number out of my coat pocket, crumpled it into a tight ball, and threw it into my desk drawer. That's just exactly what I was like, too. Never quite getting rid of something all the way. I mean, I could have thrown his number in the trash.

• • • •

School was pretty much a drag. First off came science class with me doing everything humanly possible not to look at Peter Hutchinson and him seeming to look nowhere else but at me. This was followed by a methodical math lesson and a vapid round of English Lit, after which CJ and I headed for the back hall where we always ate our lunch. Nobody went to the back hall except us, which is precisely why we liked it. None of the crew tagging after us, driving us nuts.

I couldn't figure out how guys looked at me. CJ said I was a hot little chickie, but I sure didn't feel that way. I felt like maybe if my ears would lie flat and I could get rid of that pimple that floated perpetually around my face and if my hair would thicken up a bit and my nose would perhaps tilt upward to the sunny sky, then maybe I'd be okay.

I got asked out a lot and stuff, but I usually said no on account of the guys in the crew being pretty boring.

Sometimes I'd fool myself into thinking one of them had the shine—like this guy Ricky Johnson who'd been tagging behind me right around then on account of my kind of wanting him to—but it would always turn out that they didn't. Ricky, I had thought, was a real shiner, with his long purple hair floating down the hall behind him, strutting to the john for a cigarette, T-shirt tight, nipple rings popping, and that delicious smell of patchouli that rolled off him when he'd lean over me in math class to steal an answer. But that was, of course, before Henry's party.

We poked at our lunches for a bit, both of us saddled with way leftover leftovers.

"Let's split." CJ tossed her turkey sandwich back into the brown bag. I had been thinking along those lines myself, thinking now that I had the Flame, why not make full use of her. We weren't actually allowed out for lunch on account of our not being seniors, and we didn't have a pass or anything, but CJ looked old enough, and we knew the guard was this old geezer with a soft spot for young girls, so I nodded and CJ yanked her boots back into place and said, "Darling, let's roll!"

We ran to the car without our coats. The winter wind was taking more of a hold each day, but we couldn't risk going into the main hallway to get them. I revved the Flame up a bit, getting her warm, then we took off past the guard, smiling and waving, with him just smiling and waving back.

"Piece of cake," said CJ.

"Sucker!" I shouted, feeling pretty good. Feeling how easy the Flame was making my life, thinking about how it was a new week and hopefully Henry would give me a ring-ding and we could begin where we left off, sans the alcohol. CJ, true to her carnivorous nature, wanted to go to McDonald's, but I flat-out refused: (1) because I was the driver and what I said went, (2) because McDonald's food is gross as shit, not to mention their horrible environmental policies, (3) because fat, stupid, gross people went there, and (4) because going to the health-food store took us right past the Edwards house, and I could scope out Henry. Just a glimpse of his Mustang or even his bedroom window would thrill me no end.

So we shot past the Edwards driveway, my heart jumping every which way even though the driveway turned out to be empty. Henry wasn't home, and I knew he wasn't home, and that somehow connected us. Twisted, right? Was that how my mom operated, I wondered with some disgust, the more you know, no matter how minute, the more you make it yours? I pulled into the strip mall that held our one health-food-only haven, with CJ already moaning about the prospective tasteless fare.

"It's rabbit food."

"You sound like my dad."

"Well, maybe you should listen to him." She punched me in the arm.

The strip mall had been built on top of what was once a field of wild strawberries. It was in this field I'd found Whiz Bang, under an abandoned pickup truck that had been there so long, strawberries were growing out of the steel bed. My mom used to drag Logan and me there to help pick them in the summer. We'd eat more than what toppled into our baskets, going home with stained fingers and intense tummyaches, but we'd have the sweetest jam for months to come.

Inside Strawberry Fields, the health-food store, it smelled like ginger and beeswax and herbal tea. I ordered a tempeh, sun-dried tomato, and onion sandwich with olive paste on homemade seven-grain bread. My mouth watered just asking for it. CJ hemmed and hawed making it one-hundred-percent clear that she was not into this food.

"Don't you have anything that will stick to my bones?" she asked the guy behind the counter, but he ignored her, going to work on my carrot juice.

"Get the pasta, CJ." She squished up her face. "Pasta is pasta. Just pretend we're at McDonald's and they have a new amazing dish—*pasta!* You'd order it, right?"

"It would have a little meat in it."

"I'll give you some meat, girl," I said, making a fist.

Naturally CJ hated her lunch. She got some noodles-and-seitan dish that she just kept adding more and more salt to until I thought she'd swell up like a beach ball.

"Ummm, good!" She spun a noodle in the air and caught it with her tongue.

"You're an asshole," I said, feeling happy and full, feeling nice and content and satisfied.

We tooled back to the car, me trying to trip CJ and CJ shoving me around like a rag doll. We were cold, but it didn't matter. We were on the goof and just had to roll with it.

"Girl, you look like a hooker." I drew out my voice like a southern belle.

"All the better to work it with." She shoved me back again as I tried to knock her off her boots. This time, though, I kind of lost my balance, the parking lot being a little icy and our laughter making standing up straight a feat all its own. So I went toppling backward, knocking against some guy walking out of the liquor store, his bottle of booze hitting me square in the back.

"Hey, hey. Take it easy," said this voice, and I turned around, sort of pissed off that someone was talking to me like I was a child, and of course it turned out to be Henry. Sweet Henry, heaven beside me, smiling at me, too, like he'd known it was me all along, which I guess he probably had, and he just wanted to show me up. I froze, staring at him, him looking at me and laughing. I mean, right-out laughing, like I was the funniest thing he'd ever seen. And maybe I was, but I sure didn't mean to be.

"Hey, Let, get your sweet little ass moving, or throw me the keys," CJ yelled behind me. I was paralyzed. She waved at Henry over the top of my car.

"Your friend's calling you." Henry tilted his head in CJ's direction. He had on his tight, tight motorcycle jacket, almost too small for him, but not quite. Underneath it he'd crammed a beat-up old sweatshirt, zipper open, hood hanging down the back. He lit up a no-filter Camel, cupping his long fingers around the tip until it ignited, picking a fleck of tobacco off his tongue, the whole time looking straight at me, smiling, laughing. CJ yelled again on account of it being so dang cold and our being without jackets, so I turned to go, first mumbling, "I'm sorry I didn't call you back on Sunday and all. I pretty much didn't get the message until this morning."

He nodded, dragging on his cigarette, sliding his fingers along the curve of his chest, still smiling, making me real nervous. I thought about Ryder and how he talked so much that when he finally went silent, it was okay. When somebody can jabber a lot, then the silences are all right. But when it's silence straight out, then I want to die.

"Well, I gotta get back to school," I said, thinking how I was going to slug CJ if she yelled my name one more time.

He nodded again, blowing a smoke ring right over my head, resting the bottle of booze kind of on his hip, eyeing me up and down.

"See ya," I said, thinking how CJ and I should have just stayed in for lunch. Hung out in the back hall cracking bad jokes or maybe even tracking down Ricky Johnson.

"Hey, baby girl!" I was almost to the car, but turned back. Henry just stood there, kicking some rocks around with his feet, and I knew I was supposed to walk back over to him. CJ seemed to know this, too, because she hissed at me, "Give me the fucking keys," but I didn't. I just walked straight over to Henry, holding back a grin because I was thinking, *He's going to ask me out now,* but not being sure, because I had passed out on him, and that was weird.

"My friend's having a party Friday night." I nodded. Henry's shoulders curved forward, reminding me vaguely of the unfortunate roadkills I was always blessing, their crushed heads curled in toward their tummies. He smooshed his Camel out with the toe of his boot.

"I'll pick you up at eight if you're interested."

"Sure."

He glanced up, backed away, then turned and swaggered toward his car, his hips tossing from side to side like a ship at sea. I ran back to the Flame, jumped in, and started her up before screaming.

"It's totally groovy, but next time try letting me *in* the car before working your shit."

CJ was into it though, and I figured maybe I'd been wrong about her going after Henry that night.

She said, "Maybe he has a foxy friend and we can double." She flipped down the mirror, smearing on some lipstick. "He's happening, darling, but don't you think maybe he's a bit tall for you? You know, things may get tricky, unless of course you're lying down, then it just evens out." She flipped the mirror back up, smiling at me. "But really, he's a fox. I'd do him." She leaned over and kissed me on the cheek.

"Speaking of doing him," I said, "what should I use?"

"You mean birth control?"

"Yeah. I don't have anything. I mean should we stop at the store and get condoms or something? Do I need a diaphragm? Those are so weird. Should I be on the pill?"

"Whoa, darling. It's a bit premature for prescriptions. I have a bunch of rubbers in my bag; I'll slip you some." And CJ started digging around in her purse. "But don't worry, a cat like Henry will take care of things." Then, after whipping out three attached shiny blue condom packs, she shouted, "Bingo!" My stomach went a little queasy.

"Shit, CJ, I don't know what to do with those things."

"Do you want me to show you?"

"Okay," I said, though I wasn't sure how she was going to pull that one off. She detached one of the packages and ripped it open.

"All right," she said, "first you open it like this, along the edge so you don't wreck the goods inside. Look, there's a white dotted line."

I glanced over and sure enough there was a line.

"Okay," I said.

"Sometimes they're tricky to get open and you have to use your teeth, but don't worry, mostly the guy opens them anyway."

"Okay," I said again. It was as if someone was explaining to me where the capital of Turkey was and how to navigate myself around the town center once I arrived. It was all very simple, very logical, but very exciting.

"Once you have it out, darling, the fun begins. Hold it like this." CJ gingerly held the rim, which appeared to be the entirety of the condom rolled up, between her thumb and index finger. It was milky and shiny in the light and poked up on the top like the nipple on a baby's bottle. "Do you want to touch it?" she asked, watching me look at it. I was having a hard enough time concentrating on the road as it was, but I reached over and copped a feel. It was cool and slippery like the gook you slide your hands into at a haunted house. I jumped.

"That's just the lubrication," said CJ, laughing. "So nothing gets stuck."

"But won't I already be lubricated?" I said, mentally reviewing some books I'd sneaked out of my mom's closet, not to mention a little firsthand experimentation.

"Depends on how things are going and what round you're on." As I swerved a bit too close to the guard rail, CJ shouted, "Hey, watch out!"

"What next?"

"Hold it like this." She held it in front of me so I could see her thumb on one side and her index and middle fingers on the other. "Then slowly, delicately, inch it down his dick. Got it? Do it with some purpose and kind of massage him at the same time. Guys love it when you do that." And she slid the condom down her three middle fingers on the opposite hand. The Flame took on the faint odor of balloons.

"Massage him? Where?"

"His balls, with your spare hand. Or if you're unrolling it with your left, smooth it down with your right, or vice versa. Believe me, if you know how to put a rubber on, that guy is yours for life."

CJ now had the condom extended all the way down and it flopped over the tips of her fingers like an elf's cap. I touched it again. This time it felt all right.

"Do you want to try?" she said. "I have some spares."

I suddenly became overwhelmed at the whole notion of applying that roll of latex that dangled from CJ's fingers to any part of Henry, especially his most secretive. I tried to imagine it inside of me, and I just had to clear my head. "No, I got it," I said. "Rip, rim, gently unroll, massage."

"He'll be eating out of your hand in no time." She threw the condom out the window, then split the remaining two in half, shoved one in my pocket and dropped the other back in her purse.

"One for you and one for me," she said. "Now we can both have fun."

Fun, I thought, watching the condom disappear in my rearview mirror and thinking how bad it was to litter and should I turn back and get it, but what if somebody pulled up just as I was scooping it up. Peter Hutchinson, say, or worse yet, Henry. I wanted to ask CJ what to do once the condom was in place, but hoped that part would be self-explanatory.

We got back into school okay, the guard waving us through like the damn welcome wagon, and I suddenly felt bad that we'd tricked him. What if we'd been caught and had gotten in trouble. That would have gotten him in trouble, too. It was a lousy enough job without getting in trouble for being nice to tricky girls. I realized, too, that I'd been so absorbed with CJ's condom demo, I'd completely messed up my roadkill count, and that wasn't cool. Plus we were late and were written up by the hall monitor, some squirmy kid from my English Lit class, but it didn't matter. I knew how to slip on a condom like a pro, so I thanked him for my pink skip with an unexpected wink and slid into History where I had to sit next to Peter Hutchinson again. This time his lingering glances didn't faze me.

• • • •

That night at home I was a nervous wreck about my date with Henry, and it was only Monday. I made a beeline for my closet, tried everything on; nothing looked right. I called CJ, asked to borrow her stuff, lay on my bed, fantasized about Henry. I contemplated practicing the condom technique, but that would have left me condomless, and a trip to the drugstore seemed daunting, so I passed.

My mom was in one of her "I am woman" moods, meaning my dad and I were in for lots of trouble, but mostly my dad. Dr. Applegate was back on the payroll, I could tell. Usually when my dad got in, she'd ask him lots of stupid questions like, "How was work?" and "Did you close on any new accounts?" When she was on one of her rolls, though, she didn't give two hoots about my dad and his workday. What she cared about most was getting her needs met, and as my dad didn't seem to know how to do that, or else she couldn't get clear on what her needs were, or maybe a little of both, things would really start getting crazy. Dinner was pork chops with peas in mint sauce, and a salad. I poked around at my peas a bit, trying to make them last on account of peas and salad not being the most filling of meals, but I knew better than to mention it that night.

"The chops are a bit overdone," my dad said.

"Well, then cook them yourself." My mom grabbed his plate and tossed it into the sink, instead of staring at the wall like she usually did.

"Oh, Christ, Maude. I was eating that."

"Well, I wouldn't want you to eat something that is not bringing you complete satisfaction." She ripped shreds of pork off a bone with her front teeth, pushed it aside. It distended her cheek as she spoke. Grease pooled on her lips.

"Oh, not this again." My dad pushed away from the table, picked up the folded newspaper from the counter, and headed down toward the TV room. I kept my eyes on my plate, feeling my appetite wane.

"Eat your supper, missy." My mom pointed at my minted peas.

"I'm not hungry."

"What did I do, Lord, to deserve such an ungrateful family?" She motioned up toward heaven with clasped hands. Then she grabbed my plate and slammed it into the sink, too, so I got up to leave.

"And where do you think you're going, missy? There are dishes that need to be done." And sure enough there was a whole pile of dishes to be cleaned. I turned on the water.

"I've decided I'm fucking tired of the way I'm treated around here. From now on, if you and your father want supper, you make it. I quit." She was working on the bone now, carnivorous suction sounds belting forth. I stared out the window over our sink.

"Everything is going to change. Everything. Starting with your helping out around here instead of daydreaming about the Edwards boy like he was some kind of matinee idol. And your brother is going to learn a little respect, too. No more coming and going like the wind. When he is in this house, I expect him to carry on civil conversations with me." She paused for another suck, then: "And as for your father, that's a whole different story. I've begun looking for an apartment in town. He's kept me down long enough; it's time to make the big move."

She lit up a Winston, holding the tip right under my nose practically. I opened the window a crack. She jumped up and slammed it shut.

"Oh, no, missy. This is my house, at least for the time being," she went on, "and Dr. Applegate says I cater to you far too much. You don't like my cigarette-smoking, you go live somewhere else."

My mom was looking for apartments in town just about every other week, but nothing ever came of it. Just like nothing ever came of any of her threats. She made herself powerless by threatening to do something drastic just about every five minutes.

I finished the dishes and went upstairs to nail some homework. Final exams were looming near, and as per usual I hadn't studied. That night, though, I was feeling kind of restless and couldn't seem to get through the murder of Alyona Ivanovna and her sister Lisaveta even though I'd read it a million times before. I had a book report due on it before the holidays began. So what I did was start talking out loud about how different my life would be when I lived out of my parents' house. "I will take in every stray that needs a home. I will have a husband who looks me in the eye and likes my cooking. I will have children who are nice to me." After a bit, though, my spirits sank. I snuggled up in bed, thanked God for giving me Whiz Bang, and fell asleep.

• • • •

Around two or three in the morning, I woke to things smashing about downstairs and my mom screaming and yelling like she always did when she was seeing Dr. Applegate.

"You goddamn cold fucking asshole!" she screamed, really laying on the cusswords, forgetting her proscriptive

British roots completely. "You're like living with a fucking fish! I need some attention! I am a woman! Look at me! Look at my body! Touch me! Be with me!" I could tell she was crying pretty hard on account of the hiccuping sounds in between words.

And the thing was, my dad *was* kind of cold. I mean, he could be distant, and you never knew where you stood with him, because he never seemed to tell you what he was feeling, or show it too much, either. Sometimes, if you sat down calmly with him—and he was in an okay mood—and pressed him, really and truly stayed on him, he might let a feeling slip out, but otherwise he was the Wall. That's what Logan called him, the Wall of Resistance, because when you'd fight with him, he'd just cross his arms tight across his chest, and not a word would slide past his white lips. You could do anything, I mean anything, kick and scream and roll on the floor foaming at the mouth, slash your wrists, and he'd just watch, all stony-faced.

"I can't go on like this," she said. "I need you to need me, to want me! Look at me! Look at me!" she screamed, then something big crashed. "Want me!"

"Maude, I think you're getting a bit hysterical," my dad said. "Why don't you make some warm milk and try to get some sleep."

"Warm milk! Warm milk! Fuck you and your warm milk! I am leaving, do you hear me? *Leaving!* I am looking for an apartment away from you and the goddamned kids. I do not need this shit in my life. All you three do is take and take and take. I need somebody to give to me for a change."

My dad started laughing the way he did when he got real nervous or uncomfortable, so my mom started screaming,

"Fuck you!" at the top of her lungs, and I knew my dad would be worried about waking the neighbors again, even though they lived a fair distance away. Then the garage door slammed, followed by the screech of her car's engine. I heard my dad shuffling around in the living room, turning off lights, not bothering to pick up the mess. Then he collected his things from their bedroom, transferred them into the guest room next to mine.

"She'll be back." He leaned into my room, knowing I was awake, his eyes glowing in the darkness.

"I know," I said, pulling Whiz Bang toward me, listening for the car to return.

I finally heard the garage door open while the sky was still dark. From the shadows of the staircase, I watched my mom reheat the morning's unused coffee and pick a crossword from the top of her pile of *New York Times* Sunday editions, then flop out on the living-room couch. She looked worn and old, her hair a tumble, makeup smeared. She lit up a Winston, and the smoke drifted up the stairs toward me. I lifted a hand and waved it away.

6

Sex. The driving force behind almost every teenage decision, and no doubt adult decisions, too, although my parents were not representative of this, if you know what I mean. I'd spent the entire week doing everything right, just so that my going out with Henry would go uncontested, perhaps even unnoticed, which might be a bit of a stretch, although with the way things were going then, you just never knew.

My dad had woken me early on Tuesday morning to get in a little preschool jog. I was tired as hell on account of not having slept much the night before, waiting up to see if my mom was still a part of the family unit. Outside it had been bitter cold and sunless. We could see our breath racing down Peavey Lane ahead of us.

"Try to keep an even pace, and don't let your feet drag," my dad had instructed, practically running circles around me. "You need to keep your anaerobic heart rate at a nice steady pace, open up your arteries, keep the blood flowing." He had hedged and dodged in front of me, throwing old boxer's punches into the air.

"What do you do if they come at you from the right?" he'd asked, running backward and stopping his fist just before connecting with the side of my head. I'd blocked with my left arm, ducked my head, and fake-punched his gut with my right.

"Good," he said, "now how about this?" And he went for my gut, so I'd dropped both hands down to block it.

"No, no, no. You'll get yourself killed," he said. "Never leave yourself open. You drop both hands and your opponent will have a field day on your bean counter." His fists flurried about my face. My chest had been heaving from running and concentrating at the same time, but my dad's steps were as springy and lively as a kid's in a toy store. "Keep your fists up at all times, block with your elbows, and counter immediately."

When we got back to the house, all the doors had been locked, so we had to knock the bathroom window out to get in. Inside, my mom was sitting at the kitchen table, drinking coffee, reading one of her books.

"Christ, Maude, what is the matter with you? We've been out there banging and banging. Are you deaf?" My mom didn't stir. "Don't you think you are being a little melodramatic?"

"Violet, will you please tell your father that, yes, I did hear his knocking, but assumed, being the perfect husband that he is, he would have his keys with him at all times. And tell him, no, I am not being melodramatic. I am simply prioritizing my life and taking care of myself first."

She had two thick blond streaks running down the front of her bob, and I remember thinking then, *How is it possible to rebel against somebody who is following in your footsteps?*

The thing was, by that night we seemed to be her priority again, as she whipped up some half-veggie, half-meat dinner cooked just the right amount. My dad had taped a piece of thick cardboard over the bathroom window, and other than an eerie darkness in that room, it was as if nothing had happened. By the time Friday rolled around, it was all a thing of the past, and I knew Dr. Applegate was temporarily unemployed again.

• • • •

Upstairs, in my bathroom, I kicked around the piles of Friday-night-gear rejects, trying to find the black eyeliner Whiz Bang had knocked off the counter. When I straightened up, liner in hand, my mom was standing there, leaning forward into my mirror, pulling back the skin of her face.

"It just keeps going down." She opened her eyes as wide as they could go, like that game at the carnival where if you rolled the ball in the clown's mouth, his eyes lit up and clicked open and closed. I flicked the liner pencil back and forth between my thumb and forefinger.

"Is that what you are wearing?" She glanced over at my vinyl black jeans and white T-shirt, then returned to inspecting the lines around her lips.

I nodded.

"Don't you think a dress would be a little more in the mood of things?" She motioned her hands in the shape of a woman's body.

"No."

"Well, I do, dolly girl. If I were you, I would slip into that little black dress you wore for Mary Hampton's wedding, with the pantyhose and heels. You looked mag-nificent that night."

"Mom, I'm going to a party. Nobody wears panty hose."

"I know, dolly girl, but men love them, don't they?" She winked at me, then picked up my blush brush and started rubbing some on. "Oooh, this is a good color for me." She tilted her head from side to side.

"Mom, I need to get ready."

"Well, go ahead. I'm not stopping you. I just wanted to make sure you were prepared for tonight."

"Prepared how?"

"Birth control, Violet. Do you have adequate birth con-trol? The way I see things, I am far too young to be a grandmother." She clucked her tongue and twisted her hand in the air like she was screwing in a lightbulb.

"I'm fine."

"Are you sure? Because if you need anything, I would like to pay for it. It would be just between you and me."

"No, Mom, I'm fine," I said, concentrating hard on lin-ing my eyes in black, but feeling the warmth of my very own condom deep in my boot where I'd shoved it just moments ago.

"All right, dolly girl. Don't say I didn't warn you." And she went downstairs, taking my blush with her.

• • • •

"What time is this clown coming?" asked my dad when I walked into the living room. He was reading the evening paper.

"Eight."

"Is that what you're wearing?"

I nodded.

He shook his head. "When I was your age, young ladies dressed like young ladies, not like police officers. And what is the matter with your eye makeup?"

"Nothing." I blinked, knowing full well I'd botched a last-minute attempt to remove the eyeliner, leaving smears that lay halfway between Brigitte Bardot and Mike Tyson.

"Well, Violet, I'm sure you realize I'm not crazy about the idea of you going out with this young man. He's several years older than you, and we don't know much about him other than he's Joe and Verna's son. And even that makes him questionable."

"Be sure to phone if you're going to be late," my mom said from behind my dad's shoulder.

"Dad, even Logan said he'd heard okay things about him. Just because he didn't go to college doesn't make him a total loser."

"I understand that, young lady, but I have my concerns, and I want you to be careful tonight."

My mom shook her head back and forth, spinning her finger in circles next to her ear.

Logan had called earlier to tell my parents not to freak about Henry because his roommate at school knew him pretty well and said he was just a loner kind of guy, that was all. And that was A-OK with me, being a loner kind of girl. It made me feel good, too, to have Logan stick up for Henry like that.

"So, where are we going?" asked my mom.

"Some party."

"I was more in the mood for a romantic dinner and candlelight."

"Out of luck."

"Perhaps I can persuade him otherwise." She had walked over and poked me in the side. My dad surveyed the sports section.

. . . .

"Now, don't play me for a fool, Henry. I have a son of my own, and I know marijuana when I smell it. I may have no jurisdiction over what you do with the rest of your time, but when you're out with my daughter, her mother and I would appreciate it if you're not smoking that crap." My dad began the second Henry was through the door. I was in the kitchen at that point with my mom, drumming my nails against the table.

"Don't go out there yet. Let him have to wait a bit, get his dander up," she said, blowing smoke out a crack in the window. I furrowed my brow, waited a minute, then went into the living room.

"Hi!" I said. Next to my dad, Henry's sloping shoulders seemed more conspicuous. "People who can't hold their shoulders back take no pride in themselves," my dad used to say as Logan and I had marched around the kitchen, balancing baskets on our small heads. I wanted to get Henry out of there fast.

"Well, I hope you two have a magnificent time." My mom stood right up close to Henry, her cigarette clamped between her teeth, rearranging the way the hood from his sweatshirt hung down the back of his leather jacket. I let my parents kiss me good-bye and dropped the house key in my boot alongside my lipstick and other goodies.

"Remember, Henry, I want my daughter home by midnight at the latest. Don't make me come looking for you." My dad shook Henry's hand while placing the other firmly on his receding shoulder. He looked so serious and small trying to somehow harness all of Henry's sweet heaven vibe.

Outside, the night air hit me with relief.

"Your parents are really into you." Henry hopped in his side of the car.

"Yeah, I guess they pretty much are."

"I'm not so sure they're into me though," he said, and smiled at me across the bucket seats. I caught a glimpse of his chipped tooth. I looked out my window. My parents had opened the front door and stood before the glass panel, waving at me like I was leaving for a school trip. I rubbed my hands against the glass to clear the fog.

• • • •

The party turned out to be four of us hanging around, drinking gin and tonics, and listening to old Hendrix CDs on some super–hi-tech stereo system. Me, Henry, his friend Tony, and Tony's girlfriend, Marsha. On the way over, Henry had held my hand a little bit, kissing it in between tokes on this skinny joint he had rolled. Getting me stoned, too, which was something kind of new.

Tony worked in advertising and I guess was pretty good at his job. He had this superslick apartment in one of those new developments where they first slaughter all the trees, creating this hollow, until the new ones that you buy from your local landscaper take root. Henry had spent no small amount of time stopping in front of each looks-exactly-alike complex, trying to figure if we'd arrived yet. Tony and Henry had grown up together—although Henry was a couple of years younger—and they kind of resembled each other, except Tony had flawless teeth and a budding beer belly.

Marsha was nice, I guess, but not too bright, so I spent most of the evening shooting the breeze with her boyfriend. He was one of those people who had an opinion on everything, so it made discussions pretty easy. I just nodded, saying "Oh, really" a lot, and he'd respond, "Never doubt it, sweetheart," pointing his finger and thumb at me as if they were a gun. Actually he was fairly interesting, and I was learning stuff from him about golf, Spanish cooking, a German director named Herzog, but mostly about Henry's blossoming role in the advertising industry.

"Now Edwards is a real talent. Nothing pussy about him. Didn't go to school or anything. Just picked it up along the way. I try to throw him whatever jobs I can. The better he gets, the bigger the jobs. Plus I love him like a brother. I want to see him do well." He was mixing me my second gin and tonic, adding a twist of lime. I found myself drinking a lot more around Henry than I did with most folks. It was like he threw my nerves way out in left field and the drinking helped bring them back to center. Henry was sitting on the far end of the couch, jammed right up against Marsha.

Marsha started laughing from her corner of the couch. Henry put his finger in front of her mouth to quiet her, but I could tell he was laughing, too.

"Let me try it again," she said. Henry slid the cherry from his drink carefully on to her extended pink tongue. Marsha sucked on the fruit for what seemed like an hour, then tried to tie its stem in a knot. Her mouth twisted coquettishly around, and Henry leaned in closer.

"Shit!" She spat it out. "That chick on TV made it look like a cinch, but it's bullshit. You know, if I can't do it, nobody can." Then they fell into these fits of hysteria again. I watched, twisting my tongue around an imaginary stem and contemplating my sweet Henry from a distance.

It was the way he moved, I decided, that made him so seductive. Long, easy gestures and he touched his own body a lot, right in the spots you'd want to be. He'd stroke that curve in his chest, where the two bones met, serpentine fingers meandering up and down, up and down while he listened to you speak; or he'd play with his bottom lip, kind of running a finger just inside the curve. But his pièce de résistance was when he stretched out that long body of his, fingers wedged deep inside his leathers while he spoke—with you absolutely spellbound—as if nothing was going on.

So then what happened was Tony leaned over my shoulder, whispering, "Don't worry, sweetheart. They're always like that. A harmless flirtation that's been going on forever."

"Really?"

"Never doubt it, sweetheart." He handed me a fresh drink and flipped his head toward the bedroom. "Come with me a minute," he said. "I got just the thing to cheer you up."

I followed him into his dark red room lit only by these matching gilt sconces hanging on either side of his bed.

"Sit down, sweetheart." He pointed toward the bed and started rummaging through drawers.

I positioned myself gingerly on the edge of what turned out to be a fairly turbulent water bed and wondered what Henry and Marsha were doing together in the other room. Tony pulled out a small packet of white powder, and I knew right off it was blow on account of having seen it a million times before, just always choosing not to partake. Fairy dust, as Logan called it. Tony laid out four lines on a mirror he kept on his dresser, then he pulled a twenty-dollar bill out of his pocket and rolled it up into a tight tube, offering it to me like a birthday present.

"I don't know what to do," I said, drunk enough to be truthful.

Tony looked surprised, then said, "Watch me." So I did. Then tried it myself, pressing the bill-tube against my nose, closing off one nostril and sucking up. One long heat wave shot through me, then my head cleared. I figured I probably shouldn't be doing this, but then Henry probably shouldn't be flirting his butt off with Marsha, either.

"Good," Tony said, "now try the other side." So I did that side, too, remembering how the Tat had taught me one of the yogic principles was balance. Tony laid out more lines. When we strolled back into the living room, my world was upside down.

"What were you guys doing in there?" Henry asked. I sat down next to him, grinding my teeth.

"A little pick-me-up," said Tony, leaning over with my fifth or sixth gin and tonic, slipping me a wink. I watched my hand move forward in super slo-mo, without feeling any particular connection to that body part or any of the others.

"Pull it out."

"Yeah, honey bunch, don't be such a holdout," said Marsha, putting on some lipstick. She used the metal tube as a mirror. Tony went in the bedroom and came back with the stash.

"Go wild." He dropped it in Henry's lap.

When my turn rolled around, I tooted it up just like I had before, only this time, instead of going up and in, it poured back down onto the mirror. Henry started laughing. I was mortified but in a dull, nonreactive kind of way, which, to tell you the truth, kind of scared me. I remember I kept thinking, *If the building catches on fire, will I understand the need to leave?* I knew somewhere in my buzz that I had lost control and would just have to wait and see what my body would do next. Tony reached out for the bill-tube. Temporarily immobile, I felt like a kid safety-belted into the backseat of a car, who wants to play the radio. Even Marsha, with the brain of a tick, seemed more mature than I. To compensate, I began to disagree with everything that was said, especially by Henry.

Well, I must have driven everybody crazy, because even before midnight rolled around, Henry was pulling me out of there. Of course, by then I was sorry I'd been such a jerk. Tony was nice and Marsha was okay, too, I guess, if you went in for that kind of thing. Tony closed the evening by giving me a pinch on the ass.

"Watch out for Edwards; he's a sly fox," he warned with a wink.

"Oh, really," I responded for good measure.

"Never doubt it, sweetheart!" He looked mighty pleased with himself and fired his gun at me one last time. Marsha flittered her fingers from the couch. "So nice to have met you," she said, but I sensed that she was flipping me off as I turned my back. Henry laughed again. Or at least I thought he did. I wasn't exactly sure what was going on anymore. My head was spinning now, full tilt, way beyond my dizziness at the Edwards party. *Did I grab all my stuff?* I wondered, contemplating the three or four flights of exposed stairs that loomed right beneath my toes.

I leaned way over to make sure my house key and stupid tube of lipstick, which I hadn't even used, and my precious condom, which I hoped, though it seemed unlikely, I would be using soon, were still in my boot and came within inches of taking a nosedive onto the pavement below. Henry caught me with a "Whoa, baby girl. Where ya going in such a rush?" Now I knew without question he was laughing. I wanted to slug him.

For the life of me, I couldn't figure out how to get down the stairs, no matter how long I stared at them, so finally Henry shoved his arm under mine and around my back, kind of lifting half my body onto his shoulder. In one beautiful swoosh, he lit up a filterless Camel with his spare hand, picking the tobacco off his tongue like he always did. My mind drifted to rooms plump with goose-feather pillows and cozy sleeping bags. It felt so nice, I didn't want to leave.

"Hang on there, baby girl." He pushed me into the car, my body a jumble of limp rags. Once inside, I became obsessed with the idea of sleeping with Henry that night, preferably at his apartment, but if that wouldn't do, then right there in Tony and Marsha's denuded parking lot. Henry slammed some hard-rock tape into the car stereo that I kind of liked, so I jerked my head back and forth a bit, and the next thing I knew, I was feeling all right.

"Sorry," I said, meaning for the word to cover the night in its entirety, and naturally the passing-out night, too, although I was hoping he'd kind of let that little number slip from his mind. His hand fell against my knee, almost as if by accident, though that's how most all his movements were. My body tightened. I felt his blood twitch through my vinyls. I'd been in situations like this with guys before, sometimes even liking it, but this was different. I felt less confined. It was like seeing a map of America for the first time and realizing how many places there were to go.

"So what now?" I asked, feeling kind of jittery. Henry's mouth moved toward mine, his fingers meandering up my leg. I slid my tongue in, tasting stale cigarettes and gin. I liked it. It tasted forceful and vaguely menacing. He tried pulling me toward him, but I fell backward against the door, knocking my elbow painfully against the armrest. Henry climbed on top of me then, his full weight thrusting down on my tummy, crushing my neck into a peculiar angle. The tape had run out, and Henry's slow breathing filled the car. The windows fogged.

Then I started to feel sick. I mean the kind where you know you're just not going to make it. Henry was working his hand up my shirt, and everything was feeling all right, the way I guess it's supposed to feel, when I couldn't hold it anymore. I shoved Henry off me, which was no small feat, considering his size, and rolled out the door, barfing modestly behind the Mustang's rear fender. When I got back in, he revved the engine and tore out, my door still swinging open.

"Sorry." My head tossed along the ridge of the headrest. Henry drove with his knees for a minute in order to light up a Camel, the orange tip glowing in the shadows of the car.

"I'm sorry," I said again.

"I know you are." He kept his eyes on the road.

"I didn't do it on purpose, you know."

"Well, intentionally or unintentionally, it's still a drag, baby girl." The car was beginning to fill up with smoke, so I cracked my window.

"Tony's the one who gave me all the drinks and the blow. It's not my fault, you know."

He nodded a couple of times, steaming right ahead like he couldn't get me out of his car fast enough, and I can't say that I blamed him. The thing about me, though, is nothing eggs me on like a little home-brewed rejection, so armed with barf breath, I started leaning in toward him, rubbing his crotch and trying to kiss him, but he pushed me aside.

The thing was, I really was getting twitchy then, differently than I'd ever been before. I wanted that sweet pressure of his hard-on against my pleasure dome. That's what Logan called the Tat's secret place. I heard him one night through the thin wall that separated our bedrooms. "Come on, baby, let little Wilbur play in your pleasure dome," he'd whined, and from the sounds that had followed, I figured little Wilbur had scored a home run.

· 110 ·

"Jesus, Violet, ease up," he said, pushing back my hand again. What I wanted to do then was to hop out of the speeding car and march myself right back to Tony and Marsha's. The only question was what would I do once I got there? Walk in on them in position number 372, so they could laugh and tell me what a little kid I was? I suppose I could have hopped out and phoned my dad. He would have come, no questions asked, but there was that old sinking feeling again. I was well into the land of the definite wrongs. I slumped back into the corner. What I really wanted, really and truly wanted, was to go to bed.

"Look, it's not that I don't find you attractive. It just has to feel right."

"If you find me so attractive, how come you spent all night talking to Miss Marsha No-Brains?" I asked.

"'Cuz I thought you and Fieldstone were having a good time getting to know each other. Watch your mouth about Marsha. She's an old friend."

"Yeah, so I heard." I slipped my hands beneath my legs to quell the urge to slug him. Everything he did was making me sick. He lit up another cigarette with the tip of the first. I rolled down my window all the way, even though it was about twenty below out, and let my head dangle. We were driving pretty fast and my hair whipped back around my neck.

But even in my frustration I couldn't help thinking about what being with Henry would be like. And what his favorite position might be. The Tat said she preferred being on top. It gave her more control and allowed her to get off better. I couldn't even begin to actually picture Logan and the Tat making it, even though I had heard them through the walls a couple of times. Once, when my parents were gone, they went at it all night in my mom and dad's bed. It was pretty creepy. Then the Tat had left her diaphragm drying on their bathroom sink, and my dad just about had a heart attack when he found out what it was. Having never seen one before, he had at first mistaken it for one of my mother's kitchen utensils and chided her for leaving it in the bathroom. "It's Anna's diaphragm, William," my mom had explained, and before he could respond, she'd added, "and we should be thankful they have the good sense to use proper protection." She'd snapped it into its case and returned it to Logan the next day with a fresh tube of spermicide.

Henry looked at me now the way Logan did when I was driving him supernuts. He flicked the cigarette across my nose and out the window.

"You can close it now." I half expected him to add *Bean Brain*. We drove home in silence, just the whir of the heating system, which started lulling me off to sleep. I could feel the weight of Whiz Bang snuggled in my arms, and more than anything I wanted to be with her.

• • • •

"Watch out for little animals," I said as we turned onto the dim side streets, making a furtive cross against my chest. I had counted seven roadkills, a high count for this time of year, on the way home, but with the murkiness of my brain, I wasn't certain which were first-timers who needed one cross and which had been there already, requiring two. Plus we'd driven down Butter Lane, so I passed all the ones

I missed with CJ during my apparently unnecessary condom demonstration, and I wasn't exactly sure how to rectify that now. Things in the roadkill department were getting tricky.

My house was well lit, but it was only about one o'clock, so I figured as long as I didn't have to breathe on my parents, I wouldn't be in too much trouble. Henry brooded over the steering wheel, cracking his narrow knuckles, but I was reluctant to ask him what was wrong. The date had sucked, but my bed was within reach now, so I leaned over and kissed him on the cheek. My confidence that evening had seemed to come in fits and spurts, as my dad would say. Everything about my family was always coming and going in fits and spurts: the laughter, the roses, the sunny summer days. Fits and spurts that we just learned to roll with.

"Thanks for a fun evening," I said, sounding like I was talking to CJ's parents after they had taken us out to dinner and a flick. I knew Henry was thinking I was too young, but I was beginning to see that that was part of my allure. Can't corrupt what's already been corrupted. Find 'em fresh. I had sobered up enough to slide across the seats and wet his face with a pretty decent kiss. And as I headed toward the house, he rolled down his window to say he'd call me tomorrow. He wanted to be with me, I could sense that much. I just had to handle my liquor and whatnot a little better the next time.

Inside, my parents called to me from the TV room. I yawned and headed toward the stairs. Yes, I had fun. Yes, Henry was nice to me. No, it was just one other couple. I could hear my dad start to get up at that perhaps too forthright answer, but my mom stopped him. *You failed with Logan,* I could almost hear her saying. *I'll handle this one.*

"Sweet dreams," she called out. I tackled the stairs.

Whiz Bang was all over me in the bathroom. I missed with the toothpaste four or five times before I hit the brush, and she kept swatting at the goo as it fell.

"No, pumpkin, don't eat that." I gently pushed her outstretched paw away. "It's icky. It'll give you a tummyache."

I spoke to Whiz Bang as if she could actually assimilate information, but she stuck her paw in a glob anyway, then shook her head fiercely from smelling the mint. I laughed. It felt good to release my facial muscles. I leaned way forward into the mirror. Wrinkles. I was getting wrinkles on my forehead at age sixteen. My mom had gone completely gray at twenty-three, so Logan and I both checked regularly for early signs of that.

I made it into bed before feeling my contacts locked against my eyes. I figured I'd just leave them on the bedside table and soak them in saline in the morning. Whiz Bang gave them the old one-two, looking like she wanted to make a meal of the things, so I fashioned an open book into a protective tent.

I guess I fell asleep for a bit, but woke up in a panic, my sheets soaked with sweat. Right smack in my lace-and-gingham bedroom were Tony and Marsha and Henry, all in their regular clothing, while I was feeling pretty stupid in my pj's. Before the night was out, they'd vanished and reappeared a dozen times each, progressing along like a PG-rated peep show. And the whole time they were there,

I was having conversations with them, as if they were not just hallucinations but real people.

I can't say I got much sleep that night, but once I got used to the ghostly visitors, it was kind of fun. *So I didn't get laid after all,* I thought, and I've clearly got a lot to learn about blow, both the inhaling of it and the maintenance of oneself once it's safely inside. But still and all, I knew Henry wanted me, and that felt all right. In fact, that felt more than all right; it felt divine.

7

Morning. Creeping up all around me, enveloping me in its endless possibilities and promises of adventure, if only I could separate my head from the comfort of the pillow. How people managed this, day in and day out, I just couldn't figure. Whiz Bang was stretched grandly across my chest, twitching her nose and paws in rhythm with her jungle dreams. I was reluctant to move her, so I lay there a while, kind of poke-stroking her awake. My elbow stung fiercely with each caress, but I couldn't think why.

After a bit, the soothing smell of cinnamon worked its way beneath the comforter I'd wrangled over my head, giving me hope of some form of gin-absorbing dough—pancakes, waffles, or crumpets—which would help settle my queasy stomach. My feet hit the floor with a thud, and I slid my body down to meet them. Then in one smooth, electrifying boost, I was in motion.

Downstairs, my mom had a huge pot of steaming tea for me, kept warm by a pristine red-and-white cozy that she knit fresh the first week of every year. This one's days were numbered. She was busy at the stove, flipping buckwheat pancakes and sticking them in the toasty oven. I was barely able to move my head, narrowing my vision to what lay directly in front of me, which made me think about Logan when, freshly sixteen, he'd come back from Vegas quite a booze hound himself. Night upon night, he had burst in, knocking over any unattended object that blocked his path. Normally forceful and determined in his movements, he would be bumping randomly off counters, dropping jars of sweets or pickles as we tried to sleep. The thing was, there was nothing we could do about it. The nights my dad tried to intervene erupted into violent episodes of broken fists and flying chairs. I would sit on the stairs, Whiz Bang tucked up beneath my pajama top, her head poking out the neck, while my mom screamed, following them from room to room, a tangle of saliva, flannel, and leopard-print jeans.

That was when the distance began: Logan quitting the football team, tennis, even track, which he had loved more than anything. Shoving all the different, special kinds of shoes in the back of his closet. Done with it, he'd said. Done with it all. It was just a car, I'd said, thinking he was in trouble for selling the Firebird. It wasn't the car at all, Logan told me. It wasn't the car. Just forget it. So I kind of had, only nothing had ever gone back to normal after that. Never really.

Then after months and months and months of this, Logan just gave the drinking up and started in with the pot. Its musty scent permeated the whole house but kept Logan mellow, so I guess my parents figured it was the lesser of two evils and pretty much let it slide. That was when they began to let everything about Logan slide. And

Logan did start sliding, too. Grades dropping at school, hardly going out anymore. All the phone calls that came in on our line were for me then, which was way weird, I might add.

"So, love, how is Henry when one gets him all alone?" My mom slid some pancakes onto my plate. She was hip to Logan's caffeine-and-pancakes combo, so it appeared my I'm-not-really-fucked-up antics the previous night had flopped. The thing with my mom was, if she was somebody else's mom, CJ's, say, or the Tat's, you'd probably think she was the greatest with all her understanding and clairvoyance and not getting all bent out of shape about things like hangovers and older guys. But somehow when it was your own mom, you just wished she'd ground you or something, set some kind of boundaries. Or at least tell you older guys were only after one thing and to say no, no matter what.

"Fine."

"Now you are being careful, aren't you? You remember what we discussed?" She winked at me, then bit into one of the apple slices I had just put on my plate. I thought of my condom, a bit worn and torn, but basically still intact, nestled at the bottom of my boot.

"It's not like that."

"Well, I don't ever want you to feel inadequate. These are dangerous times to be a young woman." She winked again, this time clinking her tongue afterward.

I took my pancakes and wandered into the TV room. The air was heavy and slightly itchy from the early morning resumption of heat. My dad practically shut the heat off at night. "We were asleep anyway," he'd say. "If I didn't tell you, you wouldn't even know." But the truth was, you did know. It got pretty damn cold in our house at night. I suppose he was right, but the thing was, even without knowing exactly how much my dad made, I did know it was definitely enough to keep us warm. That whole poverty background of theirs had wacked them out in a lot of ways. The highlights of the Virginia Slims Navratilova/ Sabatini match were the only source of light in the darkened room.

"It's a damn shame Martina lost," my dad said the second he heard my footfall behind him. "That Sabatini isn't worth the cement they're playing on." He used the remote to gesture toward the huge screen. Martina's body bounded about in almost life-size proportions.

My dad was a major tennis fan. He thought that Martina Navratilova was just about the greatest player to ever set foot on the court. I was a Steffi Graf fan myself. She had just about the most amazing legs I'd ever seen. My dad had turned me on to tennis one Fourth of July weekend when he'd woken me at dawn just to watch Boris Becker win Wimbledon. We'd squeezed pitcherfuls of fresh orange juice and eaten heaps of grapefruit, bananas, and walnuts, both of us being too lazy to cook, resulting in a pair of intense stomachaches that lasted well into the next day.

"Living proof that a healthy mind and healthy body are absolutely fused."

He flipped his hand at the TV as if dunking a basketball. Even if it wasn't true, you would have believed him, the way his words kind of thumped out in a fury like they were bulletproof-vested or something. That was the way he said most things, though. To doubt him, you had to listen really carefully.

"I bet Steffi breaks all her records," I said, my mouth jammed full of buckwheat, berries, and ginger.

"Not likely! And don't speak with your mouth full, young lady. People will think you were raised in a zoo." I mouthed the last part along with him.

Logan had brought home a literary magazine from school a few years back with William Faulkner on the cover. He and my dad could have been brothers. Same broad face and scratchy mustache. He'd grown that mustache for me when I was little. I'd seen some flick as a kid where the dad sported one and had bugged him to do the same. But he'd refused. Then I went off to this God-awful summer camp—where all I did was try to think of ways to get myself home again, mailing daily schemes to my no doubt quite disturbed parents, although they left me there the full time—and what do you know, when my dad came to pick me up, he was sporting a mustache. I took it as a true sign of love: sticking something on your face you don't even want there, just because your daughter had a rotten time at camp. He'd had it for so long now, I figured at this point it belonged to him. I tried to imagine what it must be like to kiss a man with a mustache, all that roughness tangling with my mouth, but squelched the thought as it vibed vaguely incestuous. Then the sensation of Henry's thick, hot mouth whirled through me, and I shivered.

"Everything all right?" my dad asked.

"Yeah, fine."

Just then my phone started ringing, its jingles barely audible over the thwacks of the tennis balls. I bolted up both sets of stairs, two at a time, to get it before the machine picked up, my head throbbing with each leap and jump. I prayed, *Let it be Henry, let it be Henry, let it be Henry.*

"Careful running up those stairs," my dad called after me. "You're liable to break your neck!" we shouted out in unison.

I picked up the receiver, chest heaving in and out.

"Let, man. How you doing?"

"Ryder?"

"Yeah. Hey, listen, sorry to call so early, but truth is, my stomach is a-rumblin', and I wondered if you wanted to join me for a little brunch on this Masterful day?"

I checked myself in the mirror while he spoke. Okay, so darkness circled my eyes and my lids looked kind of swollen up or something, plus that thickness in my mouth was back, but I figured, Why not? A little hot water, some swanky clothes, I could pretty much pull it together. It was better than sitting around here all day placating my parents.

"All right. Pick me up in an hour." I rattled off the directions as best I could.

Ryder kind of rambled on about this and that, cracking a couple of jokes, and was pretty funny if you thought about it. He was easy to listen to. None of those weird silent times like with Henry where you picked at your nails and stared out windows. Finally I said I had to get off the phone, because my mom was calling me. And she really was, too. So I wandered back downstairs to see what was up.

All the way down I was preoccupied by Henry's kisses and my barfing and how the two didn't go together well and how I'd most likely not be seeing him again and how much that sucked and how it was weird that Ryder had phoned, like maybe he thought I had the shine, and boy, oh, boy, was he ever wrong, although I was actively searching. And all this was working its way around my head, so I was at the bottom step before I noticed Henry, sweet as honey, standing rigidly right there smack in the middle of our living room, pink, purple, and blue light swirling about his head.

The morning light caught his chip and beyond into the pinkness of his soft tongue. His dark hair flip-flopped into his eyes. Same clothes as last night. I could smell the stale sweat kind of thrusting its way into the room, and it got me twitching. My stomach pushed up against my heart. I ran my hands over the flannel pajama top and sweat pants I had snarled up about my unbathed, makeup-less body. I could sense, without touching, a pimple bursting forth between my eyes or, perhaps worse, on the end of my nose.

"I always wanted a convertible myself," my mom was saying, standing right up close to him, waiting for a drop or two of his nectar, "but you know how husbands are. William thought I'd get into too much trouble." Seeing me on the stairs, she added, "Didn't he, love?"

"He wouldn't let any of us get convertibles on account of not thinking that they're practical enough. Too much heat leakage and all."

"Oh, my. Was that the only reason?" She winked at Henry. "Well, I know how to keep the heat in just fine. Maybe I'll find that husband of mine and renegotiate." And she squashed her shoulders up about her ears and wiggled her fingers good-bye, then walked toward the kitchen. I wondered just exactly what she would do if one time someone called her on her stuff. What if Henry, for instance, unfamiliar with the ooze, said, "Oh, Mrs. Hitchcock, why don't you just step outside with me now and show me how to keep my Mustang warm." What would she do then?

"I was headed to John's and thought you might be needing something yourself, baby girl." Henry smiled, and I felt my pleasure dome tighten.

In the light of a new day, I kind of blamed Marsha and her stem trick for the downward spiral last night had taken. If she had just kept her tongue in her mouth, I would never have gone into the bedroom with Tony in the first place, and if I'd never gone into the bedroom with Tony, I would never have gotten so high, and if I hadn't gotten so high, I never would have barfed. And if I hadn't barfed, well, I might be looking at myself in the mirror real differently. But meanwhile, Henry was in my living room, which was wild. So I just had to figure how not to blow it again.

"I just ate. My mom made me pancakes. You can have some if you want. She won't care."

"That's okay," he said, leaning against the white wall, looking pretty uncomfortable. I thought about last night and how good his weight had felt pushing down into me. I remembered then why my elbow hurt and breathed in deeply, touching it with the tips of my fingers.

"Didya just get up?" He outlined my attire with his hand.

"Yeah, pretty much." I was trying to finger-brush my hair without him noticing. We were silent for a bit. Me on the bottom step, not daring to move closer and actually kind of wishing he would leave, while at the same time thinking it was so happening that he was there, and him just staring at me like I was from Mars or something.

"Well, how 'bout it, baby girl? Ready for a little spin around the park?" The corners of his eyes turned up. He sunk his fingers deep into his leathers.

"Yeah, that sounds cool. I just have to get changed. If you want, you can watch Virginia Slims with my dad in the TV room." I gestured toward the short flight of stairs that led down to it, immediately feeling foolish. I figured the women he was used to being with would have invited him up to soap their backs or polish their toenails—you know, something sophisticated like that. Me, I was inviting him to watch TV and eat pancakes with my parents, so I started thinking about something a little more alluring, perhaps even mysterious, to say to make myself more enticing. But just then, just to make everything worse, my dad came bouncing up the stairs with my empty pancake plate in his hand. Henry jerked away from the wall.

"Well, Henry, you're up early!" My dad's voice exploded into the room. He was still in his pajamas and robe, a matching pale blue set with raised white lines ending in thickly cuffed sleeves and hems, belted high almost more around his lower chest than waist. And on his feet, thick leather slippers, the kind you had to struggle into because they enveloped your feet, taking them over, making them into little horse's or donkey's hooves. So that in the end, he resembled one of those guards you'd read about in a child's fairy tale, say *Alice's Adventures in Wonderland* or something by Dr. Seuss. All puffy-chested and straight, stiff-bodied, chin thrusting forward in anticipation. The whole thing was depressing as hell, but I just couldn't make it stop.

"Yes, sir." Henry flicked into his polite mode. "I just came by to see if Violet here wanted to get a little something to eat."

"I'm afraid she just finished breakfast, son." He held out my syrupy plate as evidence. "But there's plenty more if you'd like some." Then he yelled into the kitchen, "Maude! Henry Edwards is here and would like some of your pancakes."

At the time I couldn't quite figure out my dad's burst of enthusiasm over Henry's appearance in his house, when the night before he'd been lecturing him on the perils of pot, doing so with a look of serious mistrust in his eyes. Looking back, which I've had more than sufficient time to do, I've since realized he sensed this pot-smoking, leather-clad, rancid-smelling older guy was getting potentially serious about his daughter, and he wanted to figure out how to prevent it from going any further. So he was pursuing his number-one business rule of attack—know your enemy. Whatever his motive was, it gave me some time to clean up.

The second I got into my room, Logan phoned. It was pretty weird actually, because I couldn't remember a time where he'd called just me before. I could tell right off he was toasted, on account of the crazy way he was talking. Normally I would have been into conversing with him, flattered that he'd phoned and all, but right at that particular moment, my mind was pretty far gone into the Henry-zone.

"Hey, Beans, Beans, Beans."

"Yeah."

"Hey, listen, little Beans-o'-mine, have you spoken with my fine girlfriend?" His words dry, thick, kind of sticking to the trans-state phone wires, as if I had to twitch my end just to work them through.

"Yeah, she phoned yesterday. Why?"

"Well, what did she want, Beany-bean?"

"She wanted to know how things were going with Henry. She said she'd call me back today to get the scoop. Why?"

"And did she, Beans?"

"Did she what?"

"Call, Bean Brain. Did she call yet?"

"No, not yet. What's up?"

"Listen, Beany-bean Head, if she calls, let me know, all right? And try to find out where she is, but don't you go telling her I was checking. Okay?"

"What's going on, Logan?"

"Ah, just some shit. You know, whatever, whatever, whatever. I'll call you later to check in."

I hung up feeling pretty strange, like maybe there was something I was supposed to know that for some reason, no doubt my fault, I just didn't.

Whiz Bang dove in the shower after me. I shaved my legs twice to be on the safe side and ran hot water around my distended eyes. I kept thinking about Henry eating pancakes with my parents, and it made me kind of nervous.

I shoved my favorite old black T-shirt into my cargo pants, then searched out my boots, somehow located deep under the recess of my bed even though I wore them every day. Strangely the condom wasn't in there anymore, nor could I find it anywhere nearby. I looked here and there, in my bathtub, between the sheets, but I figured I wasn't going to get laid for the first time on a Saturday afternoon in the backseat of a Mustang convertible in the winter anyway, so why bother? Then I whipped open my contact case only to find two empty pools of saline. Figuring that maybe I slept in them or something, I leaned in real close to the mirror and kind of picked at my iris, trying to break the suction of day-old air and slick membrane. No luck until I recalled having whipped up the protective tent-book just hours earlier. I found them hard and shriveled beyond repair, but soaked the suckers anyway, just because it seemed like the thing to do. Plus Logan was always telling me, You just never know. Sometimes you think something is going to happen one way, and then it happens another. I poked at the shrunken bits of plastic a full five minutes, before giving up and sloshing them down the drain.

Then I remembered Ryder. I guess I must have kind of remembered him all along, but didn't want to deal with it on account of what a drag it was going to be to call him, but I figured it would be worse for me if he came by and I wasn't there. My parents would freak. Good manners and all that other swanky social stuff were important to them. So I routed out his number, crumpled and worn from my drawer, and gave him a ring-ding. First I had to get through about fifty million different nosy, smart-ass guys on the hall phone while they tried to track Ryder down— all of them thinking they were the shit—before he finally surfaced.

"Hey Ryder, it's Let. Listen, I'm supersorry, but my parents didn't tell me that we had company coming over, and they just freaked when I said I was leaving. Anyway, they pretty much told me I have to stay home. I'm supersorry."

But the thing was, I didn't feel that sorry. In reality I was kind of mad at him. I figured he knew better than to phone me; we were both candles, that was clear. Therefore, if he had just stuck by the rules in the first place, rules I knew he knew—only pursue people with the shine—I wouldn't have had to lie. I guess way deep down, in that hidden part of my tummy where I kept a running count of right and wrong, maybe down there I did feel kind of bad. I mean he sounded bummed and all, but what could I do?

I hung up, this time tossing Ryder's number in the garbage where it belonged, and studied myself in the mirror, staring hard right into the center of my reflected eyes, which looked back all flickering shades of green and brown, strangely alert, like this was it, like life was beginning now and all I had to do was roll with it. Then, as if caught on some lazy fisherman's line, I eased forward from my waist, not wriggling and fighting, but smoothly and fluidly until my lips met those of my reflection's. I closed my eyes and laid a big one across my open mouth, feeling the lipstick smear against the cool glass. Then, as if the angler had let loose his line, I unwound, rolling my fingers in the pink smear. The heat from my breath filled the imprint until evaporating into the stillness of my room. I fixed my mouth and smiled. Things were going all right for a change.

Downstairs a snarl of prattle about tea roses, Dainty Besses, and Lady Hillingtons intertwined with morbid and precise career probing so that the one was hardly distinguishable from the other, as if Henry's career consisted of photographing huge, blooming rose gardens. I went in, pushing back my hair and smoothing my skin.

My parents had Henry squeezed between them at the table, where he was still eating. Wiping up the remaining puddles of syrup with his blue-black pancake, held not with a fork, but grasped between his long, long fingers, so when he was done he had to lick each one clean, sucking off the syrup, before leaving a streak of saliva down his leathers, and unsettling my heart.

"So Henry, love, you are being careful with my little girl, aren't you?" my mom said loudly when I walked into the room. She slid Henry's cigarette out of his hand, without even asking, and used the burning tip to light hers.

My dad said, "Christ, Maude, she's sixteen. She can take care of herself." I figured my parents just disagreed on everything out of habit. They could easily have switched sides.

"I know that, William, but I want to make sure my daughter is in good hands." She winked at Henry. "They look strong enough to me," she said, glancing down at his hands, which were lying flat out across the table, then stared at him. She drew heavily on her Winston. My dad folded his arms across his chest.

I sat down in Logan's chair, looking at our kitchen from a different perspective. From Logan's place you could see clear out the window and into the white worn thickness beyond. My mom's diamond solitaire kaleidoscoped across the walls. Moving his legs under the table, Henry forced the steel tip of his boot up against mine. I could feel the tension in his leg surge through me. He smiled, and seeing him do so, my mom smiled, too. To tell you the truth, the whole thing was making me nervous, and I wanted to get out of there fast.

• • • •

Outside, the sun was intense, but the Michigan wind was cold, so I wrapped up to keep warm. Henry had on his leather jacket again, sweatshirt beneath. His hands were bare, dark hair growing beneath the knuckles, and he drummed them against the wheel as the car warmed up.

"Your parents really seem to like you, baby girl," he said, just like he had before. I thought of us in his car last night. His weight hard into me, my body tense and damp, the rhythm of his breathing, in and out, in and out.

"I know, I know." I nodded. "What did you guys talk about, anyway?"

"Oh, nothing much. You know, just shit like what my life plans are, what kind of income I have, how many women I've been with, and how do I feel about children." He turned to back out of the driveway, and I glimpsed my dad's retreating figure through the living-room window. I liked how Henry was being. He made me feel like his girl-friend, so I busted a few jokes about being a mess and apologized for the night before.

"Don't sweat it," Henry said. I looked hard out my window.

As we'd eaten, we decided to go to a movie, but it didn't start for an hour, so we tooled around the dirt roads that surrounded my neighborhood. The houses there were mansions, with tower libraries flown over brick by brick from England, Olympic-size swimming pools, full-time gardeners and cooks, and practically ladies-in-waiting. And each of these splendors was enveloped by massive stone walls, impenetrable, but swirls of barbed wire slashed the tops anyway and guard dogs could be heard growling and pacing behind them. I mean, my folks were rich, but this was ridiculous. These people were in a whole other league.

I thought about how CJ's dad wanted all of upper-class, white America to look like this. Compounds. While outside the walls, he must imagine bedlam unfolding, all the nonwhite and all the white-but-poor-and-uneducated people killing and raping and terrorizing one another until they just did themselves in. I couldn't quite figure what the people who lived in the compounds did. Did they start growing food and create schools and hospitals on their massive backyards? And how did they communicate with one another—computers and telephones? And what about marriages and dating and sex? How did you meet someone outside of your compound? Did you venture out in tanks or armored vehicles, almost certain to meet death?

And where was the government this whole time? And *who* was the government?

I figured I'd be part of the Jenkinses' "us," the people in the compound, but what happened if I got put into a lousy one? What if a huge wall went up around our house so that it was just me and my mom and my dad—not even Logan, because he would be away studying, compounded at his school?

Henry lit up a cigarette, his face briefly cast orange by the car lighter even in the brightness of day. At the time, the gesture seemed so defined to me, like something my dad would do, that the sureness of it turned me on. Then he pulled a fleck of tobacco off his tongue, like he always did after he lit up. Half the time I don't even think there was anything there. I think it was just his way of touching those secret places again, knowing you were watching. Knowing you wanted to be touching them, too.

After a while we worked our way onto the asphalt roads that led to the movie house that showed alternative films. You know, small-budget, art, or foreign numbers, nothing with Sylvester Stallone, say, or Brad Pitt. We got there just minutes before the flick started, but Henry strolled to the ticket booth, his heavy boots clanking against the pavement a few steps ahead of me. A bouquet of sweetly swaying hips, stale sweat, and easy detachment, like he wasn't going to ever really let me in, no matter what I did. Like this was it, this was as good as it got. Then lighting up for a few final puffs, picking at the tobacco, letting his fingers linger against the pink while he looked over at me to make sure I was still there. And me, kind of quivering, full of expectations and uncertainty. I didn't even know what flick we were seeing until right then.

"*The Last Seduction*," Henry said. "Fieldstone said the actress was hot."

I checked my reflection in the booth glass, looking young and tired and no doubt dull as can be, then dragged behind him into the back-row seats.

The flick seemed to be about this wife murdering her husband while working a series of supershort black skirts, super-duper high heels, and a heavily reddened mouth like my mom's—the effect of which was clear to me despite the no-contacts focus. There wasn't a lot of sex, per se, but she was sexy. The way she sucked her cigarettes and the sound of her morning-after voice.

Right when we sat down, Henry worked his hand into mine, the roughness beneath each finger scratching my soft padding. His skinny thigh, thickened by the leathers, pushed into me. His knee was hard against my leg. He stretched over and flipped his tongue beneath my upper lip a bit before becoming totally absorbed by the film. After a while I freed my hand on account of all the sweat that was building up between us. Things like that really freaked me out. I spent the rest of the movie trying to figure out Henry.

Outside, out in the failing daylight, I blinked and squinched up my eyes, trying to adjust to the last of the sun. Henry flicked on a pair of those black wraparound biker glasses and lit up, cupping his long fingers around the cigarette tip until it ignited. The thing about hangovers is, they come and go in waves. Mine was checking in for the dinner shift.

Right off, Henry started explaining to me something called film noir.

"Dark passions, violent crimes, urban atmosphere," he expounded. "A lot of night-for-night shooting, which creates harsh contrast between the light and dark areas of the frame. Dark always predominates."

I nodded, kind of half listening.

"Directors use it a lot as a way to illustrate the moral chaos in the world."

He went on for a bit, showing off all the stuff he knew and I didn't. He never mentioned Fieldstone's hot actress, but she was there between us anyway.

"That plot was so easy to figure," I said. "I knew what was going to happen at the end, halfway through the flick." In reality, I didn't have the vaguest opinion on the movie. If someone had said, "So what did you think of it?" I would have been baffled. All I knew was I was nothing like that girl.

"Did you, baby girl?"

He spoke as if I were a child who held a gold-starred test in her tiny hand, looking for praise. I thought how those two words, *baby girl,* sounded when Henry was leaning over me in the dark of his parents' guest room or when he was kicking rocks in the snow of the Strawberry Fields parking lot, trying to ask me out without making it look like he was, or even in the stark light of my house, my living room, when he stood, hands in pockets, wanting me. And how those words sounded now, dismissive, reproachful, altered with a simple change of intonation. I wanted to tell him what an asshole he was and that I was hip to his game, but I wasn't feeling too good so I flipped through the radio channels until I thought I'd driven him just about out of his mind, but he didn't say a word.

The sky was darkening into a puddle of purple, blue, and black, as if God had accidentally combined a series of contrasting paints. Henry headed toward my house, lighting up a joint and passing it to me. As I took it from his lips and put the wet paper to my own, I felt a heavy dose of the twitch coming on, imperceptible to anyone but me. I took a couple of hits, then handed it back.

What happened next was, just before my street began, Henry turned down a narrow path that led into these woods that belonged to Mrs. Henderson, this old lady who refused to sell them but lived in another town. All the burns hung out there in the summer and got stoned, and sometimes part of the crew did, too. Nobody was there that day. Henry pulled the car around behind some scrappy bushes and slid the Mustang into park.

"Now, what did you want to tell me about that movie, baby girl?" he asked, playing with my hand.

"Nothing."

"Nothing?"

I shook my head, feeling nervous as hell; like maybe this was it, like maybe if I didn't barf or pass out, like if I could just relax and play it cool, I'd get to be initiated into the cult of Henry.

"Not even this?" He pulled me over to him, stretching my back out weird so that it hurt. "Come on, baby girl, tell me how the movie was so easy to figure out," he said, "or how the girl wasn't your type."

I pulled back into my corner, and he leaned over me, forcing my legs apart and unzipping his pants. I watched with a mixture of excitement and horror as his hard-on bulged from the tops of his leathers. He leaned forward and slid his tongue between my lips. My heart began racing like an overwound toy-monkey drummer. I closed my eyes and began counting to one hundred, which actually was old advice from one of my mom's notes about how not to flunk an exam.

The whole thing was over in ten minutes flat. CJ was right—Henry was the kind of guy to take care of things like condoms, though he slid it on himself, arching back in the prettiest way, and I didn't get to try my hand at unrolling it. When we were done, he tossed the used condom out the window just the way CJ had, and again rather than enforcing my no-littering rule, I let it slide. As we pulled away, I saw it lying there and thought it looked kind of pretty, carrying on each side a part of one of us. We drove the rest of the way home in silence, the inside of my legs burning something fierce. Once we got to my house, I invited him in, although in truth I kind of wanted to be alone.

"Darkroom," he said, tapping the dashboard clock with his hard pack of cigs.

"I could help," I said, working up my mouth into a perfect little flower. Of course he declined, but with a sugar-pie smile.

I thought about the possibility that Ryder might have been the better choice after all, even though I did get to do the nasty with Henry and that was nice, I guess. Something about it just didn't seem right, but as Mom would say, "What's done is done, and there's never any going back." So I made my way to Henry's side of the car and kissed him lightly on the lips. He closed his eyes, then dug his tongue deep into my mouth, tasting like popcorn and ice.

"Call me," I said, turning back toward him, working my hips hard as I neared the front door. He nodded and lit up a Camel, a shock of light against the darkening sky.

8

I sometimes felt, before all this happened, as if my life was a daisy chain. It looked so pretty and whole to the observer, when all the while, all it really was was these random explosions of color held together by tenuous strands, at best. Snap one strand—break the chain.

Needless to say, I didn't hear from Henry the whole week, despite the fifty million or so hang-ups I left on his machine, which I knew he knew was me. I should have figured then this guy was a creep, the type Logan used to warn me about—in it just for the chase; the more complicated, the more of a turn-on. But the thing was, his hot again–cold again routine was reminiscent of my whole family dynamic; therefore, easy for me to hang in with.

Ricky Johnson had another party that Saturday, so CJ and I tooled over to check it out.

"Will Henry be there?" asked my mom, finishing up her ten-zillionth crossword of the evening.

"Doubt it." I slid on my pink vinyl coat with the sparkly buttons.

"Thank God," my dad said, strolling into the kitchen, tennis racket under his arm.

"Ignore your father. He's just jealous because his better years are behind him. He was once quite a hunk himself." She rose and wiggled her hips alongside my dad, actually almost touching him.

"Christ, Maude, what are you doing?"

She leaned into the kitchen cupboard where she kept her stash and pulled out a fresh pack of cigarettes. She smacked it against her hand, knocking the tobacco into place, then lit up.

"I'm meeting Guy Perkins at the club," my dad said. "I'll be home late." He pulled on his car coat then grabbed his gym bag. "Violet, I want you home on time tonight. No horsing around. Midnight, and that is final."

In the background, my mom rolled her eyes.

"And drive carefully. Remember, you never know what the other guy is going to do, so keep alert."

"Yes, sir," I said, saluting him.

"Don't get wise with me, young lady, or you'll find yourself having a private party in your room."

I nodded.

"Now have a nice time, but be careful."

• • • •

Back in the Flame, in replay, everything turned out just the way it was supposed to. When I saluted my dad, he laughed. When I said I was going out to a party, my mom said, "Oh, how lovely. Have a nice time and don't talk to strange boys." From behind the wheel I watched the road stretch out before me like a tight-wound tape measure, releasing itself with the pressure of my foot. It was full of possibilities, and I had only just reached *Go.*

Ricky's party seemed unbearably infantile. A prowling congregation of muscle-bound jocks and scrawny long-haired burns drunk on hand-me-down liquor, or worse yet, just faking like they were. And girls wiggling frenetically through mountains of this sweating, fluttering flesh, working it for these jerk-offs, as if they were their meal ticket to something more than just repeating the doldrums of Mom and Dad.

Right off, I spied Ricky Johnson eyeing me across the room, but I hung close to CJ. At one point in my life, visions of Ricky had floated around in my head. I guess maybe I'd gone so far as to let out the word that I was interested, and he'd gone so far as to break up with his girlfriend. My not showing up at his last week's party was a minor detail that he was apparently still rebounding from, therefore playing it cool. The thing was, my Ricky interest had come before my having laid eyes, a second time, on Henry's narrow, swaying hips—which I could almost feel now pressing hard into me as he forced himself in and out, staring out the window at God knows what—which had immediately induced the state within me of *Ricky who?* Then Henry blows me off for a week, and I'm standing in Ricky's living room, like maybe he is the hottest thing around, like maybe going out with him would be pretty cool, like maybe I should just roll the dice and move already.

Some annoying music was blasting, and my throat was starting to burn from all the yelling I had to do just to be heard. CJ intertwined her fingers with mine, guiding me toward the bar. I was driving that night, so I knew not to drink, but I figured one mixer early on wasn't going to kill me. CJ handed me a Jack Daniel's and Coke and we hung low near the bar, already pretty bored, and the night had just begun. The whiskey was rough on my tummy, but I figured that would force me into some slow sipping.

Ricky was still staring, looking pretty dazzling if you want to know the truth, his long purple hair buzzed off into a blond crew, nursing a drinkie-wink of his own. A tinge of electricity shot through my stomach with the realization it was pretty easy to be attracted to several people at once. I mean, think about being in a room with Brad Pitt, Johnny Depp, and Leonardo DiCaprio. What— are you going to pick and choose among them or just go hog wild on all three? Ricky started to make his way over, but CJ jerked me into the next room, her feet aching from the platforms she was working. We plopped down on the couch, scanning the masses.

"Well, I'd say it's a bust. Just the regular crew. By the by, looks like Ricky's on the prowl for you." She ran her fingers through my hair a couple of times, then smoothed it down my back. I leaned into the cushions and stared at the ceiling for a bit.

This kid, who was already in college, sat down beside CJ and started flirting with her big-time, the type of lowbrow flirting CJ normally blows off, but this time she didn't, so I was left out in the cold. I got up and gave the party the once-over, which in a way was a stupid thing to do on account of my running into Ricky Johnson and it appearing as if I was looking for him, which I wasn't, even though I'd been considering it.

"Howdy," he said, which didn't exactly sweep me off my feet.

"Hey, Ricky. How are you doing? Sorry I couldn't make it to last week's party. My parents' friends had a get-together, and I was sort of forced into attending. You know how it gets." All these invented parental get-togethers of mine were making my parents very social indeed.

He shrugged.

"So how's everything going?" I pushed on, thinking he wasn't like Johnny Depp or Brad Pitt or Leonardo DiCaprio at all.

"It's cool." He looked at his drink a long time and picked something up off the ice. "Did you hear about Mathieson getting tossed for exploding a bomb in the john?" He evidently thought it was a pretty cool story.

"No. What happened?"

"He rigged this bomb to blow during fifth period, so we'd all get to split early, figuring it was safe to do it during class, because who the fuck uses the john then? But old mealy-mouth Hudson does, and he just about got his ass blown off while taking a crap in the next stall." Ricky started cracking up big then, like this was perhaps the funniest story he had ever heard.

"Is Billy okay?" Billy was Hudson's first name.

"Oh, shit, yeah. Broke his arm and messed up his face a bit. They'll let him out next week."

Then the weirdest thought went through my head. I wished Ryder was there. Not Henry like you'd think I'd be hankering for, on account of having just lost my virginity to him the week before, but little Ryder and his wide-open spaces and his Masterly love. I knew he'd never tell me a story about somebody almost getting their arm blown off, unless it was to illustrate what an asshole, how un-Masterly, the bomb builder was. The back of my throat started getting itchy, and I knew I wanted to go.

"I'm going to get a drink," I said. "Do you want one?" Ricky shrugged, and I split.

I headed straight for CJ, only, of course, she wasn't on the couch anymore, and it took some real fancy footwork on my part to locate her without running smack into Ricky Johnson again. I found her in one of the back bedrooms, doing lines with the older college guy, whose name turned out to be Tim.

"Let's split," I said.

"Where to?"

"I know of a party in one of those Hillstream mansions," Tim said. "Reggie Landwehr, you know, as in Landwehr Construction? His parents are throwing him some intense shindig, loads of everything: booze, pills, the works, because no cop is going to cross Harold Landwehr. You know what I'm saying? Plus he and his new grade-school wife are into partying."

"Shit, let's go," I said. CJ finished her lines, not before offering me one, but I declined on account of my remembering how I felt the last time from doing that stuff, and knowing I'd never be able to drive if I did it now.

Finally we slid out the door, CJ packing a stolen bottle of Jack Daniel's under her fake mink, and Ricky eyeing me in disbelief from the kitchen. Outside, it was clear, but the sky was thickening into a swirl of blue, black, and white. I was doing okay behind the wheel, hardly crossing the yellow line at all, and taking only the most minuscule of sips from the Tennessee sour mash. This time I made sure to concentrate on my roadkill count, though it was all feeling like such a mess that I wasn't sure whether I should just dump the current tally and start anew with everybody a fresh roadkill (therefore, all at the number one), or try and find a moment of calm (yeah, right) to sit down and reconstruct the layout in my mind. We whizzed past the Edwardses, skidding out a bit as I squinted up, making out Henry's parked car and blazing apartment. I still hadn't told my parents about my trashed contacts. Waiting for the right time and all.

A twisted tumble of turrets and towers and towering trees rose before us, and we drove through massive iron gates into the vastness that lay beyond. A gigantic Tudor mansion, an American palace of sorts, miles and miles away, connected to us by a yawning driveway. Ten-thirty and cars were jammed everywhere. We had to walk a full five minutes in some busting cold just to get to the door.

Inside, we warmed our feet by banging them hard against the floor, and I flashed back to when I was a kid and our kitchen had been invaded by red ants. We had all pulled on our winter boots even though it had been a thick summer day and stomped them until they were ant soup. The whole thing had made me sad as hell. And later, in the solitude of my room, I'd made a secret vow to God that I would never kill anything again. Which was really the beginning of my whole roadkill thing.

We were greeted by a maid who was old and shriveled, like a Granny Smith left in the sun too long, dolled up in one of those traditional black-and-whites, frilly white cap, and apron. Only everything about her outfit was sort of not quite right and for a minute, it made me feel even sadder than remembering the ants had. She balanced our heavy jackets across one frail arm, the weight tilting her body toward CJ's purple fake mink before she disappeared through a distant door.

"Perhaps the wife of the bartender," I said, thinking about the old geezer at Henry's party.

"Huh?" CJ and Tim said in unison.

We took off through the Tudor labyrinth, my ears popping in the silence, like at church or something, before we finally landed on the party. I would have searched the halls half the night, but CJ had a nose for booze. The room we walked into first had a thick glass ceiling, crisscrossed with shiny metal supports, moonshine skimming across it like a skipping stone. Smack in the middle was a swimming pool, all lit up in baby pink and baby blue with a couple of losers, all nice and toasty, already skinny-dipping, their pink shriveled bodies casting weird shadows across the water.

"No shit," said CJ, "I could live like this. Never have to leave the house."

"Couldn't find your way out, anyway," I said.

"I'm going to locate the bar," said Tim, and disappeared into the crowd.

• • • •

For the next hour or so, I watched CJ flirt with about fifty million guys, having lost track of Tim from the get-go. To tell you the truth, I was starting to get that depressed feeling again, like nothing was quite the way I wanted it to be. Finally CJ grew weary of her admirers, wrapped my hand in hers, and dragged me down a dark, musty hallway and into the rosewood library beyond.

Inside, I felt more at ease. As I mentioned before, books have a calming effect on me, and there were a lot of hand-bound originals, titles delicately embossed with gold leaf, delightfully alphabetized in an iridescent swirl about the room. They smelled like heaven, musty and worn, full of old tired ink and tumbling pages. They filled my senses, blocking out the rank odor of too many losers in too small a space. CJ beelined it right to the bar, handed me a glass of champagne, used hers to wash down the three bright yellow pills she had just finished chewing.

"What's on the menu tonight?" I asked.

"I don't know. Some guy gave them to me by the pool. Said it would make me feel groovy." She plopped onto the couch, waiting for the payoff. I perused the books for a bit, sliding my fingers along the cool spines, closing my eyes and waiting for the dip between volumes, trying to guess what letter I was in. By the time I'd reached the *L*'s, I needed a fresh drink. I wasn't feeling buzzed, and, like I said, the rest of the place was depressing the hell out of me.

I polished off the champagne, then flopped down along-side CJ on the couch, feeling the stale heat of its former occupant seeping into me. I poked at CJ a bit, but she was nodding. *Better get going.* I leaned my head against CJ's shoulder. Darkness roared through my emptying mind, and I rode it like a surfer who'd been waiting in the stretches of bluey-blue for the perfect break. It curved round me, a seven-footer or more. I released my body into it and slept.

．．．．

"Hey. What are you, man, one of those narcoleptics or something?" Ryder loomed over me, shifting in and out of focus in unison with the pounding in my head, which in turn seemed to be vaguely connected with the rhythmic swishing of my tummy.

"I was just resting a minute." I strained a kick toward CJ, but her legs were skewed too far to the left for me to connect.

"I didn't know you knew Reggie." Ryder flopped down next to me, mashing me hard between him and CJ. The additional weight shifted the couch, forcing my head into an uncomfortable upward position. He reeked of Southern Comfort.

"I don't really. I mean, I met him and all, but I don't know him. How about you?"

"Yeah, he goes to Hillstream."

"So, you've been here before?" I asked, distracted by this old geezer with a champagne-laden tray who bent down so far to serve us, I was kind of afraid he'd never get back up again.

"Yeah, man. Many a time, many a time. Mr. Landwehr believes in sharing the wealth, which is really what it's all about. It's like a river; you've got to keep it flowing, or it will strangle the life force," he said in all seriousness, look-ing at me as if I were then expected to kiss the ground in reverence—although not quite that intense, more like maybe I should just bow my head or shed a tear. "Do you want to see the sights?"

I figured, Why not? Hell, this guy kept turning up every which way that I did and the thing was, when I was with him, I kind of liked him. Plus, at Ricky's I'd actually been *wanting* him to be there. He didn't make my palms sweat, you know, or drive me into a fit of idiotic witticisms. I just felt okay. I gave CJ a perfunctory poke, but she was well into nod-nod land, so I trailed behind Ryder, feeling a strange twinge of excitement.

Out of the library, Ryder and I wrangled through myriad vacuum-sealed halls, each as lifeless as the last. Room after room slid by. Dark and secretive, the air heavy with pine disinfectant. Ryder pointing, saying, "The library. The den. The rec room." And so on. After a while we landed in one of the fifty million or so over-upholstered bedrooms that were attached to this great sea monster of a dwelling. Ryder fumbled for the light switch. We didn't need it because the full moon was blasting down on us through the bay window, which got me thinking about how that was what God must feel like, pure radiance, but without the heat.

"The Master at his height," Ryder said, giving up on the switch. "Absolute radiance. No oppression."

I wanted a drink pretty badly at that point, not only because Ryder had this freaky habit of reading my mind, but also on account of this fluttering in my lungs, which were heavy with something, but I didn't know what. I was having a hard time taking in a full breath of air. Right on cue, Ryder slid out his flask, and we sat on the edge of the hard bed, sharing swigs of Southern Comfort and following the swing of my boots.

"This is my favorite room in the whole place," he said, staring outside, "because the sight of the moon through the window is always perfect. If this were my place, I'd never leave this room."

"Just order in a lot," I said.

"Yeah." He smiled. "But truth, I'd just put a little fridge over there and one of those countertop stoves over there, and I'd use the bathroom sink to wash dishes and to get water for soup. I've had the rooms; I've had the stuff upon stuff; I've had all the fancy gadgets, but when you've got a view like this, what do they matter?"

I looked at the moon, and it was pretty, too. No doubt about it, but I knew I wasn't feeling it the way Ryder was.

"All you need is a little bit of good company," he went on, "the moonshine all over the place and, and . . ."

And he suddenly drew up my hands to his swollen mouth, kissed the tip of each finger supersweetly, but a little roughly, too, like maybe he wasn't used to doing it. I thought of how Henry made you feel like whatever was going on was meant to be. Somewhere between fate and a really happening accident, while Ryder's movements were precise and determined. He began sucking on each tip, then rubbing my palms against his flushed face. And me just kind of sitting there watching it all, the bumps in the bed working their way hard up against my ass.

So what happened next was Ryder kind of pounced on me, knocking me back on the bed with a grunt. Took me by surprise, but I liked it. He nuzzled his face down hard on my neck, his sharp breath working its way into me, making my nose tickle, and I wanted to laugh as he started in on a good-size hickey, but I didn't. He was so sincere and looked cute as hell squirming around on top of me, his tiny ass pumping up and down as he dry-humped my leg. And I remember especially now how the smell of soap took everything over, like Betty had just finished scrubbing him up, clothes and all, with a big chunk of whiteness and a huge cotton cloth. And I felt safe and clean and important.

Then he took a breather, raising his head and chest, forcing his belt buckle into my pleasure dome. I squirmed around a bit, but he just pushed harder and harder and it started to hurt. I could feel his hard-on hot against my leg, tiny pulses in and out, straining against the confines of his zipper. He was really worked up, his face twisted strangely, his girlish lips wet in the corners. Logan had told me it was kind of painful if you couldn't get off when you wanted to, but I should never, ever let some guy use that as a sob story on me. A good steady hand was all anybody needed to relieve the pain.

I shifted again, but the belt buckle was digging further into me, and to tell you the truth, was driving me a little bit nuts. Then Ryder started doing the trippiest thing. He started saying my name over and over again, like a weird chant or something, a mantra, although then I didn't even know what that word meant, and it kind of gave me the creeps. I stared up at the ceiling and tried to relax, even gave the Tat's breathing one more try, and it was working better than the night with Henry, but then Ryder shoved his cold hand up my shirt and started feeling around. It tickled and I was getting annoyed, losing the twitchy vibe I'd had earlier. Then he drew me up toward him, his tongue flicking, his pink lips rounding wider and wider and at that moment—the golden moonshine painting his pompadour the color of daisies, his eyes the bluey-blue of a fading sky—he looked so damn pretty to me that I started to like it again, and began shifting beneath him.

Then, just when everything was feeling all right, and I was wondering if this was the night I should have shoved a condom into my boot, or were thoughts like that jumping the gun, and if they weren't jumping the gun, perhaps Ryder would have the condom, and how did you know what you were supposed to do what night and with whom, a thick knot of Southern Comfort–infused saliva landed in my mouth and made me want to barf. A few drops even rolled down my chin, and before I could even think about it, I drew my knees up to his stomach and pushed as hard as I could. He toppled backward off the edge of the bed, miraculously landed on his feet and backpedaled until he hit the wall. I could see his hard-on still bulging in his Wranglers.

"I'm going to find CJ," I said, hopping up, untangling my clothes. The room took a fast swerve to the left, then settled in. Ryder trailed me down the hall. In reality, I mostly trailed him because I couldn't figure out where the hell I was going. But it felt like he was trailing me, the way he kept apologizing and pushing his hair around.

• • • •

"Listen, Let, I'm sorry, man. I don't know. I don't know. It just felt so right, like it would be beautiful, you know. And truth, I thought you wanted it, man." He did sound sorry, and damned embarrassed, too. I was sorry and embarrassed myself. And the thing was, I *had* wanted it. But not like that. I was beginning to realize that I consistently hit a level with my drinking where everything just seemed wrong, no matter what. With a bad mood hot on its heels.

The hall lights turned our pale figures into creations of Henry's film noir. Long shadows shot down the hall, closer to the comforts of home than I was. Ryder tugged at my hand, wanting to talk. I wanted to sleep. That was my second realization of the evening—liquor made me tired. Pass-out kind of tired. I started thinking about how many times I'd fallen asleep in strange places lately, and it made me feel weird. First at the Edwardses', then at Hillstream, and most recently at this stupid party.

Actually now that we were out of that bedroom, Ryder looked all right to me again. I had a strong inclination to lead him back into that moonlight radiance, but it seemed like too much work. Was that how Henry felt about me? By the time we got to the good stuff, he was exhausted from all the baby-sitting. I made a mental note to be more agreeable next time I was with him.

"Forget it, Ryder. It really doesn't matter," I said after his fifty-millionth apology. And the funny thing was, it really didn't. I pushed back his hair, heavy still with Montana sun, brilliantine building up between my fingers. I thought of his phone number crumpled up in my garbage, and it made me sad. I was still in a lousy mood, though, fantasizing about my bed and wanting to be in it.

"We're both like candles," I said, thinking back to the way I felt the day I met him.

"You're wrong, man. The fire is within." Ryder kind of freaked me out that way, how he always knew just what I meant and all, even when maybe sometimes I didn't. His face fell in and out of shadow as he shifted his heavy Ropers about, heavier even than the jackboots that Henry wore, designed and built for ranching. *Spirit breakers,* I thought, picturing them digging in hard to the sides of wide-stretching horses. *Freedom riders* would have been his counter had he heard me.

"Think about it, man. Stop the search because it's already there." His nose was broadened by the coarse hall lights, his mouth more swollen than ever, thick and parted, wet with Southern Comfort and the tangle of our saliva. He headed down the hall and was eventually absorbed into the labyrinth.

I stared at the emptiness before me and tried to figure what to do next. For the longest time it was hard to think straight. It felt like it had been weeks since I had a clear thought.

CJ was as I had left her, a rumpled mass of vinyl, nylon, and princess-pink nail polish. She refused to respond to my persistent nudges, only tossing her head from side to side, as if rolling dough. I plopped down next to her. I could feel the pull of my bed, the weight of my comforter, the lushness of my pillow. I didn't know what time it was but figured it had to be past curfew. Doomed, I picked at my nails, then roused CJ with some double-intensity pokes.

Somehow I got her up and moving and began dragging her down the hall, like a slow dance of sorts, like with one of those dorks who you just can't say no to, because you feel so bad for them, but at the same time you can't wait for the dance to end, because you're kind of dragging them around the floor. And the weird thing was, nobody even noticed us, or if they did, thought it was just hunky-dory that a little thing like me was lugging this dead weight down a hall that stretched out for about forty million miles, with the door—the size of a peanut—barely visible in the distance.

When we got there, I propped CJ up against a wall and managed to locate our coats. We had definitely lost track of Tim, which was fine with me, on account of not wanting to have to drive him home. I rammed CJ's limp arms into her purple fake mink, and tugged it across her bulging chest, squashing and squishing like crazy, but I couldn't get it to close. She kept mumbling about the damn couch. "You busted me outta my crib, darling. Take me back." And endless shit like that. That was the downside to CJ. In every other way just about, except maybe how all the guys fell for her, even mine, she was the coolest, but at parties she always had to try stuff out. Any stuff, too. It didn't matter. Just tell her it would make her feel great, and she'd pop it or drink it or sniff it or smoke it or toot it, stopping only at needles. Looking for the perfect high that never seemed to come. Logan said it was because her old man was such a jerk-off; she didn't have much of a role model.

Outside, it was cold as shit. Winter had landed. I raced for the car parked miles in the distance, but CJ moved like she was caught up in a gigantic rubber band. I was harboring the ridiculous hope that Henry would eventually get around to calling me, and I wanted to be available for a date, rather than grounded on account of CJ and her pills. The Flame turned over slowly and it was a while before the heat came on. I blew into my hands, filling my nostrils with the sickeningly sweet stench of Southern Comfort and Ivory soap—Ryder.

"Shit, Let, crank the heat," CJ said, then passed out, her head tilting forward like maybe her neck would break if I pushed on it. I swung out hard, the back end whipping round, wheels spinning, white flying like a Sno-Kone machine out of whack, coming within inches, the most minuscule of inches, of scraping swanky lined-up cars, before flooring it down the drive. At the road I hit the brakes. I would be no killer-of-little-animals. I tried the Tat's breathing again to calm myself and this time it seemed to help. After a bit I felt all right. I was like some kind of human yo-yo, only it wasn't my finger working the string.

I rubbed my forehead hard, trying to think. Turned out it was only 12:30, and I figured if I got in by 1:00, I'd be A-OK. The lines in the road were playing a wicked game of leapfrog and my head was all aswirl trying to sort things through, so I plodded along, ten miles an hour, tops. I figured we could walk home faster, so I concentrated on picking up some speed. Only just then the Edwards house popped up, and Henry's place was still blazing hot against the dark sky, so I figured I'd pull in. I don't know, for some reason it made perfect sense at the time. The main house was in total darkness, so the chances of old Mrs. Edwards nailing me were slim.

CJ was totally out, so I locked her in the car, leaving on the overhead light and her favorite CD in case she woke. I figured I'd just be a minute, but you never know—she might freak in the dark. Henry's door hung heavy and black alongside the white slats of the garage, like a Motherwell, or one of those other painters from his time, illuminated by my headlights, which the safety timer hadn't yet shut off. I knocked once, the crack echoing for a million miles, yet barely audible against the wood. No response. I jumped up and down to keep warm and also so I wouldn't have to think too much, keeping my brain concentrating on how to land safely and all. "Take action or lose out; there's no other way of looking at it," my dad would say. So I tried again, this time with some force, and sure enough, I heard Henry padding down the stairs, my heart exploding into a series of cartwheels.

"Hey, baby girl," Henry said, with no hint of surprise, like he knew I was coming all along, like he was just biding his time waiting for me. He was dragging on a Camel, surrounded by a halo of smoke, barefoot, bare-chested, just his leathers between the two of us. He kind of rubbed his chest bone up and down real gently, his dark nipples hard from the sudden cold, the smell of his body seeping out into the night. And me silent, startled, without words. And him just smiling. Waiting it out.

"D'ya wanna come in?" he asked finally, glancing at my car, taking in all the weird details like CJ and the loud jams, but didn't ask any questions. He closed the door behind us, and I followed his rank scent up the stairs. Guys my age didn't smell like Henry. Guys my age smelled like Mom stuff: Tide and Prell and Ivory soap.

His apartment was pretty busting. A string of low-hanging track lights, each focused specifically on one of his photographs that lined the walls in uneven rows. Photos of cars and trucks and minivans; shot in studios or out in the open on a road near water or something. Then low across the heavy wooden windowsill, a whole series of black-and-whites, printed small so that you could shove one in your pocket and take off with it, and nobody would even notice. Girls in sexy poses, like bent across a bed or painting their toenails in some swanky baby-doll nightie, the light so hard against their faces that their features were almost erased. But the thing was, each girl seemed detached, like what was happening was just for that second and nothing else.

"Who are the girls?" I asked.

"Friends." I was getting that same feeling that I got with my dad when I wasn't sure whether he wanted me there or not. When you thought maybe he did, it would turn out he barely had time to spit at you. But when you'd give up and split, he'd be yanking you back, full of sweet talk. You just never knew which mood he was in. Henry lit up a joint and passed it over.

He looked different to me. Sitting pretty, as Logan would say, eyes somehow darker, body more defined, like something great had happened. I took a tiny hit of the joint, remembering how I still had to get home, and I was really staying only a minute anyway. I positioned myself on the couch. Henry sat down next to me, his leg almost touching mine. I concentrated on breathing deeply, even puffing up my chest a bit into a birdlike posture, staring straight ahead at his walk-in kitchen.

"So, where have you been?" I asked, turning my head the most minuscule amount to look at him. He had the joint dangling from his pink bottom lip, his fingers jammed into the tops of his leathers. He looked good, and it got me twitchy.

"Tooling around some." He took a long toke before passing back the joint. I hit it again, feeling the paper, wet from his lips, against mine. Everything around me kind of grew and shrank simultaneously, except for sweet Henry. He became absolutely crystal clear.

"Like where?"

"Checking out some colleges I might like to join." He winked at me.

I took another hit, working hard on controlling my head, which kept rolling forward like a bowling ball. But in reality, I felt good. I stretched back onto the couch, resting my feet on some old beat-up trunk Henry used as a table, checking out the room some more. Cameras everywhere, but not much else, like if you didn't already know something about Henry, you sure weren't going to discover it here. Henry sauntered off for a minute and came back with two bottles of ice-cold beer and this little stash bag. The land of the fairies.

We did a couple of lines each, this time the fairy dust staying up my nose, and I kept thinking, *I gotta go, I gotta go,* but I just didn't seem to be able to get my feet facing in the right direction. And I'll tell you, Henry was in no hurry to get me out the door. He stretched back out again along the couch, ramming right up hard against me, wiggling his bare feet on the trunk alongside my dirty boots. And I was feeling twitchy as hell, but nervous, on account of things probably being a little different in a bedroom than in a car. More room to move around and do stuff. Stuff I didn't know how to do, such as the condom maneuver. In the car Henry slid it on himself, and made it look pretty easy, but would it be my turn tonight? And in that moment, that pause, with all the attention on me, would I be able to rise to the occasion? And as I'm thinking about this and more, too, in pretty graphic detail, I caught sight of his kitchen clock—an old bashed-on hubcap with a plastic face nailed into the center. It was closing in on one-thirty. I jumped up fast, spinning toward the door, causing Henry to have a good chuckle or two.

"Hey, hey, baby girl, where ya going?" He caught hold of my hand, pulling me toward him, fingering my palm; examining every cut, every crinkle, every vein.

"I'm supposed to be home by now," I said. But I didn't move. Instead I let Henry lead me into his bedroom and lay me across rumpled sheets, smelling thickly of him, as if they'd been on the bed for weeks and weeks; so unlike Ryder's unsoiled routine. Then Henry walked to the side table and flicked on the lamp, angling it directly at my body, tilting the shade a couple of times until he came up with the lighting he was searching for. The strange thing was, I suddenly wasn't nervous. I just fell into it, like this was the moment I'd been anticipating that day in front of the mirror.

Henry climbed up on the bed, straddling my body, locking bent knees hard into my sides. I wasn't sure what to do, but Henry kind of guided me along, slipping off my sweater set with his teeth. Unlike Ryder's, his hands were warm, lingering, well trained, and I was squirming, arching forward, pushing hard into him, everything loose and fluid, but tightened up, too, in anticipation. I closed my eyes and breathed deeply.

"Open your eyes, baby girl."

He bent over and angled the light so it fell more on my body, less on my face. Then he pushed up my skirt and unzipped his leathers. He shifted the shade one more time so that it included him, pulled my body into a particular placement, then bore down hard on me, keeping his lips from mine.

When it was over, Henry lit up a Camel, while I looked at his bedside clock—2:45. I was dead. Henry went into the kitchen and came back with a beer. The smoke was making my head pound. I took a swig, then slipped into my sweater set. A smaller selection of girls observed me from his dresser. I was feeling lousy. Right up until then, I'd been feeling pretty good, but then I just felt lousy again. Henry watched me dress.

"Where's the bathroom?" I asked.

He pointed to an open door. En route I had to step over the condom I managed to slip on unassisted without making too much of a fool of myself, though I'd forgotten about the massage-the-balls part until it was too late. I closed the door behind me and stared into the mirror a full minute before doing anything. What was I doing here? I missed my curfew yet again, and I was so high I could hardly focus on myself in the mirror. I leaned way in to check for pimples, but my skin seemed okay. I squashed some Ultra Brite on my finger, mushing it around my mouth a bit, then shut off the light. When I got out, Henry was still in bed.

"You all right?" he asked, trying to finger my hand, but I pulled away. I was too sick to talk, so I just left. He didn't try to follow me or anything. Just stayed in bed in those little white Calvins and smoked some more cigarettes. Something just didn't seem right, but I couldn't figure out what. I really couldn't.

• • • •

Outside, the winter's first snow had begun. When we were young, Logan and I had carved forts from the mighty snowdrifts that had built up between the neighbors' property and ours. The rooms were so big, you could walk right through them without ducking your head. In reality, our dad had been the true craftsman, but Logan and I had done our share, spraying the water to create gigantic room-connecting ice slides, carving windows in the small, medium, and epic rooms, turning the ousted snow into snowmen with crooked carrots for noses and garden rocks for eyes.

We would spend hours whizzing about in ski pants, wearing down their backsides, sliding from one room to the next, finally exhausting ourselves, forced to retreat inside to brimming pots of tea and freshly baked mincemeat pies my mom would have waiting for us. Each fortress would last for days or weeks, depending on the temperament of the weather. And even then, even when the neighbors' snow had melted into shapeless mush, ours would stand firm in the brilliant winter light, blinding.

My headlights were flickering in the darkness, barely casting light at all. I figured maybe CJ had woken up and had been playing around with the controls. Inside the car, it was freezing. CJ was still sleeping, oblivious to the hour or temperature. I turned the key, listening to the Flame hack and jerk, hack and jerk. I tried again, with a similar result. She just sputtered and coughed, weakening with each pass until on the final turn, her pains were all but inaudible.

It was then that I noticed how the inside light was kind of blinking on and off too, just like my headlights had been, and I figured they must not have been in the safety shut-off mode after all. They must have been in the use-up-all-the-juice-it-takes-to-run-your-car mode. I rested my forehead against the steering wheel for a minute, blowing hot air clouds into the frosty night, thinking about what to do next. CJ was snoring away like nothing was wrong, which made me want to kill her, so I shook her. She sat straight up, looking at me with heavy lids.

"What?"

"What? What? It's fucking freezing out, and my car is dead! That's what!" I slapped the steering wheel for emphasis.

"How'd it die?" She didn't seem all that interested, if you want to know the truth.

"It died because I left some stuff on for you so that you wouldn't be uncomfortable, just in case you happened to actually wake up."

"Why'd ya leave me in the car, darling?" She was rubbing her eyes and straightening out her hair a bit.

"Listen, CJ, just forget it, okay? The car is dead, and we've got to get out of here. My parents are going to kill me."

"What time is it?" She did some sort of abbreviated seat stretch.

"What are you, the queen of questions tonight? It's three o'clock, and we've got to get the fuck out of here!"

I jumped out of the car, deciding at that moment that the only thing to do was to walk to the nearest gas station and phone my dad. Waking up the Edwardses or going back up to face Henry was out of the question. Two or three yards into my journey, I saw a car sweep into the driveway, the headlights blinding me; a raspy voice spread out through the falling snow.

"Violet, is that you, dear?" It was old Mrs. Edwards, not sounding too startled, either, at seeing me in her drive at three in the morning.

"Yes, Mrs. Edwards, it's me. CJ and I were having some car trouble, so I pulled into your drive hoping maybe Henry or Mr. Edwards could fix it, but nobody was home. And while we were sitting here waiting for one of you to maybe return, my car pretty much died all the way, so I don't know what to do." I stopped for air.

"Have you been sitting here long?" queried Mr. Edwards, his voice muffled through the glass. He lifted himself out of the driver's seat and trudged toward me.

"I don't know, maybe an hour or two, I guess." I paced back and forth, chock-full of this weird nervous energy.

"An hour or two. Sweetheart, didn't your father teach you how to jump-start a car?" He smelled like chocolate and wine, his words slurring when he spoke. I was kind of relieved, figuring this would make him less likely to notice the state I was in.

"Maybe the girls should come in the house while you look at the car, dear," old Mrs. Edwards said out her half-rolled-down window. I could see her breath as she spoke.

"Yes, that seems reasonable." Mr. Edwards had already tried turning over the engine himself. Now he had the hood up, his head buried in the workings, workings that I wished I'd paid more attention to during my daddy-daughter car lessons. "Put some coffee on, will you?"

I tried to decline. I didn't know what to expect out of CJ, and the last thing I wanted was to spend time with old Mrs. Edwards. Plus, my parents. Plus, Henry. I *had* to get home. I could still smell Henry rising up through my clothes. *He's marked me,* I thought, and smiled. Mr. Edwards looked up from the engine and smiled back.

• • • •

Inside, I phoned my parents while old Mrs. Edwards prattled on about the party they'd just been to. CJ seemed to be doing all right. She had walked unassisted over the slippery snow and into the house and was propped up on a kitchen chair, looking like she was actually listening to the old bird cackle. My dad was relieved that I was alive and kicking, but I knew an earful awaited me when I got home. My chest pushed up inside my throat. Why, oh, why was I having such difficulty getting my little teenage body home on time?

Old Mrs. Edwards slid me a cup of hot chocolate, holding back the rum-spiked mug for herself. The thick, bitter scent made my stomach turn, and I noticed CJ had pushed hers aside. She started telling us how divine her party had been, full of all the local society and whatnot. She simply couldn't understand why my parents didn't participate more in the goings-on of the community. "If I want to see a bunch of monkeys putting on a show I can pay five dollars and go to the zoo," my dad would say whenever my mom wanted to attend one of those functions.

I hated when my dad talked about the monkeys, because I hated zoos. Animals in cages really bummed me out. I mean, big-time, too. It was up there with roadkills. Pet shops; zoos; birds behind wire, wings clipped, propped in front of the open window; glassed-in fish swimming the same tiny circle all their lives; hamsters poking in and out of their plastic houses, running and running and running the wheel, waiting, praying for their minute of freedom. They all depressed the hell out of me. They really did.

"My Joe hired me as his secretary," old Mrs. Edwards was saying, "back in the days when it was a respectable profession. He was married at the time, but the passion had gone out of the relationship."

Passion. That was how my mom described the old days with my dad, and the word made me itchy. The days in the trailer when things had still been nice between them. "Your father would bring me these magnificent armfuls of freshly opened violets that he'd collected from a field down the way from our trailer park. His eyes dancing at the sight of me. That's why I named you Violet, love. So your father would always remember how he had once adored me."

Logan said our mom was insatiable. Meaning nothing would ever fill her up. He said it was because she had lived this deprived life when she was young, even though now she had everything money could buy, and it still wasn't enough. But it was in just this way I felt certain I took after her and often wondered if she hadn't brought me into this world solely to carry on her hunt. Thing was, she didn't seem to know what she was hunting for any more than I did, just something to fill her up, something to make her breathe long, easy breaths. Something pure. Something that burned inside when she got near it. The shine.

Mr. Edwards finally came stomping in, blowing into his hands, cutting off his wife's story before the truly gruesome details began.

"Well, you're up and running again, sweetheart." His eyes looked pretty bloodshot in the kitchen light, and his hands struggled against the vagaries of gravity. I studied him while he fumbled with his coat and could clearly see the rounded shoulders of Henry as well as the sharply structured nose and dark, descending eyes. The windowsill cheekbones were all his mother's, though, in addition to the lean body. Mr. Edwards was built like an old-time hockey player.

"Thank you so much, Mr. Edwards. I'm sorry to have inconvenienced you and all." I stood up and grabbed my coat, watching the second hand tick by on the kitchen clock.

"No trouble, sweetheart, no trouble at all. After all, you are William Hitchcock's daughter, and I must make sure that you are always safe and sound and treated well. Is that a cold you have coming on, Violet?" He was referring to the way I couldn't stop wiping my nose, as it felt like the coke I snorted at Henry's was suddenly falling out.

"No, Mr. Edwards. I feel fine."

We were all doing a good job of ignoring CJ's snoring, which was escalating by the minute. I managed to slug her the minute the Edwardses turned away, but it didn't do any good. Just then, old Mrs. Edwards came up with the happening idea that we should spend the night. Before I could even protest, she had my dad on the phone working it out.

I knew my dad would think I was somehow behind this change of plans, but in reality, home was the one place I *did* want to be. Eventually old Mrs. Edwards got us situated, me in the guest room and CJ in Henry's old room, which she ended up in on account of our walking in there first and her just passing out cold on top of the bed. I slid off her boots and pulled the comforter up to her neck, sniffing it first for remnants of Henry's teenage years.

The guest room was mine. Mrs. Edwards had lent me an old pair of Henry's pajamas to sleep in. They must have been from junior high because they fit me just fine. She held them close to her face before handing them over, saying, "He was such a dear child," and she suddenly looked all young and happy, and I could tell how much she loved her son. It was like with CJ's folks, or for that matter probably mine, too. There was so much about them to just drive you nuts, but when it got right down to it, our parents were pretty much all-right people. You just had to look at it the right way.

I liked how my nakedness felt inside Henry's worn flannel, and rubbed off thinking about Henry. I awoke with a start, my ears ringing in the stillness. I tiptoed to the bathroom to splash my face and finger-brush my teeth before dressing quickly and making the bed. I left the pajamas folded neatly across the pillow. I was tempted to leave without CJ. Waking her easily seemed unlikely, but to my surprise she was sitting up in bed reading *Vogue.* Her boots were pulled up high about her thighs, and she looked like hell.

"Guess they were downers," she whispered. We weaseled through the halls.

Before exiting this time, I made sure to leave the Edwardses a big, warm thank-you note saying how sorry we were that we couldn't wait till they woke up, but CJ had to be home in time for church and all, which was not so off the mark, as Mr. Jenkins was a total church freak. God spoke to him on a regular basis, guiding him through every step he made. Which was how I felt sometimes, too, that God was guiding me. But I couldn't quite figure out how the same God could be leading us both into such incompatible positions.

The door slammed behind us, but no one stirred. I prayed the Flame would start and was blessed with the roar of an engine. It was only six-thirty. I was beat. CJ's eyes were puffy, her stale breath filling the car. I imagined I wasn't faring much better, the effects of the toothpaste having already worn off. I considered another round at the IHOP, but changed my mind, on account of just wanting to get home and get it over with. Plus, I missed Whiz Bang like crazy. It was my second night without her this month. So I dropped CJ off, wishing her luck, and pulled into my driveway around seven. Not surprisingly, my parents were waiting for me at the breakfast table sans the hangover remedy, so I knew right off I was well into the kingdom of the definite wrongs.

9

I woke up Saturday afternoon to the sounds of my dad getting in a round of off-schedule calisthenics, of which I was
no doubt the root cause, although he was not the type to
mention it. "One and two and three and four!" he was
shouting, and I could hear his hands clapping in unison, so
I knew he was doing those push-ups where you have your
feet on a chair and your body is angled over the floor, then
you lower yourself down and as you push up, you clap your
hands, then descend again.

And all the while I'm listening to this, I'm realizing I
can't see a damn thing even though I could tell my eyes
were wide open. I thought, for at least a full minute, I
might even be dead, just that nobody had got around to
noticing yet, but I could move my limbs fine. Plus I had
no memory of any accident. I'd always read that when you
have any kind of accident, you remembered it in crystal-
clear detail, with all sorts of heightened trippy colors and
sensaround sound. Then Whiz Bang shifted her weight,
and I caught a glimpse of Kurt Cobain checking me out
from my wall, and I knew I was definitely alive, so I rolled

Whiz Bang off my head and just lay there for a while, staring at the ceiling, thinking.

First off, I thought about trying to get my parents to send me away to boarding school. One of those ivy-laden get-outs in England would be cool. I thought they might go for it because of all our relatives over there. Then I thought about how it rains in the afternoon and how Whiz Bang would get stuck in customs for six months and I'd have to go visit her every day, riding one of those rickety English bikes through gray streets, and poke at her through the bars of some horrid little cage. Exhausted from a series of rigorous classes that had begun at 5:00 A.M. and that I would be behind on anyway, due to my inferior American schooling. Not quite the answer I was looking for. I suddenly had a burning itch to talk to Logan, to see if he had figured his way out of this stuff, but the thing was, at some gut level, I knew he never had.

Las Vegas. That's when everything began to change around this place. Change from what, though? I could barely remember a time when things had been anything but the way they were now. Like an abandoned switchboard. All the wires dangling loose, waiting on the operator who never shows. But somehow, in the vague reaches of my mind, I knew it had been different before Logan took off, taking with him my last chance of a happy home.

When he and the Tat were gone, my mom had paced the kitchen, lighting one cigarette with the tip of another, until the house smelled stale and old, and the ashtrays overflowed. I'd wondered when she'd remember to open some windows and start cleaning again, but my bed went unmade the whole week Logan was gone and we ate John's pizza every night, brought home by my dad and cold from the car ride.

"Something might have happened to them," my mom would whisper when she thought I was out of earshot.

"For Christ's sake, Maude, they're fine," my dad would say, riffling through some papers. "He's just blowing off some goddamn steam. They'll be back soon enough."

"But I'm worried he may do something foolish."

"Well, he certainly has one hell of a role model for that, doesn't he?"

And my mom would cry some more.

Like I mentioned, before Logan left he was kind of a big-deal athlete, on a bunch of teams and stuff. When he came back and gave everything up, the coaches would call the house, getting my dad all worked up, and father and son would go at it, resulting in some pretty snarling fights, but eventually everybody seemed to have gotten the message. Logan had retired.

To pick up the slack, I had joined the seventh-grade track team, developing shinsplints within the first week, but turned into a pretty good sprinter nevertheless. That was when my dad started getting me up at five-thirty on a regular basis to get in some extra training before school. It was right after Logan got back from Vegas that all the journals started. Before that he'd never been home long enough to write down his own name, but once the pot replaced the booze, he hardly ever left his room. He'd just sit up there getting way toasted, reading some books and writing like a madman. The Tat used to come by all the time then, and she'd spend half the nights in the guest room without even calling her parents to let them know. It got confusing at times, though, when my dad was also sleeping in the guest room, so eventually my parents just let her sleep in Logan's room. Sometimes when Logan and the Tat did go out for the evening, I'd sneak into his room and stare at all his journals piled on the desk, the dresser, everywhere, really. I'd rub my hands over the smooth covers and press the coolness against my cheek, my heart pounding in my ears. But I never once opened one. If I wasn't able to vibe anything through touch, then it wasn't meant to be.

· · · ·

I squirmed around in bed a bit, looking at my watch. Five P.M. and hungry as hell, but the thing was, I didn't want to go downstairs. The lecture that morning had been short and to the point: Get it together or else.

"You are moving into dangerous territory, young lady, and I will not tolerate it in my house. If you choose to move out, then you would have complete freedom, but while you are under my jurisdiction, you will behave."

"William, remember our discussion?" my mom had said, lighting up a Winston with the tip of her last.

"Christ, Maude, of course I remember it. I don't happen to agree with all of it, that's all!"

My mom had turned away from us and looked out the window.

"Now, Violet, I am all for grounding you, because I find your behavior inexcusable, but your mother seems to think you are finding yourself or some such nonsense. So let me make this clear: From this point forward, if you are not able to get yourself home exactly on time, you will lose the use of your car and will face a severe grounding. Am I making myself perfectly clear?"

"Perfectly," I'd said, rolling my eyes like I was bored or something, which I wasn't. What I was was tired and still a bit strung out and scared, too.

"I have just about had it with your sarcasm, young lady. Now get up to your room, and stay there until I tell you you can come down."

I should never have gone to Henry's. I felt the soreness between my legs and pulled my comforter closer around me. Then I thought about Ryder. Eyes as old and worn as a Persian rug, bluey-blue always in the blue sky of day or the moonshine of dark. But I couldn't hold the thought long because Henry slunk in. So sweet, he made my mouth ache. But I couldn't say I understood him. I couldn't say I understood him too well at all, and maybe that was just what I wanted, something that made no sense. "There's never been any logic to our family, Bean Brain," Logan would say, "so don't wear yourself out looking for it."

I climbed cautiously out of bed—Whiz Bang lolling on her back in the gingham sheets—and headed to the bathroom, spying en route a carefully folded piece of paper slipped beneath my door. The goo.

"My only daughter," I read, "I see that you are struggling to find your path, and I want so much to show it to you, but I am not able. First, because I simply do not hold those answers in my hand, for you or for myself, which has brought a lifetime of subservience upon me. But, much more important, Dr. Applegate tells me that these are the most vital and revealing years of life. To attempt to mold them would mar them irreparably. Therefore, know that I

· 173 ·

watch your journey with great love and compassion, and I hope that you have the ability to rise above that which I was unable to. With special love, M."

The usual sense of dread filled me. She wrote as if she had just finished about fifty million of those Gothic romances, not at all in the manner she spoke, but I couldn't help but feel she was completely sincere, which of course then led to my regular dose of guilt. The dose that revolved around not loving her enough. If I loved her more, we could just sit down and talk openly about these issues, rather than her feeling obligated to leave me these weird missives. Instinctively I knew it was my fault, I really did, but to tell you the truth, the note still made me sick.

I took a mildly invigorating shower and toweled off to the tail end of a message from CJ. She was grounded for the week, on account of her not going home last night, and the real zinger was her parents considered *me* a bad influence, which, I have to tell you, was a complete joke, considering CJ had first gotten me high in eighth grade and her older brothers were the first to get me drunk.

I headed downstairs, but felt a sudden draw toward Logan's room. So I turned back. His door creaked against my hands, and I froze, half in and half out of the darkness. Whiz Bang shot past me. It was actually my old bedroom, but it didn't feel like mine anymore. It didn't feel like Logan's, either, because when I moved into his room he was already away at school, so my dad just loaded all his stuff into all these boxes and stacked them in orderly piles along the far wall. The furniture had all been switched around, too, so this was his stuff, but there was no vibe to it. It was like going to an amusement park when all the rides had been shut off. Everything was there, but nothing was happening.

I could hear my parents moving about downstairs, so I was sure they could hear me, too. I tiptoed toward the closest box and laid my hand across the top. I knew his journals were inside, or if not this box, the next. Whiz Bang was having a ball—the dark, the new smells. She was already halfway into a box when I grabbed her. It wasn't right, being in here like this. If Logan wanted me to know why he left, he would tell me. The same with my parents. Clearly no one thought it was something necessary for me to know. Or maybe they were just waiting for me to ask.

• • • •

"Sleep well?" my dad asked when I got downstairs, as if nothing peculiar had occurred. That was his way: Voice your opinion and move on. I nodded and headed for the kitchen. My mom was reading one of her books when I walked in, a mound of butts in the ashtray alongside her elbow.

"Well, love, I'll bet you're hungry." She opened up the kitchen window to air the place out. I noticed she'd posted the serenity prayer on the fridge.

"Sort of."

"Well, I'm just going to pull together some leftovers. If you want some, eat. If not, you can just watch us."

She ran water over her Winston and tossed it in the trash, then pulled out these meticulously packed bowls filled with every bit of food we didn't finish that week, along with a tossed salad, crusty bread, and cheese. Very British, really. But then when you got right down to it, we were a very British family. Open the closets and shove everything in.

"Why did Logan go to Vegas?" I asked when my dad had joined us and we were all seated around the dinner table, eating.

My mom said, "What a very peculiar question," trying to act real normal, but looking perplexed all the same.

"None of your damn business, that's why," said my dad.

"But I am a part of this family. And I want to know."

"We'll discuss it at another time, when everybody's had some decent sleep." He scooped up seconds of potato salad. My mom pushed back her chair and went to the window, gazed out at her rose beds, which were wrapped in cheesecloth and covered over with snow.

"He misunderstood some things that happened between your father and me. And unfortunately, he took them personally, which was silly of him, because they didn't concern him at all."

"Well, why would he think they did?"

"I really don't know, love. Your brother is very sensitive to things and has such an overdeveloped imagination, it's hard to know what set him off." She turned back toward the garden.

"That's enough of this kind of talk for now," said my dad. "If you don't feel like eating, Violet, go upstairs and do some homework. I hope you don't plan on bringing home any more of those B's this semester."

"B-pluses," I said, but my dad continued eating, staring at a bowl of cold string beans rather than me.

So I did go upstairs because I didn't feel like eating. Plus, I hadn't been doing much homework lately. Not that

I ever did do much on account of having what CJ referred to as my photographic memory, which meant I could study for a test the night before and get an A, which is pretty much what always happened, except for last year's science class where I'd refused to dissect the cat, opting instead for a halfhearted study of schoolyard leaves conducted with CJ. We spent most of our time heightening CJ's suntan, although we did put together what I considered to be a rather pleasant presentation. Mr. Travis had thought otherwise.

Instead of pulling out my books, I sat there on my bed, wondering what the hell the big secret was about that trip to Vegas three years back. What could have happened that nobody would share with me? It made me feel funny inside, like my head would burst right open if my mom didn't walk in the bedroom that second and fill me in. Which she didn't, so I sat there a little longer, looking up at the stars, counting to see how high I could get without blinking.

10

Five A.M. My bed as warm and reassuring as a baker's oven. My dad prodding my shoulder, poking me.

"Violet, up and at 'em." He was clad in jogging gear, the thick stripes of reflective tape too much to absorb in the glare of my overhead light.

"I'm sleeping, Dad. Can't we do it later?"

"Never put off till tomorrow what you can do today!"

"I'll do it today, just later." I rolled over and looked out my window. "Dad, it's snowing."

"A little snow never hurt anyone. It'll help open you up, get oxygen to your brain. Now up and at 'em!"

I rose slowly.

Outside, the snow was falling fairly hard, and it was difficult to keep my footing. Instead of running our normal loop, my dad branched out a bit and headed toward the woods where I'd first made it with Henry, which truth be told, were quite a distance and mostly uphill.

"Dad, this is crazy," I yelled from behind.

"Ah, stop your complaining and breathe." He got a couple of feet ahead of me, running with this nice, rhythmic stride like he always did, and after a bit I lost him in the snowfall. I called out for him, but there was only that trippy no-noise noise that you get when it's snowing hard in the early, early morning. I was getting kind of worn out but had this strange sense of doom that kept my feet moving—left, right, left, right. And after a while, after quite a bit of left-righting, I made it to the end of our road, right where the wood began, but the silence continued.

"Dad!" I called out, my heart pounding like it wanted to pop right out of me, because usually he'd be running back and forth, checking on my stride. I kept spinning around, trying to see if I couldn't spot those bright green stripes of his, but they were nowhere in sight.

So then what happened was I started running right into the heart of the woods, which was not that easy to do on account of how the snow was falling especially hard through the bare branches that hovered above my head like old crumbling lace. Strangely, in the midst of my panic, I found myself looking for the condom Henry and I'd used, as if finding it would somehow confirm my status of womanhood, which seemed a bit shaky these days. After I got past the bush where Henry had parked his car, I spotted my dad coming up out of one of the narrow side paths.

"Dad, what are you doing?"

"Well, what do you think, Violet? I'm going home." He started marching down the road, only it was in the direction that led further into the woods.

"Dad, we don't live that way." I ran up beside him, noticing his shaking hands. He turned around without saying a word and marched up the road in the right direction, stopping when he got to the top. He looked to see if I was behind him still, then let me get ahead and lead the way, but doing it like he was just pretending to wait up for me and be nice, which made me feel weird because he'd never done that before.

The cold began to catch up with us at our slowed pace. My dad's teeth started chattering, but I could tell he couldn't run right then, so we walked the distance back to our house, getting all covered in white and just about freezing to death. Once we reached our driveway, he broke ahead and stomped into the house.

"Don't you want your egg and muffins?" I yelled.

"Not now, Violet." He slammed his bedroom door shut.

• • • •

Finals week. The vacation itch. There was some kind of dance that weekend that was supposed to be this big deal and all, like if you didn't go you might as well hand in the towel right there, or paint a big red *L* on your forehead for *loser*. The regular crew was cavorting around the school, hanging streamers and signing people up for various committees, with great purport, as if they were solving world hunger and not just making arrangements for coat checks and parking attendants. First thing Monday morning, Ricky Johnson cornered me.

"So, Let, whadda ya say, do ya wanna go to the dance?"

"I don't know. I wasn't planning on it. It looks pretty much like a drag, what with the Secret Sneaky Santa committee and all. Maybe if CJ is up for it, we'll check it out."

"I meant with me, Let. Do you wanna go with me?" He looked at his feet.

The thing was, I didn't want to go with him. Not one bit, but at the same time I didn't quite know how to phrase it the way I meant it. I didn't mean I didn't want to go with him because he was a loser, although he undoubtedly was, even though just about any girl at Courier would have told you otherwise. I didn't want to go with him on account of knowing he was without the shine. I knew that to be a fact then. And I knew it infallibly. Henry Edwards was living proof.

"You know, Let, I don't get you one bit. No, siree. CJ let me know that I should dump Pamela, 'cuz of you. So I did. And now what? You avoid me like I have the plague or something. It's not right," Ricky said, and I might add that he looked mighty appealing with his neck muscles popping like that. And what he had unwittingly done was to put me in the land of right vs. wrong.

"Okay," I said, feeling kind of sick inside. "You're right. I'll go."

"No, forget it. I don't want any of your highfalutin charity, Let. You don't wanna go with me. Peace. I'll ask somebody else. See ya."

He stormed down the hall and I was left with that same sinking feeling I always got when faced with the *W* word. *Wrong.* Definite wrongs. It was wrong of me to have liked Ricky Johnson enough to get him to break up with his girlfriend of a year or so and then change my mind about it. At the time, though, I didn't know it was wrong. That was the trick. Learning to recognize wrong while it was happening, not afterward when all you could do was try to make amends.

CJ and I had English Lit together right before lunch.

"Going to the dance?" she asked me. We were seated in side-by-side desks.

"No. Are you?"

She nodded.

"No way. With who?"

"Ricky Johnson," she said, like there'd never been a thing between us, which I guess there really hadn't been. All the same she surprised the hell out of me.

Our teacher was one of those mealy-looking people; you know, they look like they need to spend a few days in the sun and clear some of that rotting meat out of their system. CJ and I had worked out this plan where first I'd pretend I wanted to get some water, then she'd pretend she needed something from her locker, and the next thing you know we'd both be cruising down the hall, headed for the Flame. Mrs. Swanson didn't seem to care whether we were there or not.

Our plan went off without a hitch and we waved at the old-geezer guard on our way out, me of course wanting to stop and make sure his kids loved him okay and whatnot. CJ started putting up this stink that she wasn't going back to the health-food store, no matter what. She leaned way far over, so I could hear her gum cracking in my ear, and cranked the wheel in the opposite direction as I was turning.

"McDonald's!" she screamed. "Darling, I want to lay some hot beef and fries in my veins before I die. Dig?"

I dug. It was my car, but I figured CJ would have done the same for me.

McDonald's was packed, and that tummy-tantalizing aroma of grease oozed forth into the world, which is a pretty hard smell to walk away from, even for a veggie-head like me. I figured a milk shake and some fries wouldn't kill me. CJ got one of those double-everything-hold-nothing cheeseburger extravaganzas.

As we were sitting there eating in one of those rounded orange vinyl booths, who should have walked in but Ryder and a couple of his boarding-school buddies. They all had that wholesome but naughty vibe, straight out of a Bruce Weber book. Ryder swaggered right over, just like nothing weird had happened between us a mere forty-eight hours or so ago.

"Hey, Let. How are you doing?" He flopped alongside me and munched on a few of my fries. "These are some of my bros, man. This is Let."

CJ was looking at me, like who the hell is this? I'd been getting the vibe from her off and on for a while that she thought I wasn't quite on track lately. Which was wild coming from her, because it was hard to know just what her track even was. The whole Ricky thing had kind of capped it off, as if she were saying, "Look it, if you want to fuck up your life, groovy, but don't expect me to help you out." Which I couldn't quite figure out, on account of her doing way more crazy stuff than I'd ever attempted.

"Still searching?" he asked, referring back to our last conversation, about our being or not being candles and where the true fire lies.

I shrugged, and smiled at him. "Maybe. How about you?"

"No, man. Never searching. Exploring. Exploration takes you everywhere you need to go."

"Is that a fact?" I said. I could tell CJ thought Ryder was a real wacko, so just to be contrary, I asked Ryder if I could have a sip.

"A sip of what, man?" he asked, with one of those shit-eating grins smacked right across his face.

"Of whatever is left in your rodeo flask." The top of which was poking out of his back pocket. So he passed it to me, looking me right in the eye, like he was a priest or something, absolving me with the holy sacrament. CJ and Ryder looked at me, as did the guys Ryder had come with, no doubt because we were surrounded by families and McDonald's employees, so I just unscrewed the top and took a swig. It went down nice and nobody noticed a thing. Then I started coughing up a storm, which I knew CJ thought was a hoot, so I swung the bottle back to Ryder and turned my head in the other direction. CJ had finished her meal, and I could tell she wanted to go. She was giving me all the warning signs—complete and utter silence or these real polite smiles if I looked in her direction. I wanted to slug her.

"Don't you girls have school today?" asked one of the Hillstream guys.

"Don't you boys?" CJ shot back, like she always did when she wasn't getting her way.

"No. We're done for the winter. No school till '95." Two of the guys hi-fived each other.

"Everybody else is gone already," chimed in another kid. "We're the leftovers."

"Leftovers?"

"Well, not all of us, man. Not all of us. What it gets down to is Freddie, Marvin, and me. Orphans, man. We're the true orphans. The rest of them are just getting a late start."

"We'll have a blast alone in that fucking dorm," said the kid who I figured was Freddie, on account of his looking too athletic to be saddled with a name like Marvin. "Briggs is too feeble to bust us for doing shit, so let's paaaarrrty!"

"Truth," said Ryder. "Freedom we will have." Then he whispered to me, "But the true freedom comes from within."

Finally CJ, looking at her watch every ten seconds, gave up on the hints and said, "Let, darling, we gotta slide back to the schoolyard. It's been groovy to hang, but we gotta split, now."

So we did, only the thing was, Ryder came, too.

• • • •

The whole way back we passed the flask around, CJ going for a couple nips herself, then staring out the window, like if she didn't get out of the car soon she might just go stark raving mad. I couldn't see what the big deal was, so I cranked up the radio and sang along at the top of my lungs.

"When are you going to get it through your sweet little head that you cannot sing worth shit, darling? You dig?"

"When are you going to get it through your sweet little head that this is 1994, darling? You dig, you groovy cat, you?"

"Fuck you, Let."

"No, fuck you. You've been giving me attitude all week, and I'm not into it. Why don't you just take your attitude and ride it back to school."

I pulled the Flame over hard onto the side of the road, but what with that morning's snowstorm and my liquid lunch, she pulled a bit more easily than anticipated. My heart went clammy with the screechy-scratchy sound that followed.

"Oh, this is just fucking great!" I hopped out and examined a pretty deep gash along the passenger side of my car where I'd run it into this low brick wall some clown had built around his property.

"Is it all right?" CJ hung her head out the window.

"No, it's not fucking all right. There's a gash from here to Timbuktu, and my dad is going to fucking flip! Shit, I'm in enough trouble already."

"Maybe you should ease up on the booze."

"Maybe you should learn to be respectful of people who are driving you places and not cause them to smash up their brand-new cars on account of your fucked-up ways."

"You mean that?"

"Full-on!" I shouted. "Full-fucking-on!"

"Well, fuck you." And she swung her door open, banging it against the wall, putting another pretty little ding in the paint.

"Nice," I said. "Real nice." She just flipped me off, pulling her fake fur closer around her, and started down the road.

"Long-standing love," Ryder said. "Always makes folks do the craziest things."

So we passed CJ and just kept going. I figured it would take her about twenty minutes to walk back, making her late for class and damn cold to boot. I knew it was wrong to leave her. I knew it was a definite wrong, and I knew it while it was happening.

When we got back to school, we sat in the parking lot by the football field for a bit, shooting the shit.

"So why aren't you going home for Christmas?"

"You go where you're wanted, man. You go where you are wanted."

"Your parents don't want you to go home?"

"Well, yeah, along those lines. Michael got booked on this shoot in some awesome location, and they just don't see how they'd have the time to fit kids in. The truth of it is, man, I wasn't really counting on going home in the first place, although I did want to see the ranch. They bought one. A beaut, so I'm told. A real beaut. And they got our horses back, which is beautiful. Really makes everything all right."

"What about your little brother? Where's he?"

"Oh, Declan doesn't really qualify as a kid, man. He's some sort of special assistant to Michael, so he gets to go."

"Doesn't that make you feel lousy?"

"No, really it doesn't. They're just trying to get through their lives the best way they know how."

"Ignoring you?"

"Truth, but that's not how they see it. And you've always got to try to see it from another's point of view, otherwise everything we do is in vain."

"But sometimes the point of view is wrong." It made me nervous just to say that word.

"No, man, not necessarily. Sometimes it's wrong, beating a child, murdering somebody, that's wrong, truth. But most of it is just perspective. I can see that goal post," and he pointed at the football field, "as beautiful or ugly or in between, and that perspective affects my life."

"But some things are definitely ugly and some are definitely beautiful. There's hardly ever an in-between."

"Name something that's definitely ugly."

"Name an in-between."

"Lo . . . ," Ryder started and I'm sure he was about to finish with *v* and *e,* but CJ emerged from the road behind us, reminding me I was late for class.

"Hey, cruise around a bit and come back for me at three, okay?" I jumped out of the driver's seat.

"Cool, man. Three it is."

And I dashed off into the empty halls.

• • • •

Right off, history was a drag. There I was next to Peter Hutchinson, my cream dream, only this time he was looking at me pretty strangely. In fact, the whole goddamn row kept glancing over with these weird looks on their faces. Naturally I thought something must be wrong, like food in my hair or a huge pimple, so I scrambled all over myself but couldn't find anything askew.

Then the thought occurred to me that maybe I was looking cute, and that's what was drawing all the attention, so the next time everybody looked my way I flashed them a smile and they all started nudging one another and winking and stuff. Finally Peter Hutchinson leaned over toward me right when the teacher was drawing a map of medieval England on the board. My heart was racing, because I was pretty sure he was going to ask me to that goddamned dance, and the thought of turning two guys down in one day was a bit much. But I've got to tell you, it did make me feel pretty good, because Ricky Johnson and Peter Hutchinson both were these big deals in our school, even though they didn't thrill the hell out of me.

"A little liquid lunch, huh, Let? You'd better pop some gum before Bobbins catches a whiff of you, or you'll be paying Marshalston a visit!" Peter said. Saying it like it was the funniest thing he'd ever had to say, too. Holding back a big old laugh because Mr. Bobbins turned around to face the class again. Mr. Bobbins was a real stickler for following school rules. Marshalston was our principal, and one thing he simply could not abide was underage drinking and smoking. He made these wacko announcements over the loudspeaker almost every morning about how alcohol and drugs were poisoning our society. "Keep on the right track. Stay smart. Stay clean." He was liable to toss you flat out of school, even for your first offense.

Everybody kept leaning over to look at me, only now I wasn't smiling. I was blushing clean up to my baby-fine hair, thinking about every zit on my face and my stick-outy ears, and any other thing that would make me feel lousy about myself. Then I thought about Ryder driving around drunk in my new car and I just about had a heart attack. Whatever buzz I had going was fading fast.

Let me tell you I was out the door before the final bell even rang, tripping over my feet to get free, and there she was, the Flame, parked right alongside the steps leading up to Courier. Ryder was jamming to some music, thumping his fingers against the wheel and bobbing his head, and I've got to admit, it made me happy to see him sitting there waiting for me. He didn't appear to have noticed me, so what I did was dash back to my locker to get my coat and stuff, only on the way back, I ran right smack into CJ.

"Hey, CJ," I said, smiling. Now that Ryder had turned up with my car, I was feeling okay again.

"Hi, Let." She sounded very serious, making it clear I wasn't high on her list of favorite people.

"Want a ride home?" I'd been driving her home every day since I got my car.

"No, thanks, darling. I'd rather walk."

"Hey, sorry about that, CJ. I don't know, I guess I was pretty much bummed about the scratch, thinking about how my dad's going to kill me. I don't know. But everything is great now. I'm supersorry. Really."

"Well, isn't that just groovy? I freeze my pretty little ass off getting back to this place, while you prowl around with that crazy cat with the flask. And now that I'm safe and warm again, you're sorry."

"Hey, you hopped out of the car. Denting the door, too, you know?"

"Listen, you've turned into quite the blamer. 'Whose fault can I make it now?' Well, whose fault is it that practically every time you go out at night, you never make it home again? And that every time you see a foxy guy, you think he's the one that's going to change your life."

I just looked at her. I'd learned that little trick from Henry. Keep silent and eventually the other person will make a fool out of themselves. Plus it gives the illusion that you know something when in reality you don't.

"Let, you're my best friend, but you've been doing some tripped-out stuff lately. Like leaving me in the car when I could have frozen to death and jerking Ricky around after you made such a big deal about liking him. Then today getting drunk at McDonald's with that Ryder cat."

"If you hadn't have popped those pills, I could have woken you up."

"Oh, yeah, that would have been so fine to watch Henry laying you across his big bad bed."

"All I'm saying is, you're not so perfect yourself, CJ. You know?"

"No one expects it of me. I'm not like you. You're smart, Let, and pretty and headed for something big. Everybody knows that. But lately it's like you've been on the prowl for trouble. And I do not dig it."

To tell you the truth, she was kind of getting to me, looking oh-so-sincere, like she wasn't so into saying all this, but felt obligated or something. So I decided to split.

"See you later, CJ," I said, real nastylike. "I'm going to go home and work on being perfect now. I'll call you when I've got it down."

Ryder had the car all toasty warm and a pint of Southern Comfort sat wrapped in a paper sack on the seat between us, but the thing was, my enthusiasm was waning. So what I did was to drive Ryder back to Hillstream, dropping him off lickety-split, him seeming kind of bummed, saying, "Lunch, man, Wednesday." Me nodding in agreement, then heading home with the unwavering determination that I was going to do everything just exactly right and please the hell out of my parents. It made me pretty sad thinking about Ryder all alone in that big old school, like a young Scrooge, but there wasn't much I could do about it. I was battling the wrongs and losing.

. . . .

I actually did go home, too. Right off, I went upstairs and finished all my homework, reading every page of my history book with great care and completing each geometry question with such precision, you would swear my life depended on it. In a way it did. I couldn't shake this gnawing feeling that something was just not quite the way it ought to be, but I couldn't put my finger on why.

I knew when my dad got home on account of the weird silence that swept through the house. Not that my mom had been doing anything real noisy to begin with, like singing or maybe whistling, because she hadn't, but somehow when you put those two in a room together, it was like hell froze over, as Logan would say. And it was, too. Like big slabs of ice were working their way around our house, and it was best to steer clear of them on account of ice being deathly cold and kind of sharp-edged, too.

When I went downstairs, I laid out all the silverware and helped my mom drain the pasta and made sure my dad found the paper okay for his half hour of reading before we ate. He didn't mention one word about that morning, so I didn't, either, because in truth, it was a pretty strange morning, and I didn't want to deal with it. Finally I called my dad in, and we all sat down to dinner. Whiz Bang balanced on my legs, swatted food straight off my plate, then ate it from my lap.

"That's a disgusting habit," my dad said as he always did, but he never did anything about it.

"How was school today, love?" my mom asked, serving up this huge portion of pasta with the fresh basil from one of her windowsill pots, sun-dried tomatoes, loads and loads of garlic, and ground pepper fresh from the spice mill.

"It was good."

"Prepared for your finals?" My dad glanced up from his steaming plate. He had a piece of roasted chicken alongside his pasta.

"Totally prepared. I was studying the whole time, right up until you came home. I only quit to help Mom get dinner ready."

"You can never be too prepared. You may think you are ready, and then it will turn out you were wrong. Keep at those books. That's how you get ahead in life, always being more prepared than the other guy." He cut into his chicken breast, scrunching up his face. "A bit undercooked, Maude."

My mom looked out the window dramatically, like maybe if she held the pose long enough the Academy would rush right over and lay an Oscar on her.

"Ellen Harding phoned today to say that Jeffrey isn't doing well," she countered, right on schedule with her let's-discuss-someone-else's-troubles technique. She pushed aside her plate, even though she'd hardly eaten a thing, and lit up a Winston, despite knowing that I couldn't stand it when she smoked during dinner. We were all of us looking in some opposite direction.

"Really? What seems to be the matter with him?"

"Well, they don't know, but he's been complaining of a pain in his chest for several months now and has refused to go to the doctor."

"Damn right of him, too. Nothing those quacks can do for him that a little fresh air and exercise wouldn't cure."

My mom was silent, looking as though whatever my dad had said had been a mortal blow to her. It was funny how I used to think when Logan went away to school that maybe our dinners would get better. Things had been so extra-dramatic when he lived with us, it was almost impossible to get through a meal without having a coronary from the stress alone. But nothing much had changed.

"Sometimes, William, doctors are necessary. They do serve a purpose."

"The only purpose they serve is robbing people, who don't know better, of their hard-earned money. If these numskulls would get out there and get their juices flowing, instead of marching off to the doctor's office every time their head hurts, it might help to unclog their brains so that they could think clearly enough to know that all that medicine stuff is a bunch of malarkey." This was one area where my dad and I strongly agreed.

"Sometimes, William, running a mile or two a day doesn't fix everything." My mom rose and shoved her untouched food into the sink.

"Name one instance."

"Us, for one. Our marriage. Your interminable running hasn't done one damn thing for this relationship."

My dad chewed his chicken carefully and looked at her, arms folded across his chest.

"Hell, I don't even reap the benefits of increased sexual stamina." Her eyes widened as she lit up another cigarette.

"Christ, Maude."

"What, do you think Violet doesn't know? Ask her if she's ever heard her parents in the throes of passion late at night." I looked at my plate. "Or at any time for that matter!"

"Maude, calm yourself."

"Oh, I'm calm all right. And you know what else your running doesn't help? Your losing your marbles. Your running does not prevent you from losing your marbles one iota. Keep your brain ticking? It's ticking all right. It's ticking marbles, one by one, out your ear."

My dad stared at her a minute with coated eyes, while my mom glared out the window behind the table.

"I would suggest that you finish your meal, and we'll discuss this later," he finally said.

"I would suggest that you go to hell," she said, taking her pack of cigarettes with her into the TV room.

I noticed that ever since I got the Flame, things at the dinner table had deteriorated. Before, my parents would at least ask me questions like, whose mother was picking me up tonight or did I need them to drive me anywhere. Dumb stuff like that, but the thing was, it was distracting and ate away at a lot of otherwise dead time.

Now they hardly said a word to me and even less to each other, that night being an obvious exception. Sometimes my mom, no doubt having had her nose in some self-help book all day, would come up with these rehearsed kinds of safe dinnertime topics for a rebellious teenage daughter, but my dad wouldn't play ball. And when that happened, she usually threw in the towel, which I thought was totally weird. Of course, anything that went wrong as a result of her thwarted attempts to change her life she blamed on him.

I thought about CJ for a minute and how she said I was a blamer. It made my stomach hurt to even consider I'd inherited that quality. Maybe things were sliding a bit.

Maybe CJ did have a bit of a point. But nothing beyond my control. I mean, it wasn't like I'd killed somebody or anything. Anything short of that could be fixed.

Right after dinner, I cleaned off all the dishes and wiped down the counters and got the leftovers stacked exactly right in their containers, while my dad went down to the TV room, acting as if I did stuff like that every night.

When I finished, I went downstairs to join them and walked in on the middle of *The MacNeil/Lehrer Newshour,* the gentleman's news. And the thing was, they were sitting there, in opposite chairs, of course, as per usual, acting as if nothing had happened. Which in a way nothing had, because they fought like that with great regularity.

I was feeling sluggish at that point from all the Southern Comfort, so I flopped out along the floor. TV time was always good for us, on account of our being perhaps abnormally opinionated on just about every topic under the sun. Therefore, TV was the perfect vehicle, because we could voice our likes, dislikes, or previous knowledge of an event without ever having to speak to one another. We just said it out loud, almost to the television. Then you could choose to respond or not, and it didn't matter. No one's feeling were hurt, because no one had been addressed in the first place. It was perfect.

When about an hour had passed, I announced I had some more homework to do, and headed upstairs. Whiz Bang bounced behind me. For some reason I got this nutty idea in my head that Henry was going to ask me out for New Year's Eve, which was pretty absurd, considering it wasn't even Christmas yet, not to mention the minor detail that he hadn't phoned me since Friday night. Still, once a thought landed in my head, it took root pretty quickly, so instead of doing homework, I climbed into bed and tossed that one around a bit, before finally dozing off to visions of champagne and fairy dust and Henry's worn leathers.

11

Logan phoned pretty late that night, which right off got my heart racing, because naturally I thought something terrible had happened to him or the Tat. But he just jabbered away about school and Ann Arbor and pointless stuff like that. I mean, stuff we could have discussed in the light of day. So then I got really nervous, wondering what was this all leading up to, and if it was nothing, then what the hell was he calling and waking me up for?

"So, Beans, has Anna been by the house lately?" he asked finally, and it wasn't too weird of him to ask me that. The Tat *had* spent a lot of time at our house over the years. And she did used to come by by herself a lot and hang out when Logan had something else to do, but that hadn't happened since they had begun college.

"No, why?"

"Just tell her I've been looking for her."

"Looking for her?"

"Looking high and low."

I laid the phone alongside my ear and tried to stay

awake the way you do when you want to catch the end of a late-night flick.

After a bit Logan asked, "So how are things with you and that Henry dude? You guys still hanging?"

"Some," I said, waking up now.

"Huh. I met him up here last weekend, visiting that old school buddy of his."

"Did he know you were my brother?"

"Yeah, he knew. Didn't seem to want to hang with me too much. Probably thought I was going to lay some trip on him. Whatever. But he seems cool enough. What does the old man think of him?"

"Not much."

"I'll slip in a good word or two. Meanwhile you keep me posted on Anna."

"Okey-dokey," I said, and we hung up. By that point I was wide awake and weirded out, if you want to know the truth, so I didn't sleep too well the rest of the night.

• • • •

All day I waited for Logan to call with some sort of follow-up explanation, but he never did. I wasn't too keen on calling him on account of not wanting to speak with him directly and his not having an answering machine in his room. That was the great thing about growing up in the age of answering machines, you could sort out all kinds of weird stuff without ever having to actually speak with another person. Then I thought about all those boxes stacked in his room, and I walked to his door.

The second I was in, my heart started pounding, so much so that when I looked down, I could see my sweater moving in and out, in and out. Whiz Bang was in heaven, prying the cardboard boxes open again, hopping in, sitting around for a while, then jumping back out. I opened the first box I saw; it was full of all these projects and reports Logan had done in grammar school—"The Lost Race on Mars" with some crazy drawing—stuff like that. After about twenty minutes of snooping, I came across a box that was full of his journals. All sizes and colors, worn and frayed the way I remembered them. I went to the door to listen for my mom, but couldn't hear a thing. So I went back, squatted before this most holy abyss, and slid in both hands.

The journals were cold and clammy from being packed together for so long. Many were sealed, but a couple just had rubber bands around them, with scraps of torn paper tucked inside. I figured Logan must have had some system where he memorized the placement of the papers, therefore immediately recognizing the traces of a spy; like how James Bond hid matches in his hotel door to be certain no one was inside when he returned from a SPECTRE-fighting day. I didn't think Logan would still remember the code, so I snapped off a few rubber bands and opened the first journal. The handwriting was so minuscule, I could barely make it out.

He wrote about school and missing playing sports, which surprised the hell out of me on account of his never acting like he missed them. He wrote about this teacher or that kid in his class who was really and truly driving him crazy. He wrote a lot about going away to the University of Michigan in the fall and a whole shitload of stuff on the Tat and their sexual antics, which was way too weird to read.

I thumbed through about four or five of these journals, and to tell you the truth, most of them were actually pretty boring. A lot of complaining, which was strange, because Logan brooded or sulked—but never a grumble. So what I did then was jimmy open one of the locked diaries. The second its pages parted, I knew I'd hit the mother lode. I took these entries to be his first, on account of the earliness of the dates. They were written in red ink, his favorite color, the print large and careful, like a documentation, like he wanted it to be found someday. They read like this:

Wednesday. Sometime in March, 1992.
  Never going back to what was. Disgusted by it all. Locked doors. Locked mind. Locked heart. Hard to breathe, have to get away. Where is the love? Where is the trust? Where is the truth?

Friday, March 27
  Her naked flesh chasing me, calling me, crying outside my door. This is my mother? This is my goddamned fucking mother!!! I have to get away.
  Later—phoned Anna, told all. Agreed to come with me to Vegas. Leave tonight. Never, never NEVER coming back. NEVER!! Old man is a jerk-off, too. Leaping to her defense, saying she needed a certain kind of caring that he couldn't give. Do I tell the Beans? Shatter her illusion of family? So eager to trust. So sensitive. Wants love so badly, she'll blind herself to many wrongs. Perhaps post her a note once settled. Good-bye, house. Good-bye, room. See ya, Mother and Father.

Monday, March 30, 1992—Las Vegas

Checked into Golden Nugget. Anna missing home. Gambled away most of money from sale of Firebird. Still have charge card.

Tuesday.

Got wicked tattoos today. Anna got my name up her inner thigh. Hurt so much she cried through most of it. Mine is this wild garden scene with tripped-out snakes and exploding flowers all centered around the words I Shall Not Want. *Because that is how I feel life should be. If you don't want things, like a normal life and normal parents, then you're never let down. No wanting, no bumming. I got the words from some psalm Kevin Quinn (tattoo guy—super-famous, too) had tattooed on this dude's back. You know, "The Lord is my shepherd, I shall not want. . . ." Only it was just that handful of words that caught me up. Rang true. Because from now on, that is me. No wanting. No needing. And never going back.*

It's been a while since I wrote. Don't know date. Sometime in April. Anna wigged and wanted to split, so here we are. Home, home on the range. Tackling the bullshit. B-U-L-L-S-H-I-T!

There were no more entries until the following fall, then they appeared in a longer, less haphazard form. There were no further clues as to what had happened in March. I figured the long writing gap was on account of the drinking habit Logan brought back with him. He had been too drunk most of the time to tie his own shoelaces, let alone clarify his collapsing thoughts enough to jot them down.

I sat there a couple of minutes more, feeling all-out lousy, trying to make sense of Logan's cryptics, but I guess not trying very hard, because as I look back now, it was really all there. The whole gruesome story, I just didn't want to see it. After a bit, I starting dumping the books back into the cardboard box from which I had more or less stolen them, not even bothering to straighten up, just tossing them in; acting like Logan, wanting someone to know what I now knew without my having to tell them.

After a bit my mom yelled up that supper was ready.

"I'm not hungry," I called back, then returned to my room and closed the door, my stomach shifting in anticipation of a dinner that wasn't coming. I wasn't one of those people whose emotions affected their appetites. No, I was a steady and solid eater, although no one could ever figure where the food went on my miniature frame. Logan said it fueled my mouth, because when I did get talking, you couldn't shut me up. I was feeling hungry and damn confused and kind of depressed too, although I couldn't tell you exactly why, except maybe because I knew something really had happened that had altered us in some irreversible way.

I picked up a picture I had stuck in the corner of my mirror years back. It was from some vacation when Logan and I were young, where we were all gathered up together, like a bouquet, shoulders rubbing shoulders, white teeth flashing, and the thing was, we all looked kind of happy. Even Logan was in the thick of it, working a goofy smile and leaning up against my dad. I looked hard into each set of eyes and tried to bring it back, tried to remember Logan laughing, or my parents not minding if their bodies touched. But it was gone. So I did then what I suspect any teenage girl in my state of confusion would do. I sneaked out my bedroom window, walked along the roof, and slid down the drainpipe.

· · · ·

Outside, the wind blew so cold, I could feel it creeping through my coat, my sweater, my skin, nestling itself in my bones. I hurried toward the Flame, thankful that the garage was distant enough from the kitchen that it was unlikely my parents would hear a thing. Driving down our road, I had no vision of where I was headed, I merely turned the wheel and hummed out loud, which I wrote off as nerves, since I certainly wasn't feeling lighthearted. Of course my initial instinct was to pay a call on CJ and catch up on the white-supremacist movement, but that was out of the question for obvious reasons.

I really didn't have any other friends. Over the years CJ and I had managed to blow off anyone that tried to join our two-girl gang, and I guess I was realizing the cost. There was always Ryder, but Hillstream could be such a complicated place to get into, plus he just didn't strike my fancy right at that moment. I decided to drive to the health-food store and get myself one of their double-hummus and avocado sandwiches, the one where they added layers of roasted red peppers, olives, and sauerkraut if you asked them to. I'd gotten my roadkill count sorted (I'd spent a couple of hours drawing a map and working it through, methodically, with pink and purple markers) and was back on track, making sure to stay hyper-attentive from now on.

I tooled right over to Strawberry Fields, scanning the shoulders, but of course en route I had to drive down the very street on which the Edwardses live. And of course I had to pull in their driveway just to see if Henry was home. And of course he was, too. I knocked on his door, and after a long, long while, he came down.

I said, "Hey, Henry," and smiled. "Wondered if you wanted to get some dinner?"

I was feeling A-OK around him this time, sort of a curious, but not unpleasant, combination of nervousness and expectancy. He lit up a cigarette, the smoke enveloping him like a halo, like he was some kind of malfunctioning angel. He had on his leathers, of course, and a white kind of ruffled shirt that hung open, sliding backward off his shoulders, exposing that hard, sunken chest of his for all the world to see.

"Let. Hey." He looked at me and didn't say anything else. Well, I'd practiced his technique a bit with CJ, so it took a little longer than usual to sucker me in.

"So do you want to grab some food or something? I was headed for Strawberry Fields, thought you might want to join me."

He leaned against the doorjamb. "Why aren't you eating at home tonight, baby girl?" He was doing that touching-his-chest thing again, making me all twitchy out there in the cold.

"What, are you my father? Do you want to go to dinner or no?" I flashed him my pearly whites.

"No," he said, "not tonight."

A perfectly formed smoke circle floated over my head, and I noticed he was actually smoking one of those Djarums for a change. I recognized it because the Tat smokes them, too, so the scent was familiar.

"Oh, what have you got, some hot date?" I smiled as coyly as I knew how.

"Maybe."

Another circle up and over. But he didn't move. He didn't close the door. In fact, his eyes slid down my body a couple of times, making my palms sweat.

"Okay. Can I just use your bathroom for a minute?" Just get my foot in the door, I figured, then the rest would be a piece of cake.

"Not tonight, baby girl." He tossed the sparkling remains of his cigarette into the snow.

"Okay. Maybe tomorrow night?"

"If you can hold it that long."

He had the door practically all the way shut when I stuck in my foot and pleaded, "Call me, okay?"

He nodded, clinked the lock shut, his beautiful arrangement of limbs and skin and smell cut from my view. Looking up, I swear I saw the curtains in the window above his front door waver for a moment, then stop.

I took off for the goddamned store anyway, because I really was hungry, only not quite so much as before. I ordered my sandwich and a carrot juice, but I couldn't stop thinking about Henry blowing me off like that. And who the hell was behind that curtain? That made me think of my mother naked in front of Logan's door, which totally freaked me out, not to mention making me nervous as hell, which I was feeling in general anyway on account of the list of wrongs I had committed in the last few hours: breaking and entering into Logan's room, reading Logan's journal, not going down to dinner when called, not writing the book report that was due on Friday, sneaking out of the house without a word, trying to sneak up into Henry's apartment for a little of the old one-two, even though I still wasn't convinced I liked it with him, and then back to the rejection. And the curtain.

I wondered if my parents had noticed I was missing yet. I imagined that my mom must have gone up by now to see if I was okay and could feel my parents' disappointment when she found my room empty, but in reality it was their own fault, wasn't it? Whatever it was they had done to Logan, well, now they were doing it to me. Round two. Ding, ding.

I ate my dinner in about five minutes flat, then took my next logical step. I went and got Ryder. This, though, wasn't quite as easy as it sounds. On the way over I guess I was thinking about my mixed-up life a bit too much and not paying enough attention to the road, despite my prior pledge, because before I knew it, this squirrel dashed out in front of me and I hit the brakes so hard I did two 360s and ended up with the front of the Flame knocked up against an oak on the other side of the road. Luckily, it was a back road, and no other cars had been around, but when I stopped shaking long enough and went out to survey the damage, my left headlight was bashed in, though it still vaguely worked, and there was a long scratch across the front fender.

I sat down on a snowbank for a minute. I wanted to cry, I truly did, and I even tried, but nothing would come of it. So I sat there for a while, nobody driving past, until this squirrel, I imagined the same one I'd almost murdered, popped up on the opposite bank. He sat on his hind legs and made chucking noises that sounded a bit like laughter. I looked at him, then the Flame, then at him again, and I laughed, too. I mean, what else was there to do? I wondered what Helios would have had to say had Phaëthon been so disrespectful of his chariot. When I got back in the car, I noticed I had a red mark on my forehead where I'd banged my head against the steering wheel, but I felt okay, so I slipped her into reverse and moved on.

Ryder, it turned out, was pretty happy to see me. It was still early, seven or seven-thirty, and the guard was apparently on vacation with the rest of the dorm. Only the elusive Mr. Briggs, a resident advisor, had been left behind to mind the orphaned boarders, and he was nowhere to be found. I figured I could hang out with Ryder for a bit and still get home before my unofficial bedtime of ten o'clock. Hillstream was deserted, the full moon reflecting off patches of ice like cat's eyes. The rare hoot of an owl could be heard, and bare, worn trees looked like stragglers in the distance, lonesome for long summer nights and the lingering warmth of the sun. I found Ryder right off, in the library where we'd first met, curled up in the same chair.

"Let, man, cool!" he said when he saw me. So unlike Henry and his halos of smoke. "What's up?"

"Driving and thinking. Thinking and driving." I opted not to tell him about the squirrel. He'd find out soon enough anyway when he saw the smashed headlight, which kind of twinkled as I drove.

"Truth," he said. "Come with me to the thinking pad." And he took me by the hand, putting his finger to his lips so that I would know to be quiet. We tiptoed up the curving staircase, a velvet runner beneath our feet, and arrived finally in Ryder's room.

I realized then I'd always been curious about this room. What it smelled like, the color of its walls, the sheets on his bed. And none of it was what I had expected. It was plain and white at its core. White sheets, white curtains. White-painted furniture. Stacked on a chair were the white T-shirts he always wore. But covering his side of the room was a collage of vistas. Layers of beautiful settings torn out from magazines and travel books. The sheer density and variety of color was intense enough to put you in the hospital for a week. Everything was represented, from the cold, season-long darkness of Alaska to the jungles of Vietnam.

"The shine," he said, remembering the word I'd shared with him days before, or maybe not remembering it at all. Maybe it was a part of his vocabulary, too. I guess if you're actively looking for something, at some point you learn its name.

"Is it?"

"Man, this is the true shine, Let. Feel it."

He led me over to this old wooden chair, straight-backed and carved with these beautiful swirls of birds and flowers and trees, and indicated that I should sit.

"Now look at it long and hard, feel it flowing into you, because it's the whole fucking world you're taking in. Then close your eyes and just be."

I looked at Ryder's collage a good long time, so long, in fact, that it began spinning out like a kaleidoscope, a huge swirl of color and light. Then I closed my eyes, the back of the chair pushing my body up and forward, forcing me toward this inner light I had never felt before—a tremendous explosion of whiteness generating from a point between my eyes, rushing down my spine, then up again, out the top of my head. The shine. A minuscule, slippery moment in the vastness of time. Then it was gone.

I opened my eyes to Ryder grinning at me, holding out a half-empty bottle of Southern Comfort.

"Where's the cowboy?"

"He's just for traveling, man. Here is where I keep the reserves." And he flipped up the bedspread, which hung low around the floor, revealing an army of whiskey lined up, ready for battle.

"Shit, Ryder. How did you get all that in here?"

"You just have to have faith, and whatever you want to have happen will happen."

"Do you want to go out Friday?" I asked, surprising myself, but apparently not Ryder. He already had plans in mind.

"Be delighted. I know the place to be. Pick me up at eight o'clock, man, by the theater. I'm without wheels."

For some reason I started to feel sad for Ryder, and sad for myself, too, thinking about my parents and their screwy marriage, and thinking about Logan and our twisted family. It was as if I wasn't part of my family. That's how I saw Ryder, too, without grounding, without comfort. Only I viewed him as even further along. *In the free fall,* I thought, not knowing exactly what I meant. *In the fucking free fall,* and the words made me feel strangely at peace.

Nine-thirty, or thereabouts, I split. Ryder taught me how to climb down this close-growing tree and jump to the ground without being seen. He told me to memorize his window in case I came back another night when Mr. Briggs was more visible. Two floors up, next to the wide-spreading maple.

The lights were still on at my house. I parked the car, touching the headlight as if I held the magic to repair it with my fingers, shimmied back up the drainpipe—no easy feat, especially for someone of my less than heroic stature—scuttled across the roof, and reentered my room in a tumble. Whiz Bang turned a couple of circles at the sight of me, purring, and shoved her head into my leg. My door was still closed, and there was no sign of entry, although I don't know what kind there could have been. I got changed, washed up, and climbed into bed, considered calling down good night, but thought, *Why push my luck?* I didn't sleep, though. I lay there, full of expectancy, until finally my dad passed by my bedroom door.

"Good night, Violet. I hope you feel better," he whispered.

"Thanks. Good night," I called back, instantly strung out on my regular dose of guilt. It had been so easy to slip back into my bed, completely undetected—too easy. And the night's exhilaration drained out of me like a wrung towel.

Way deep down I thought maybe I perceived the faintest hint of anger, which was causing a strange tightening in my lungs, no doubt a result of my parents' not even noticing I was missing. Not even bothering to leave the kitchen table to see if I was all right, even though that was about the first time I could remember not going right down to dinner when called. I could hear my mom shifting around downstairs, then she, too, meandered past my door, tight-lipped in her nightly doings.

I thought about my parents, both individually and as a unit, and I didn't feel much trust toward them anymore. I couldn't put my finger on exactly why. They hadn't done anything to me directly, at least not that I knew of, but somehow everything was changed. Like when you're having fun at a party, then somebody looks at you strangely, or at least you think they do. They might be looking behind you or at you, thinking about something else, but you're convinced it's *at* you and *about* you, so you get weirded out and want to leave. That's how reading Logan's journal had made me feel. I wanted to leave.

12

Wednesday morning was upon me in a flash, bringing with it a sense of foreboding I was beginning to get accustomed to. In the bright morning light of the kitchen, I made my own breakfast. My mom was busy painting her fingernails the color of blood and reading out crossword questions that she couldn't get.

"Western with Pitt," she said. "Now that's one any full-blooded woman should know."

"Legends of the Fall."

"Oooh, very good. I see I've raised my daughter to share in my exquisite taste." She put her wet fingernails to her lips and made a kissing sound. Knock him off my dream list. I tried, for a moment, to imagine her naked, chasing Logan, crying outside his door, but couldn't hold the thought.

"Make me some tea, would you, Violet?" she said when the whistle blew. "I probably won't be here today when you get home from school. I'm meeting with a realtor to look at apartments in Nottingham."

My chest tightened up like it always did when she spoke like that, even though way deep down I couldn't help feeling a sense of relief at the thought of my parents finally splitting up, releasing Logan and me from this crazy Ping-Pong game of a marriage.

"Okay."

"Well, don't feel obliged to show too much interest on my account. After all, I'm only your mother, and I'm only considering moving out on my own once and for all. Last night was the last straw. I know you heard what a bastard he was, even though you'd sequestered yourself away. I refuse to tolerate such coldness in my life anymore. I'm worth a hell of a lot more than the bullshit I'm given to chew on around here." And she punched the air with her fist.

I let my yogurt curl up in my bowl and stared at my feet. No wonder they hadn't noticed I was gone.

"Well, I can tell you don't give a shit about this, and why should you? It's not you who is married to that bastard, is it? No, you're too busy chasing around boys too old for you to know what to do with to notice the unrest in your own home."

"I notice it."

"Oh, well that *is* good to know." She blew on her nails. "A real comfort to me in my time of need."

"I thought you didn't *need* anything," I said. "I thought this whole process you were going through was about releasing yourself from need and becoming completely self-reliant."

"Don't twist my words, missy. It's the need of your father I'm releasing myself from. And I've mastered that one pretty well, if I do say so myself. But a true mother always needs her children's love and support, especially at moments of great turmoil such as this."

I knew she was about to launch into another one of her anti-my-dad spiels, which were really about how to never take responsibility for anything, how to blame others for your lousy circumstances.

It was right then I made my vow—sitting at the breakfast table, Logan's words filling my head, the morning light pushing through the slatted wooden shutters—to never, in any way, shape, or form, be like my mom. And I think she knew it, too, because she just shut right up and went back to her crossword rather than giving me the ooze. I think she knew something irreparable had happened between us, but at that point, couldn't figure out what.

• • • •

I left my mom sitting there and drove to Courier. It made me sad to see the state the Flame had deteriorated into. She looked like an alley cat who'd had one too many fights. I was half expecting a note of reprimand from my dad to be stuck under the windshield wipers, since his car was parked right next to mine, but there was none to be found. I was starting to miss hanging out with CJ, picking her up for school and whatnot, but didn't know how to make up with her on account of her being pretty much right and my not wanting to tell her that, or at least at that time not knowing how.

I've told her since then, of course. Just last week when she came to visit me here I let her know she had been right all along and not to feel bad about anything that happened because she couldn't have prevented it, even if we had stayed friends the way we used to be and not just the polite acquaintances we'd become. And she really couldn't have,

I wasn't just saying it out of sentiment, although I was feeling pretty sentimental at the time, no doubt due to all the drugs they had loaded up my "temple" with.

I managed to make it through my first three classes without dying of boredom, because the week before break is always a joke. Finally lunch rolled around, and there was Ryder grinning at me from way down at the other end of the hall. He looked so strange standing in Courier's '70s blandness—low, windowed halls, orange doors with emergency-exit bars, far away from the romantic hush of generations of profound learning nurtured at Hillstream.

I was able to study him closely there, as if I'd collected a woodland specimen and brought it home to my laboratory to ponder. The girlish swelling of his mouth, the unruliness of his hair. Even from my distance, I was aware of his childlike cleanliness that seemed to wear off as the day progressed, needing revitalization the following morn. And as I headed in his direction, it was as if time had slowed down and things didn't seem to matter so much anymore. He walked me to the parking lot, his Carhartt jacket and thick Roper boots exuding a hint of the cold that awaited me.

"Freddie Newhouser's," he said, pointing to a brand-spanking-new cobalt blue Camaro. "He was going to come with me, but didn't wake up in time, so I decided, man, why bum him out with the tediums of kept appointments or not-kept appointments, so I spared him the trouble and came to get you myself."

"Won't he mind?"

"Once I get my car, man, I'll repay him with the first spin."

"When will that be?"

Ryder got that distant look of his, what Logan called the dream state when they finally met. "Can't really tell you, but the Master must have some kind of plan brewing for my wheels. Betty's been telling me they're on their way for many a moon now, many a moon, but it's all in the way you look at things. We have ourselves a fine set of wheels here just for the taking."

I smiled, thinking about how Ryder thought just about everything was just for the taking, and who knew, maybe he was right, but it sure went against the way I was raised where *nothing* was for the taking, unless you had earned it first, then it wasn't taking at all, it was a reward.

"Ready, man?" He slid the flask out of his pocket and took a slug, then passed it to me. I realized then I'd been waiting all morning for its sweet charm. Ryder Hadley's guaranteed good time. It hadn't really guaranteed me too many good times at all, but I didn't think about that right then. We were hurtling down the road at about a hundred miles an hour, and I didn't much mind where we were headed, because the forward motion was enough to satisfy me, as if I wanted nothing more than to be thrown headlong into the future. We don't *always* have to know *everything* that's happened to us. Or if we do, we don't have to let it influence our lives unnecessarily.

But the thing was, the whole time I'm running this rap in my head I'm thinking of my mom pounding and pleading and scratching on Logan's door, because of course at that point I'd blown it well beyond what I had read, and I'm wondering what in the hell happened in my house. And where was I? Sleeping? Doubtful. At school? More likely, or perhaps at CJ's back in the days when we spoke to each other.

The Southern Comfort was sinking in fast, and I began reconsidering my acquiescence to CJ's point of view. I wasn't spinning out of control. Not even close. Hell, I just wanted to have fun. Let go. Kick back. Ride the wave. It could have been sugar water I was lapping up. I was in search of the release. And right on target, just like he always was, Ryder rolled down his window and let out these tummy-jolting yelps that had me jumping all over my seat to do the same. I opened my mouth wide, icy-cold air wafting in, and let out such a whoop, I startled myself. But I've got to tell you, it felt good.

Ryder was all grins and brilliantine, still holding on to the steering wheel, although just barely, sticking his whole goddamned head out the window and screaming like the world was coming to an end, so not to be one-upped, which is a hard-core Hitchcock trait, always having to be the best, I knelt on my seat, hanging my head so far out the window that I felt certain it would blow off, or at least get knocked against a passing tree, or perhaps I would get sucked right out of Freddie Newhouser's car by the sheer force of the outside world that we were cutting our way through, and whatever the result I did not care one bit, because the hoots and howls I let out felt so fine, they were worth dying over.

Ryder tugged on my jacket and motioned toward me with a freshly opened bottle of whiskey, so I knew he'd already finished off the flask, and I drew myself back in to enjoy a little warmer-upper. And we continued on that way until we reached the wooded borders of Hillstream, in all its magnificent glory, having weathered more students than Ryder and I could ever imagine and showing us with her thickly rooted elms, heavy with lichen, and her dark-berried hawthorn, that she could weather us, too. I remember feeling particularly happy at that moment, as if I'd found a lucky penny, only better. It was like when Whiz Bang came out from under that strawberry-laden truck just for me. Not anybody else, no matter how hard they'd tried. Just right straight to me, without a moment's hesitation. She was mine and not even my mom could touch that. That was how Ryder felt at that moment—entirely mine.

We hoisted ourselves up the twisted maple that led to Ryder's room, on account of wanting to make sure of not running into Mr. Briggs. Although not a true disciplinarian at heart, he had laid down an explicit no-girls-in-the-rooms rule, and Ryder, pretty much liking the guy, was loath to break it. Inside was a smorgasbord of ill health: cold pizza; chips and dip—the kind of dip that comes in those plastic containers with metal pull-off lids; coagulating nachos; and culminating in what I imagined to be some sort of soggy Greek salad.

"I didn't know how you ate, man, so I went for a little bit of it all." He slipped off his coat and flannel shirt (white T-shirt stretched across his chest), and pulled out a fresh bottle of Southern Comfort from beneath his bed. "To the abundance of the Master." He took a swig, then handed it to me. It was like *The Cat in the Hat* and Ryder and I were the kids who had been left all alone.

• • • •

"You have my book," Ryder said later, lying flat out along the floor. We had gorged ourselves on a bit of everything, and I was lying alongside him.

"What book?"

"*Walden,* man. I left it in your car the day we visited the museum."

"Oh, right. What's it about?"

I passed back the empty bottle of Southern Comfort. I remember wondering how long I had been there, but not really caring too much.

"Simplification, man. Simplify, simplify, simplify."

"How?" I asked, and meant it, too.

How on earth do you simplify something like your mom going bananas every other day—one minute whipping you up everything your heart desires, the next, painting her fingernails red and hardly noticing you're in the room; and your dad working out like a fiend the whole time his brain is not ticking quite the way he had intended, although he has not seemed to catch on to this little detail yet, so long runs in snowstorms prove to be alarming; and your brother hardly speaking to the family, except of course at weird hours of the night, with weird questions, which somehow makes it worse than his not phoning at all?

And not to forget, Henry Edwards, lurking out there in the dark creases of my life; waiting on me, barefoot, shirtless, stoned just enough, deciding, no doubt, only at the moment of my actual arrival, just what he would do with me that night. Maybe not even deciding upon first sight, stringing me along, tossing a few possibilities around in his head, then selecting on a whim. And me, always the sucker, for the whole gang of them, figuring if something didn't feel right, it had to be on account of something I had done wrong. Simplify this.

"The Master, man. Look to the Master."

"What the fuck is that supposed to mean?" I was a little drunk at that point, if you want to know the truth.

"That's not for me to tell you. It's for you to find."

"Find how? How do I find the Master in this world of collapsing words and downward-spiraling dreams?" The liquor was making me wax a bit poetic.

"Truth," he said, and I've got to tell you right now, I didn't know what the hell he meant by that, but it shut me up anyway on account of his voice sounding so low and scary, full of finality, which was one thing I had a hard time with. I liked to have that little open space in which to breathe. After a while there was this sudden knocking at the door, and the handle started to turn. Instinct alone caused me to roll over and under the bed, bashing down Ryder's upright brigade of whiskey. I stared at Mr. Briggs's—or at least I assumed it was Mr. Briggs's—expensive wingtips and abnormally thin ankles, and I remember thinking, *God, please, if you get me out of this one, I'll stay on the straight and narrow. Please just let me get home without getting in trouble, and I swear this time I'll remember and will erase the wrongs from my life.* His voice was mild, almost tender as he tried to rouse Ryder.

"Hey, man," Ryder said. The room was in complete upheaval, the empty bottle of Southern Comfort alongside Ryder's head. Trodden-down chips and wads of nacho cheese were scattered in a kaleidoscopic pattern across the wide wooden planks, as were the little paper cups which once held these chocolates that Ryder had proudly offered up for dessert.

"Hey, man. Mr. Briggs. What's up?" He took hold of Mr. Briggs's hand for a pull-me-up.

"Mr. Hadley. Is everything all right in here?"

"Fine, man. Things are fine." I imagined Ryder must be surveying the room, trying to think fast. "I must have been thinking about Christmas, man, and not being able to meet up with my family and it got the better of me. I apologize." There was a silence. I stared at the springs above my head. A thick coating of dust had formed over each one so I tried not to move.

"I can certainly understand that would be extremely disconcerting for a boy your age, Mr. Hadley. My situation is quite different. Yes, quite. I am full grown, and most of my family has passed on; therefore, I elected to stay on at Hillstream over the holidays. Yet with you and the other two boys, it's not the same. Doesn't seem quite right to me. Not right at all."

He really did sound perplexed about the whole thing, too. I shimmied myself to the edge of the bed, so I could see better. Ryder came into view and shot me a death glance, but the elusive Mr. Briggs remained hidden. He must have noticed the bottle of Southern Comfort—it would have been hard for him not to—because he continued: "A boy your age shouldn't be in possession of that, Mr. Hadley. I will not question how you managed to procure it, but I will hope that you will amend your actions in the future." Strange thing was, he didn't sound angry at all, just sad.

"You're absolutely right, Mr. Briggs. And I will do so, man." Ryder's feet looked solid and unwavering.

"Would you care to come down to my room for some coffee, Mr. Hadley? Not the type of thing I should be offering a resident here, but I feel at this moment it may be appropriate."

"Thank you very much, Mr. Briggs, but I am otherwise engaged for the evening. Thank you though, man, sincerely. It comes from the heart, I can feel."

There was silence again. Probably just a few seconds or even less, but it felt like much more. Then Mr. Briggs moved toward the door, and I heard his hand grasp the handle.

"Next time you are feeling so inclined, Mr. Hadley, please feel free to pay me a visit. I may not look it now, but I was once young and remember a little bit of the torments of youth."

Then he was gone. I lay under the bed a minute longer, feeling pretty lousy. Mr. Briggs was a real heartbreaker. Ryder must have felt the same way, because when I finally crawled out, he was sitting at his desk with his head between his hands. It was going on five-thirty, I'd missed my afternoon classes, and my brain felt like the first battalion was lining up to march. I touched him on the shoulder, but he didn't look up.

"Hey," I whispered, "I gotta go."

• • • •

I reached my house right before my dad, barely slipping out of my coat before he came huffing in. I was three hours past my usual time, without so much as a phone call, and I was certain I smelled like a bar. I was hoping to reach my mom's gum drawer before engaging in conversation, but I was out of luck.

"Are you just getting in, Violet?" my dad inquired. We were shoulder to shoulder at the hall closet.

"Mm-hm."

"Track?"

"Not really. I ended up driving CJ home, and I guess we got to talking."

My dad seemed to buy it. In reality, what was there not to buy? My best friend, or at least he still thought she was, needed a lift, and we got carried away on solving the world's problems or just down-home gossip. I could smell the lemony-pepper scent of a dinner cooking, so I knew my mom was home and had not found herself a new residence, having, in reality, probably not even looked.

"I made a special treat tonight," my mom said to me, even though it was obviously directed at my dad, on account of the special treat being scrod, which I wouldn't eat if you paid me one million dollars. Anything with eyes was out of the question.

"Great," I said, looking around for my dish, finally spying the veggie-pasta thing she was always making, which was good, too, so I wasn't complaining.

We all slid into our chairs, and I couldn't help watching my mom, then my dad cut into their fish. First off, because there weren't too many other places to look and secondly, because the way the bones cracked as the knives went through was alluring to me in one of those nauseating ways. Like in horror flicks when the kid getting his head chopped off is really the last thing you want to be watching, but you look anyway.

"I had lunch with Margaret today," my mom began. "Apparently Keith and Jennifer are planning to divorce." She frowned, looking out the window, munching right through her fish bones, as was my dad, I might add. Little bits of cartilage slipping out between her lips before being sucked in and eaten up. One of the more unappealing English customs, up there with drippings. There was this long silence where my dad served himself some of my pasta, so I finally said, "Wow, that's too bad. Why?"

Of course, the why was long and dramatic and allowed plenty of space for my mom to expound upon the difficulties of being forced into a loveless marriage without any way out; and for my dad to say that was baloney. Every situation had a way out. It was all a matter of choice.

Well, it didn't take a rocket scientist to figure out that they were discussing their own marriage. Probably even Logan's cryptic journal entry, which, whatever that was about, no doubt came up again and again in their fights, and I just never knew it. Things escalated a bit more, then my mom started crying and ran out of the room.

I waited for what I considered to be a respectable moment, then put my plate in the sink and made my way upstairs. Of course, they hadn't even noticed I was drunk. On the landing I ran into my mom who had a folded-up note in her hand. My heart sank just looking at it.

"It's from CJ," she said conspiratorially, I guess having overheard what I told my dad regarding my after-school whereabouts and indicating she knew otherwise. "She came by while you were out." Her eyes were dry now, and it was hard to gauge just which mom was lurking behind them right at that particular moment.

"Thanks," I said, slipping it from her hand.

"Henry's always welcome here, love," she said. "Better it's happening under my roof where you're safe, than out in the wilds."

"I wasn't with Henry," I told her, but she gave me this confiding look that seemed to say, "Nonsense, there is no need to lie to me. I'm your mother; I know all about you," then she turned on her heel and went back down to finish her dinner.

Up in my room, I lay across my bed and read CJ's note, short and to the point as it was, pretty much apologizing for everything she had said to me and begging back my friendship. I crumpled it right up, tossing it across my room into the garbage can. Whiz Bang flew through the air after it.

I realize now I wanted somebody to fault me for something. I wanted to get caught doing just one thing wrong, on account of otherwise not being allowed a full grasp of right, which by the way, I still wasn't clear on even though I'd been thinking about it enough. I didn't know this at the time. All I knew then was I was feeling stagnant and claustrophobic, except with Ryder, although occasionally with him, too, which led me to think something was definitely lacking within myself if I couldn't squeeze but two minutes of satisfaction from my day, the result of which was to amp up my search for the shine.

13

CJ and I made up, in a way. We both knew she was right, despite her retraction in the note, I *was* slipping somehow, and therefore, nothing felt quite the same between us, even though we wanted it to. We ended up eating lunches in the cafeteria with the crew (effectively avoiding awkward back-hall silences), which meant sharing a table with both Peter Hutchinson and Ricky Johnson, resulting in my picking at my food mostly, staring through the huge glass door at the courtyard where all the smokers hung out. CJ had been riding to school with her big brother, then taking the bus home or copping a ride from one of her fifty million new friends. Since splitting with me she'd fallen headlong into the in-crowd we'd always avoided, so these lunches were really the only opportunity we had to talk.

"Plans tonight, darling?"

"Yeah, going out with Ryder."

"Where to?"

"I don't know," I said, and I really didn't, either. Ryder's was a life without plans.

I got home from school early on Friday, having aced all my finals, or at least I was pretty sure, and even finishing the book report that had been haunting me all week, though I couldn't say it was my finest work. My mom was nowhere to be found, which was way weird, since she hardly ever went out except maybe to get some groceries or pick up a fresh bottle of nail polish. Almost everything in our house, furniture included, was catalog–born and raised. It was all nice stuff, too, on account of there being so many nice catalogs out there, most of which were sent to our house with great regularity.

My mom passed many an evening sitting at the kitchen table, leafing through this preposterous pile with the just-so attitude she applied to such a task: folding down corners, circling color choices with a wax marker she bought just for that purpose (from an office-supply catalog!), filling in order forms with her extra-sharp crossword puzzle pencil (a pen being far too arrogant), starting a pile of envelopes to be walked to the mailbox the following morning, then the wait. Four or five, sometimes six, days for smaller items, like sheets and blenders and mixing bowls with matching coffee mugs. Weeks or months for the furniture.

Then bingo, it arrives. Does it work? Is the color nice? Does it smell the way you thought it would? Final decisions, the hassle of the return, the agony of parting with something that was almost yours, that could be yours if only you were a little more open-minded, could just get used to it somehow. The arrangement of the keepers. Then, the cycle beginning anew. "It's a good thing we have so many rooms," my dad would say, eyeing the expanding stacks of catalogs. Logan said it all had to do with that insatiable streak of our mom's, a result of the twisted childhood she'd been dealt. "Poverty will leave you with a thirst for life that you and I can't even imagine," he'd say, then add, "but it still doesn't make what she does to us right."

Whiz Bang and I stretched out on the couch and flicked on the larger-than-life TV. Right off, there was nothing on, so I flipped through the channels, finally landing on one of those Christian stations, you know, the kind with the con-artist preachers. This guy had on these huge plastic glasses, which were dwarfed only by his enormous buckteeth, and he was gesticulating about, his arms spread wide, no doubt meaning to embrace every loser watching; then he jerked them back in, fingers to chest, creating these two semicircles, and I couldn't help noticing they were the exact configuration needed to drag some poor captive, kicking and fighting, securely by his head, to the destination of this preacher-man's choice.

His voice was caramel-coated southern drawl and his expounding went something like this: "I accept Jesus as my savior, therefore all my sins are forgiven me. The unbelievers, the spiritually blind, they will attack your faith. They will ask, 'Well, what do you have to do to deserve the Lord's grace?' I tell them, 'I trust in the Lord Jesus Christ, it's that simple.' And they will see your authority, and they will continue to doubt. Those that would scorn us feel a sense of guilt, because they see in us what they should have within themselves and have not! The sweet love of the Lord Jesus."

I pictured a bunch of little old ladies sending this charlatan their life savings. Believing not only were they forgiven, but were superior because of it. While this preacher with his false oration was living in some mansion with bikini-clad jailbait combing his waning hair before being whisked off to the casino (of which he was undoubtedly a full partner) in a swanky white limo.

But to tell you the truth, there was something in it that rang true, making me remain on that channel, because in a way I did accept God as my savior, although I didn't view it exactly that way. Like I said before, it was more of a business arrangement we had. I kept an eye on certain things for him down here, and he kept an overall eye on me. I started figuring maybe that was why I was never getting caught at anything. God kept intervening. So I concluded I must be doing an A-OK job with my part of the bargain, because he was doing a terrific job with his, and I didn't feel so bad about stuff anymore, on account of realizing it was all part of the setup. And from that point forward, right up until I landed here on New Year's Day, I thought it was just that simple: Make a few crosses, say a couple of prayers, heartfelt though they were, keep God happy, and transform yourself into an untouchable. But I've since learned life isn't that straightforward.

I remember talking to the Tat just the other day about how Ryder was so nonjudgmental and all. Telling how he opened me up. Taught me a lot about living. And she responded, without missing a beat, "That's because he had no sense of judgment. One is the continuation of the other." At first, of course, I didn't want to hear that. I didn't want to hear anything bad about Ryder then, but now I realize she is absolutely right, and in fact, I had known it myself all along. It was how I picked up on his thinking that everything was there for the taking, and I looked at that as a kind of special sense of freedom that he had, which in a way it was, but it was also a lack of judgment, which became pretty obvious as time went on. I think that's the hardest thing about growing up, being forced to look at people you love for who they are. That's even harder for me than looking closely at myself, which I've started to do a bit here, too, because the Tat frequently tricks me into it with the daily meditations and whatnot.

· · · ·

My mom got in around five-thirty, and I knew right off she'd been to see Dr. Applegate and he'd given her the super-duper, all-that-matters-is-you pill. She waltzed right over and shut off the television, so I knew some kind of scene was brewing.

"All right, missy, up and at 'em. You're cooking supper tonight."

"But I don't know how to cook." My right hip was killing me from lying prone so long, but I dared not move and run the risk of catching her eye. No telling what might happen around this place if you suddenly made eye contact.

"Well, it's high time you learned then, isn't it?" She brushed Whiz Bang off the couch and pulled me up by the arm.

"Mom, that hurt," I whined, which wasn't totally whining, because it really did hurt.

"In the kitchen."

So we marched up the stairs, Whiz Bang wisely staying behind. My mom started pulling down piles of everything, slamming them onto the counter. Boxes of pasta, bags of flour, cans of corn, and whole, peeled tomatoes. I stared unwaveringly at them right up until she walked out of the room.

"Jesus fuck," I said when she was gone.

"I heard that," she yelled, marching back in, this time a cigarette glowing in her right hand. "I do not want one word of complaint. Not one. Do you understand me, missy?"

"Mom, don't you think you are acting a bit crazy? After all it's just—" and I started to say *dinner,* but she whacked me across the face with such tremendous force I fell back against the counter.

"Do not ever call me crazy again," she said through tightly locked teeth, glaring at me with those trippy, glassy eyes of hers.

"You're fucking nuts," I said, not caring anymore. *Whack,* again across my other cheek, and I discovered that that cheap-novel burning sensation was indeed real.

"Make the fucking dinner, Violet."

"What should I make?" I asked, starting to cry a bit, on account of feeling like my life was sliding beyond my control. This was a slightly different version of the crazy mother than I was accustomed to. This was a version that actually backed up its threats, therefore I didn't know what to expect next.

"You're a big girl, you figure it out." She lit up another Winston with the tip of her last and tossed the old butt into the sink. "I'm taking a bath. I'll be ready at six."

"Sorry," I said, but she didn't respond. "I said I was sorry." My words sounded rushed.

"I know, I heard you." And I listened as she climbed up the stairs to her land beyond the reaches of us. I stood paralyzed there a moment more, touching the rawness on my face, then slowly set about making dinner.

· · · ·

What I came up with was a huge tossed salad and these vegetable sandwiches, with some extra cheese thrown on my dad's.

"Christ, Maude, I had a sandwich for lunch. If I'd wanted another one I could have eaten in the goddamned cafeteria," my dad said when we were all at the table.

"Speak to your daughter about it," said my mom, using her tongue to shove a wad of bread and avocado into her cheek.

"Violet made the supper tonight?"

"Violet, tell your father how you slaved over this outstanding meal so that when he came home from his ball-busting day at the office he would have nothing but peace and tasty nourishment awaiting him."

"Christ, Maude. I think you need to slow down with that Dr. Applegate."

That was the first time I've ever heard my dad mention the doctor, and for a minute or two, maybe more, my heart stood dead still.

"Violet, tell your father, please, that I have no intention of discontinuing my sessions with Dr. Applegate, and if he doesn't like it, he can move himself out."

"Maude, calm yourself. You are being ridiculous."

And the whole time this is going on my dad is eating his meal just like everything was normal (which I guess in a sense it was), while my mom had, of course, pushed hers aside and lit up. I'd made my way through about half a sandwich, but couldn't stomach the rest.

"*I'm* being ridiculous? Do you know that is exactly what Dr. Applegate says about you? 'What a ridiculous man,' he says. 'Losing his marbles all over the place and isn't aware one bit. It's a wonder how you have the patience to remain married to such a preposterous fool.'" My mom was always using these long, animated words that I think she picked up from doing too many crosswords.

"So the good doctor thinks we ought to divorce?"

"I would say he clearly does."

"I love it. I pay this clown one hundred and fifty dollars a session so that he can tell my wife she'd be better off without me. Who does he think will buy his next motorboat once I'm out of the picture?"

My mom just stared out the window and inhaled her cigarette, looking like maybe she'd pushed it too far and was having second thoughts. I took another bite of my sandwich, but had to chew it about a million times before I could get it down.

"I see now how things are," said my dad, using his deep, solemn voice.

"So now you see." My mom put out her Winston in the uneaten sandwich, which made me feel kind of lousy.

I did all the dishes and cleaned up the whole kitchen, then ran upstairs to get ready because Ryder was probably halfway to my house already. I kept my jeans on, just changed from my sweater into a tight-fitting, long-sleeved T-shirt, white of course, which if I haven't mentioned yet, is my favorite color, that and red. I wore white almost every day and would have liked my bedroom redone into an all-white place of peace, like Ryder's room at Hillstream.

I figured I had to remind my parents about my date, because you would think, after the rigmarole that had just transpired, it would have slipped their minds. I'd told them about Ryder earlier in the week, his living at Hillstream, coming from Montana and his dad being a big fashion photographer, which I'd already told my mom about when I first met him, and which hadn't impressed my dad one bit. When I went back downstairs I was surprised to find my mom had her newest *Harper's Bazaar* out and was examining a layout that I instinctively knew to be Michael Hadley's.

"He's magnificent," she said, keeping the magazine tilted toward her so that I couldn't see it. My dad was nowhere in sight.

I sat down opposite my mom, feeling for the first time strangely intimidated by her presence. I glanced repeatedly at my watch, hoping Ryder wasn't the type who was late.

"Do you remember that I have a date with Ryder tonight?"

"Of course, love. Why wouldn't I?" She looked up at me, her glassy eyes shining in the overhead light.

"I don't know. I just thought what with all . . ."

"Oh, that. Your father was just blowing off steam. Trying to come to terms with the new me. I don't take shit from anybody anymore, and he is just going to have to adjust to what that means for him." She looked back down and flipped a page.

"Did Dad remember?"

"Remember what, love?"

"My date with Ryder." I have to tell you the word *date* lined up next to *Ryder* sounded mighty strange to my ears. Mighty strange indeed.

"How should I know? What do I look like, a switchboard operator?"

Just then the bell rang, and I hopped up to get it, but my mom held me back, grabbing on to my wrist.

"Don't appear too anxious, missy. He'll get the wrong idea."

I thought, *No, he'll get exactly the right idea—that I want to get the hell out of my house.* But by the time she released me, my dad had already let Ryder in. I waited in the kitchen about five full minutes, which seemed like a lifetime, watching my mom flip through her magazine, waiting for my dad to call my name, which usually took about thirty seconds on account of his never liking any guy I was seeing.

But no call came, so I walked out into the living room, and there was Ryder and my dad, sitting down in the two big overstuffed chairs that looked out over the front rose garden, which was all wrapped up now in burlap and whatnot, but that was the view nevertheless. They were hanging out, talking, like old war buddies. So much so that Ryder didn't even look up when I walked into the room. He was telling some story about Montana ranchers that had my dad in stitches.

"I always knew those cowboys had no common sense. You can lead them to horses, but you can't make them ride," my dad said with a chuckle, and Ryder joined him.

It was strange to see the two of them sitting there, enjoying each other's company so much. My dad looked relaxed and happy, as if an hour ago he hadn't been swapping insults with his wife, and Ryder looked, as always, like life had just begun.

"Hey, Ryder," I finally had to say, just to get some attention.

"Let, man. William here is crankin' cool. We were just getting to know each other. Learning the lay of the land."

My dad was kind of beaming, which was way weird, since Ryder certainly was not your daughter's dream date, despite the Ivory soap. But he did have that charm, which, I was noticing more and more, worked its magic in myriad situations.

My mom popped out to see us off, and I could tell she was sizing Ryder up and finding him lacking despite the fact he was mine. Seeing my mom and dad standing there, more or less side by side after the weird dinner we three had just shared, was too much for me. I squirmed in my jeans, dying to leave, while Ryder droned on and on about this and that, and that and this. Finally, without my curfew being mentioned once, we split. Freddie's car awaited us. I climbed in, letting out a sigh of relief.

• • • •

The party turned out to be in the same mass of minipalaces as the Landwehrs' house had been the week before, which, by the way, seemed about a million years ago; like when you finish a book and the characters kind of linger in your head a bit, but the vitality and force that had once caught you up are gone. Just like when I drove to the Landwehrs', we had to pass by the Edwards house, and naturally I scoped out Henry's car, which it turned out was parked right smack out front, and seeing it got me twitching hard, like I always did when I so much as thought about that one. My heart sank halfway to my tummy as I looked at Ryder, trying hard to figure what I was doing with him. When we pulled up in front of the mongo-dwelling of yet another of Ryder's school buddies, neither one of us felt much like going in. Instead we sat in Freddie's car, with the motor running, a real eco no-no, trading sips from Ryder's flask.

"What are you going to do on Christmas Eve? You and Freddie and Briggs have something planned?"

"Don't forget Marvin, man. Never Marvin, because he is such a trip."

"Okay, Marvin, too. What's the scoop?"

"My parents phoned up the Chop House, and made arrangements for me to dine in splendor on that day of thanks."

"Which means?"

"I'm to join my uncle at eight o'clock sharp. 'Don't be late,' says Michael, 'you never know how long his heart will hold out, and that's one bill we don't want to get stuck with.'"

"But isn't that the uncle who never shows up?"

"Truth. I feel it, too. He'll never show."

"You can come by our house," I said, the words just

rolling on out before I'd had time to give them true consideration. "The Tat's always there for Christmas, so it would be no problem."

"Well, that would be mighty nice, man. I'll be glad to take you up on such a sweet offer." I smiled at him and he at me, and I felt A-OK, like inviting Ryder over for Christmas Eve was the right thing to do and a definite right at that, which was an experience I'd rarely had before. We'd emptied the flask by then, so we tooled inside the house, Ryder taking my hand, leading me in through the thick oak doors that creaked as they shut, and straight to the bar. He tried to find some Southern Comfort, but they didn't have any, so we settled for two gin and tonics apiece, which was a bit perky after the slow, mellow vibe of whiskey, but, as always, I adjusted to it fine.

· · · ·

Well, the house itself was incredible, more like something from the East Coast beaches than Midwestern suburbs material. So much so, in fact, that I kept waiting for Gatsby himself to pop around the corner, dressed in white. Harold Morgan was the kid throwing this bash on account of his parents being away, off somewhere picking up a little preholiday tan. Harold, who for some inexplicable reason went by the pseudonym of Wolf, which his thin, wiry nervousness in no way resembled, took to me right away and was pretty hard to shake the entire time we were in his house. Ryder fortunately stuck by my side.

"Ryder, sweetie! It's too fabulous that you're here," said this voice from behind us as Wolf droned away, and I watched as two thin, pale arms encircled what I was considering more and more to be my date.

"India, man. You look beautiful. Truly beautiful. Tell me what you've been stirring up."

It was strange how, until that moment, I'd never thought about Ryder having a past life. I mean, I knew about his family—which made me feel kind of sad when I thought about it, although mine wasn't all that much better—but I had never thought about prior girlfriends. I suppose I had considered him untouched, although deep down I had always known otherwise on account of his eyes, which were languid and overexperienced.

I slid up closer to Ryder and slipped my hand into his. I'll admit I was a little tipsy at the time, liking the sensation of his closing his hand around mine. The girl didn't even seem to notice. I don't think she even was aware I was there, or if she was, she didn't care. Ryder seemed pleased to see her, but he was like that with everyone. I kind of became what you might call obsessed with this girl's beauty, because she was a real knockout by anybody's standards, with her long blond hair and model-thin body, and pretty soon I got that sinking feeling in my stomach, so I was just about to take off and get myself another drink when Ryder got around to introducing us.

"Let, man, this is India. India, Let."

"Delighted," she said, looking straight at Ryder the whole time, like we were in one of those old flicks or something, and she was playing the society bitch-vamp. From what I could gather of their conversation, they had grown up in Kalispell together, neighbors on Flathead Lake and just a street or two apart in the town. She was a few years older, attending U of M, and had driven down our way for this here party.

India droned on and on, like some off-hours TV show, while Wolf kept up a fresh supply of drinkie-winks. I started scoping out the room, when who should I see across the way, but my sweet angel-man, looking way beautiful in his leathers and the same white ruffled shirt he'd had on the night I'd seen him last, when he wouldn't let me in. Had I seen a movement in the window above his door, I wondered, thinking back to that evening, or was I imagining things now, the way you do when time has distanced you from the facts? Our eyes met, and he smiled, flashing the chip. I was overwhelmed by a rush of panic, dropping Ryder's hand just before Henry slid between us, his long fingers wrapped around a bottle of beer.

"Baby girl," he said, and smiled again.

"Hey, Henry. Whadda ya doin' here?"

"Friend of Art's." Art was Wolf's older brother. He was having a miniparty of his own in the basement. "Fieldstone hires him a lot for graphics."

I prayed Marsha wasn't lurking about. Henry seemed to pick up on the way I was swaying side to side pretty fast, even though I had been fairly certain it was all in my head, because the next thing he said was, "Do you want to sit down?" I nodded, thinking about what a loser date Ryder was, leaving me standing there that whole time while he chatted up Miss Priss from cow-fuck Montana, while Henry, being a true gentleman, had immediately familiarized himself with my situation and sought my relief. We sat without speaking, thigh to thigh on the couch for about five minutes, me glancing over just to make sure he

· 241 ·

was really there. His eyes were way bloodshot, toasted big-time. I laughed, thinking about how it wasn't my needs he was looking to meet after all.

"Jesus, you're really wasted, aren't you, baby girl?" He leaned back next to me; he smelled warm and used. Ryder had disappeared from my sight on account of Wolf and some of his buddies having closed ranks around him.

"I'm fine," I said, wondering if the movement of my lips was actually producing the words I intended. "Why didn't you call me? Didn't you have fun the other night?" My face slid toward my mouth, and I jerked my head back.

"Of course." He pushed his hand through his dark hair.

"Well, where ya been?"

"Here and there."

He took a slug of beer, licking the lingering foam from his lips. The twitch set in. His hand swept against mine as if by accident. I reached out toward it, but he shifted away. I recognized our movements now as part one of his lead-in and relaxed into it, knowing what would follow. Ryder appeared, sprawled in the chair across from us. I could smell him long before my contactless eyes could recognize his blur.

"So Let, man, who's your pal?" Ryder asked, leaning forward, elbows on his knees.

"Henry."

"Henry. Pleased to meet you, man. I'm Ryder."

And he put out his hand, but Henry just nodded, then after a minute or so of silence, flicked his head to the side, indicating that I should follow him, which I did, leaving, I guess, Ryder just sitting in the chair, but I'm not exactly sure, since much of that evening remains a blur to me.

I finally got my new contacts the other day and the Tat said my not having worn them for so long was symbolic of my not wanting to deal with life. Wanting to see clearly again was a positive sign of my recovery of lost dreams and whatnot.

After a bit Henry led me into this way small bathroom off one of the sitting rooms, which felt too claustrophobic to be affiliated with such a colossal dwelling, and whipped out a small plastic bag of fairy dust. I rolled up the dollar bill he handed me, while he cut lines on the counter with the jackknife he carried on his key chain.

"Fly, baby girl," he whispered.

I bent over, closed off my left nostril, and sucked through my right. I felt the burning rush work its way clear into my brain. I pushed the remainder up with my middle finger and watched Henry take his turn. Then we switched sides. I was again impressed by the balance in this; its ritualism struck me as somehow pure. Henry wiped his finger over the counter and slid the remaining dust across my upper gum and down my tongue, numbing both with his touch.

"Ready?" he asked, and I nodded, zipping up my coat, which I hadn't bothered taking off, and we sneaked out of the party via the back door.

Naturally we drove to his house in silence, which even though I couldn't stop chewing on my bottom lip was fine with me. The drowsiness from the liquor mixed in with the kick of the blow was making me feel weird. There was a moment of complete darkness and silence when Henry shut off the Mustang and turned to me to see if I was okay to get out of the car by myself, and in this tiny reprieve I thought exclusively of Ryder, and I wished it was he I was with. Then the moment was gone.

Henry's apartment was warm and tranquil, although still without life. He sauntered into the kitchen to grab some beers. I noticed a pack of Djarums lying crumpled alongside the telephone, devoid of any joints. *Maybe he's out,* I considered, but he came back in with one of his skinny ones dangling from his lips, handing me a Budweiser with one hand and passing me the joint with his mouth. I missed the pass, so Henry caught it up and held the paper to my lips as I inhaled. Then he took another toke, flipping it inside out so the lit end was hidden in his pinkness, a thin trail of smoke sneaking out the chip. I was impressed, but fearful to try myself, so he taught me how to shotgun, which meant I inhaled his exhalation, and I've got to tell you, this combination of substances had me feeling a wide variety of things at once, each competing to claim the moment as its own, reducing the instant of superheightened awareness to just a passing flash in time.

I followed Henry's swaying hips down the hall and into the bedroom, where once again, he laid me out across the dirty sheets and positioned the bedside lamps just so until the light fell on me the way he desired, then mounted me with all the force and determination that he never showed outside of the bedroom.

"Pretty little girl," he said, latching his teeth on to the bottom of my T-shirt, pulling it up toward my breasts like a dog. He kissed my tummy, licked my neck, my lips, my cheeks. Every move I made, every touch, every sigh, was encouraged, even coached. He was forming me into his natural lover, of whom he planned to take full possession, if only for a few moments here and there. And we rocked the bed for hours in this guided rhythm. When I grew weary between my legs, Henry taught me the mysteries of saliva, and when weary in my head, Henry showed me the endless pleasures of the fairies. It was a night without end. A true slide into the dark side, and I loved every minute of it.

14

It's funny how everything can seem A-OK at night; in fact, it can seem just exactly right, then morning hits and whoosh, what a sinking feeling of doubt sweeps over you. Henry lying there so thin in the morning glare, lighting up a joint and finishing off the beer from the bedside table, while I shifted about on the sheets in search of an unstained corner.

We tried to mess around again when we woke, but nothing came of it. I just couldn't get going, and even with the miracles of saliva and lubricated condoms (which I was now expertly unrolling), it hurt like hell, so Henry pulled out and swung off into the kitchen to whip up our dandy little breakfast. Meanwhile I sneaked in a shower, letting the hot water pelt down on my swollen eyes. Then, flipping my underpants inside out, I slid back into the Henry-zone.

"Do you see other women?" I'd asked him, when he returned with our tray.

"What do you think?"

"Was someone here when I came by the other night?" I hadn't been able to shake that vision of the moving curtain.

"Do you really want to know?"

"I guess not."

Henry lay back onto his pillow, chugging a fresh beer and folding his toast in half before wolfing it down. He looked kind of saintly in a way I can't quite describe, except maybe to mention the hollowness of his body, which prone across the bed as it was, seemed to sink right down into the bowels of the earth, giving him this martyr vibe.

Around ten-thirty or so, after managing to ignore me quite well while sorting through photos and contact sheets and cleaning some of his Nikon lenses, he drove me home. A plaintive ride full of strangely comforting silences—the sole thing about Henry that felt consistently natural, it being a continuation of my family dinner table.

When I got home, no one was about, which was pretty weird because like I mentioned before, my mom never left the house much, and being that it was midmorning, Dad should have been back from his tennis match, that is, if he even went at all, what with his daughter missing. I cooked myself up a big pot of Oatmeal and All, but just looking at it made me want to barf, so I pulled down a box of saltines, poured myself a nice glass of water, and sat in Logan's chair at the kitchen table, looking out the window; wondering if my parents were making the rounds of every hospital, jail, and drug center this side of the Mississippi looking for me. Finally I heard my mom's car pull in, at which point I took a deep breath and waited.

• • • •

"So the wanderer returns," said my mom, plopping down in the chair opposite mine, snatching some crackers off my plate. "Make me some coffee, will you?" I sat there a moment as if glued to my chair. "Are we going deaf, missy? Make me some coffee."

I rose slowly, still under the influence of nausea, although the crackers had helped, and pulled down the coffeemaker. I plugged it in, ground the beans, scooped them into the white filter, filled the back compartment with water, and pushed the button, the whole time waiting for my mom to say something that would explain what was going on in our house, but she never did. When I turned back she had started a crossword that had been tucked into the pencil/gum drawer and was so immersed in it that she didn't even look up when I placed her coffee on a London Bridge coaster near her right elbow.

"Where's Dad?"

"Your father has moved out," she said.

"What?"

"Are you losing your marbles, too? I said he has moved out." And she pushed her lips way forward to form the word *moved*.

"When?"

"Last night, I believe. When I woke this morning he was gone."

"Well, how do you know he's not just playing tennis or something?"

"Because one does not usually take two suitcases full of belongings to a tennis match, does one?" She stirred two heaping spoonfuls of sugar into her brew and lit up a Winston. "I suppose you want to discuss it?" I shook my head, even though in reality I did want to know what happened.

"Well, then one thing we can discuss, missy, is *your* where-abouts last night."

"I'm sorry," I said, looking at my feet, feeling tears of horror and uncertainty—and resignation to the fact that my life would always be vaguely unpleasant—well up in me.

"I'm sure you are, missy. I'm sure you are. So would you like to share with your mother just what happened?" I shook my head again.

"Oh well, that's a nice how-do-you-do. Just pick the hours you wish to come and go, treat me as if I run a boardinghouse, but when the chips are down, a real tight-lipped dolly girl."

I continued staring at my feet, wondering where on earth my dad was.

"Well, I think I can guess where you were. You were in some dark alley or parked along some deserted lake with that charming young man of yours, Mr. Ryder Hadley, son of the world-renowned fashion photographer. Don't think I don't know what you get up to. Don't think just because I'm not there with you, I'm not thinking about you every minute, living the experience with you in my head." My stomach welled into my lungs. "Well, missy, I'm afraid you leave me no choice but to ground you. Upstairs."

I turned to put my glass in the sink, perhaps a minor moment of hesitation or shock that I feel I was rightfully entitled to, considering the circumstances, but before I reached the stainless steel basin, she yelled, "Go!" so I took off at the speed of light, trying to figure what had happened to the teenage-rebellion-and-space-to-grow theory. It was as if she was thrilled to be rid of my dad, so she could lay down some much-needed right-and-wrong rules, her version. And I've got to tell you, she was the last person I thought would ever be finally punishing me for a wrong, especially for spending the night with a guy which, in truth, had never come with a right or wrong sticker attached.

. . . .

When I got upstairs, I called CJ. Even though things hadn't been feeling exactly right between us, sometimes something happens and you just have to share it with your best friend even when, technically, she's not really your best friend anymore. Right off, things were out of sorts. CJ's voice was stressed, and I could hear her dad in the background speaking gruffly about something or other like he always was, and one of her brothers doing the old yes-sir routine, although in real life they were about the most impolite, sleazy assholes you could meet.

"I can't really talk now," CJ said.

"Okay. No problemo," I said.

"What's the scoop anyway, darling?"

"Nothing. Just wanted to tell you about last night with Henry."

"I thought you were out with Ryder."

"Oh, I was," I said, picking at my nails. I thought about Ryder sitting in that chair, trying to shake hands with Henry, and it made me a little sick that I'd just left him like that. But he'd left me for that Asia chick, or India, whoever. I knew I was blaming again, I could feel it, but in that moment, it felt like the only thing to do. "But then I ran into Henry and you know . . ."

"You are living one free-and-easy life."

"No, I'm not. It's not like Ryder is my boyfriend or anything." I hadn't spoken with CJ on the phone in ages, and I was wishing I hadn't broken the streak now.

"And Henry is?"

"What's that supposed to mean?"

"Wake up, darling. Henry is there for the picking, and he doesn't mind whose basket he falls into."

"Are you trying to tell me something, CJ?"

"Yeah, I'm trying to tell you to wake up. That guy is bad news. Not that Ryder is the hippest cat in town, but at least he treats you well."

"Were you there the other night, CJ, considering you've become such an expert on Henry and all?"

"What is that supposed to mean?"

"Behind the curtain?"

"Let, I don't know what you are talking about, but you are pissing me off, so I'm gonna split. You live life the way you want for a while, then call me when you're back. Dig?"

• • • •

Sometimes life deals you blows that you just weren't expecting, except that when you think about it later, you realize you really were expecting it; you just didn't want to deal with it, which is not such a bad way to live, because if I prepared myself for every single bad thing I was expecting, I would be much more high-strung and anxious than I already am.

When I got off the phone with CJ, I took a bath and tried to stop thinking for a bit. But I couldn't. Mostly I thought about my dad and wondered if I would see him again. And was he happy? And did he miss me, too? I thought about my mom as well and wondered if she'd ever let me out of my room again, and if so, when and for how long, and what kind of restrictions would apply. Punishment wasn't quite having the healing qualities I was hoping for, though I suppose it was a bit early to tell. Then I wrapped myself in a gigantic white towel, crawled into bed, and like so many times as of late, I dozed off in the middle of what seemed to be a snowy winter's day.

"So, Bean Brain, I hear you pulled a full-on toaster last night."

Logan sat next to me on the bed—clad in his well-worn gold leathers with lace-up crotch, and some explosive–tiny flower shirt, like a trip you couldn't come off, which I had never seen before, so I figured it was from some dank, patchouli-scented store in Ann Arbor—looking pretty beat himself.

"Yeah." I looked at the bump my upright toes were making beneath the comforter. "Did you just get home? Where's the Tat?" It was weird she wasn't there. It was even weirder Logan had come up to my room and woken me. I started to get that nervous vibe, where I instantly think I've done something wrong.

"I dropped her off at her parents'. She's coming by tonight for dinner, if there is one."

"So you heard about Dad?"

"Oh, yeah. I heard about the old man all right. That and plenty more." There was an awkward silence, and my nakedness began to feel uncomfortable beneath the sheets. "So listen, punk, give me the lowdown on your night of

revelry. What happened with this jerk from Hillstream?"
He leaned back on his elbows so that the tips of them
rubbed against my leg.

"I wasn't with him. I was with Henry."

"Henry? What are you hanging with that jerk-off for?"

"I thought you liked him."

"Yeah, well not so much anymore. Steer clear, Beans.
That's today's advice. Steer clear."

"It's kind of too late."

"What?"

"What, what?"

"Jesus, Beans, what have you been up to?"

I've got to tell you, the whole situation was making me
nervous, me in bed naked, Logan practically in bed with
me, not that I felt anything inappropriate would happen,
but we just weren't that kind of family. We were intensely
private in all our doings, most especially those involving
any element of our bodies. Plus Logan had never asked me
shit about any boyfriend before, so suddenly discussing
my sex life with him did not come naturally, but stutter-
ing and spurting as I was, I did manage to convey the gist
of it to him nonetheless.

When I was finished, he said, "Get up and get dressed,
I'm treating you to lunch." Logan looked a lot like my
mom, I thought, studying his oval face and straight nose.
His hair fell forward, and he wound it behind his ears.
"Looks like you need to locate a little clothing first." He
pinched my bare shoulder. "I'll meet you downstairs."

• • • •

Before going downstairs I was caught up by the compulsion to phone Ryder. I couldn't shake the ickiness that surrounded the memory of just leaving him there. I did try to reach him, too, but I've got to admit, I was relieved when I couldn't find his number. The garbage had been emptied and there was no answer at the Hillstream number the *très* perky info lady gave me. I even, with palpitating heart, tried to get a listing for a Mr. Briggs—*nada.* Ryder did not want to speak with me anyhow, I figured. That little moment in my life was definitely kaput.

I met up with Logan in the TV room where he was sprawled out in our dad's chair, legs dangling over an arm, reading *National Geographic,* which my parents had subscribed to ever since Logan and I were little kids.

"Ready?"

"Ready."

We headed out to the Flame, Logan seeming distant and distracted in a vague, dreamy kind of way, which was hard to pinpoint, since he was always kind of vague and dreamy, but this was different.

"Where'd Mom go?" I asked, noticing that her car was missing.

"Bookstore, Beans, no doubt to find you a cure." He knocked his fist lightly up against the side of my head. I squirmed away.

"Hey, I'm not supposed to be out. I'm grounded."

"Life is for the taking, little sister. Remember what the old man says—you snooze, you lose." Though when Logan caught sight of the Flame he said, "Shit, Beans. I guess you've been taking life a little bit too much," but thankfully, he left it at that. After driving a bit, while I scoped out roadkills to see if my system still worked from the passiveness of the passenger seat, Logan got back to Henry.

"So you're really hot for this Henry dude?"

"Yeah, I guess." I looked down at my feet, feeling more bad Henry-warnings coming on.

"Keep away, Let. That's all I say. Keep the fuck away."

"Why?"

I rubbed the steamy side window with my hand and looked out at snow-covered strip malls and oversize subdivisions and all the other ugliness that had begun to take over our land. No wonder the roadkill rate was way up, there was nowhere left for the little critters to go.

"Why? 'Cuz I say so. Trust me on this one." And he lit up a cigarette, which he hadn't done since he full-out quit drinking three years back.

We were quiet for a bit, then I said, "Why'd you go to Vegas, Logan?" I wasn't planning on asking him this; it just slipped out.

"That's a weird question."

"Yeah, apparently so. And no one wants to answer."

"Some shit happened I needed to get away from." We were silent through three red lights, with the only sound being that of Logan hitting his cigarette, hard, before I said, "Then, why did you come back?"

"Because I missed you."

"I'm serious."

"Why are we here? Why are we on this topic?" He sounded kind of frustrated, too, but I didn't seem to be able to stop. At the same time I couldn't tell the truth, either. I couldn't say, "Well, we're here because I sneaked into your room and read your locked-up, boxed-up journals," could

I? So I said, "I don't know. Sometimes I think about running away." Which wasn't really true. Boy, the lies were piling up.

"Yeah?" Logan looked at me all serious, and I was instantly sorry I'd lied to him. Instantly sorry I'd sneaked in and read his journals. "With Henry?"

"No, not with fucking Henry." As sorry as I felt, I wished Logan would get off Henry already.

"Good. Stay away from him."

"I know. I know. You told me that."

We were silent again, then Logan said, "I came back because it was the right thing to do."

"But maybe there was an in-between." I'd been thinking about this in-between theory of Ryder's but not getting anywhere with it.

"A what?"

"An in-between." I could tell from Logan's voice that he knew just what I'd said and he thought it was stupid, so I didn't even want to repeat it.

"An in-between?"

"Yeah, something that's not a definite right and not a definite wrong."

"Who the fuck told you that?"

"A friend."

"Hen—"

"No, not Henry. Another friend."

"That Hillstream punk?"

"Yeah, Ryder."

"He sounds like a real winner."

"I didn't say I agreed with him," I said, wishing for once I had something I did believe that stood in contrast to

Logan—just so I could acknowledge that I actually had a brain of my own rather than an auxiliary of his.

"You'd better not," he said. "That kind of thinking will get you nothing but trouble."

Eventually we ended up at John's. Logan ordered up a thin-crust pizza, loaded with the works, half without meat, which made me smile, because he rarely acknowledged things like that about me except in a teasing way.

"Do you think Dad will come back?" I asked as I picked off some toppings and popped them in my mouth.

"Hard to say, Beans. Does it matter anyway? The two of them are so fucking unhappy, I can't see how where they live would make one bit of difference."

"Are they?"

"Trust me. I know about these things. We all live our lives fighting the demons and some of us are less well-equipped. Now eat up."

How well equipped was I? How fucking well equipped was I?

. . . .

Back at the house, around threeish, my mom came home with a gift-wrapped book for me from the local chain bookstore, which, by the by, was managing to drive all the other local, hippie-head bookstores out of existence.

"For you, love," she said, handing me a book while flicking her lighter with a free hand. I was tempted to inquire as to my grounding status, but thought better of it. Logan smirked at me from our dad's chair where he was sprawled out again across the room. We'd been watching reruns of *The Avengers* when my mom came in—actually first-time viewings for both of us, since we hadn't even been born when the show was originally on.

"Oh, doesn't she just look devastating?" said my mom, hands on hips, admiring Diana Rigg. "She was a real hot number in her day."

"Hard core," said Logan. My mom looked at him, then turned to me. "Violet, love, open your present."

So I ripped open the green-swirled paper that temporarily shielded me from the impending unhappy experience.

"Read the card first, dolly girl," my mom said, sitting on the footstool beside me. She held her cigarette way out behind her, and waved frantically over my head. I could smell her Joy 1000 pulsating from sweat glands along her neck as I read the card: "I love you so very, very much, my youthful, blooming flower. You are like a jewel nestled against the pebbles on the beach, in time you will be discovered. XXOO Mom."

"Thanks," I said.

"Well, open it up."

I finished ripping the paper and stared at the book: *When Life Becomes Unmanageable*—subtitled *25 Easy Ways to Stop Drinking, Smoking, and Losing Control.* On the front cover there was a picture of the author—a doctor with a furrowed brow and these lopsided plastic glasses. I dropped it into my lap and smiled. My mom shifted forward and leaned her elbows on my knee.

"Dr. Applegate says it's marvelous. Just the thing you need to get you back on track."

"I *am* on track," I said, looking her right in the eye.

"Well"—her steady I'm-in-control-now voice that had been building since her double-slapping me in the kitchen didn't waver one iota—"I would like to think you are, too. Perhaps this book will help shed some light." She smiled.

I felt as if I were living out one of the standard worst nightmare scenarios, where you are arrested or kidnapped and end up under the control of a crazy person and there is nothing you can do legally, morally, or physically to change that. So you just keep trying to wake up until the punch line comes and you realize you are awake.

· · · ·

The Tat came by for dinner, but it would have been almost better if she hadn't. It became readily apparent she and Logan weren't hanging out much at school and that her being at our house at all was some kind of perfunctory agreement, though my mom seemed oblivious to this. Or else she was enjoying it in some way. I wasn't sure, and either scenario was icky. After dinner, the Tat walked herself to the door while Logan sat at the table and stared out the window.

That night I could hardly sleep, suffocating in the heat my mom had left running full tilt. I rose and opened my window, leaned my forehead against the cold glass. After contemplating the moon for an hour or so, I decided the thing for me was a little chamomile tea and some late-night telly—mind pollution as Logan calls it, although he watched it plenty. I wandered downstairs but skipped the kitchen; something instinctively pulled me into the darkened TV room. Logan was slumped in my dad's leather chair, his feet sprawled wide across the ottoman, and even though I later realized I was expecting him to be there all along, I still jumped.

"Hell, Logan, you scared me."

"Did I? Sorry, Beans."

I couldn't quite make his face out in the dark.

"What are you doing?" I whispered.

"I might ask the same question of you, little sister. It must be past your bedtime." I didn't like the edge to his voice. I sat on the couch and pulled a blanket up around me, despite the oppressive heat.

"Do you want to watch some TV?" I asked after about a million hours of silence.

"Nope."

I wondered how long Logan had just been sitting in the dark like that. All hunkered down against the straight-up back of the chair, he looked like one of those solid little tugs that haul in ships from the sea. He shifted about for a minute, finally pulled a Ziploc bag out of his pocket.

"Wanna get stoned?"

I nodded, watched him roll a fresh joint. His heavy blond streaks glowed strangely in the moonlight that shone through the uncurtained sliding doors. First he worked the herb through his fingers, breaking it up in his left palm. Then he slipped a paper out of his brown cardboard pack, made a crease, laid it on top of the pot, closed his palms together, and flipped them over so that the paper ended up on the bottom of his right hand. He rolled it into a tight tube, licked the edge to seal it, sucking lightly on the ends, and twisted them closed. Though not a pothead myself, I recognized his expertise.

"Here," he said, offering up his masterpiece. I reached over and took a hit, passed it back, repeated this a couple more times until I was well toasted and had to decline, leaving Logan to his own devices, which turned out to be finishing that joint and starting another.

"Wanna drink, Beans? Celebrate our ruling family?" He stood and tumbled toward the liquor cabinet.

"Sure," I said, not totally certain I did. He slopped together two Jack Daniel's and Cokes, handed me mine with a kind of semiberserk smile I wasn't familiar with.

"I don't drink anymore, as you know, but, Bean Brain, tonight I am in the mood." And he downed his in one gulp, while I placed mine on the floor beneath me.

"Bean Brain, Bean Brain"—he slurred the words slightly, bending toward my J.D. in an unnaturally awkward motion—"drink up."

"I don't want it, Logan."

"Well, if Bean Brain doesn't want it, then I'll drink it for her. Don't mind if I do." He nodded to my drink and swallowed it whole. Then he grabbed the bottle and went back to his chair. My heart started pounding, and I couldn't help but wish my dad were around so that maybe he could suddenly wake up and intervene. It was beginning to feel more and more like the old days, only this round I was onstage rather than in the audience.

"Don't look so forlorn, little sister; things aren't that bad."

I stared at my feet.

"For Christ's sake, just 'cuz Anna's off banging some fucking jerk asshole doesn't mean we can't have ourselves a little fun."

He took a swig and offered it to me. I shook my head, wishing I hadn't smoked the pot after all. Actually wishing I hadn't even come down.

"Don't you even want to know who it is Anna's seeing? Aren't you even the littlest, tiniest bit curious?"

Logan squished up his fingers into smaller and smaller increments as he bent toward my face. The thing was, I really wasn't curious about who the Tat was seeing. In that moment, I didn't want to know about that or anything else—where my dad was, why my mom was naked in the hall. I wanted to shut it all off. *Go to bed,* I repeated endlessly, hoping Logan would feel my thoughts through the room. *Go to fucking bed.*

Logan fell back into the thickness of my dad's chair, which was molded perfectly to my dad's shape and size, a permanent head indentation, oiled slightly from his hair tonic, near the top. Logan pushed aside a needlepoint cushion my mom had made years ago. We were silent so long, I thought he'd fallen asleep.

"You really don't know why I left?"

"I don't." The room suddenly felt too big and I pulled the blanket tighter around me.

"You really don't know about the old lady?" He was flipping the cushion relentlessly in circles with his fingers.

"No," I said. Then after a bit, "What about her?"

"She's tragic, isn't she, Let? So fucking tragic. And the old man is tragic, too. In a different way, of course, because he never lets the tragedy touch him. And that's the most tragic thing of all, because if no tragedy touches you, then you remain untouched period. Like some kind of greased-up freak-head out in the rain. You don't get wet, but you don't get clean, either."

I didn't like the way Logan was speaking. It scared me. I didn't want to sit in our darkened TV room at odd hours of the night and look at my parents as tragic or greased-up freak-heads. He was trying to pull me into his quagmire. I would not go.

"I used to think there was some sort of rhythm to life that I just had to learn and follow. You know, like the way everything around here is in such perfect order. Keep it neat, and life is sweet. Go astray, and you gotta pay. Then I realized that that was all bullshit. Bullshit that the folks had invented to keep us from knowing how tragic our fucking home really is." His body was rigid, but his head bobbed gently from side to side like a free-floating balloon. "There's no love here, Violet; it's a loveless nest we've been brought into, you and me. I know, and I know you know, although you may not want to admit it. But I really don't think they know it. I think they think this is love. Even this latest stunt. It won't last. He'll be back, righteous and vindicated, feeling he's proved some pointless point, but nothing will have changed. Just our empty house and all of us coming and going from it, like blood pumping in and out of the heart."

"Maybe they're doing the best they can."

"Little sister, that is just your guilt talking. I know, because I used to have it. But I got rid of mine." He paused. "I got rid of mine the day I found our helpless, neglected mother fucking the shit out of a stranger in this perfect house of ours."

My breath cut short.

"Don't tell me you really didn't know," Logan said, leaning forward a bit to gaze at me as if through a dirty windshield.

I shook my head, wanting to cry, but holding back the tears on account of feeling a little afraid of Logan and just wanting the whole thing to be over with.

"Sit back, Bean-o-rama, and let me tell you about this family of ours."

He drank deeply from the bottle, and this time, when he passed it my way, I joined him.

"It was the shoes I saw first—galoshes next to the front door, which, as you know, the old man never wears 'cuz he thinks they're pussy as hell. And he's right. The house was silent, just the buzz of the termites trying to bring it all down, which was strange, right? Because usually you were around doing something, at least fucking breathing, or the old lady was cooking or pruning her plants. But not this day. I was home early from practice. Coach Hurly had the flu and his assistant didn't want to risk that any of us would get it, so he sent us packing. One of those freaks of nature that makes you believe there must be a God, warped though he is." Logan took another swig before continuing.

"So I checked out the kitchen, the living room, the study, the TV room, everything downstairs, but nobody was about, and in the back of my head I'm thinking, *Well, whose fucking galoshes are those?*" Pause for a swig. "Well, Beans, it turns out the old lady had sent you over to the neighbors to help with a little jam-making or something, so you were nowhere to be found, and as I creaked up those stairs there was only the three of us here—the old man was, naturally, at work, where he's hidden out all these years. Just the three of us: me, the old lady, and her lover."

Logan paused so long, I again thought he'd fallen asleep. I shifted beneath my blanket and chewed my bottom lip until it began to bleed, wondering how many of the things I'd always considered our mom was faking was she actually capable of following through. Did she really want to show Henry how to heat his Mustang? Was she really hankering for some interstate trouble in the Flame? Would she one day show up with a key to an apartment of her, our, own in Nottingham, far from the safety of the walls I knew so well?

"Somehow I made it all the way to the top step," Logan began again, "without being heard or hearing a thing myself, although I couldn't quite shake the nagging sensation I should turn back, but I didn't. Instead I made it all the way to their fucking door, which was wide open. And there, little sister, was the old lady, stretched gloriously out on the old man's bed, for all the world to see, some old fuck banging the shit out of her, moaning and groaning, the old lady's tits rocking back and forth, looking old and tired, and the smell of their bodies making me want to puke."

He twisted the front strands of his hair around his forefinger, staring at the ceiling, then guzzled a good portion of the remaining J.D.

"So the next thing you know, the old lady is chasing me down the hall naked as the day she was born, and I'm locking myself in my room, swearing I will never, ever leave it again."

"How did she know you were there?" I asked, uncertain as to why an unnecessary detail like that seemed so important at the time.

"I dropped my books. The whole time I'd been hanging on to my fucking school books, lugging them up the stairs with me rather than leaving them on the kitchen table. You know I've always thought back on how fucking weird it was that I'd carried my books up with me, as if I knew they would be my giveaway. The mind can be visionary that way, Beans, without you ever knowing."

"So then Vegas?"

"Then Vegas. And what a time that was. Everything you could ever want is in Vegas." His gold leathers glistened in the moonlight.

"Did Dad know?"

"Ah, yes, the old man most certainly knew. Indeed. What a pathetic fool. He defended her, or at least tried. He didn't know how to love her in the way she needed to be loved, he said. Try to understand. So I nodded, trying to look like I understood. And then I left."

"And when you came back everything was different," I said. The bottomless fights, the hard, broken words, the busting silences: everything awful that had come to roost at our house.

"Shit, yeah, it was different. 'Never going back,' I told myself. Never."

"Back to what?"

"Truth. Back to truth and trust and believing what you see is the way it is, because it's not. The saddest part of all is that you just repeat what you know. Like with Anna two-timing me. Just like the old lady. And I took her back, just the way the old man did. And you know what, she did it again with the same guy. Believe me, Beans. Only fools trust."

We sat a moment longer in the silence. *This is it,* I thought. This is our little secret. This is why there are no toasters on the counter. This is why my mom leaves in the middle of the night and returns hours later, sunken, frayed. This is why the clouds wash down, enveloping my dad; why he doesn't know which way to turn with me. This is why he doesn't have a sense of who I might become or can barely see who I am now. Not because of the affair, not because of what Logan saw, but because of what he understood: the truth getting fucked. Logan had said we lived in a loveless nest, but it was worse, we lived in a house without trust, a house without foundation. And without that, your home will tumble. Just watch the news when an earthquake hits. It's always the folks with the shaky foundations who lose their homes first. A bunch of the rest remain standing, even if they're neighbors, even if they share the same fault line.

"But I thought you said you believed in right and wrong."

"Did I? When?"

"In the car, on the way to John's. You said you came home because it was a right and that there are no in-betweens."

Logan paused a moment. "Shit, Beans. Don't listen to me. I don't know what the fuck I'm saying half the time." I knew he was drunk. I knew he was talking nonsense, but nevertheless every organ inside of me that could go queasy in that moment did. If Logan didn't know what was going on, then who did? I mean if Logan didn't know about stuff like family and right and wrong and who was appropriate to date and who wasn't, then how was I supposed to know? "I just said that so you wouldn't end up like this." And his voice got all soft, like Whiz Bang's belly in the morning.

"I didn't want you to lose your sense of right and wrong, lose your compass through this fucking awful life."

"I don't have a sense of right and wrong to lose."

"Yes, you do, Beans. You've just got to trust it."

I watched the moonlight flickering across the ceiling in ever-changing patterns as the wind blew hard and strong outside. I was indoors, safe, needing to be held and comforted. Wanting someone to take from me all this knowledge that had been dumped on me over the past few weeks. Since my birthday, really. Since the Flame.

A long, muffled noise caught my attention, then short choppy noises: the sound of Logan crying. In all my sixteen years I had never seen him cry, never even imagined that he needed to. I was paralyzed at first, unable to comfort him until he knelt on the floor, resting his shaking head on the ottoman. Then I too knelt and touched his back.

"I love you," I said to Logan, uttering those words for possibly the first time in my life to someone other than Whiz Bang. "It's okay. It really is. You didn't do anything wrong."

I added that bit from my heart, on account of every time I was upset, that was exactly what I wanted somebody to say to me.

Logan said, "I love you, too." He hugged me close. That may have been one of the first times I'd ever heard those words said to me, and I started crying, too. Logan suddenly straightened up, knocking my arms back down, then laid his head against the arm of the chair, cramming his body into the seat. I crawled back onto the couch. Neither of us wanted to be alone.

"Logan," I whispered after a long buzzing silence, "thanks for always protecting me."

"I wasn't protecting you, Violet. I was just trying to figure shit out."

"I'm sorry it happened that way. You know, with the Tat and Mom and stuff."

"It's all right, Bean Brain. It's all past. It's just you and me now."

15

Six days till Christmas and no word from my dad. No word from Henry, either. There was this awkward new-found closeness with Logan and sporadic moments of nausea with my mom, who in two days had changed in ways I had not imagined possible. She was a full-blown hurricane, ordering Logan and me around until every piece of silver, every sliver of wood, every fold of curtain, was absolutely spic-and-span. Then we cooked. It turned out Logan had learned to make outstanding rice and beans from a Mexican woman who lived down the hall from him at school, and it seemed we might be living solely on variations of that until finally my mom broke down and gave us a three-hour reprieve to Woodsbury Mall.

"You drive, love," said my mom, dangling her fingers in front of me, "I don't want to smudge anything."

I reached out grudgingly, thinking about her with her lover, and not wanting our skin to touch, but Logan swiped the keys out of my hand. He seemed to have rebounded easily from the other night's turn of events, though he smiled at me now, when my mom wasn't looking, in such tender ways that seemed to indicate I'd been initiated into some sort of special club and he wanted to make sure I was holding up all right.

"I want to take that baby for one more spin," Logan said. "Or what's left of her." And we sped off to Woodsbury, me catching the views from the backseat, because naturally my mom wasn't going to sit there even if it was my car.

"Any news from Dad yet?" I asked.

"No, missy. No news from your father."

"Aren't you worried?" Logan asked.

"Why should I be?" She gingerly slid on her sunglasses (even though the sky was gray) and blew on her nails some more, peering at them over the huge black tops of her Jackie-O's.

"Well, don't you think something might have happened to him?"

"I *know* what happened to him. He moved out."

"But it's pretty unlike him, don't you think, to just move out and never phone?" Logan's voice had an exasperated edge.

"No, I don't think so." She handed me back her purse. "Pull out my cigarettes, will you, love?" She was now smoking Winston 100s. Then she turned toward Logan and said, "I also don't think it's any of your business." She pushed in my virgin cigarette lighter and waited for the coils to heat.

"None of my business? He's our fucking father!"

"Yes, and the last I heard, I'm your fucking mother!"

She lit up and looked hard out the front window. I tried to imagine her having sex in the middle of a school-day afternoon with a stranger. It made my stomach hurt.

"What's that supposed to mean?"

I could see foam resting in the corner of Logan's mouth the way it always did when he was especially mad. It was the precursor to the rage, a clear sign to seek cover, though it had been a while since it had paid us a visit, so maybe I was wrong.

"What it means is, it would be nice if you two had some of the same concern for me as you do for your father. I'm the one who's been walked out on, you know?" My head started throbbing on account of all the smoke and the whole parental thing.

"We know that, Mom, and we are concerned about you, but we're perhaps more concerned about Dad at the moment, because we don't know where the fuck he is."

"He's fine."

She pulled out my virgin ashtray, flicked in some glowing ash.

"How do you know?"

"Because your father is *always* all right. Okay? Can we talk about something else, please?" We drove the rest of the way to Woodsbury Mall in blessed Hitchcock silence.

At the mall we agreed to go our separate ways. I hadn't bought any presents yet and was contemplating what to get for my dad, even though I wasn't sure I'd see him, when I spotted Ryder. He looked clean and sweet, flipping through a copy of *Leaves of Grass* and humming, while pinkish, twinkling lights encircled his head like a halo.

"Hey, Let," he said when he looked up and saw me.

"Hey." I chewed on my inner lip, aggravating the soreness from the Saturday-night marathon with Logan.

"Merry Christmas, man." He moved closer.

"Sorry." I flipped through some book like maybe I was reading the flaps or something, which I wasn't. What I was doing was feeling lousy. I kept picturing Ryder sitting there in that chair, and it got me all sad. I couldn't make heads nor tails of this Ryder/Henry juggling act I seemed to have going on.

"I know, man. I know."

"I guess I got a bit too drunk. You know, lack of judgment. But it was wrong, and I'm sorry."

"Truth. It's over."

I nodded, Ryder's use of *truth* striking me a bit differently now. He didn't seem surprised to see me, though I noticed he still held the book in his hands, tossing it back and forth in a slow, kind of restless rhythm.

"Shopping?"

"Some."

"Me too."

Ryder set the book down on the display table, smiling up at me with astonishing grace. For a moment I thought I saw a sparkling of the shine behind the bluey-blue of his eyes, but it was gone before I could be certain. We drifted through the mall, which was scented with cinnamon and real fir trees, no cheeseball stuff. Ryder's arms dangled next to mine, and I remember I felt strangely happy then, as if there were no nicer time on earth than that particular moment.

Tiffany's was surprisingly empty when we sauntered through, and I picked out a sterling water-can key chain for my mom to replace the green-vinyl number one of my dad's clients had passed her way. While it was being gift-wrapped, I checked out the glass display cases full of knickknacks, which were about as high on my list of things to have as chicken pox, but this angel sitting on a cloud of Tiffany-blue velvet caught my eye. It was no bigger than my thumb, cast in sterling silver, and there was something about the curve of the angel's wing and the tilt of the head seemingly drawn back by the weight of its halo that made me want it.

"Pretty," I said, feeling somewhat silly when Ryder walked up.

"A guardian, man," Ryder said.

"How can you tell?"

"Look at the weight of the halo. The heavier the halo, the more intense the mission." And I was struck again by Ryder's knack for staying in line with my thoughts.

· · · ·

Ryder and I met up with my mom and Logan beneath one of the giant Christmas trees. My mom looked wired, pacing back and forth while Logan sprawled out on a bench, feet spread, staring off into the far distance. She seemed to take it for granted that Ryder was with me and hustled him toward the car with a "You must join us for dinner, love. It's too horrible to think of you alone in that boarding school of yours."

"Thank you," Ryder said. "I'd love to, but I'm not alone, you know. Freddie, Marvin, Briggs. We're like a family, because it's not about blood, it's about truth."

It was around then that I started noticing how in a lot of ways Ryder was wise beyond his years. I mean, he was only sixteen, same as I was, but he knew what made, and unmade, a family. To tell you the truth, I didn't know what was up with my mom, inviting Ryder over like that when she'd been making us live such cloistered lives, and hadn't seemed to like him in the first place, but it was A-OK with me.

I started getting that Christmas tickle where you just feel happy no matter what. I liked Christmas. We attended midnight Mass every year. I loved all the pomp and circumstance. I'd inhale my mom's perfume, heavier than ever, because on Christmas she always wore the real thing, no dabbling with eau de cologne. And I'd squish between Logan and my dad, waiting for the hymns, remaining silent as my father's voice rose so passionately above the rest. Plus, I felt it gave me a formal way to communicate with God, and before entering the candlelit chapel, I always made sure my roadkill lists were in order.

During the ride home, Logan and Ryder were getting along like old pals, which was weird, considering Logan never paid attention to anyone my age. Ryder kept leaning over Logan's seat, jabbering about Montana.

"How about the cowboys?" Logan said. "I bet they're real jerk-off dickheads."

"Some of them are. Some of them get it, though."

"Get what?"

"It's about the land, the beauty, the vastness. It's about the whole and breathing into it, being part of the one."

"Right on," Logan said, although I'd never heard him say one thing about the whole before—his spiel usually harped on the individual and how to endure. My mom, of course, suddenly thought Ryder was the cat's pajamas on account of his sounding like those New Age self-help books she was always sticking her nose in. For once, this turned out to be okay, because when we got home, instead of insisting Logan and I cook again, my mom traipsed into the kitchen, flipped on the radio, spun around to some old dance tunes, and whipped up a shepherd's pie for "the boys" and a truly yummy stir-fry for me.

. . . .

After dinner, Ryder and I locked ourselves away in the sun room. Ryder stretched out in the armchair, feet spread wide in front of him, toes turned out, just the way Logan always sat, as if an hour or two of my brother had changed his very being. I remember looking at him really closely then, as if I needed to memorize his features for a final exam, and seeing in the swelling of his lips, in the strain of his neck, in the hushed spread of his shoulders, something of Logan— a caged frenzy to the eyes on an otherwise placid face.

"How the English do eat." He grinned in my direction, slid the flask out of his back pocket and took a swig. "Your mom seems divided. Split energy. Like a daisy chain pulled apart."

I nodded. "Well, my dad's missing, or at least she says he is, so I guess that has her a bit more crazy than usual. But she's pretty much crazy anyway. It's like she's falling or something, only I'm not sure what's going to catch her."

I was surprised at my own words, having never discussed my family this way, except maybe the other night with Logan. Ryder didn't say anything, but he didn't look bored, either, so I continued.

"I think she knows she's falling, because she tries to latch on to us to kind of break the descent or at least slow it. I don't know how to explain it—she's just crazy. Trust me."

"Truth. My parents are crazy, too, man. Completely crazed."

"How?"

"Shit, man, I don't know. Michael's a crazy bastard. But Betty loves him too much to be free. When he's sober and not hung over, which is a tough combo to land, he's cool. Used to be real athletic, but now he's lost most of his stamina and agility. That's the real reason we gave up the horses. He tried to ride one day and couldn't keep his seat. Shit, he barely even got on Mercy in the first place. One of the hands had to shove him up and tie the reins to his wrists. Every time he fell he'd pull the horse's head down with him. Finally he started kicking Mercy and screaming at her. Punching her in the face. A bunch of us pulled him off, but Mercy was never the same. Not after that."

"What happened to her?"

"The ranch we boarded her and Vengeance at bought them. So Betty and I used to drive out sometimes for a visit, but it started to depress Betty, so we had to quit."

"Didn't all the drinking and stuff affect your dad's work?"

"In his field, they almost encourage assholes. It makes you more interesting."

Ryder reached toward me for the flask.

"How come it never seems to upset you? I mean, you seem so okay about the way your family treats you."

"Well, what am I going to do?"

"I don't know. Get angry."

"Get angry at what, man? They're just people, too."

"But they're not just people. They're your parents."

"No, man, if you lock them in that cage of expectation, you're just going to get hurt."

"So are you saying I shouldn't trust my own parents?"

"Trust? Whoa, where did that come from? No, trust is good. Where you can find it. Expectations that others should be the way that you want them to be. That's what will get you into trouble." And he touched my face so gently, it was as if a butterfly had swept by.

. . . .

After a bit, my mom came in to tell me my dad had finally phoned. He was staying at the Peacetown Hotel and would be joining us for Christmas Eve.

"Didn't he want to speak with me? Did Logan talk to him?"

"He sent his love," she said. "I'm sure he'll give you a call in the morning."

When my mom left the room, I noticed how my whole body hurt and that my breath seemed caught in my chest.

"It's all right," Ryder said. "It doesn't change anything in here." And he put his hand to his heart. But it felt as if he'd put it on mine.

"Do you want to sleep here?" I asked, noticing the late hour on the grandfather clock. "I mean, will you get in trouble with Mr. Briggs or anything?"

Ryder shook his head, so I led him upstairs. His hand felt small in mine, but secure. He squeezed my fingers in time with every step. On the landing I considered drawing him into my room. I doubted that my mother would even notice. I doubted that she noticed Ryder wasn't already halfway back to school, nor had she considered how he'd get there, what with me grounded, Logan already cloistered in his room, and Ryder without a car. But a voice in the back of my head said, *Not yet*. I wanted this to be right. I wanted this to feel like nothing that had come before.

"The guest room is cool," Ryder said, squeezing my hand again. I directed him there, hoping my dad didn't decide to make a surprise visit in the dead of night.

I helped him pull back the sheets and showed him where the bathroom was and what towels to use. I found myself taking longer with the details than was really necessary. A strange, nervous calm spread through my body.

"It's all right," Ryder finally said. "There's no rush."

I wasn't sure that I agreed with him. I inexplicably felt there was a rush. In fact, I felt myself inseparable from the rush, but I wasn't sure where the surge was taking me.

• • • •

Later, in my room, I was overwhelmed and couldn't sleep. I felt as if I needed to put closure on Henry; that he still somehow held a part of me that needed to be freed before I could be with Ryder.

I wrote him a letter. I meant it to distance us, hoping that the formality of the written word would help me wrench back that part of my soul that was still so addicted to him. I chose the words carefully, using my thesaurus a lot so that he would be impressed, but I suppose the sentiment was a little off. Henry was like a bar and I was a binger. As long as I steered clear of his street and found healthy alternatives to his sweet taste, I was all right. But even a baby toe back on his block, and my body ached. Thinking I could write him a good-bye letter was foolish.

But I did it all the same. I wrote about what he had meant to me, how he'd changed my life and how good it was that we'd both moved on. It was all very positive and forward, but between the lines was the space for more of the same. In retrospect I suppose I was balancing the unfamiliar feelings of secure and reliable affection with the familiar feelings of chaos and doubt. But that night as I snuggled back deep beneath the flannel sheets, drawing Whiz Bang's tiny purring body toward mine, I felt strangely elated and comforted by this Henry-outpouring, as if a mere stroke of the pen could change my life.

But my life was already changing. Because that night in the sun room, shrouded in failing daylight, I had begun to descend into the astonishingly electric quicksand of Ryder Hadley.

16

In the morning I was given a temporary reprieve to drive Ryder home. My mom seemed to take it for granted that Ryder had spent the night, as if that was the way it should be.

"Can never have too many men in the house," she'd said, poking me in the side. Logan was still in his room. When I dropped Ryder off at the foot of the Greek theater, he kissed me good-bye. He somehow tasted of jelly beans, and it made me laugh. I liked Ryder. I really did, but it was like something inside of me wouldn't let me like him all the way. I was going to fix that.

On the way back from Hillstream I'd pulled onto the Edwards grounds, walked the tree-lined path to Henry's door, and slipped my letter beneath it. I sat in his drive for a bit, listening to my blood trickle its shine-free course through my veins. I could feel Henry through the morning air, and just knowing he was up there—sleeping or moving around, eating, smoking one of those skinny joints like he always rolled, or taking a shower, washing out the sleepy dust caught in his sweet eyes—let me feel the heat of his body, the sunken curve of his chest, the saltiness of his mouth, and I was nervous that it would take more than a letter to free me. So I consciously drew on my British roots and vowed that any future Henry-feelings I would simply repress.

• • • •

Ryder came by a few nights later for dinner. He and Logan were horsing around in the den while I helped my mom whip up some rabbit stew, which grossed me out beyond description. I was working on the regulation salad and bread/cheese fare that accompanied everything we Hitchcocks ate.

"So is Dad still coming for dinner on Saturday?" I asked, Saturday being Christmas Eve.

"As far as I know he is, but you never can tell with that man, can you?"

I had always felt like you *could* tell, that maybe his moods were a bit swingy, no doubt due to having a head full of clouds, but, yes, you could tell. You definitely could tell.

"What time will he be by?"

"Well, let me see, where was it I posted his itinerary?" My mom lit up a cigarette with one hand and stirred the stew with the other. She never used to smoke while cooking.

"Is he going to spend the night?"

"I imagine so." A slight wiggle of happiness wrestled its way up my spine, thinking about my dad being home again, even if just for one night. Being trapped in the house as I was, I'd been losing touch with the roadkills, and I took a minute then to think about every one I'd most recently passed and did some in-my-head cross work, preparing for our night at church.

. . . .

After dinner, Ryder followed me upstairs when I went to grab my sweater. I sat on the bed and watched him in the mirror while he seemed to touch everything in my room. Even CJ had never taken such an interest in my stuff.

"Cool," he said, smiling. He was always smiling at me. "It's nice to be in a real room again."

"Don't you ever want to go back there? To Montana, I mean?"

"All the time, man. All the time."

"Well, why don't you?"

"You can only be in one place at a time, and right now it's here with you." Ryder had moved closer to me and lowered himself to the bed. His voice became heavy, unnatural. I thought about Henry for a minute. I wondered if he'd read my letter and what he thought of it. I wondered if someone had been behind the curtain that night or if it had just been the breeze. I wondered if he thought about me when I wasn't around, the way I thought about him. I wondered if when he was about to kiss another girl, which I hoped was never, I popped up in his head and what I felt like there. I wondered if he'd care that I was with Ryder, and guessed the answer was probably no. And then I repressed the thoughts.

I knew Ryder was going to kiss me even before he did it. I knew, in that moment, I was going to like it, too, but before we got very far, Logan shouted up the stairs, "What's taking you guys so long?" So we had to go join him.

• • • •

Later, when Ryder was asleep in the guest room, which seemed to be fast becoming his second residence—third, really, if you count Montana—and Logan was hidden away in his room and my mom was God knows where, my phone began ringing. Although I was wide awake, the late-night intrusion, for it must have been at least midnight, startled me—angered me, too, depending, of course, on who it turned out to be. Henry? My long-lost dad? I picked it up on the third ring.

"Hello." I made my voice sound slower, thicker than I was actually feeling.

"I read your letter, baby. Keep the fuck away from him!" A familiar voice. A voice I knew and trusted.

"What? Who is this?"

"You know who this is. Henry is mine. *Mine!* Keep your distance."

"Anna?" I said, my voice quivering in the night. But the line was dead.

• • • •

So that was the first I learned of Henry and the Tat, although it seemed preposterous and in the fierce morning light, I couldn't be absolutely certain it was the Tat's voice after all.

The second circuit of insight occurred the following afternoon when Logan, Ryder, and I were sitting around my bedroom, enjoying a bottle of Southern Comfort Ryder had managed to sneak in with him. Logan had a harried, desperate look about him, perhaps due to not having shaved for a day or two, which was way unlike him. Ryder, as per normal, looked rested and peaceful.

"Perfect," Ryder said.

"Perfect, what?" Logan asked.

"Perfect moment, man." He passed the bottle back to Logan, skipping over me. I was taking a breather.

"Right on," Logan said, streaks of sunlight resting on the worn skin beneath his eyes. It was strange to see Logan drinking again, although no bad had come of it yet. Outside, it was clear and bright, despite the cold. The bottle was circulating freely, as was my mind, and it was only one o'clock or perhaps two. We three were alone in the house, Ryder's absence seemingly unnoticed at Hillstream, me still grounded, which struck me as vaguely absurd since my mom wasn't around enough to keep track of me anyhow, and Logan not seeming to want to stir, content to sit with us and drink. It was all kind of nice. It was like *The Cat in the Hat* again, only now Logan was there with us, too. Then the phone rang.

"Hello," I said, staring out the window, remembering the feel of hot sun on my face. Logan and Ryder were behind me, laughing.

"Baby girl," came his voice, and my heart beat frenetically within my chest, though I tried and tried to calm it.

"Hey."

"We need to talk."

"Do we?"

"We do indeed, baby girl. I got your letter." He dangled it like a string before a kitten. I remained silent. Uncertain. Electrified.

"Baby girl, baby girl. I didn't know how much you cared."

"Why did you let the Tat read it and all?"

"Who?"

But I couldn't bring myself to say her real name.

"We need to talk. You need to understand."

"Understand what?" I whispered, on account of my voice going all soft and limp and because at the mention of the Tat, Logan had hushed up; I felt him behind me, listening. Ryder was silent, too.

"About us, baby girl. Come by."

"I'm grounded."

"You'll find a way."

And everything I'd repressed was free again.

I hung up and turned toward my brother's expectant face.

"So you know?" said Logan, looking right through me with wide, burning eyes, green, so very green they were almost the color of grass. I nodded, close to tears.

"For how long?"

"The Tat phoned last night."

"What did she say?"

I shrugged.

"What did she say, Let?"

I looked down at my feet, feeling as if I'd betrayed both brother and almost boyfriend in the simple motion of lifting the receiver from its cradle, allowing the darkness in.

"She said to keep away from Henry."

"What?"

"She told me to keep the fuck away from Henry," I said, looking defiantly at the both of them, then sat on the edge of my bed and cried. I was suddenly overwhelmed by the complexity of it all. By the sheer frustration of hankering for someone who sometimes hankers for you and sometimes doesn't, but seems to mostly want you right when you're feeling kind of settled without him. Right when you're feeling kind of settled with somebody else. And the humiliation of knowing on a way-deep gut level that you're smarter than the mess you've gotten yourself into, but it doesn't matter. You are in deep.

Logan bolted from my room, ricocheting off the door frame on the way out, leaving me with Ryder. And part of me thought, *Perfect. Sitting here alone with Ryder is perfect.* And the other part thought, *I wonder what my mom would do if I broke my grounding?*

· · · ·

After a bit, my mom came home from wherever it was she had been, several more blond streaks gracing her hair, although far more subtle than the copycat versions that ran down the front.

"What's for lunch?" she yelled up the stairs, but none of us stirred. "Is there anyone in this house besides me?"

I could hear her shuffling bags of something around. I went down, feeling drowsy and depressed.

"What's for lunch, missy?" she asked again when I walked into the kitchen. She had a glass of wine in one hand and a glowing Winston in the other.

"I dunno. We haven't eaten yet, either."

"Where's your brother? And is that Ryder still here?"

I nodded.

"Don't you think that they might miss him back at school? Lord knows I don't want a copper knocking on my door." She leaned against the counter, smoothing her hair with her cigarette hand.

"I thought you liked him."

"Like him, smike him. He's a boy who needs proper supervision like the rest of you."

I wasn't sure if this was an indication of Dr. Applegate's return or not. In fact I couldn't vibe from any of her recent actions Dr. Applegate's current status.

"You didn't seem to mind that he was staying here before."

She looked distracted, only half aware of my presence or even where she was.

"Stay here? He can die here for all I care, just as long as he has the proper permission from that school of his. Make sure he does, missy, or it's on your head. I can't be expected to watch his every move, can I? If he insists on staying with us, like an orphan in a storm, then it's rather out of my hands. Now lunch, missy. I'm famished."

. . . .

And so it went—Logan, Ryder, and me more or less living as we chose, never leaving the house, except for the one time Logan took Ryder back to school to collect his things and, I suppose, make arrangements with Mr. Briggs; then there was another trip to the liquor store to fortify our stock of Southern Comfort, which we'd all begun drinking with great relish, but most especially Logan, who'd continued to slip beyond my reach.

We became oddly domestic, sharing the chores of ordering in food, rinsing out the glasses, though anything that required the outside world Logan took care of. My mom had hidden the keys to the Flame, and Ryder refused to leave me.

One night when we were all tucked in our beds, I heard my door creak open. At first I thought it was my mother suddenly wanting to bond, so I faked sleep. Then I felt his sweet breath across my closed eyes, and I knew it was Ryder.

He didn't have a condom with him, so I managed to find the one CJ had given me, what felt like a lifetime ago. Ryder and I squirmed and giggled under the bed trying to locate it, and he kissed me so many times, in so many delicious ways, that I banged my head on the box springs before routing it out.

Ryder wasn't an expert at putting on condoms. He couldn't arch back, looking all pretty, and slip it on at the same time. He didn't seem to notice if the light was on or off, let alone direct it in some way. He didn't call me baby girl. And he didn't roll over and grab his beer when we were through.

Instead, he held me until it was morning, then sneaked back into the guest room right before my mother got up.

• • • •

"I'd really love to cream that fucking punk," Logan said. Our mom was out, and Logan, Ryder, and I had left the confines of my bedroom and were seated around the kitchen table. It felt almost eerie to be in there again, like when you go back to the house you grew up in, but somebody else lives there now. We were drinking my mom's wine, as the Southern Comfort had run dry, and waiting for the Chinese food we'd ordered to arrive. Though to tell you the truth, it felt as if we were waiting for more than carryout. It felt as if we were waiting for enlightenment.

Logan pushed aside his glass and began drinking straight from the bottle. He tilted his chair back and rested it against the countertop, looking completely wild in his snakeskin leathers and purple satin shirt. Logan was still talking about Henry.

"I hear you, man," said Ryder, "but release it. Feel the now."

Ryder pushed his knee up against mine under the table, and we had interlaced our fingers. Logan, with the sheer speed of light, shot out of his chair, grabbed Ryder by his T-shirt, and jammed his finger right into his face. Our hands came undone, and my heart started racing.

"Listen, you little punk. Don't go telling me what to do. I got more muscle in my pinkie than you do in your whole body. If I want to be bummed that my old lady is fucking my sister's boyfriend, then I'll be bummed. You got that?"

"Truth," Ryder said, holding up both hands above his head as if he were being robbed.

Logan held on to him a moment longer, spit building in the corners of his mouth—the rage, I thought, nervous at the possibility it was surfacing again—then set him free. He sat down again, leaning back into his chair and pulling a joint from his shirt pocket, then lit up and passed it around.

"He wasn't really my boyfriend," I said, after a bit, staring at the crackling glow I held between my fingers, "I mean, not really, you know." I felt uncomfortable speaking about Henry like this with Ryder there, plus the aforementioned not-being-accustomed-to-discussing-my-sex-life-with-Logan scenario and the two situations combined felt like a bit much.

"That's nice, Bean Brain. You're just fucking the guy, but he's not your boyfriend. The old folks did a fine job raising you."

My eyes swelled with tears.

"It's in the past," Ryder said. He squeezed my hand again beneath the table.

"Let it go, right?" Logan looked like he was going to lunge again, but he didn't.

After a bit I said, "How'd you find out anyway?"

"She went back for her fucking book." And I thought for a moment about the yoga book lying on the carved-up wooden table at John's and how easy it would have been to swing back to the café when we realized we'd left it behind and how insistent the Tat had been that she could just get it later. I wondered if she'd been planning what was happening now from the second she first saw Henry. And strangely I was glad. Not that Logan was hurting. But that it was somehow through chasing down Henry that I arrived at Ryder.

"I was flipping through it one day, killing time, and there on the front page the fucker had written, 'For a good time, call' and his number."

He took another swig.

"After Anna confessed to everything I broke it off with her. Six years out the window. But I took her back and now she's chasing after that asshole again." He stopped here, as if saying the words had somehow caused his throat to seal up. His jaw tightened, and his fingers moved in and out of a fist. Then everyone grew silent.

Finally the food arrived and over the chop suey, Logan said, "Sorry."

"Peace," said Ryder.

"I'm sorry about Anna," I said. That was the second time I'd comforted my brother in a matter of days, and to tell you the truth, it didn't feel exactly right.

Then Logan opened another bottle of wine. And that was it. We were a family again.

• • • •

Later that night, when we four were all tucked into our separate beds, I had the overwhelming urge to hear Henry's voice, and I hoped that soon Logan would stop talking about him. I wanted to find out what it was he had called to tell me, although I already knew. Some unexpected twang of guilt had forced him to call with an apology of sorts, an explanation for the havoc he was wreaking on my family, all of which he thought could be forgiven with a simple "we need to talk," knowing the talk would never take place, the basic act of offering it being enough to get him off the hook.

Then I heard the creak of my door and could see Ryder outlined in the faint light, and I smiled. He was out of his clothes before he even reached the bed.

"When we're old and gray," he whispered in my ear.

"And have a family of our own," I whispered back.

"We'll always be happy."

And in that moment I could see Ryder was just like the rest of us. He was looking for family, too.

17

A thick, glowing light sneaked beneath my door. I lay in bed, tucked between red flannel sheets. Ryder had tiptoed back to his bed just before dawn, allowing me a couple hours of sleep. I could hear the familiar huff and click of feet against the ceramic kitchen floor downstairs. I lay there a minute, allowing the sweet calm that only such a simple sound could produce to fill me. It was the footfall of my dad. Then I dashed downstairs, jumping them two at a time, anticipating the hard sweep of his embrace. But there was none.

It was Christmas Eve.

My dad sat at the kitchen table, the newspaper spread before him, looking dazed and worn—a shipwrecked sailor on land again after weeks and weeks at sea.

"Good morning, Violet," he said, extending his cheek a little to the right, perhaps in preparation for a kiss, but I slunk away.

"Good morning." I went to the stove, heated water for my tea.

"How have things been?"

I shrugged, thinking about Ryder asleep upstairs between crisp white sheets and Logan staring out his window, waiting to be missed before appearing, and all the drunk-up bottles of booze knocking around beneath my bed on account of our not having figured how to get them out of the house.

"Okay, I guess." I dunked my tea bag around a bit and sat down opposite him. "How about you? Are you still at the Peacetown?" It felt like a strange question to ask my dad.

"I am and I have a damn nice room, too. You and Logan will have to visit soon."

"Are you coming home?"

"No. I don't think so, Violet. At least not right now."

"Why?"

"Because things are not as they should be, are they? They're all rather cockeyed and out of order."

"Ryder says order is just a way of not dealing with the truth."

"He did, did he?" He paused a moment, then looked at the paper. "Have you been seeing more of Ryder lately?"

"He's been kind of staying here." My dad looked back up, his moon-face open, round and smooth, unlined by time.

"Staying here. Did Hillstream send him down?"

"No. I think he just got lonely there and all. Plus what with Mom grounding me, it can be a bit boring here, just me and Logan, so it's been nice to have him around."

I looked out the window. The first major storm of the winter was brewing, blackening the sky. I heard the floorboards above our heads creak and knew from the noise's placement Ryder was up.

"I see," said my dad, feeling, I knew, uncertain of his

place of command now. Ryder staying in the house disturbed him, but it was no longer his domain, his kingdom. Or was it?

. . . .

Later that day I ran into Henry. My father, seeming to forget my grounding, had sent me to Kroger's, while keeping Ryder behind. Henry and I met among the cans of cranberries and brightly colored boxes of Jell-O.

"What did you want to tell me?" I asked, smelling his smell creeping up me and trying to force it down.

"Not here," he said, leaning against a shelf of cereal, sliding his fingers into his leathers like he always did.

"Well, where?"

"Not here. Later. Somewhere else." He looked at me leisurely, as if deciding whether to bid or not when I hit the block.

"I already know," I said.

"I know you do."

"Well, then what is there really to discuss and all?"

"You tell me."

He slid his fingers along the hollow of his chest.

"Well, why did you phone me?" My hands were still resting on the handle of my cart. I flipped around some bananas I'd selected, arranging them more becomingly in the red plastic seat.

"Why do you think?"

I shrugged. "Because you felt lousy about fucking my brother's girlfriend?"

"I didn't know she was your brother's girlfriend at the time."

"So you just thought she was a friend of mine and that was just fine. I wouldn't mind if you were fucking one of my friends. Who cares, right?"

"Whoa, baby girl. I don't see a collar around my neck." And he stuck his hands up in the air as if I held a gun.

"Well then, why did you call?" I kind of yelled, though I didn't want to. My chest heaved up and down, while Henry tilted his head to the side and waited. So I waited, too, waited for him to say, "Because I really do care, because I really am crazy for you, because your letter, your sweet letter, helped me see the error of my ways." And I wondered what I would do if he did say all that.

"I dunno, baby girl. I truly don't. I felt bad, that's all. I like you. You're a nice kid, and once Anna told me about Logan knowing, I didn't want you to misunderstand."

"Misunderstand? What is there to misunderstand? You were fucking my brother's girlfriend. And you let her read my fucking letter. What's there to misunderstand in that?"

"Listen, baby girl. I like you. I liked you from the first time I saw you, but I'm not ready to get married or anything. You got that?"

"And the Tat? Do you like the Tat, too?"

He nodded, his dark hair flipping back and forth in rhythm with his fine head.

"Do you like her more than me?"

"No, not more. Differently."

"Are there others?"

"There were always others. I never pretended otherwise."

"But you did," I said. "You did pretend otherwise."

"You misunderstood."

He pushed his long body forward from his shoulders

and turned back to his cart. And I remember wanting him then, with the most supernatural kind of lust ever known on this earth. He rolled, hip by hip, away from me, sweatshirt hood dangling down his narrow back, keys jangling, boots clanking, and I abandoned my cart to dash after him, grab him by the wrist.

"It doesn't have to be this way."

"What way?"

"Like this. We could go to your place right now. We could do whatever you wanted."

He'd let his wrist lie firmly in my grasp, but began to wiggle free.

"Let, stop it."

"No, take me there, Henry. Please take me there."

"No. You're making a fool out of yourself." And he slid free. I thought of Ryder. My trippy cowboy who crossed his heart every night before slipping from my room. "This is forever, man," he'd say, and I would stare at my ceiling, draw Whiz Bang to my chest, and cry.

• • • •

When I told Logan I'd seen Henry, told him privately after pulling him into a corner of the TV room, he flipped. I'm not sure why I told him. I suppose I felt obligated now. Plus I needed to release a little of my own anger and hurt. Clearly, Logan wasn't the person to release it to.

After he kicked over the coffee table and couch, both my parents and Ryder were in the room, watching. I tried to calm Logan, but I don't think he heard a word I was saying. Ryder tried, too, but Logan turned on him so fast that my dad had to intervene.

"What exactly is going on here?" he said. His voice halfway between order and alarm.

"Nothing you're not already familiar with," Logan said. Spit shot out of the side of his mouth.

"Logan, I don't know what you're talking about. Why don't we clean up the mess and discuss this later?"

"Because later always sucks just as much as now."

My father had started to right the table, but Logan kicked it back again, jostling my father into the wall.

"Christ, Logan, now you are getting out of line." My dad drew himself up and moved toward Logan. They stood so close, you could sense the heat leaving one and entering the other.

"Am I? And here I thought I was following right straight in your line."

"What the hell are you going on about?" My dad's voice remained eerily calm.

"Anna and Henry." My dad just stared at him, so Logan continued. "Anna fucking Henry. My girlfriend going out on me. Deceiving me. Breaking my trust. Then my taking her back, like an asshole. Sound familiar?"

I thought my dad was going to slap Logan right then, and he probably would have, except my mom started crying and dashed out of the room.

"Logan, you can really be an ass," my dad said.

"Yeah, well, I had a good teacher."

My heart was pounding so hard, it made me nauseous.

"Logan, goddamn it, you get up to your room this instant, or so help me God, you'll be sorry. I may not live here anymore, but I am still your father!" My dad's face blazed red. It was the first time I'd ever heard him yell. Ryder wrapped his hand around mine. I could tell he wanted to say something that would make things better, but didn't know what.

"Oh, yeah, like I'm really afraid of you. What are you going to do to me? Same as you did to Mom and her lover man? Which was nothing. The Big Nothing."

"How dare you!"

"How dare I? I'll tell you how I dare. I don't just sit around on my pussy ass and let things happen to me. That's how I dare. My girlfriend started fucking around on me, and, yes, I had a moment of weakness, admittedly so, but you don't see her here tonight, do you?"

"I suggest that you calm yourself, son, then apologize to your mother. You and I will continue this discussion at a later time."

"No. I don't want to calm down. That's how things happen to you, when you're calm and untouchable. I don't want to apologize to my mother. What she did was disgusting. She ought to fucking apologize to me. I don't want to discuss this at a later time. I want to get it right out in the open now. There's no reason Let shouldn't hear, it involves her, too."

"Logan, this is not the appropriate time for this type of conversation."

"Why? Because we have company?" He gestured toward Ryder. "Or because it's fucking Christmas Eve and everyone is supposed to be full of thanks and good cheer? Well, maybe I don't have any good cheer in me. Maybe that bloodsucker upstairs sucked me dry while you calmly waited for the appropriate time to deal with it."

Then I saw my dad do something I'd never seen him do before. He began to cry. First his chest heaved a little bit as if he were choking, then his eyes became bloodshot, welling with tears that flowed down his cheeks. He remained like this for what seemed a lifetime, while I contemplated soothing him, but before I could make my decision, he simply walked out of the room.

Logan looked at Ryder and me, then walked out, too.

And for a moment it felt as if the house were tipping sideways, as if the weight of the foundation had somehow shifted. And I realized it was because, for once, nothing was in its right place.

· · · ·

My mom had prepared a feast for dinner, turkey, brandied sweet potatoes, Yorkshire pudding, the works, but none of us ate it. When it was time to leave for church, most of it was still on the kitchen table.

"Is Logan coming?" I asked, the four of us lined up awkwardly in the hall while my dad fumbled for his keys.

"No," he answered, preoccupied with pockets and drawers.

The dam was breaking, and he hadn't enough fingers to plug the holes. But I could already see him begin to try. I could see by the way he stood a little in front of my mother the rest of the evening or the way he answered all the questions directed at her that he was back in the role of protector, fearful of what would happen if he deserted her. Would she survive? And I realized then he savored that role.

This is not what I want from love, I thought.

"I want to say good-bye, then." I raced up the stairs before they could complain and knocked on his door.

"Logan, it's me, Let."

"What do you want?"

"Merry Christmas, Logan."

"Merry Christmas."

"Logan?"

"What?"

"Come to church, Logan." *Come to dinner, Logan. Come downstairs, Logan. Come, Logan, come.*

"I can't."

"Why not?"

"It's obvious."

"Ryder and I want you to." I leaned my cheek against his door, holding the brass knob in my hand.

"Go away, Let."

"But, Logan—"

"Go away!"

Downstairs my mom and dad waited by the door, their coats buttoned high, their gloves fitting snugly. Ryder leaned against the white wall, watching me. *What more is there to know?* I wondered. *What other secrets linger in this house, sleep undetected on old blankets in the boiler room, pace tirelessly in the attic? And what power do secrets hold? What happens to a secret when it's no longer a secret? And what happens to the people involved?*

I could hear the car warming in the drive outside. A light snow was falling, a hoax played by the morning's dark brew; distant neighbors' Christmas lights twinkling like stars in a fallen sky.

"Ready?" asked my dad, and I nodded, feeling Ryder at my side. On the way to church, we sat two in the front, two in the back, each head turned out as in a synchronized water ballet. But I reached across the cool leather seat and squeezed Ryder's waiting hand.

18

When we left midnight Mass, the storm was in full course, so my dad spent the night after all, leaving Ryder to the couch. Ryder had woken me early, sliding out of his pj's and into my bed, encircling me from behind.

"A gift, man," he'd said, laying a blue Tiffany's box across my pillow.

"My angel." I lifted out the tiny silver guardian, heavy halo, glowing skull.

"So nobody can fuck with you." And he pushed my hair from my face, crossing his heart like he always did when he spoke sweet-talk to me.

I'd placed my angel on the sill above my bed, figuring she'd keep an eye on me and all, while I slept.

"The Guardian, man."

"The Guardian." And I'd nestled my head into the comfort of Ryder's chest, sleeping soundly until the sun rose.

· · · ·

Right off, when I went downstairs, I ran into my dad, who was tending the fire and humming to himself.

"I'm sorry about how things have been lately," I said impulsively. "You know, all the drinking and stuff. I'm not going to be like that anymore."

"I know you're sorry," he said with a softened voice, and I wanted him to take me up in his heavy arms and let me know that he loved me no matter what, but he turned back toward the hearth, stirring the logs with his long brass poker. I stood behind him for several minutes more, waiting, but he never turned back. Later my mom came down, looking surprisingly fresh and alert, followed by Ryder, and lastly Logan, looking the worse for wear, as my mom would say, his face gray and lifeless, his hair a snarl of refusal.

We emptied our stockings—a makeshift sock hung for Ryder—and opened our presents. Then we ate tomato bread and drank tea. My dad showed no signs of leaving, instead setting up shop in the den as he always had before. And Ryder was allowed to stay on, or else his presence was simply forgotten, which was more than likely the case, since Logan and I weren't paid much heed, either. Things returned to normal, I suppose, but there was this weird undertow of never-never land which kept me thinking if I didn't swim hard enough, I'd end up there, too.

I was still grounded, although it was to end in time for New Year's Eve. Ricky Johnson was, of course, having a bash that CJ and I were planning to attend, the plans having been made before our falling out. I hadn't seen her at all during vacation and had only spoken with her once when she phoned, no doubt out of obligation, to see how the holidays were going. I think we both hoped the night out would miraculously make things better between us.

I wasn't sure how I felt about venturing out into the world again. Ryder, Logan, and I had created our own world right here on Peavey Lane. Despite his place in Ann Arbor, Logan seemed content to hang with Ryder and me, though he grew more despondent every day, just a fierce shadow about the house, grizzly beard, fading skin, green-grass eyes. Thoughts of school and CJ and even the Flame seemed overwhelming. Sometimes just leaving my room felt like too much, and I'd send Ryder downstairs for anything I might need.

The three of us spent that week, the week between Christmas and New Year's, getting full-on looped in my bedroom, though it seemed to me Ryder was drinking slightly less. My mom and dad were scarcely around to notice a thing. It wasn't as if they'd fallen back in love or anything, if they really ever were. It was more like the weirdness that had brought them together in the first place had somehow intensified. Plus, Logan's being so difficult again, and what with all the problems with me, gave them plenty of issues in common. I suppose to some, that is love, warped though it is. To them, it seemed to feel A-OK.

"Man, I'm telling you, leave it be," said Ryder. It was two o'clock and we were already well-lit; my parents were M.I.A.

"Christ, I know. I know. But I miss her sometimes. You know. She was my one and only." Logan was stretched out across my bed, white pointy boots dangling off the end.

"If it was meant to be, it'll happen. Trust in it."

"But maybe my calling her will make it be. If we're both just sitting around waiting for things to be, nothing will ever happen."

"Truth. But you've got to trust in the Master. Free your mind to the now."

"Yeah, but my now sucks."

"Thanks," I said.

"Nah, Beans, you know what I mean." I did know what he meant. But I was actually doing okay in my now. Sort of. I mean, while Logan and Ryder debated calling up the Tat, I did think about Henry. I thought about his narrow, writhing hips, wondered if he had moved them for the Tat the same way he'd moved them for me. I thought about his sunken, smooth chest—dark, dark nipples popping in the cast light—and I wondered if he had stroked it in the same way for her. Had he arranged the light just so, just exactly so? Had he jumped and bucked, twisted and fallen into the same rhythm as with me, with the same steady breath, the same stretching fingers? Had I and the Tat both rolled in the same dirty sheets, drunk from the same unwashed glass? Had she showered just before I had?

And believe me, it didn't make me feel great to think she'd been where I'd been right before or even right after, but it didn't make me feel lousy anymore, either. I looked at Ryder and wondered if maybe the shine came in a different form than I'd originally figured, wondered if it wasn't all glossy and sleek, but rather something simpler and drenched in sun. But, of course, I still wasn't getting it. I still wasn't absorbing what Ryder had been saying all along about the shine and where you really find it, because if I had really been getting it, I probably wouldn't have thought about Henry at all.

"Pass the bottle, Beans," Logan said.

"It's empty." I held the last of our stash above my head. I was seated on my wide-planked cowgirl-floor, leaning against my desk drawers.

"I'll get more." Logan rose unsteadily to his feet.

"Are you sure you should drive, man?"

"Yeah, I'm sure." His long limbs wavered to and fro.

"We can just raid the liquor cabinet, man. I'll run down. You stay here." Ryder stood up, too.

"Well, ain't you a sweet guest? 'We can just raid the liquor cabinet, man.' Who died and made you king here?" Logan moved closer to Ryder, pushing his chest up against him.

"Peace," said Ryder, holding his hands above his head, the way he'd been doing lately when Logan acted like this.

"Peace. Peace. Why the fuck do you talk like that?"

"It's just an expression, man. No harm intended."

"No harm intended. Here we go again."

Ryder remained silent and watched Logan, who was staring out the window pretty hard and breathing deep hard breaths. I thought about that weird breathing the Tat had been doing the day I got my car and wondered if Logan wasn't practicing that himself. It did seem to be calming him down. Finally he said, "Why do you stay here?"

"I stay here because it's where my heart is," said Ryder, and I couldn't help but smile, despite the tension in the room. Then he asked, "Why do you?"

Logan sat on my bed and stared a bit more, then said in this voice I wasn't familiar with, "I stay because I've got nowhere else to go." I thought about his place in Ann Arbor, which I thought certainly counted as a place to go—way more of a place than my bedroom—and it made me feel funny. It was like in some way I'd become responsible for him, which was exactly opposite of the way I figured life to be.

"Is that why you came back from Vegas?"

"No. Fuck no. Anna got sick, and we ran out of money. I had no choice."

Ryder remained silent. I was picking at my nails a lot and chewing the sore spot on my lip. I didn't much like that the two of them were disagreeing, but I wasn't sure where I fit in, and since no one was looking to include me, I just kept quiet.

"We always have the choice of how we perceive things."

"Is that right, Mr. Hillstream-orphan?" Logan said, and I thought it was strange how he picked that word, *orphan,* not only because Ryder had used it to describe himself, but because that was sometimes how I thought of Logan and me. Orphans of a life we wanted but could never have. "How do you perceive this?" And he flipped Ryder off.

"You're missing the point," said Ryder.

"Oh, yeah? Is there actually a point here?"

"Do you think you're the only one who's had a parent break his trust?" Ryder said. And he said it all soft, too. It wasn't what I expected him to say. I don't think it was what Logan expected him to say, either. There was a bit of a silence, then Logan said, "No, of course I don't think that."

"Then why do you act like what's happening in your house has never happened anywhere else before? Why do you act like it's all so precious and not just part of the plan?"

Logan sat on the bed a bit longer without doing the special breathing thing, then he stood up, very, very slowly. He looked at Ryder, and he looked at me, and he smiled, but it wasn't like a real smile. He looked kind of crazy, if you want to know the truth. "I'm going to get more booze," he said.

So Logan left, and I lit up the remaining joint, but Ryder passed.

· · · ·

After a bit, we heard voices downstairs, and I knew my parents were home. Ryder slid open my window to air out the place; an unnecessary precaution, since they hadn't been in my room once since Christmas. I sat silently staring at my angel. I had been doing that ever since Ryder gave it to me, whenever I felt that something was off. But suddenly I was distracted by a loud smash in the hall and Logan screaming "fucking Christ," unaware of my parents' return. Or perhaps just not caring, since he was well into never-never land himself, just a slightly different latitude. Suddenly my parents and Logan were all in my room. Logan's silver shirt was drenched, and his knees and hands were cut from the broken glass. His eyes pirouetted fiercely, spinning balls of green.

"What is going on up here?" my dad hollered, holding Logan by his ear while Logan offered no resistance. Ryder and I sat still and waited. My dad shoved Logan into my chair, then swept up the many scattered empty bottles into the electric air.

My mom said, "William, careful, you'll hurt yourself." She bent forward with him, disengaging bottles from his hand.

"What is happening in this house?" he yelled, staring at Logan and me, then focusing his rage on Ryder.

"You"—he placed his red, red finger hard against Ryder's chest—"out! You are out of here!" Ryder raised his head, looking my dad dead in the eyes.

"If it's the way it should be, man, who am I to fight it?"

My dad grabbed him by the shoulders.

"Don't talk goddamned nonsense to me, son. I know your ways." Then silence loomed over our heads. We waited to see who would look away first. Ryder held his own and more, and it was my dad who turned his gaze.

"You should know better," he said to Logan, his voice suddenly low and defeated.

"Know better than what?"

"This." He spread his arms wide, taking in the shambles of my room. My mom stood behind him, watching his every move, ready to catch him should he fall.

"It's not so bad," said Logan, still all crazy-eyed. "It could be worse, you know. It is what you make it."

"Oh, Christ, now you sound like him," said my dad, pointing at Ryder who he suddenly turned back toward.

"Pack your bags, son," he said. "I'll drive you home."

So Ryder left us then, his small frame edging out the door ahead of my dad. From Logan's window we watched him go, our foreheads pressed against the glass.

"Shit," said Logan.

"He'll be back," I said, pleased at how much Logan approved of my wayward friend, despite their altercation. He shook his head.

"I've got a bad vibe, Beans. There's a storm brewing."

"No there's not," I said, but I felt it, too.

19

My parents' comings and goings had become haphazard, full of whims and sudden impulses. They had slid into some warped, prechildren love affair that made my stomach queasy. On New Year's Eve, though, they stayed in. I was in, too, on account of having had my grounding extended until the school year started back up. And even then, it was as per my parents' discretion. It didn't really bother me that much. I mean, I had nowhere else to go, did I? Logan continued to hang about the house like rags on a beggar man. Strangely, he'd been grounded, too, but I figured that since he really did have a second home of his own, despite his comments to Ryder, he'd just up and leave. But he didn't.

I missed Ryder like crazy, and falling asleep without him had become tricky. Even the warmth of Whiz Bang purring against my chest did little to soothe my overticking brain. The Southern Comfort was gone, the empty bottles beneath my bed had been routed out and removed. Logan and I hadn't had a drop in three days, and, speaking for myself, my mood swings had been intense. Hyperexhilaration, radical depression. I even went so far as to pull out the book my mom had given me on unmanageable lives—crawling into bed, armed with a red marker with which to test my crisis level, figuring if I could hold the pen, then technically, right off, I should pass.

Expecting questions that ran along the lines of Do you prefer gin or vodka? I was taken aback by the more probing tone. Do you come from a troubled, repressed, or dysfunctional family? (Who in America could answer no?) Do you take things personally? (Is there something wrong with that?) Do you feel a lot of guilt? (Only when I know I should.) My score rose, coaxing with it my teenage heartbeat. I threw the book back under my bed and closed my eyes to life.

· · · ·

At eleven-thirty, my parents turned in. I heard my mother's crisp footsteps down the hall, then my father's soft padding. He slipped into my room, thinking I was asleep, and kissed me on the forehead, then closed the door behind him.

Ryder phoned just about exactly the minute my dad hit the hall.

"Man, get me out of here!" he said. We'd spoken every day since the ousting, but each time his voice gave me a new thrill.

"I can't, Ryder. You know I'm grounded and all."

"Well, unground yourself and all, man. It's fucking New Year's. The Master is granting us another try."

And I wanted to go, too. I thought about the night I had sneaked out, how my parents had never even noticed

I was gone. My heart began pounding. I could hear the radio buzzing in the background and Logan moving about in his room.

"I don't know, Ryder. I'm in so much trouble already."

"Don't think in the extremes, Let. Life happens breath by breath."

I was silent. I needed to think.

"Meet me at the Greek theater in half an hour," I said.

• • • •

I splashed my face, smoothed down my hair, not bothering to change, since I had crawled into bed while still in my clothes, and did a little Master dance before my full-length mirror.

Logan's figure flashed in the glass.

"Logan, shit, you scared me!"

"Where ya going, Beans?" Red and green, his eyes flared beneath heavy lids.

"Out," I said, sensing Logan to be in one of his moods.

"Out with Henry?"

"No! Not out with Henry."

"What then, just getting ready in case he crawls through your window and wants to get it on? Huh?"

"Fuck you!"

"Whoa," he said. "Listen to Miss Get-Around-Town and her fancy words." He leaned in the doorway and tucked his hands beneath his armpits, looking just like our dad. Looking just like the Wall we both hated so.

"Fuck you, Logan," I said again, and I meant it, too. *Fuck you and your snide remarks. Just because the Tat has been an asshole to you doesn't mean you get to be one to me.* That's what I wanted to say to him, but of course I didn't. Instead, I shook with tears, exhausted from this endless, endless search of mine for the shine, but it was more than that. I realized it was the first time my thoughts had run counter to Logan's, and it felt strange. Granted, I hadn't verbalized them; they had been safely confined to the privacy of my mind, but they startled me nevertheless. Logan stood beside me, his body softened into an embrace, catching me up, pulling me close, close, closer still. *We smell alike,* I thought. *Orphans of the wanting-war.*

• • • •

Logan joined me, changing first into his swanky leopard jeans ("for good luck"), his exploding floral shirt, and a full-length leather trench coat. We hopped out my window—Whiz Bang mewing from behind the glass—slid down the drain, and circled around to the front of the house.

The Flame, black, thunderous, her nicks and scratches and busted headlight endured in a queenly manner of reticence and grace, sat waiting patiently in the drive. I smiled when I saw her again. It had been so long since the two of us had been out into the blacky-black of night. Logan had located the keys easily enough; they were in my mom's gum/pencil drawer.

"Hello, friend," I said, climbing in, rubbing her smooth exterior gloss with my hand. Snow fell on the Flame as I backed her down the drive, the headlight twinkling like a fallen star. Not a sound. No wind. No fellow travelers. No lonely dogs whining in the night. Just me and Logan. As if we'd been placed inside a snow globe, all hushed. Not an absence of sound that once was, but rather a place where sound had never been.

The Greek theater lay white and smooth beneath a canopy of dark, bare branches and moonless clouds.

Logan said, "Where is he?"

I shrugged.

"I'll go look," he said, rolling sideways out of his door.

"I'll go with you." I felt the creeps creeping on me.

We carved a path across the fresh snow, our footsteps echoing into the vastness.

"Ryder!" Logan called, while my heart beat hard against my chest. We paused, then walked in farther, entering the theater through the far side, past the empty pool and the statue of Artemis.

"Ryder!" Logan called again, and again my heart jerked about.

"Are you sure he said to meet him here, Beans?"

I nodded, spinning around. And then we saw him, crumpled up low upon one of the heaven-bound rows of benches. I slid my hand into my pocket, fingering the Guardian that I had shoved in there after Logan's white vinyl boot had knocked it from its perch upon my sill on our way out.

"Christ," said Logan, suddenly energized and dashing forward. I knew he thought Ryder was dead, because I thought the same thing, but I remained planted, catching snowflakes on my tongue, until Logan got there and roused our little cherub from his sleep. We three moved forward, through fields of white down, rhythmically passing Ryder's bottle of whiskey amongst us until we reached the car.

Logan said, "I'll drive. You two get in the back." I tossed him my keys without a hint of hesitation, though I knew he was well stoned.

"Watch out for the little animals." I adjusted my body to the familiar curve of Ryder's chest.

"Do you think I'd go killing anything on New Year's Eve, Beans?" I could see his eyes watching me in the rearview mirror.

"Just be careful, Logan."

"Yes, sir, Mommy-o!" And he gave me a salute. Then he reached deep into his pocket, the car swerving to the right, and withdrew a Ziploc of pot and papers.

"Roll us up a doob, Beans," he said, tossing the bag onto my lap. To be honest, I'd never rolled a joint in my life, but I'd watched Logan and Henry do it often enough so that I produced a first-place winner.

"Didn't know you had it in you," Logan said with a smirk, lighting up with the Flame's coil. We were headed down Dakota Avenue. "Where to, kiddy-winks?" He looked at us in the rearview mirror again.

The road was strangely empty. Only blackness broken briefly by harsh artificial light. It felt as if we were the only people left on earth.

"To the zoo, man!" shouted Ryder, popping forward from my body, leaning over the seat, throwing his hand onto Logan's shoulder. "Briggs told me, just this afternoon, how the chimpanzees aren't being treated right. Not being treated right at all. I say let's free them. I say let's bust them out!"

"Just how do you figure we'll do that?" Logan asked. He offered Ryder the joint, but Ryder passed it to me without taking a hit.

"With love, man. With the Master's love guiding us, we'll let them loose." He turned to grin at me, then leaned in for a kiss. "You'll be into it, right, Let? Helping the little animals to be free." I looked out the window. I wasn't into it at all—the thought of being at the zoo with all those caged animals, whom we knew we'd never be able to release, overwhelmed me—but I knew I didn't need to say as much, since Logan would never drive us there anyway. "Mercy and Vengeance, never again."

"Right on!" shouted Logan, and I felt my stomach tighten. He grabbed the bottle from me and took an enormous swig.

I'd once read a story by C. S. Lewis about parallel universes where identical things were happening, only the outcomes would be different, depending on the choices your parallel person made, and at that moment I had the overwhelming desire to beam on over to my counterpart.

Logan drove us to the zoo.

. . . .

My mom told me later she found Ryder's desire to free the chimps symbolic of his own feelings of entrapment and neglect. Perhaps Logan's falling in so eagerly reflected likewise, although I figure it was all the alcohol and pot he'd been loading up on.

Naturally enough, when we arrived at the zoo, the gates were locked, but Ryder hopped right out anyway, disappearing around the side. Logan and I sat silently in the car, until Ryder's face appeared on the far side of the thick black poles that, tightly lined up as they were, encased in brick on top and bottom, served as a fence. He waved us in.

"Logan . . ."

"Come on, Beans," he said. "It's okay."

Out I slid, looking back at the Flame while Ryder jimmied open a door, and we were in.

Logan said, "Have you done this before or what?"

I thought about the lady who'd sneaked into a zoo somewhere and been eaten by a lion not too long ago. Combine that with Ryder's comings and goings at the museum, and I had known it was doable from the get-go.

Ryder just smiled. Then we were inside the zoo, with me doubting my every move, yet seeing my brother make the same moves and not having it in me to doubt *him*. At least not yet.

"Where are the chimps?" asked Logan, hands shoved deep into his pockets, his coat flying behind him in the rising wind so that he looked like Raskolnikov loose in the streets of St. Petersburg rather than trapped here, with Ryder and me.

"Somewhere, man. But while we're here, we ought to free them all!" Ryder yelled, spinning around and around music-box style.

"Right on," said Logan, picking up his pace a bit, on account of trying to indicate leadership.

All around us were locked buildings. Caged animals. Spooking the night with their lonesome calls. To tell you the truth, I wanted them freed, too. But what on earth would we do with them all? Take them home to Peavey Lane? We couldn't just let them go free right there in Detroit. First off, they'd be roadkills within minutes. My lungs closed up. I tried to pretend it was just like when CJ and I were on the goof about something, but it sure didn't feel that way.

Ryder had disappeared from sight, and Logan was giving me this weird cold-shoulder thing, which was probably because he knew we shouldn't be there, too.

"Logan!" Ryder called out from the whiteness. And Logan took off, leaving me alone in the night.

· · · ·

I sat on a bench for a while, listening to the animals cry. Then there was this crash. And even though I didn't know exactly what had happened, I knew we should really be in bed and not in the middle of the zoo. "God," I said right smack out loud, addressing myself to the swirling clouds of snow, "this is a definite, definite wrong. Get me out of here, get me home safely, and I swear I will never leave your chosen path again." And this time I meant it with all my heart. Eventually Logan came running up, the same hand he'd cut with the broken-up bottle of Southern Comfort at my parents' house bleeding again.

"Shit, Logan, what happened?" I asked, not really in the mood for the answer. We were well into the land of definite wrongs, and I wanted out.

"Ryder was trying to open the door, and it wouldn't budge. Jammed. Totally jammed. So I socked it for him."

"Shit, are you okay?"

"Whatever, whatever, whatever. Does it matter? Am I okay? Are you okay? Ryder is definitely not okay. But strangely, I don't think he's drunk."

Logan's eyes were sort of crossed, greener than wet grass, and ticking, ticking, ticking. And I wanted to say something, but couldn't find the words. I wanted to say, "What is happening to you, Logan? Why are you unraveling so?" And that missed moment in time stays with me now, in my green-white room, like a husk upon the corn.

So then what happened was I started to cry, what with Logan looking all wacked-out and not knowing where Ryder was and all the little critters trapped in these God-awful man-made environments, on display like some freak show. It was too much.

"I want to go," I said to Logan. He nodded, but didn't move. Instead, he took my scarf and wrapped his hand in it.

"I want to go, Logan. Now." It had felt strange to think oppositional thoughts to Logan's, and it felt stranger still to verbalize them. As if standing up for a definite right somehow created a definite wrong.

"Whoa," said Logan finally. "Listen to Miss Smartie Pants here." He didn't even seem to notice my tears.

"I want to go, Logan. I. Want. To. Go."

"Yeah, well, I want a lot of things, Beans. Life just isn't always so accommodating."

I didn't like how Logan was being, and I was drawing up the courage to tell him so, when Ryder appeared and started saying, "Let, man, I love you, Let. I love you, man. Truth, I do."

"Oh, Christ," said Logan, rolling his eyes, but I could tell he thought it was all right. It took me by surprise. It was the first time a guy had ever said he loved me, not counting Logan that night in the TV room, and for a moment I couldn't tell whether or not my heart was beating. Something about it didn't feel totally right though. He was drunk. Or at least, I assumed he was. But Logan was right, Ryder hadn't been drinking his usual amount that night. He hadn't been drinking his usual amount his last few days at the house, either. And I couldn't remember the last time I saw him take a hit of a joint.

"I know you're just thinking I'm drunk, man, and babbling, but I'm not. I swear. And I mean it. I mean, I fucking love you." But I couldn't absorb it then. I couldn't feel what he was saying. In fact, I was starting to not feel much at all, and that scared me.

"I want to go," I said again—slowly, clearly. "I want to get out of here."

"Beans, are you listening to this boy?" said Logan, suddenly very gung-ho about the whole thing, probably because it distracted from the tension that was building between us. "He said he loves you! There ain't nothing like a little love in this world to make it all worthwhile. Get it while you can, little sister, because when you turn back, it may be gone."

Ryder seated himself beside me, taking my hand in his, while Logan threw snowballs at a nearby tree, missing every time. I wished Whiz Bang was there. Suddenly Logan turned toward us, looking all serious, and said, "I came back because I was worried about Let."

Ryder and I looked at him.

"I didn't want her to turn out like me. I needed to warn her."

I felt my head go loose, like when you let go of a balloon and it drifts off into the universe.

"You came back because you didn't want to be anywhere else," said Ryder. "You didn't know how." And in that moment everything became quite still.

"What do you know about it?" Logan's words sounded thick now in the night, like boots moving through mud.

"Did you look for a job? Did you look for an apartment? Did you make a go at setting up a life there?"

"Anna didn't feel well."

Logan threw more snowballs.

"When someone breaks your trust, you can feel it," Ryder said. "And it changes everything. You can feel it so hard, you feel like you're going mad, but as long as it's there and you know it's there you can start to try again. But if you never feel it. If you never even acknowledge that anything hurt, then it stays inside you and gets bigger, man. And then it's beyond your control."

"Okay, so we've both had our trust broken. What makes you such a know-it-all?" he said, but he didn't say it meanly. He just said it as if he were curious.

"I never thought my parents were perfect."

"I sure as fuck don't think mine are." The snowballs hit the tree now with a steady rhythm, like raindrops falling from a branch into a puddle.

"Don't you?" Ryder said quietly. And it made me hurt inside because I knew he was talking to me, too. It was all the expectations stuff again. Logan was trying to act like he didn't have expectations, like his tattoo, *I Shall Not Want,* but he wanted just as much as the next guy, maybe more so. He wanted to be loved and liked and have life turn out in reality the way it was in his head. And a little pretty-colored ink saturated into his skin wasn't going to change that one iota. It was the same with me.

"I wanted to protect Let," Logan said again, over the smack of a snowball.

"But I want to feel it, Logan," I said, interrupting Ryder, who was starting to say something about being true to yourself. I wasn't planning on interrupting Ryder. I wasn't planning on getting involved at all, but the words just came out. "Whatever it is you want to numb, I want to feel."

And suddenly I did feel. I felt that free fall I'd first sensed in Ryder the day he showed me the shine. Only now I knew the comfort and the grounding came from yourself. And that wasn't a sad thing at all. I knew something in me had started to shift and even if I fought it, I was headed somewhere new.

• • • •

When he was tired of throwing snowballs, Logan said, "Let's go."

"Yes," I said, relieved. "Let's go home."

"Nah," Logan said. "It's New Year's Eve. We're not going home."

"Hey, man," said Ryder, "I think it might be smart. Tonight's probably done us all in." And even though Logan and Ryder now appeared to be all right with each other, I could tell Logan was irritated.

"Tonight hasn't done me in. In fact, watching the two of you lovebirds has got my blood all itchy for my love, and I'm going to go find her."

"You want to find Anna?" I said. I couldn't believe it.

"I'm glad one of you is paying attention."

"But Logan, it's so late. And the roads are turning into shit. And we don't even know if she's here or in Ann Arbor." I wanted to add "And you are drunk off your ass and not thinking straight," but it felt especially wrong to oppose him now.

"Look, I'm going to find Anna. Now you two wimps can join me, or I can drop you at home. Whatever suits you."

"Trust me," Ryder said. "Let's get some sleep and find Anna in the morning."

"You're not listening," Logan said again, all drawn out and kind of creepy.

"I am listening," said Ryder. "I just don't agree."

"Is that a fact? Well, let's flip a coin, huh? Heads, we search for Anna; tails, we go to bed." And he started scrummaging around in his pocket for a quarter. "No," he said, suddenly looking at me. "There's three of us here. Three adults living in a democracy. Let's take a vote. I say we go find Anna."

"I say we go to bed," said Ryder.

They both looked at me. I examined my feet some more. I knew what the right thing to do was. I knew it in my gut and in my heart and in my mind. I knew it, and yet I still couldn't bring myself to counter Logan. Plus, like I said before, I wasn't sure crossing Logan wasn't a definite wrong in itself. I wasn't convinced that going against the family wasn't about as wrong as it could get.

"Let's go," I said, kicking around some rocks I nudged out of the snow.

"Home, man. Right on," said Ryder.

"No," I said, looking Logan right in the eye. "Let's go find Anna." Logan smiled at me, then, just a little. I could tell he wanted to full-out grin but held back. In that moment I felt like I could see everything, the strictures in his veins, the gash in his lungs, the places his heart sank, the black-and-blue spots, the welts. *Just don't let him drive,* I thought. *Take the fucking keys.* But I already knew I wouldn't.

And so off we went, down the path of brick, past the closed-up critter prisons; Logan stumbling behind, then ahead of us, his grizzled beard flecked with ice and snow. *What is a family?* I remember thinking. *Is it the obvious blood flow from one generation to the next, or is it something more? Is it to know and love and* trust *someone? That, together, you form a foundation against all the complications that life can bring and share in all the fun, too?* And while my heart said, *Yes, that is family,* my mind said, *No, family is the rights and wrongs, and opposing Logan is wrong, and therefore, breaks the family.*

. . . .

Before we got to the car, Ryder swiped the keys from Logan's pocket. Logan didn't even get mad; he just turned and faced Ryder with his palm open.

Ryder said, "No way, man, should you be driving."

And Logan said, "Oh, and you should?"

"No, man. None of us should." And he was right. Because even though Ryder was drinking considerably less, he was still drinking enough.

"Then how do you propose we get home? Or perhaps we should just sleep here with your beloved chimpanzees?"

Ryder started to say something, but I cut him off. "Give him the keys, Ryder." I could feel Logan's chest rise and his shoulders thrust back. He kept his hand out. Ryder looked at me, but I couldn't look back.

"Okay, man, what the fuck," he said. "Maybe I'm just being too heavy. Let's go find Anna and get you some winterly love." And he said it all so genuinely, I think he really meant it, too. And suddenly, with his smile, he lifted his mood, he lifted Logan's mood, and he lifted my mood, too. Though not all the way. Ryder was right. And I knew it. He slipped his hand in mine, and we crawled into the backseat. Logan hopped in front and looked at us in the rearview mirror.

"Ah, look at the lovebirds," he said. And he was all happy now, laughing. As if nothing contrary had just occurred. And Ryder got all happy, too, and gave me a sweet kiss. And, in a certain way, I was also happy. I remember thinking, *This is family.* Then right on cue Ryder said, "You guys are my family, man," turning first to me, then patting Logan on the shoulder.

"Right on," said Logan with a big brotherly smirk usually reserved for me. "I feel the same."

And while things didn't feel exactly right, they didn't feel exactly wrong, either. *Perhaps this is what the in-betweens are like,* I thought, but I didn't have too much time to mull it over because Logan flipped the Flame into reverse and we headed out toward the highway.

20

So Logan drove, sucking down the remainder of the Southern Comfort and tossing me back the bag to roll another joint. Technically, I suppose I was still drunk, but the euphoria was well gone.

"We should've planned it better," Logan said. "We should have had some kind of plan." The Flame swerved well onto the shoulder and back again as he turned toward us to check on the joint.

"Watch the car," I said.

"Yeah, right. Like you'd notice if there was a new ding," he said, all goofy and normal-like, as if everything was just as it had been, which perhaps it was, but it didn't exactly feel that way. "You should have sold this baby the day you got it, like I did. At least you'd have a pocket full of cash and you could get out of here. Take Ryder with you."

Like that helped you a lot, I wanted to say. Escaping, as if being on another part of the planet makes your family not be true, but Ryder passed the joint forward, then wrapped his arm around me, pulling me in toward his heat, and I relaxed. We were headed, at a fairly fast clip I might add, in search of the Tat.

We finished the joint right when we pulled in front of the Burbanks' house, just as if we'd timed it that way. It must have been around two-thirty then, figuring it backward from what time I ended up here. Everything was dark.

"So, man, what do you think? She home or what?"

Logan shrugged. We watched him get out of the Flame and zigzag toward the redbrick Colonial, our hearts leaping when, at the driveway, the automatic outdoor lights flashed on, paralyzing him in midstep, but after the shock wore down, he continued on. I scoped out the upper windows for movement, but everything was deadly still.

Ryder took the opportunity then to slide himself on top of me, forcing me down onto the seat. And I remember looking at him in minute detail, examining each and every crevice and line of his face, the way married couples are said to do when divorce is looming near. I was still searching for the shine, a habit I couldn't seem to shake, and coming up empty. But the thing was, it didn't matter anymore.

"You know now, don't you, man?" His lips paused above mine.

"Know what?"

"It's within. It's always within." And this time I was not surprised to find that our thoughts had kept pace with each other, side by side, as they had done so many times before. Everything already understood, like with Whiz Bang, whom I held to be the forerunner.

"Quickly," I said, "before Logan comes back."

And so we broke in the new year, my cowboy and I, warming my pleasure dome in the dead of night under a vinyl roof beneath a snow-white sky. And this time when he crossed his heart and said, "Forever," I felt it, too. And when he whispered, "I love you," first in my right ear and then my left, I felt it inside, way, way deep, where it seemed thus far only the bad things had gone. And in the moment I whispered "I love you" back, nothing had felt more right in my life.

· · · ·

Logan came dashing toward the car just as Ryder was zipping up his pants. Sliding in for a homer, Logan flew feet-first into the side of the Flame. Ryder leaned forward and thrust open the door.

"Shit," Logan said. He pulled his left leg behind him and hopped in. I looked at the house. Lights were flipping on all over it like a pinball machine gone wild. Logan jammed the gas with his good leg and steered with his good hand, and we swerved along the narrow road before he regained control and got us out of there.

"What happened, man?"

"I fucked up which room and landed in her old man's instead."

He seemed surprisingly calm, even lucid, for having taken such a wrong turn. I've since learned this is a trick of alcohol; it can take you so far around the bend, you seem almost back to where you began—clean-cold-sober—but you're not.

We drove along for a while, headed for Ann Arbor, I supposed, since home was just down the block. Ryder had kind of drifted off to sleep, though not in a passed-out-drunk way, but more, it seemed, out of contentment. His head was in my lap, his baby-body curled up next to mine, and it got me thinking about my warm bed and how nice it would be to be in it right then. I conjured up after-sleep breakfast waffles dripping with maple syrup, crowned with bananas, cinnamon, and ginger; along with some fresh OJ and a pot of tea.

And I rambled further ahead and thought about how cool it would be when I had the Flame back again, legally and all, and how I would get her scratches and dents fixed up, her headlight mended, how I would take perfect care of her, and keep her well away from the burning sun, choosing right then to most definitely not follow in Phaëthon's footsteps, although I was vaguely aware I'd made such vows before, but this time was different, though I knew I'd said that before, too. But this time was.

I pictured how nice it would be to drive over to Hill-stream and meet Ryder for lunch, become friendly with Mr. Briggs because he seemed like a nice-enough guy, maybe include him in a couple outings, too, just for good measure. And maybe if things kept going well between Ryder and me, I could even visit him during the summer at his parents' ranch, hang in Montana, meet the Master, learn how to ride. That was, of course, if *he* even got an invite home for the summer. Otherwise, maybe he could just come and live with us again, only this time we would do it right. It would be practice for when we got older and could have a place of our own. And my mind just kept kicking this corny love stuff about like a popcorn machine on the blink.

And not once during that whole evening did I think about Henry Edwards, or even want him to be there.

Logan was picking up speed, and when next I glanced out the window, I found we were cruising down the expressway. I stroked Ryder's hair, the brilliantine thick between my fingers, watching him drift in and out of sleep. I remember at that moment feeling peculiarly content, which somehow gave me the courage to say, "Maybe Ryder was right. Maybe we should just go home and find the Tat tomorrow." My voice shook a bit, and I hoped Logan didn't notice.

"Excuse me," said Logan, with this fake serious tone of voice, though I wasn't sure how fake it was.

"We can turn back," I said, and this time my voice didn't quiver or come out all mousy. Standing up to Logan wasn't as hard as I'd always pictured it to be, though it wasn't exactly a walk in the park, either.

"Ah, come on, Beans," he said, suddenly all sweet. "We'll be there in no time. And if you're still nervous about our communal state of inebriation, we can crash at my place. Ryder is passed out anyway, so he has no clue what's going on."

"Maybe things are the way they should be, and we should just respect that."

"Ah geez, now you sound like Ryder. Relax. Everything is fine."

"But it's not fine, Logan," I said, though he acted as if he hadn't heard me. The weight of Ryder's head in my lap was the same as when Whiz Bang snuggled up there, and it felt vaguely reassuring. There was still hardly anybody on the road, and the snow had turned soggy. When the CD he was playing finished, Logan didn't change it, so we drove along to the squeaking of the wipers. The snow fell thicker and thicker.

Our vision narrowed, but Logan seemed undeterred. In a way it was very peaceful. The smell of Ryder on my hands, the whiteness all around. I wanted to fall asleep, to be enveloped by these comforting sensations, but instead, I kept thinking back on those animals trapped in the zoo. Their sad eyes behind bars and glass and crumbling brick. It made me sick as hell.

Then the car started to shift. At first I wasn't sure what was going on, because everywhere I looked I saw white, like we were inside a snowball that was getting bigger by the moment. We'd been driving along pretty quickly, and that same force seemed to be propelling us sideways. Then I was jarred forward, my head cracking against the front seat, and I felt the weight of Ryder lift from me. There was an all-encompassing shattering and the car seemed to fill with ice.

Then we were rolling over and over and over again, Logan's head bobbing in front of me like a piñata. He seemed strangely powerless, his strong arms flopping up and down, back and forth, and even though the whole thing was probably over in less than a minute, being there felt like we had all the time in the world. I calmly rolled down my window and stuck both hands out to try to stop the motion. We slid what seemed like downhill, then flipped upright, and stopped.

Logan twisted around, his face distorted by fear. "Are you all right?" he shouted at me, forcing his way out of his seat belt and climbing in back. He drew me to him, digging his nails into my neck and pushing my head hard against his chest. "Are you okay?" He kept screaming that at me. Pulling me in and pushing back again to look at my face. "Oh, Jesus Christ. Jesus fucking Christ!" He wiped the sleeve of his coat across my forehead. The leather darkened.

"Where's Ryder?" I asked, my voice echoing in my ears. I couldn't figure what was going on, why Logan was clutching me to him, or where Ryder had disappeared to.

Suddenly Logan became frantic, as if he'd forgotten Ryder was supposed to be with us. He crawled over me, digging his boot into my leg and forcing open the door. It was freezing out, and I wanted to hug myself for warmth, but my arms flopped before me like fish on a line. I heard Logan's screams pealing off into the darkness, being absorbed by the heavy snow, then beginning again like synchronized church bells. So before I even saw Ryder, I already knew he was dead.

It was funny how in a split second it all came together. I knew we'd been in a car accident. I knew my head was bleeding and my arms were broken. And without moving from my hollow within the broken glass, I knew Ryder was gone.

. . . .

I walked slowly over to my brother, fish-arms dangling by my sides. I felt no pain at all, which the doctor here later told me was on account of a severe case of shock that I suppose I should be grateful for, and in retrospect, I am. Logan had Ryder's head propped up in his lap, and his shoulders were heaving. Ryder looked completely untouched, as if he were simply resting, although his jaw was twisted strangely away from the rest of his face.

"Oh, Christ, Let. He's dead! He's fucking dead! And I fucking killed him!"

I knelt down next to them, the snow seeping into my kneecaps, and caught up Logan as best I could in my arms. I figured I must have been crying, too, but I didn't feel it. All I felt was my brother's pain. He was almost unrecognizable to me, his face having shifted into this type of living death mask. His eyes receded far back into his narrow skull, while Ryder's were open, seemingly alert, like he was counting stars or something, which is just the kind of thing he would definitely stop and do.

"It's the rage, Violet. It's the fucking rage! I knew it would catch me one day, but I always thought it would be me that would pay the cost. Me! Fucking *me*!"

"No, Logan," I said, "it wasn't the rage."

But I knew that it was. I knew that rage had been eating at him so long that it had a life of its own. I knew how he had fought it, tried to throw it out, tried to suppress it, but it didn't do any good; it never went fully away. It had a fine home in my brother, where it was nursed and treated well. Family runs thickly in your veins, I realized then. It can feel unfightable, unchangeable. But in the end, it's really only you, dressed up in someone else's clothing.

Logan calmed a moment and bent over to close Ryder's eyes.

"I wish I had a camera," I said, straightening up. Ryder lay there looking, with his twisted jaw, somehow like one of my roadkills. But different, too—lighter, as if already transcending. Warm enough still that the snow melted on his cheeks, and pretty as the sky above. My touchstone. My fading light.

"I don't have any pictures of him, you know," I said. "Not one."

• • • •

Blinded as I was by the light, I thought God was paying me a visit. But He wasn't. It was a man in a big brown car. Drunk as hell. Stopping off to help us. He wobbled down, sliding against the incline.

"Is he all right?" he asked, flopping a finger in Ryder's direction. I looked up into his bloodshot eyes and shook my head. Then the man tried to move Ryder. I don't know what he was thinking. Maybe he just wanted to get him into his car, get him home and into bed all safe and sound. Something I would have liked, too, but it just wasn't going to happen.

Ryder wasn't bloody or anything, so he would have fit in the car just fine without making a mess, but at the drunk's first lunge, Logan went berserk. He grabbed the man by his coat collar and shoved him all the way back up the hill. A massive adrenaline rush firing him, considering the steepness of the incline and the ice and all. When Logan had jumped up, he'd knocked Ryder's head against the ground, causing his eyelids to shift, and I remember thinking, just for that split second, just for that minuscule amount of time, that we had been mistaken and Ryder was alive. Then he returned to his motionless state.

At the top of the incline, Logan had somehow secured a rock and was smashing it over and over again against the stranger's car. A trucker and somebody else had pulled up, and I guess they figured the drunk had crashed into Logan on account of Logan not seeming drunk himself, just plain crazy, which I guess at that moment he was. So the trucker started trying to restrain the drunk who was trying to stop Logan from wrecking his car.

Then this woman came up by my side—nicely dressed, I remember, in a pink wool coat and tall black riding boots. Strange that you even notice things like that during such moments, but I've heard a bit about that kind of experience since I've been here, and apparently it happens all the time. During a crisis you notice everything, like it's blown up to twice its size, chock-full of all these busting colors and scents. Like this lady, smelling of roses. Smelling exactly like my parents' gardens when the summer breeze lifted their sweet aroma into our house.

She took one look at Ryder, and I knew she wanted to barf. Her face went white as the snow. But I thought he looked so pretty lying there, as if he were about to make a snow angel or something, and I couldn't relate to her alarm. In fact, what I wanted to do right then was to move his arms up and down a bit, create the wings, but as I was leaning forward to try to do just that, the rose-scented lady grabbed me by my fish-hand and pulled me up the hill, screaming to a man in a puffy parka trimmed with dead animals.

When we reached the man, she spoke to him in unintelligible words, though I sensed they were English, and she motioned down the incline. I turned to see what all the hullabaloo was about. Ryder lay so still that the morning snow had begun to pile softly on top of him, taking his features for itself. His body, just barely within reach of the headlights, took on the attitude of a film-noir flick, like the one Henry had taken me to. Dark passions, he'd said, violent crimes.

The trucker had managed to subdue both Logan and the drunk, and Logan was now walking in circles, punching himself in the head, while the drunk sat in his smashed-up car trying to figure what to do next. The man in the dead-animal parka leaned into his Jeep, pulled out a cellular phone. The woman stood next to him, shaking. I wanted to tell her it was all right, but to tell you the truth, I was starting to think then maybe it wasn't.

Logan kept going around and around in these circles; the trucker paced back and forth, back and forth in front of his truck, glancing over at me, then at Logan, then craning his neck to see down the incline; and the woman just kept shaking while the man spoke calmly into the tiny phone; the drunk just hung his head between his hands. All of them, in unison, seemed to be shuffling their feet to keep warm. I stood in front of the couple's Jeep, the heat of the radiator enveloping me. Waiting.

21

Ryder died on a Sunday. He once told me he thought he could walk right out across Flathead Lake, on mornings when the sun was most intense, and reach the other side without ever falling in. I figured that was just exactly what he had done, crossed the lake and all, me still standing on the shoreline, hoping to catch a glimpse of his receding figure. My pompadoured wizard, my tiny conjurer, come upon only foolishly late in the waning light of day.

His parents never showed up here at the hospital. Instead, they had his body flown to Montana and buried on their new ranch, the one he'd never seen. It makes me happy to think of Mercy and Vengeance riding over him, stamping the ground above his head, letting him know that they're A-OK.

The accident got a lot of press coverage both locally and nationally on account of Ryder's dad being more famous than Ryder had ever let on. He's in *People* magazine this week, along with this God-awful picture of Logan and me from about four years back dressed in puffy Michigan-winter coats that somehow made its way to the editor; and the E! channel did a whole special on Michael just yesterday, of course painting him out to be this top-notch dad.

My parents tell me that their phone has been ringing off the hook, so my dad yanked it out of the wall, and now friends and relatives reach them via my line. An unlisted number that has so far miraculously resisted press leakage.

Logan says he's not going back to school this semester (I'm not sure what I'll do, either), and something's brewing with him and the Tat, because lately she's started to come around when he visits—which is just about every day—instead of sneaking in alone at odd hours to make peace with me, which is what she was doing before.

Mostly Logan just stares at the wall, or maybe elaborates a bit on a book he's reading or something external like that, but it's pretty hard to concentrate on anything, on account of my seeing him all broken the way he is just reminds me of Ryder. But there is a strange closeness between us now, a base of trust, which was building anyway over the past few weeks.

The Hadleys haven't pressed civil charges against Logan, and it doesn't look like they will, and I guess my dad was more above the law than I ever figured, because the police have dropped the criminal charges, too. So Logan walked away scot-free. We both did, because I hold myself as much accountable for that night as Logan. I was so caught up in the rights and wrongs that I couldn't see what was really going on. The Tat says when I think like that it's the voice of God talking to me, but the only voice I hear now is my own, which is the way I suppose it should have been all along.

I miss Ryder like crazy, haunted as I am day and night by his rodeo ways. My guardian angel sits on my windowsill here, too, on account of her being in my coat pocket and my dad finding her there when he was organizing my stuff. He and my mom had rushed right over to the hospital that morning after one of the night-duty nurses phoned them. They hadn't even noticed we were gone. My dad had clenched me to his chest, forcing my bandaged head into his pajama top; over his shoulder, I could see my mom's quivering hand guide a cigarette to her bare lips, her eyes like marbles in the fluorescent light.

"I couldn't sleep," she'd said. "I knew something was wrong. Why didn't I check your bedrooms? Why?"

"It wouldn't have made any difference," I'd said. "You wouldn't have known where to find us."

She'd said, "I would have known," and had run her dry hand along mine while my dad had pressed me to him harder still.

Logan had been nowhere in sight then, on account of his being questioned in a back room somewhere, despite his erratic state. He appeared to me later, in the early morning light, like an apparition at my bedside, crying softly into the sheets.

Henry's never phoned me once here, although he must know what happened, on account of our dads and all, not to mention the excessive press coverage. It's funny how on that night I didn't think about Henry once, as if I'd finally cut myself free of him. But I've thought about him a lot here, and decided if ever I were to write a book about this, I would paint him out to be dark and smarmy and evil, on account of his distracting me from Ryder and distracting the Tat from Logan and distracting my mom from my dad, and if we hadn't all been so distracted from our lives in such a way, Logan, Ryder, and I would never have ended up in the Flame that night (which by the way is also dead, meeting the fate of Phaëthon after all).

But it's funny how when it gets right down to it, I still remember the sweet curve of Henry's chest, sinking back into his narrow lats; and the lazy way he looked at me with half-opened eyes, brooding darkly from well beyond my reach. And I know my portrayal of Henry would be tempered with desire.

I've been thinking a lot about Logan's rage, too, and how it's haunted him for all these years, although it seems lately to have dissipated somewhat. Since I've been in here, he's quit drinking and smoking pot altogether, and when he showed up this morning, he'd rid himself of that God-awful beard, which was a relief to us all. I think about how he always said he believed the rage would take him, and perhaps it would have, too, but that's where God comes in.

At first, when Ryder died and I understood it—I mean, really understood he was gone—I figured God had let me down. I thought about all the times He'd bailed me out of insignificant jams like illegal dorm visits and losing my way in the woods, which was cool and not to be sneered at, but those rescues started happening frequently enough that I'd come to feel protected, perhaps even indestructible, yet when it came right down to the big stuff, to the life-and-death stuff, He'd turned his back. At least that's what I figured when the tranquilizers first wore off. Let down by God Himself, I thought, after all that careful roadkill work, too (even though I would have sent the critters to heaven just the same, bargain or no).

But after a couple of days, the fuzz began to clear, and I started having these visions. Ryder would come into my room through the latched, leaded windows, even though I was on the sixth floor, and he would grin at me, just like he always did, and tell me not to be so blue, that it was all part of the plan, man, all part of the way it should be. Truth, he would say, we'll meet again. Right now, man, look at the present.

Even in my visions, Ryder didn't always make a whole lot of sense, which is why I believed it was him, but what I think he was trying to tell me was what God had done was to take Ryder in Logan's place, and I think Ryder would have been A-OK with that had he been asked. Or maybe he was asked and that's why he gave me my guardian and all, for the present, for after-he-was-gone moments. Life is a beautiful journey, he would say, you just need to sit back and enjoy the ride.

I think Ryder was in touch with a lot of things I didn't understand then, like the shine, like how he knew I was looking every which way for it, and he knew just where it lay, too. But it's the kind of thing, in the end, you have to come to on your own.

My life here progresses toward a regular pattern: my mom doing crosswords by my bed, smoking Winstons even though she's not allowed to, fanning the smoke from my head when I wake; and my dad's brain wandering helplessly amongst the clouds while here on earth he keeps on keeping it ticking; and Logan leaning over me, wiping my burning forehead gently with his hand, at a loss for words even now, even after all this.

I've always had a headful of voices fashioning my outlook on life, but now, with the death of my brilliantine cowboy, they've all gone dead, too. A citywide blackout in the bluey-blue of my mind.

And there remains only me.

EX LIBRIS

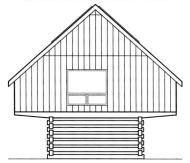

A Donation From The
Children's Defense Fund's

LANGSTON HUGHES
LIBRARY

9-25-01